D1565256

# Decebal Defiant

## Siege at Sarmizegetusa

Book Three in the Rome - Dacia Wars Series
103– 107 A.D.

## Peter Jaksa

Attention Publishing

CHICAGO, ILLINOIS

**Peter Jaksa/Attention Publishing**
**30 North Michigan Avenue, Suite 908**
**Chicago, IL 60602**
**www.addcenters.com**

Publisher's Note: This is a work of fiction. Names, characters, places, and incidents are a product of the author's imagination. Locales and public names are sometimes used for atmospheric purposes. Any resemblance to actual people, living or dead, or to businesses, companies, events, institutions, or locales is completely coincidental.

**Decebal Defiant / Peter Jaksa**. -- 1st ed.
ISBN 978-1-7367277-2-0

For all descendants of Dacia,
in Romania and around the world

*It is during our darkest moments*
*that we must focus to see the light.*

– ARISTOTLE

# Contents

> Chapter 1

# Retribution

*Iazygi territory, western Dacia, March 103 AD*

K ing Decebal watched from the saddle astride his big gray
stallion as his army closed in around the city walls. He
was there to drive out the Iazygi occupiers who took the
opportunity, one year ago, to seize this walled city in the
western part of Dacia while Decebal was in the east fighting Emperor
Trajan and the armies of Rome. The Iazygis captured the city and
claimed it as Iazygi territory.

Now the Dacian army returned to take their city back. It was time
for Dacia to reclaim its lost territories and to punish those who had
allied themselves with Rome. King Decebal made it clear that this was
a campaign for justice and retribution however, not slaughter.

"Kill no civilians," Decebal ordered Tarbus, a captain of infantry.
"Accept the surrender of any soldier who lays down his arms."

"Yes, Sire," Tarbus acknowledged. "Those who yield shall live."

General Drilgisa was feeling less merciful as he watched the Iazygi
defenders on the walls. "Ah, we'll just have to fight them again at
some later time and kill them then. It seems like a shame to let them
go now when we have them trapped."

The King considered that his General had a point. The Dacians and
Iazygis were old enemies, and Iazygis usually allied themselves with
the armies of Rome. On the other hand, Dacia had a new peace treaty
with Rome and Decebal had no wish to start a new war.

"If we must fight them again then so be it," the King said. "For now it is enough to take back our land and push them back into Iazygi territory."

"As you command, Sire," Drilgisa said respectfully. He gave a small nod towards the city walls. "But many of those soldiers have Dacian blood on their hands. They deserve punishment."

"Only if they fight back, Drilgisa."

Drilgisa gave him a wolfish grin. "Which Iazygis are sure to do." He turned his horse towards the city. "Stay with me, Tarbus. Let's go find out who is feeling peaceable and who wants to die, eh?"

"Yes, sir!" Tarbus replied with enthusiasm. He urged his horse forward with his knees to follow Drilgisa.

Decebal turned to his friend and longtime bodyguard Buri, a tall and wide bodied warrior standing and watching beside him. "Your son is taking after Drilgisa more every day. Brave and enthusiastic but not reckless."

Buri watched Tarbus ride alongside the veteran General with a look of pride on his face. "My son is a fast learner. There is no better general and leader of men than Drilgisa, so he's in good hands."

The King nodded in agreement. "We will need many more young men who are good leaders to rebuild the army of Dacia."

They turned their attention to the battle as fighting commenced. It promised to be a short battle.

The Dacian archery units opened the attack. Foot archers, horse archers, and slingers loosed a barrage of arrows and sling bullets at the defenders on the city wall. Some of the Iazygi warriors bravely tried to fight back with their own war bows and by throwing lances and spears, but they were greatly outnumbered. Those who were not hit immediately ducked for cover behind their shields or scrambled off the wall for safety.

"Let's go!" shouted the captain of the Dacian unit in charge of the battering ram. "The bastards won't show themselves now! Let's break down that gate!"

Twelve soldiers under the canopy of the battering ram's sloped roof braced themselves and pushed forward with all their strength. The six wooden wheels turned slowly and the ram moved forward. The Iazygi archers and spearmen on the wall kept their heads down. A brave few took a quick peek to see what the attackers were doing.

The battering ram was built in the Roman design. A shed like structure covered a large oak timber fitted with an iron head at the front end. The ramming timber was suspended by ropes from the slanted wooden roof. The roof was wide enough to cover the soldiers whose job was to push the machine against the city gate, then swing the iron tipped timber forward and back on the ropes to batter down the gate. After enough hits the wooden gate would splinter and give way. Dacian infantry would then storm in and finish the job.

The battering ram was pushed forward until it touched the gate. "Pull!" the captain shouted the order, and the men pulled back the oak timber by the ropes nailed to its sides.

"Loose!" he yelled when the timber reached its farthest position back away from the gate. The men let go of the ropes and the massive timber shot forward. The heavy iron tip slammed into the wooden gate with a loud bang and made the entire gate structure shudder from the impact.

"Again!" the captain shouted. "Pull!"

Two Iazygi archers leaned out to shoot flaming arrows into the roof of the battering ram. The arrows sank into water soaked animal skins and fizzled out. One archer took a Dacian arrow in his side and the two men scrambled back to safety behind the wall.

"Loose!"

Soon after the gate was breached the Iazygi defenders surrendered the city, suffering only a small number of dead and wounded. There was no sense in inviting a massacre by fighting for this Dacian city that could not be defended for long. General Drilgisa escorted a trio of Iazygi officers, stripped of all weapons and armor, to the Dacian command post outside the town.

King Decebal addressed them in a calm but firm voice. He wished for these Iazygi leaders to understand that his aim was diplomacy and not bloodshed.

"You will move your people, along with their livestock and what possessions they can carry, out of the city by mid-day. You will march them all to Iazygi territory within three days. Anyone still on Dacian land after three days will be put to death."

The leader of the officers bristled, offended by being given such orders even from a Dacian king. "This is Iazygi land! Last year it was annexed by Rome and given to us by Emperor Trajan. By your attack today you break your treaty with Rome, King Decebal."

"What is your name?" Decebal's tone was even, not imperious.

"I am Katal."

"Listen well, Katal, and take these words back to all the Iazygi chiefs." The King paused to get their full attention. "I make the law in Dacia, not Emperor Trajan or Rome. I decide who lives here or not. And I decide who lives or dies on my land."

"Do you wish to start a war with Rome?" Katal challenged him. "Emperor Trajan gave us this land as payment for our alliance with Rome in his war against you."

"You have three days to leave Dacia," Decebal reminded them. "Disobey my orders under penalty of death." He turned to the Dacian guards. "Take these men back to their people."

Drilgisa watched with mild amusement as the three officers were marched away. "They think that Rome will give them land in Dacia, and that Trajan will fight us again if we don't agree?"

Decebal gave a careless shrug. "It makes no difference what they think or what Rome wishes. Rome does not rule in Dacia."

"Nor will they ever," Drilgisa said.

"Nor will they ever," King Decebal agreed. "Not while we still live, my brother."

*Sarmizegetusa, Dacia, April 103 AD*

Titus Lucullus was in command of the Roman garrison in the holy city of Sarmizegetusa. The two hundred Roman legionnaires were there for observation, not enforcement. Lucullus saw himself as the Emperor's watchdog, tasked with keeping an eye on how well the King of Dacia was following the terms of Dacia's treaty with Rome. From what Titus had observed so far the answer was not very well, and it left the Roman feeling troubled.

Lucullus asked to meet and talk with Diegis and Vezina. Diegis was the younger brother of King Decebal and a high ranking general of infantry. The very old and very wise Vezina was the High Priest of Zamolxis, Dacia's religious leader and also the closest advisor to King Decebal and Queen Andrada. Over the years Titus had gotten to know both these men and trusted them to be honest with him. They shared that trust in him in return.

The Roman garrison was housed in tents in an open space inside the walls of Sarmizegetusa. No Romans were allowed in the royal palace by order of Queen Andrada, and so Diegis and Vezina went to see Lucullus in his tent. As was often the case Titus was occupied with administrative matters. Even a small garrison required daily record keeping and he had no clerk to do that work for him.

"Titus, put away your scribbling," Diegis greeted him lightly with an amiable smile. "How can you Romans hope to conquer the world when you spend all your time with scribbling and record keeping?"

"Who says that we hope to conquer the world?"

"Everyone says that, Titus," Vezina answered in a matter of fact voice. "It would be false modesty to deny it."

Titus conceded and gave them a half smile. "I cannot deny that people say that, but neither am I Caesar or the Senate of Rome. The ambitions of Rome are not under my command."

"Fair enough," Vezina said. "So what do you wish to discuss?"

Lucullus' expression turned serious. "King Decebal is taking land from the Iazygis, I am told. Dacia is rebuilding the mountain forts that were damaged in Rome's war with Dacia the past two years. Also I see that Dacia is constructing new field artillery and siege engines."

"All these things are true," Diegis agreed. "Dacia must protect our people against our enemies, as we always have."

Lucullus shook his head. "All these actions break the terms of the treaty agreed to by Dacia and Rome. This treaty is hardly six months old and already King Decebal acts as if there is no treaty."

"We are aware of our treaty obligations, Titus," Vezina said. "Even so the King will do what is necessary in the defense of Dacia."

"The Iazygis complain to me, and they are allies of Rome," Titus added. "This is why I must complain to you."

"Are we not also allies of Rome?" Vezina asked.

"You are, Your Holiness," Lucullus replied patiently. "However, if treaties are to work then allies must treat each other in a reasonable manner. King Decebal is reclaiming land that was taken from Dacia, and the Iazygis claim that he is also taking land that was always Iazygi land. He does this to punish the Iazygi."

Diegis gave a small shake of his head. "It is not so simple. Perhaps one day we can have a talk about the history between the Iazygi and Dacia. Borders are not always clear or agreed upon."

"I expect that will be a lengthy and complicated education," the Roman said. "For now my interest is only in keeping the peace."

"We are keeping the peace," Vezina assured him in an agreeable tone. "The Iazygi are moving back to their lands with little fighting and minimal bloodshed."

"I am asking for Dacia and King Decebal to honor the terms of our treaty. No more than that."

"That is perfectly reasonable, Titus," Vezina said. "However let us also understand that there are two things in life that often do not obey the laws of reason."

"Only two?" Diegis asked with a grin.

Lucullus gave the High Priest a small respectful bow. "I defer to your great experience and wisdom, Vezina. Tell us then, what are these powerful forces that defy the laws of reason?"

Vezina continued in a serious tone. "The first of these forces is the quick forgiveness and fierce protectiveness that a mother shows towards her children, even when her children are in the wrong. We all have seen it."

Titus gave a nod. "Yes. And the second force?"

"The second is something that few people see directly but that you and I are both familiar with. You no doubt have seen it also, Diegis."

"And what is that?" Diegis asked, now curious.

"The pride of kings."


Queen Andrada made it a rule that the evening meal include all the members of her family who were in the city at the time. This was not some display of authority but rather a simple wish to get the family together at least once a day. She was sadly aware that her family was growing smaller all the time, which made it even more imperative to keep them together when she could.

The King was often away on military or diplomatic missions. Her oldest daughter Zia was now married and living in her own quarters with her husband Tarbus. Her sister in law Tanidela was living as a captive in Rome. Her other sister in law, Dochia, and Decebal's son Cotiso were both killed in the last war with Rome.

Her youngest daughter Adila, just turned eighteen years of age, was training to be an archer of all things. Her son Dorin was five years younger and just beginning his military training. Her niece Ana, the daughter of Diegis, was twelve years old. This was her family now gathered around the dinner table.

The evening meal was roasted goose and roasted vegetables, both richly spiced with garden herbs. As always freshly baked bread was a staple with every meal along with freshly churned butter. Cow milk, goat milk, and fruit juices were provided for beverage. There was also cool water freshly drawn from mountain streams that was fed into Sarmizegetusa through large clay pipes buried underground. The beverages were served in elegant silver goblets. The palace kitchen servants brought the food and beverages quickly and efficiently.

Adila turned to her brother as she slowly spread soft butter on a thick slice of fresh warm bread. "In the morning I will be at archery practice with Tiati. He asked if you would like to join us, Brother?"

Dorin paused between bites on a roasted goose leg and shook his head no. "I don't want to learn the war bow. I will practice my swordsmanship and fight with falx and sica, like Tata."

"And also like my Tata," Ana said proudly.

"Yes," Dorin agreed. "Uncle Diegis is the best swordsman I know other than General Drilgisa."

"It would not hurt to have skill with a bow," Adila persisted. "One day it might save your life."

"I know," the boy grumbled. "Maybe some other time."

"It was very thoughtful of Tiati to ask," Andrada said to her son. She turned to her daughter. "Are you and he becoming friends?"

"Yes, Mama," Adila replied. "We are friends. And he is the best bowman I know at our age. I saw Cotiso fight with a bow and Tiati is just as good as Cotiso."

"Then he must be very good," Dorin said. "Thank you for asking me, but I will stick with the falx."

"Adila, when I am older you can teach me how to use the war bow," Ana said.

The older girl smiled at her young cousin. "I will be happy to. But first you need to get much bigger and stronger to use a war bow. And before you can kill Romans, you need to learn to kill some rabbits and squirrels first!"

The Queen gave Adila a reproachful look. "We are at peace with Rome. No one needs to be killing Romans."

"Yes, Mama," Adila said. "We are at peace with Rome. For now."

That took Ana by surprise. "What do you mean, for now? Will the Romans come back?"

Andrada sighed with exasperation. "Adila, stop with this talk of war." She gave Ana a calming smile. "The Romans are not coming back. We are at peace and will remain at peace."

"I am sorry, Ana, I did not mean to frighten you," Adila said. She placed a comforting hand on the girl's shoulder. "I did not mean that the Romans are coming back now."

"What Adila means," Andrada interjected, "is that we must be prepared if any enemies attack Dacia. It makes no difference if they are Romans, or Iazygi, or Gauls, or Germans. If enemies attack we must be ready to defend ourselves."

"I understand, Auntie," Ana said. "Tata tells me the same things when he has to go out and train our soldiers."

"Good," Adila said. "Don't be afraid of our enemies, Ana. Practice with your hunting bow for now. When you are stronger in three or four years I will teach you the war bow."

"And what are your plans?" the Queen asked her daughter. "Will you join an archery unit now that you are becoming an archer?"

"I don't know yet, Mama." Adila gave a small shrug. "I just want to be useful, and not sit around feeling helpless."

"You are not helpless, my daughter," Andrada said. "One thing you will never be is helpless."

King Decebal returned to the capital city of Sarmizegetusa several weeks later. The military campaign in the western part of Dacia against the Iazygi tribes was finished. The repair and rebuilding work on the Dacian forts on the western frontier was well underway.

Vezina and Diegis provided a report of developments on the home front. Diegis had just returned from a tour of the northern Dacian tribes and brought back fresh troops with him. The population of northern Dacia had not been touched in the war with Rome.

"Three hundred cavalry and one thousand archers," Diegis said, "in addition to the four thousand infantry. We are forming new units for them to keep men from the same tribes together."

"Well done," Decebal said. "But we'll need another five thousand infantry and at least as many archers and cavalry."

Diegis gave a nod. "Perhaps next year, Brother. The village chiefs are grumbling. They need men to harvest the crops in the summer."

"We cannot blame them for that," the King said. "And how are our Roman guests?"

"Ah, nothing different," Vezina replied. "Titus Lucullus thinks that we are poking the Roman bear too harshly."

"He would think that," Decebal said. "On the other hand we have two choices. We can either poke the bear when necessary to make our armies stronger, or we can sit idly by and wait until the bear decides to eat us."

"I agree, Sire," Vezina said. "I think that perhaps even Lucullus might agree but his loyalty to Rome comes first."

"We should not expect anything less from Titus," Diegis added.

"Can he be bought?" Decebal asked with a laugh. "We can always use men like him who are so highly dedicated."

Diegis shook his head. "Not this one. He would rather open the veins in his wrists before he would betray his duty to Rome."

"Ah, but there are others betraying Rome even as we speak," the High Priest said. "We are getting a trickle of Roman deserters coming to our camps again. Not from the garrison here because Lucullus would have them crucified, but from camps along our frontiers with Rome in the south."

Decebal raised an eyebrow. "More Roman deserters so soon, after Trajan beheaded two hundred of them just last year?"

"There will always be men who desert," Vezina said. "Some have grievances with their army officers or general grievance against Rome. And some are just plain greedy. Dacia pays them better."

"Do we want to recruit deserters, I wonder?" Diegis asked.

"That is a question worth the asking, Diegis," Vezina said. "Roman deserters joining our army is what most offended Emperor Trajan when we discussed terms of treaty."

"First we will consider what is in the best interest of Dacia," the King said. "Then consider what might offend Emperor Trajan."

"We recruit deserters then, Brother?"

"No, we don't need to recruit them. They will come to us for their own reasons. We should be selective and accept men with special skills or specialized knowledge. Those men we can use."

Diegis gave a nod. "Understood."

"Do what needs to be done," the King commanded. "We'll sort out our differences with Rome as we go along."


The practice field for archers was a large open space on the north side of the city near the military quarters. Adila and Tiati competed with each other. This drove each of them to greater effort and also made practice more enjoyable. They shot twenty arrows at targets from thirty paces away, then distanced themselves to fifty paces, seventy paces, and so on to a distance of two hundred paces. A superior foot archer could be effective from as far away as two hundred and forty paces.

Adila had a good eye in the shorter ranges but Tiati was stronger, sturdy and athletic, and he had the advantage in the longer ranges. He was two years older and began his training at a younger age, which also gave him a big advantage in experience.

"Ah! I am useless past ninety paces!" Adila complained with a laugh. "I will never be as strong as you."

"You are not useless," Tiati disagreed. "You are very deadly within ninety paces and that is good enough."

"Good enough for shooting deer, maybe."

Tiati shook his head. "You are looking at your skills the wrong way, Adila."

"What do you mean, the wrong way? You are stronger than me and more accurate at far distance. That makes you a better archer."

"From a far distance, yes. But think, Adila. Dacian archers rarely fight from long distance. We fight in the mountains and the forests, often in ambush attacks, usually at close range."

Adila sat down on the grassy turf for a rest and put her bow down beside her. "You are right. The only battle I saw in person was at Tapae, which was not typical. The armies fought on open ground and our archers attacked from both long distance and short."

Tiati sat down beside her. "Yes, but that is not how we usually fight. When I joined the army last year it was all mountain fighting, forest fighting."

"Ah, I see. You are saying then that you did not kill the enemy from a hundred paces away?"

Tiati laughed, his eyes twinkling. "In the forest you can't even see the enemy from a hundred paces away!"

"I understand. So maybe I won't be useless after all, huh?"

"If we go to war again," Tiati said in a serious tone, "you will be a very lethal forest sniper with a bow."

"Well then, my friend," Adila said, standing up, "let's get back to practice and work on our accuracy and stamina. Shall we?"

Most days the Queen and King found time to talk late in the evening. It was their only time to be alone and not be interrupted.

"Our children are growing up so fast," Andrada said. "Zia is now married. Adila is training to be an archer. And before you know it Dorin will want to join the army."

Decebal stretched out beside her on the soft woolen sheets. "I can remember a time, my dear, when your fondest wish was simply to see them grow up healthy and safe."

"Ah, you are right," Andrada said. "I am concerned as a mother, that's all."

"They are well, Andrada. We cannot do more for them, only try to protect them as we protect all our people."

"Our enemies are camped in tents outside the royal palace," the Queen said with a half smile

"They are not our enemies now. They are our guests, under terms of treaty with Rome."

Andrada sighed. "Guests, then. How long will this peace last? That is the question."

"We cannot know. It may last for a year. It may last forever."

She turned to look at him directly. "You know very well the peace will not last forever."

"Most likely not."

"Vezina says that we are poking the bear," she mused.

"There is no way around it," the King declared. "Rebuilding our army is poking the bear. So is renewing alliances with our neighbors, and driving the Iazygis from our land."

"All these things might be seen as breaking the treaty with Rome. If you were a Roman, certainly."

"Possibly. But what is the alternative?"

The Queen frowned. "Capitulation. Surrender."

"Yes. And when have you known me to surrender?"

"Never."

"Then we will do whatever is necessary for Dacia, and the bear be damned."

"What then is our aim, Husband?"

"Peace only comes through strength, not weakness. Dacia must be strong as always."

"I know. This has always been true."

"It is a truth that will never change," the King said in a firm voice. "That is why we prepare for whatever the future holds. The rest is in the hands of the gods."

Andrada gave him a wry smile. "Which gods? Zamolxis and Jupiter have different visions for the future of Dacia, I think."

Decebal returned the smile. "There is one true god. Zamolxis rules us and we show him deference and obedience. Jupiter is a statue in a temple in Rome, made from baked clay and paint. We should not be afraid of their clay gods."

"No," Andrada acknowledged. "I am not afraid of their barbaric gods. Their legions however might be a concern in the years to come."

"Exactly right, my queen. And that is why we must prepare to face their legions again. This is what keeps Dacia free and our children safe."

# Chapter 2

# The Bridge

*Rome, April 103 AD*

Games at the Circus Maximus were presented to the people of Rome as a generous gift from Emperor Marcus Ulpius Trajanus. Free admission to the games was just one more reason for the multitudes to love Caesar. They had always loved him for his military victories and his noble character. Indeed, his military achievements in Germania and Dacia were being compared to those of the Divine Julius Caesar.

On a sunny and glorious spring morning Emperor Trajan watched the chariot races from the Emperor's box, which had the best view in the stadium. His co-consul for the year, General Laberius Maximus, sat next to him. Trajan was known to reward his friends generously and Maximus deserved the highest rewards for his military successes in Dacia. Being elected as a consul of Rome was the highest political position a Roman nobleman could aspire to. The Emperor's closest friend, Licinius Sura, had been similarly rewarded with a consulship the year before.

Seated on the other side of Trajan were the Empress Pompeia Plotina and his sister Ulpia Marciana. The women were close friends and shared responsibility for managing the Trajanus household. They also shared responsibility for managing the vast financial interests and business enterprises of the Trajanus family. Many who knew the Emperor well credited Plotina and Marciana for playing key roles in

Trajan's rise to political power. He was a military mastermind who devoted most of his life to military matters, and indeed spent most of his life living in military camps while on campaign. When Trajan was away these two very capable women took care of family business in Rome.

Five of the scheduled twenty-four chariot races for the day were already completed. Maximus was in a happy mood because the team he sponsored had just won the last race. Romans bet heavily on the races and on their favorite teams and drivers, and Laberius had placed a very large bet on his team.

"How many wins does that make for your man Sirius?" Trajan wondered. Sirius was Maximus' slave and one of the most popular chariot race drivers in Rome. Slaves were trained from an early age to be professional race drivers. The most successful became stars and were treated as sports celebrities in the city.

"This is his fifth win this season," Laberius said proudly. "He has a gift for handling horses and race strategy. Ten more wins and he will earn enough to buy his freedom."

"That would be wonderful for him," Plotina said in a pleasant voice. "If he lives that long, of course."

Trajan turned to her with a patient smile. "Well, of course if he lives that long. Racing is a dangerous sport and Sirius knows that. It also gives him opportunities for fame, fortune, and freedom."

"It is a dangerous sport for team sponsors also, my dear Plotina," Maximus said. "It is hugely expensive to hire and maintain a racing team. Stables, horses, drivers, trainers, veterinarians, stable boys. If the team doesn't win you can lose a small fortune."

Marciana scoffed at his comments. "Don't tell me you do it for the money, Laberius. There are much easier ways to make money."

"No, my lady," Maximus replied. "I do it for the sport. My farms in Campania bring in more than enough money."

Marciana gave him an indulgent smile. "Then enjoy the sport and don't fret about the money."

"I bow to your wisdom, my lady," Laberius said with a nod. He was sincere in his compliment. Marciana was known among the nobility for having a very shrewd business mind.

"Ah, here comes Salonia and the girls," Plotina said. "Running late as usual, the poor dears."

Salonia Matidia was the daughter of Marciana and the only niece or nephew of the Emperor. Since Trajan had no children of his own he had always treated Salonia like a daughter. Salonia's daughters, twenty year old Mindia Matidia and nineteen year old Vibia Sabina, were like granddaughters to him. Salonia and her children lived as part of the Trajanus household since the two girls were barely past their infancy. Salonia's unfortunate husbands did not live long after marriage to her, although she was not to blame for that.

Salonia, Mindia, and Vibia took seats in the Emperor's box one row behind the royal couple. They exchanged warm but still proper and polite greetings. In private the Trajanus family was very casual in how they treated each other. In public they were always formal and well mannered. Impeccable social graces were required for public life in Caesar's family.

Salonia motioned to the guest who was following close behind her and her daughters. "Tanidela, come sit by me."

Tanidela, sister of King Decebal of Dacia, was a well-treated royal prisoner of Emperor Trajan and Rome. She gave a curt bow towards the royal couple and took a seat beside Salonia. She and Trajan's niece became fast friends in part because they were close in age, in their late thirties, and similar in tastes and temperament. They were both considered elegantly beautiful and popular with the common people of Rome.

Much to Tanidela's surprise after her arrival in Rome, being taken in by Trajan's family resulted in her being treated as a minor celebrity by the people of Rome. She made her own fashionable clothes in the Dacian fashion, white fabric embroidered with colorful designs using multiple colors of thread. Her distinctive native dresses, along with her light brown hair and striking green eyes, made her stand out in any Roman crowd and enhanced her celebrity status.

Plotina turned to greet her Dacian guest. "You did not bring little Tyra?" Tyra was Tanidela's little girl, two years old going on three. When Tanidela was captured by the army of General Maximus she had the infant Tyra with her.

"No, Empress. I left her with her nurse. She would be frightened by such a large crowd."

Marciana laughed. "It is a frightfully large crowd, isn't it? And all that noise!"

"We cannot expect one hundred and fifty thousand people to stay quiet when they are enjoying themselves, Sister," Trajan said. He also turned towards Tanidela. "You are well, lady Tanidela?"

"Yes, Caesar, I am well," she replied pleasantly. "I trust that you are well also?"

Trajan smiled at her self-assurance. One did not inquire about Caesar's health, but Tanidela was the daughter of one king and the sister of another. She refused to allow herself to be intimidated by any person or situation. He treated her well, this royal prisoner, in part because he liked her. But she was also a useful political prisoner and he would not set her free just yet. Perhaps she would never be set free because the problems with Dacia might never be fully settled.

"The next race is about to start, Tanidela. Enjoy the race."

"Yes, Caesar."

Some distance below them on the stadium floor four chariots were lined up behind the starting gate. Each was pulled by a team of horses. A race official standing to the side dropped a cloth napkin, a trumpet gave a loud blast, the starting gate was lifted via a catapult mechanism, and the teams of horses pulling the four chariots bolted out of the starting gate and raced down the track.

The crowd erupted with cheers and shouts. The chariots were bunched so close together, each looking for an advantage down the track, that it seemed impossible to Tanidela they would not crash into each other.

"How do they not get killed?" she asked Salonia, leaning close to her ear to be heard above the roar of the crowd.

Salonia gave a casual shrug. "Sometimes they do get killed. Watch when they come back this way and turn around the corners, that's when they get most daring and reckless."

Tanidela leaned back in her seat and watched. The chariots were already at the far end of the huge stadium and making a turn. They would race around the track seven times, always turning left around the corners. At the end some team would win and be rewarded with gold. Some people would rejoice and celebrate, and sometimes some drivers and horses would die. This was Rome, her new life, the world that her daughter Tyra would grow up in and call home.

The thought made her angry, but she had to keep the anger buried inside. Tyra was not in danger living among the Romans, she knew. What angered Tanidela was that her freedom to choose a life for her daughter was denied to her. She was treated well and allowed some freedom, but it was the freedom of a bird in a golden cage.

Emperor Trajan frequently enjoyed the company and counsel of his old friend Licinius Sura. Like Trajan himself, Sura was a native of Hispania who rose to the top of political power in Rome. He was a decade older and for a long time had served as a mentor to the young Trajan. With the help and influence of Sura the young General Trajan also became a friend of Senator Marcus Nerva, who in time became Emperor Nerva. Emperor Nerva later adopted Trajan as his son and heir. Trajan's path to becoming Caesar went through Licinius Sura.

"Tell me more about this bridge you wish to build, Marcus," Sura asked. "A bridge across the Danubius? It is a fantastical idea. Even at its narrowest points the river is more than half a mile wide."

Trajan grinned at Sura's dubious tone. "Yes, a bridge made of stone and timber, that spans almost a mile long from one river bank to the other. It will connect Moesia and Dacia across the Danubius. Yes, Licinius, it can be done!"

"But why would you wish to connect Moesia to Dacia? We have enough trouble as it is keeping the barbarians on the north side of the river and out of Moesia."

Trajan shook his head. "I am not worried about the barbarians. This bridge is for our use, not theirs. It will be guarded by forts and legionnaires on each side."

"Very well, it will be our bridge under our protection. Then what?"

"Then we can move troops quickly and efficiently into Dacia or any other territory north of the river. And it will allow us to transport goods south from Dacia on a very large scale."

"Ah ha!" Sura exclaimed with a smile. "I can see your greater plan unfolding. We are not finished with Dacia, then."

"No, Licinius. We are far from finished with Dacia. There is a great deal of wealth there in gold, silver, iron, cattle, and grain."

"Indeed there is, all that and more. Then we must insist that Dacia give us very favorable trade terms and access to their wealth. If they don't then we shall have to pacify or conquer Dacia."

"Exactly so," the Emperor replied. "Now you are seeing my vision."

Sura raised his wine goblet in a toast. "To the wealth of Dacia then, and to the greater glory of Rome. This bridge will be essential for both military movement and commerce."

Trajan looked up towards the door, pleased to see the two visitors being led into his study. "Hadrianus! Apollodorus! We have been waiting for you."

The two men approaching were strikingly different in every way. The tall, broadly built Hadrian looked like a young Hercules. The much shorter, slightly built Apollodorus looked like a middle aged engineer. The older man was Greek and wore his hair short and his beard neatly trimmed in the Greek style. Hadrian was a Roman who was raised within the Trajanus family, but he was also an admirer of Greek culture and wore his hair and beard in the same fashion.

Apollodorus of Damascus was widely recognized as the greatest engineer and architect of his time. He was held in very high esteem by Emperor Trajan, who had no shortage of building projects for him. The engineer carried two large map scrolls under his left arm. These were the plans for Caesar's greatest project yet.

Trajan directed them to a long polished table. "Come this way, Apollodorus. I am very eager to see your drawings."

"Yes, Caesar," the engineer said. He proudly unfurled the first scroll, a map of Moesia and southern Dacia, and placed weights on the corners to hold it down flat. "This location is by far the best suited for the bridge. The city on the lower bank is Pontes. The city on the upper bank, in Dacia, is called Drobeta."

"How wide is the Danubius at this location?" Sura wondered.

"Over half a mile," Hadrian answered eagerly. "However the river has a unique feature – "

"In the middle of the river at this spot is a very large sand bar," Apollodorus interrupted. "This will make it easier for us to divert the river, one half at a time, and build the stone and cement pillars on top of the riverbed."

Sura raised an eyebrow, still looking skeptical but willing to be convinced. Hadrian looked very irritated with the engineer for his rude manners but kept his temper. Apollodorus did not have much patience with the young man or much respect for his opinions.

"Is this not a brilliant plan?" Trajan asked happily. "Let us see your drawings of the bridge, Apollodorus."

"With pleasure, Caesar," the Greek said. He unfurled the second map scroll across the table top.

Sura took a look and gave a soft whistle in amazement. Trajan gave him a grin, pleased to see his friend's reaction. The bridge looked very long, very wide, and very solid. Twenty tall and massive stone and cement pillars held up the wooden structure of support arches, timber floors, and guard rails on each side.

"Is it to my specifications, Apollodorus?"

"Yes, Caesar. Exactly so. It is wide enough to allow two vehicles to pass in opposite directions, whether they be military vehicles or transport wagons. And in the center there will still be enough room for a column of legionnaires to march six abreast."

"That is astounding!" Sura exclaimed.

"Astounding indeed," the Emperor agreed. "Hadrian had the idea originally, we must credit him that. Apollodorus is in charge of the architectural designs and the engineering plans to make certain the bridge is strong enough. Hadrian will assist him in the construction."

Sura gave Hadrian an appreciative nod. "Well done, Hadrianus."

Hadrian acknowledged the compliment. "The hard work is still ahead of us. Apollodorus and I leave for Moesia shortly. Together we will build this bridge."

The Greek gave him a patient smile. "You shall have responsibility for the legions and for procuring the manual labor. Freedmen, slaves, legionnaires, it does not matter who but we will need a lot of men. I shall be responsible for all design and construction decisions."

Hadrian gave him a pained look. "This was my idea to begin with, Apollodorus. I have many more ideas."

"You gave Caesar an egg, and the egg was an excellent idea," the older man said. "I, however, shall give Caesar the chicken."

Trajan and Sura burst out laughing. Hadrian's face turned red. He was not amused.

The Emperor placed an arm around Hadrian's shoulder. "You are the general in charge of the legions, Hadrianus. You will be providing security and manpower. I am placing four legions in your hands and I trust that you will command them well."

"Yes, Marcus," Hadrian said. "I will command well."

"Good. You will command the men, and also you will learn from this master builder standing before us. In this important project of architecture and engineering Apollodorus is your general."

"I understand, Caesar," Hadrian said.

Trajan looked from Hadrian to Apollodorus. "You will work as a team to build me a bridge that will stand for a hundred years. A bridge of stone and timber that will transport armies and goods and make Rome master of the barbarian lands beyond the Danubius."

"It shall be done, Caesar," Apollodorus said with a slight bow. "We will require a small mountain of stone and a forest of oak trees, but we shall build this bridge to Caesar's satisfaction."

"How long will it take to completion? Your estimate?" Sura asked.

Hadrian gave a shrug and looked to Apollodorus for guidance. The Greek paused for a moment.

"Three years, perhaps four. No longer."

Trajan shook his head. "Two years, Apollodorus. We may need use of this bridge sooner than we expect."

"Yes, Caesar," Apollodorus replied and rolled up his scrolls. "Let's get to work, Hadrianus. I want to leave within the week."

"My men are eager to get started," Hadrian said. "They will be supplied and ready to march in three days."

"That's the spirit," Trajan said approvingly. "Get to work."

Sura watched the two men leave at a brisk walk. "So you think this can be done?"

"It will be done!" the Emperor declared. "Apollodorus can work miracles, and I will provide him with whatever he needs."

"Good. I believe you. The only doubt in my mind is, will those two work together?"

The question caught Trajan by surprise. "Of course they will. They will work together, Licinius, because I command it."

Sura gave him a small smile. "Then you better command it clearly, else Hadrian might kill the Greek on the banks of the Danubius."

When the Danubius River was at low tide Apollodorus of Damascus directed his work force of twenty thousand men to start digging. They diverted the water in order to uncover the muddy river bed from the Pontes side of the river out to the sand bar in the middle. Massive pillars of stone and concrete were then driven into the river bottom, then reinforced at ground level by large stone and cement structures.

The pillars had to rise one hundred and fifty feet above the river bed foundation. The bridge had to be high enough to not only clear the river at high tide but also to allow enough room under the bridge for boats travelling on the river to pass underneath.

When the pillars were completed on the Pontes half of the river, the process was repeated on the Dacian side at Drobeta. The work was difficult, grueling, and hot. Workers were driven hard, Roman legionnaires as well as many thousands of slaves and hired freedmen. Hadrian and Apollodorus used generous monetary rewards to push the free men and threats of punishment to push the slaves.

Oak forests were cut down to provide the timber for the floors of the bridge, the wooden arches supporting the upper structure, and the sturdy guard rails necessary to prevent men and animals from falling over the side. Every foot of the bridge was designed and built to the specifications of Apollodorus.

While most of the workers toiled at bridge building, others worked on building the military forts at each end of the bridge. These were needed to garrison the Roman troops and also to guard the bridge and the warehouses from attack. Emperor Trajan knew that when the bridge was finished, or perhaps sooner, it would become a military target. He counted on General Hadrian to defend it.

# Chapter 3

# Messenger to Zamolxis

*Sarmizegetusa, June 104 AD*

Dadas was captain of cavalry scouts for the Dacian army. All the scouts across Dacia reported to him, and he in turn reported the information to the High Priest Vezina. Vezina was the chief advisor to King Decebal and also the man in charge of Dacia's network of spies and informers.

The reports from Dadas after his return from southern Dacia and Moesia were troubling. The young cavalry officer, of average height but wiry and slim and able to stay in the saddle for days on end, summarized the information in his verbal report. His audience was the royal couple, the High Priest, and the generals Diegis and Drilgisa.

"The Romans recently finished construction of the walls of both forts, at Drobeta and Pontes. Each side of the river is defended by two cohorts of legionnaires. The rest of their troops are still working on bridge construction but can be deployed for military action on very short notice."

"They expect an attack on the bridge," Vezina said.

"As would I, Vezina," said King Decebal. "As would you."

Vezina gave a nod. "Indeed, Sire. That bridge has but one purpose and that is to move their armies quickly and efficiently across the Ister into Dacia." The mighty river that Romans called the Danubius was known to the people who lived on its banks as the Ister River.

Andrada gave Dadas a doubtful look. "Truly, it goes from one bank of the river to the other? That does not seem possible."

"Yes, My Queen," the scout replied. "Thus far they have the stone pillars in place, from one bank to the other. When they complete the wooden structure of the bridge on top of the pillars it will span the entire river from the Dacia side to the Moesia side."

"And how long will it take to complete?"

Dadas shook his head. "I do not know, My Queen. I don't have the knowledge of an engineer."

"It took them a year to reach this point," Vezina answered for him. "I expect it might take another year to complete it. This is the most ambitious building project I have ever heard of. Of course diverting the river and building the cement pillars was the most complicated and difficult part."

"We should attack now, before they finish it," Drilgisa said. "The longer we wait the more difficult it will be to attack it later. Once the floor is built they can use the bridge to quickly reinforce the troops on the Dacia side."

"I am thinking the same," said Diegis. "It makes the most sense from a military view."

Decebal leaned back in his chair, in silent thought. His general Drilgisa was usually inclined to take an aggressive approach. That made for successful military strategy but poor diplomatic strategy. His brother Diegis was of a similar mind. As the leader of the nation however he had to think beyond military strategy and look further ahead in time.

"There will come a time when we must fight for this bridge," the King told them, looking around at the faces waiting expectantly for his decision. "As long as it remains in Roman hands it will be a threat to Dacia and the nations north of the Ister. However, now is not the time to fight for it."

"Why not, Brother?" Diegis asked.

"For two reasons. The first is that we are not prepared for another war with Rome. We need more time, at least another year, to rebuild the army."

"I agree about the military preparations, Sire," Vezina said. "And what is the second reason?"

"The second reason," Decebal continued, "is that I do not wish to destroy the bridge. I wish to use it. We should wait until the Romans complete the structure, and then we'll capture it."

Drilgisa laughed. "I like that idea even better."

"If we capture the bridge then we will need to hold it," the Queen said. "By any turn it means war with Rome."

"Yes it does, My Queen," Vezina agreed in a serious tone. "War with Rome is coming whether we wish for it or not. That is why they are building this bridge."

Andrada sat back with a sigh. "I wish that I could disagree with you, Your Holiness, but every time I do that I eventually find that I was wrong."

Decebal addressed his chief of scouts. "Well done, Dadas. Keep us informed. I want a report every week on the progress of the bridge construction. If they start to move men or goods across the bridge I want to know immediately."

"Yes, Sire," Dadas acknowledged the order. He gave a bow towards the royal couple, then turned and walked away.

"A bridge over the Ister," Diegis said, shaking his head in wonder. "No more winter crossings across the ice, eh?"

"If Zamolxis wills it, it will be so," the High Priest said.

Drilgisa gave the priest a good natured grin. "I hear that this Greek named Apollodorus will also have a say in the matter."

"Ah! You are fortunate that Zamolxis so clearly favors you as a warrior, Drilgisa," Vezina replied with an easy smile. "Perhaps it would be wise to not repeat such sacrilege however."

"Yes, Your Holiness," the general said with a slight bow.

The High Priest took Drilgisa's joking in stride. The General could be irreverent but he was never disrespectful, as Vezina well knew.

The King turned to Vezina. "How are preparations faring for the Messenger to Zamolxis ceremony?"

"Very well, Sire. The competition will be concluded in one week. Following that the priests of Zamolxis will select the winner. Then the week after that we will have the Messenger ceremony."

"And how is my son competing?" Decebal asked.

"He is doing well, Sire. He is very young and at a disadvantage in most events. He is a most fierce competitor, however."

Andrada frowned. "Dorin is too young! He should not be involved in the competition at such a young age."

"The boy is fourteen years of age," said Decebal. "Yes, he is very young for the Messenger competition but he is old enough to decide about participating. We cannot deny him that right."

The Queen shook her head skeptically. "He is simply too young."

"The gods must be honored," Decebal said in an even tone. "If we break our own laws and traditions, then what do we become?"

Diegis caught Andrada's eye. "I watched Dorin compete in some contests. He is like a young colt running around trying to keep up with mature warriors like Boian and Tiati. He may not win but the effort will make him stronger."

"It is in the hands of the gods," declared the King.

The discussion was over.


Before he became a god Zamolxis was a very learned man and a priest of Dacia. In his youth he travelled the world to gain the knowledge of the world. He spent many years as a close discipline of Pythagoras, the great scholar widely considered to be the father of philosophy and mathematics. After many years of study he returned to his home in the mountains of Dacia and became the first High Priest of Dacia. He educated and trained his people in the sciences including medicine, mathematics, astronomy, and philosophy. After he died Zamolxis was re-born as a god, and his spirit continued to live on in the holy mountain Kogaion. Zamolxis was immortal. He would watch over his people for all time.

Zamolxis walked the earth as a mortal six hundred years before the birth of Decebal. For countless generations since, every four or five years the people of Dacia chose a Messenger from among them to deliver their hopes and prayers to Zamolxis. At first the Messenger was picked from among the men of Dacia by drawing lots. In later generations the Messenger was chosen based on a competition among the finest warriors of Dacia. The chosen Messenger had to be the best of them all. He was the bravest, strongest, fastest, most skilled in military arts, and the most handsome of face and body.

In the years when a ceremony was scheduled the young men of Dacia competed fiercely for the honor of being chosen the Messenger to Zamolxis. It was the highest honor they could aspire to and a path to immortality. They competed in running, horsemanship, contests of strength, archery on foot and on horse, swordsmanship, knife throwing, and other contests of military skill and athletic ability. They were judged as well on strength of character and on physical appearance. The Messenger had to be unblemished to be worthy of Zamolxis.

In this particular year the final six contestants included Boian, the best horseman and swordsman in the contest. It also included Tiati, friend of the Princess Adila, who was the fastest runner and the best archer on foot and horse. It included as well the promising young athlete Dorin, a fast runner and skilled horseman who was also a prince of Dacia. Being of royal blood did not provide any benefits of favoritism for Prince Dorin. The selection of the Messenger was a sacred religious duty, and for a priest of Zamolxis to show favoritism would be an unthinkable act of sacrilege.

The selection of the Messenger was performed in front of the Holy Temple of Zamolxis, built on the highest terrace in Sarmizegetusa. It was built in a round shape to symbolize the sun, as were all temples of Dacia. The Holy Temple was held up by eight great stone pillars, each covered in a thin sheath of gold. The bright summer sunshine bouncing off the gold pillars dazzled spectators in the vicinity.

A very large crowd of people gathered to watch this most sacred ritual. In the front row of the crowd, sitting on chairs reserved for them, was the royal family including the King and Queen. They sat patiently as they watched the six final contestants being led out of the temple. The High Priest Vezina led the way, resplendent in his blue robes embroidered with threads of gold and silver. After him came Mircea, his chief assistant priest. A long line of other priests followed.

Dorin was placed in the center of the line and stood next to Boian and Tiati. He looked out over the large crowd, his face tense with the knowledge that this event could change his life. He avoided looking at the faces of his parents. His only fear was that what he saw there would make it more difficult for him to keep his poise. Above all this moment called for courage, character, and poise.

High Priest Vezina walked slowly and reverently in front of the row of contestants, meeting the anxious and impatient eyes of each one. He stopped in front of the trio of Boian, Tiati, and Dorin. It was clear that one of these three would be declared the winner. Vezina looked Boian in the eye for a moment. His gaze shifted to Dorin and he did the same. Then he turned to Tiati, and with a happy smile he reached out and placed a hand on the young man's shoulder.

Vezina led Tiati, now the chosen Messenger to Zamolxis, forward a few steps so that he would be better seen by the assembled crowd. No one cheered or shouted because the occasion called for a reverent silence. Tiati let the joy show on his face. His feelings of gratitude and honor were almost overwhelming.

In the front row of the crowd King Decebal maintained a solemn expression befitting the occasion. Queen Andrada took a deep breath and let it out slowly. Princess Adila did not quite know how to feel because too many emotions were flooding her mind.

The Messenger would spend the next three days in the Temple of Zamolxis receiving a steady stream of visitors from among the people of Dacia. People of all ages spoke with the Messenger and shared their hopes and their prayers with him. Tiati listened patiently and respectfully to each person. It was his duty to carry these prayers and messages to Zamolxis.

At the end of each prayer day a public feast was given to honor both the god and his Messenger. Tiati was the guest of honor at each banquet. Traditional songs for the occasion were sung and dances were performed. People gathered around a very large bonfire and celebrated far into the night.

The Messenger to Zamolxis ceremony was held on a morning with overcast skies. The low gray clouds threatened rain but nothing fell other than a few scattered sprinkles. Another large crowd gathered in front of the Holy Temple to watch the ceremony. This was the most sacred of religious ceremonies for the people of Dacia. The last one was performed several years ago, before Dacia's war with Emperor Trajan of Rome.

A large wooden stage, about the height of a man, was built in front of the temple. Wooden stairs on one side of the stage led to the top. Four men dressed in ceremonial robes stood and waited at the top of the stage.

The High Priest Vezina led the Messenger out of the temple and walked by his side towards the stage. The assistant priest Mircea walked behind them followed by the other priests of Zamolxis. The priests gathered and stood around the sides of the raised stage.

Vezina led Tiati up the wooden steps to the top of the stage. They walked to the front and looked out over the assembled crowd of many thousands of people. The four men in ceremonial robes stood and waited behind them. They would perform their roles when directed to do so by the High Priest.

"Are you ready, my son?" Vezina asked in a soft voice.

Tiati's eyes scanned the crowd below and far into the distance. He was an orphan and had friends in the crowd but no close family. He saw Adila standing in the front row and looking up at him, but could not tell how she was feeling from the expression on her face. At the sound of Vezina's deep voice he turned from watching the crowd to face the High Priest again.

"I am prepared, Your Holiness." Tiati's expression was calm and serene. This was the highest honor that he could ever hope for. His heart was filled with pride and he was content.

"Then let us begin, my son," Vezina told him. "Zamolxis awaits you with open arms. All our hopes and prayers go with you. Honor us, and honor our god Zamolxis, as in this moment we honor you."

"Yes, Your Holiness," Tiati said. "I thank you for this blessing and this honor."

The High Priest placed two fingers on the Messenger's forehead and said a long prayer. When he finished the prayer he gave Tiati a warm smile, his eyes misty with emotion.

"Lie down on the floor, my son," Vezina instructed.

Tiati took one last look at the crowd. These were the people he was serving, and he did so joyfully. He took a quick glance down at the ground in front of the stage. Three strongly built warriors were standing together just below him. Each of them held a very long spear in his hands.

Tiati slowly knelt down on the floor of the stage, then stretched out to lie down flat on his back. He took one last look up at the gray sky. He folded his arms over his chest, then closed his eyes. He breathed easily. He was completely at peace.

The four men on the stage each took hold of one of Tiati's arms or legs. They raised him off the floor to waist level. The crowd waited in hushed silence, some holding their breath. On a signal from Vezina the four men tossed the Messenger up in the air, over their heads and out over the edge of the stage. Below them the three soldiers with the long spears prepared themselves, the spears positioned so that the long sharp blades pointed straight up.

Tiati fell heavily on top of the three upturned spears and his body shuddered with the impact. One spear blade aimed squarely at his back slid off a rib and plunged deep into his left shoulder. A second spear pierced his right side, just below the rib cage. A third spear just missed his spine in the lower back and plunged into his left hip.

The pain was blinding but Tiati gritted his teeth hard and did not make a sound. For a moment he was suspended in the air, held up by the stout spear shafts. Some people in the crowd gasped. Adila turned her head to the side, not wishing to watch her friend suffer.

The three spearmen slowly lowered their spears and brought the body to rest gently on the ground. Pools of blood formed under Tiati's shoulder and side.

The assistant priest Mircea knelt down beside Tiati's still body. The young man's face was very pale and his eyes were closed. His lips were pressed shut very tightly. Mircea could not tell if he was still breathing, so he laid his hand on top of Tiati's chest. He felt the movement of a soft breath. And then the Messenger opened his eyes.

Tiati was in shock, in great pain, and feeling very disoriented. His eyes focused on Mircea, who was kneeling above him with a look of grave concern on his face. This was not right, Tiati knew. He should now be in the heaven of Zamolxis, not lying in pain on the ground in Sarmizegetusa. Tiati's mind was reeling with pain and confusion. He tried to move his lips but found that he could not speak.

Mircea raised his head up to the gray skies and said a prayer to Zamolxis. He looked up to the edge of the stage where Vezina was looking down at them with an intense look on his face. The High Priest was wondering the same thing that every person in that vast crowd was wondering.

Mircea looked Vezina in the eye and slowly shook his head from side to side. The answer was no. Zamolxis did not accept his gift and the Messenger was still alive. That was a very rare occurrence in the

Messenger ceremony, and when it happened it was taken as a very bad omen. The worst omen.

Vezina turned to face the assembled crowd and also shook his head from side to side. The ceremony was a failure. Some people in the crowd groaned with disappointment and some started to weep. Zamolxis rejected their Messenger, and in so doing rejected their hopes and prayers. No one knew the reasons why, not even the High Priest Vezina, but all accepted the judgment of their god.

The saddened crowd slowly drifted away and headed for their homes. The priests of Zamolxis headed back inside the Holy Temple. Mircea said a prayer over Tiati, still lying prone on his back in his own blood. Then the priest stood, sadly shook his head, and followed the other priests. A rejected Messenger was treated as an object of pity and a symbol of bad luck.

Tiati felt a presence above him and opened his eyes again. He was gazing into the calm face of Adila. The look of concern and profound kindness that she gave him took him by surprise. He was a rejected messenger and an outcast now, was he not?

"I failed," Tiati said, his voice strained and hoarse. His eyes filled with tears that rolled down the side of his face. They were not tears of pain, but hot tears of shame.

"No," Adila replied in a very firm voice. "You did not fail. Neither you nor I nor the King have the power to steer the will of the gods."

Tiati shut his eyes tight. "I should be dead. What will happen to me now?"

"What happens now," Adila said, "is we take you to the surgeon's tent." She looked up at the three spearmen, still standing near the stage. "You three men! Help me carry Tiati to the surgeon."

The proud soldiers might have brushed off an order from another young woman, but not from the daughter of King Decebal with a fierce and determined look on her face. They laid down their spears and, along with Adila, carefully carried Tiati to the surgeon.

"Tell me your thoughts on this," King Decebal asked Vezina. They were in the royal dining room having their noonday meal following the Messenger ceremony. Andrada sat next to the King.

"I have no particular thoughts on it just now, Sire," Vezina replied. "The will of Zamolxis will be revealed to us over time."

"It usually is," Decebal said glumly. "I fear that this may be a very bad portend for Dacia. It is very rare for a Messenger to be rejected by Zamolxis. I cannot recall the last time it happened."

"Neither can I," said the Queen. "It has never happened during my lifetime."

Vezina paused to take a drink from his silver water goblet and gave the matter some thought. "The last time it happened, My King, you were still a very young boy."

"So almost fifty years ago?" Decebal asked.

"Yes, Sire. It has been a very long time."

Andrada raised an eyebrow, curious. "And what happened then? In the ensuing four or five years, I mean."

Vezina gave her a bemused smile. "In truth, My Queen, I do not recall. Nothing very terrible, I don't think. I would have remembered any great tragedy if it happened."

"No plagues of locusts?" she asked. "No barbarian invasions?"

Decebal turned to her with a serious look. "This is not a joking matter, Andrada. You know this. We should not tempt the gods by mocking them."

"Yes, I know this," she replied with a sigh. "On the other hand the last few years have brought more than a few disasters for Dacia. I am simply wondering, Husband, what more can happen to us now?"

Decebal leaned back in his chair. "That we cannot know. It is the will of the gods."

Vezina gave a nod. "That is so. We can only do what is right and thus hope to win the favor of the gods."

"Ah," Andrada said, looking up as Adila entered the room. "Here is a young lady who tries to always do what is right."

Adila greeted them and joined the dining table. A servant quickly brought her a bowl of stew and a tray of freshly baked bread.

"I saw that you carried Tiati to the surgeon's tent," Decebal said. He gave her a proud and approving smile. "That was very kind of you to look after him."

She paused between spoonfuls of the savory stew. "Tiati is my friend. I will not let my friend bleed to death in the field."

"You were right to do so, Adila," her mother said. "Will Tiati live?"

"Yes, Mama, he will live." She looked at each of her parents, then at Vezina, with a hint of defiance on her face. "The surgeon said that his hip is shattered and he will likely be a cripple. But he will live."

Vezina gave her a look of sympathy. "The Messenger ceremony is over. There is no purpose now for Tiati to die when he is no longer the Messenger. I hope that he lives a long life and in good health."

"If Zamolxis wills it," Adila said and returned to her food. She hoped that her comment would not be taken as impertinent, but then again perhaps it did not matter either way.

There were so many questions on Adila's mind for which she had no answers. One question was whether the gods ever listened to the hopes and wishes of mere mortals. She had asked her mother that question once. Andrada did not know either.

Her father the King seemed certain that the gods were benevolent, yet even he cursed Zamolxis on the night that her brother Cotiso was struck by lightning. Nothing in life was certain, she thought. She could trust only herself, and do only what she thought was right.

# Chapter 4

# Enemy of Rome

*Sarmizegetusa, January 105 AD*

Brasus, the son of Tarbus and Princess Zia of Dacia, was born on a cold and snowy day in January. The cold did not touch the future prince of Dacia as he was swaddled in soft and warm blankets and furs. Zia was attended by a midwife, a wet nurse, her mother the Queen, the doctor Zelma, her sister Adila, and six devoted female servants who fetched and cleaned and saw to it that their beloved princess was not lacking for any comforts. After the baby was born Tarbus stood happily by the side of his wife and son, but otherwise he knew enough to not get in the way.

King Decebal and Buri came by shortly after to visit the young parents and their first grandchild. Both men were near fifty years of age but were still fit enough for the battlefield. Both were too valuable as leaders of their nation to risk their lives in battle, so the days of fighting on a battlefield were long past.

Zia's brother Dorin and the young girls Ana and Lia accompanied the King. Dorin stayed discretely towards the back while the two girls crowded closer to Zia's bedside to see the baby.

"This is Brasus," Zia said, uncovering the tiny face of the infant she held at her bosom. "Speak softly because he is sleeping."

"He sleeps easily and that is a good sign," Andrada said. "He has a quiet spirit and an even temper."

"So far, at least," Tarbus added with a grin. "I'm sure that soon he will be keeping us awake half the night."

"Oh, he is beautiful," Ana said with wonderment.

"All babies are beautiful, Ana," her friend Lia added. "At least that's what Mama says."

Buri leaned in slightly for a closer look. "Brasus is a good name for a warrior," he said proudly.

"And also a good name for a prince," King Decebal said, his tone equally proud.

Zia gave them both an indulgent smile. "My son will be what he wishes to be. And who knows what the future holds."

"Whatever the future might hold, in his veins flows the blood of Dacian kings," Decebal told her. "Never let him forget that."

"Oh, fear not, Tata," Adila said lightly. "Zia and Tarbus will not need to remind him. Everyone else around Brasus will make sure that he never forgets!"

That made Zia laugh. She and her sister exchanged a knowing smile.

"Yes we certainly know what it's like growing up in a royal family, Adila." She glanced at her baby's sleeping face. "But I am not worried about my son. Someday he might become a king, or like Buri he might grow orchards of apples and pears."

"Why can't he do both?" Buri wondered.

Tarbus laughed. "Oh, I don't know, Father. His crown might get tangled in the branches of an apple tree?"

Picturing that made the two girls giggle loudly, which made the baby stir. Zia put a finger to her lips to silence them.

Buri turned to Decebal. "We should go and let the child sleep."

"That's a good idea," the King said. He turned to Zia to say goodbye. "I am happy for you, my daughter. Raise your son to be healthy and strong and he will choose his own path in life."

"Well said," Buri added. "That is my only wish also, that he grows up healthy and strong in a free Dacia and chooses his own path."

"That is the Dacia we all grew up in," Andrada said. She glanced at her daughter and grandson fondly. "I know that will also be the Dacia Brasus grows up in."

*Sarmizegetusa, March 105 AD*

Titus Lucullus was still troubled by reports regarding Dacian military activity. Indeed the problems appeared to be growing worse. The number of Dacian infantry garrisoned inside the city doubled in size over the past six months. The training fields were always full, and active even in the winter time. Archery practice was ongoing, on foot and particularly on horse. The skills needed to make a good horse archer required tireless practice in both horsemanship and archery.

The Dacian stables were filled with fresh horses, many of them colts that would be trained for battle by the horse archers. Dacia bred its own horses, but the needs of a large cavalry required that many more were purchased from the Sarmatians and Scythians.

Dacia had very large reserves of gold and silver and large harvests of grain every year. Sarmatia and Scythia had the wide open plains and broad steppes that made for ideal horse country. The extensive trading between these nations was highly beneficial for all, and also made them strong allies in times of peace and war. Rome was unable to compete in these kinds of trading.

The Scythian horses were not the big war stallions preferred by Sarmatians and Romans, but rather the small and fast horses that were ideal for horse archers. Dacian cavalry preferred to fight as horse archers and excelled at this type of fighting. They were more effective against Roman infantry fighting from a distance with a war bow than the regular cavalry that fought at close quarters with lance and sword.

The numbers of Dacian artillery of all types were also increasing. These included some artillery units assigned to infantry units, but also artillery positioned on top of the walls to hold off attackers against the city. Sarmizegetusa was strengthening its defenses all the way around.

Titus was witness to all these things happening around him. King Decebal was rebuilding his army at a rapid pace. This was counter to Dacia's treaty with Rome, as both the Romans and Dacians knew. Lucullus cited all these details in his written reports to Rome.

There were no return communications from Rome, and so he had no idea whether his reports were taken into consideration by anyone with the authority to act on the information from him. Titus simply did his duty as the weeks and months flew by.

The Roman camp in Sarmizegetusa was growing bored and restless with the tedium of sitting around and doing nothing. Titus Lucullus took groups of eighty men, what the Romans called a centuria, on marches along the mountain roads outside the city. There was no need to scout because nothing in the area changed, so the marches were primarily to keep the men busy and fit. The Dacians sold them food so there was no need for hunting or gathering other supplies.

On a warm March afternoon Lucullus marched his legionnaires back towards the city gates when they came across a Dacian work detail doing road repairs. Usually Titus steered his men clear of such groups of Dacians to reduce temptations on either side to stir up trouble. There had been no physical conflicts between his men and the local people, and no verbal confrontations beyond some insults and jeers directed at his men. This was normal and expected since many Dacians viewed the Romans as an occupying force.

On this particular afternoon however as the legionnaires marched past the road work detail someone in the Dacian group shouted a loud and harsh insult. Lucullus was not bothered by insults, but what caught his attention was that this was a particularly Roman insult regarding the honor of the legionnaires' mothers. If it was said on a street in Rome it would trigger a fist fight or a knife fight and blood would be spilled.

The insult was shouted again, now clearly in a Roman accent and tone. This was not an insult made by a Dacian. There was no doubt that it came from a Roman, and there was only one reason Titus could think of that a Roman would be working on a Dacian road work detail. He could not tell which of the road workers was the Roman deserter who had shouted the insult.

"Traitor!" one of the legionnaires in the column yelled towards the group of road workers.

"Eyes front!" Titus shouted it as a stern command. "No talking while in formation!"

"Asinus!" came another shouted insult in a Roman voice from the Dacian group.

Now Titus could see that one of the workers, a large and burly man dressed in Dacian work clothes, was partially turned toward the column. The man's face was red with anger.

"Traitors die!" another marching legionnaire shouted, offended by an insult from a Roman deserter.

"Eyes front! No talking!" Lucullus repeated the order.

"Vescere bracis meis!" the deserter in work clothes taunted the marching men, his free hand grabbing his lower anatomy. "Asinus! What do you get in monthly wages? I earn as much as a Praetorian!"

The Praetorian Guards were paid double the salary of an ordinary legionnaire. This was also known to be what King Decebal paid most Roman deserters.

Lucullus took a quick sidelong glance at the man as he passed him by. He was a large man in his twenties, with curly brown hair and a prominent Roman nose. His face was distorted with anger. The man met Titus' eyes very briefly and spat on the ground in disgust.

Some of the Dacian workers were now also laughing and jeering at the legionnaires. Titus noticed that three men in particular kept their heads down and stayed diligently focused on their work. They were also very likely Roman deserters. They kept their heads down because they clearly had more sense and discretion than the brown haired loudmouth.

So, Lucullus thought unhappily, there were at least four Roman deserters in a Dacian work detail outside the walls of Sarmizegetusa. Doubtless there were many more that the Dacians were keeping out of sight. He found that thought very troubling.

Some weeks later Lucullus requested another formal meeting with Vezina and General Diegis. He wished to get away from the dreary Roman camp and arranged to meet with the two men, plus Buri, at Buri's fruit orchard inside the city walls. They sat outside at a table on the edge of the orchard. Long neat rows of apple, pear, and cherry trees stretched into the distance.

Titus was always surprised to see how large an area the city of Sarmizegetusa covered inside its walls. They had room for pasture for their livestock, and even this fruit orchard for Buri. They had enough grain stored in large granaries to supply the city for years. They had a fresh supply of water carried in through clay pipes for drinking, bathing, and even for running a sewer system underneath the city. This was a city, Lucullus reminded himself once again, built to withstand a very long siege if necessary.

"Do you like my orchard?" Buri asked. "You look a little surprised."

"It is impressive, Buri. And yes I am surprised by how many fruit trees you have here," Lucullus said. "I see that some of the trees are budding. When do you get the apple and cherry blossoms? No doubt that would be impressive to see."

"Ah, not until late April or May. Come back in May to see cherry and apple trees in full bloom."

Titus shook his head. "Regrettably I cannot accept your offer. I will be in Rome then."

Vezina raised an eyebrow. "You are returning to Rome?"

"I am, Your Holiness. Caesar summons me to Rome and I leave within the week. That is why I asked to talk with you now."

"I am happy for you, Titus," Diegis said, and sincerely meant it. "You deserve better than to spend two years living in an army tent in a field in Sarmizegetusa."

"We are soldiers, Diegis. We do what is necessary."

"So tell us," Vezina wondered, "what did you wish to talk about?"

Lucullus looked around at the three Dacian men. They were friendly and treated him respectfully, yet soon they might be enemies of Rome again. This was a time for hard truths.

"I fear for the future of Dacia and Rome, and for how we treat each other," Titus said.

"As do we," Diegis replied. "But we have kept the peace for two years now, as has Rome. Why should we not continue to abide by the treaty between us?"

Titus frowned. "Because from the beginning King Decebalus has behaved as if the treaty did not exist. Come now, we cannot pretend otherwise."

"Dacia does what is necessary to protect our people," Vezina said in a reasonable tone. "King Decebal will not accept less."

"You have rebuilt your military," Titus said evenly. "And not long ago I watched legionnaires being insulted by Roman deserters, right outside the walls of Sarmizegetusa! You understand how offensive it is to Caesar and the people of Rome that Dacia still accepts deserters from the Roman army."

Vezina gave a nod. "I understand. We make some allowances for deserters and this goes against our treaty. But tell me this, how does that compare as a threat alongside the stone bridge that Rome is building across the Ister to connect Moesia to Dacia?"

"The bridge is not part of our treaty," Lucullus said.

Vezina waved the comment away, dismissive. "Come now, Titus, that is a lawyer's answer. Trajan's bridge is a pathway for the invasion of Dacia, it could not be any more clear. Of course Dacia must take all steps necessary to defend itself."

Titus leaned back in his chair for a silent moment. "Unfortunately this point is where we come to loggerheads."

"Yes," Vezina agreed. "Unfortunately."

"Will King Decebal guarantee to keep the peace?" Lucullus asked bluntly.

Diegis shrugged. "He is my brother, but I cannot say what he will do. Will Trajan guarantee not to use his new bridge to invade Dacia? Will he tear down his bridge, which is a dagger aimed at the heart of Dacia?"

"I can answer only one of those questions, Diegis," Titus said with a tone of resignation. "Caesar will not tear down his bridge even if Jupiter himself starts to hurl down thunderbolts at it. He spent two years, and a great deal of treasure and many lives, in building that bridge. There is nothing that will convince him that it should not be completed. It is part of his legacy you see, and he expects that it will stand for a hundred years."

Vezina chuckled. "Now there is a man with vision for the future. It may well be that he is right and that bridge will outlast us all."

"Loggerheads," Buri said gruffly.

"I am afraid so," Titus agreed. He turned to Vezina with a smile. "I will always remember what you told me about the pride of kings. What I can do with that knowledge, however, I do not yet know."

"Me neither, Titus," Vezina said. "I view it as something that we may understand, but I never thought it within our power to control it. Perhaps not even they, Decebal and Trajan, can control it."

*Rome, May 105 AD*

Emperor Trajan was in a thoughtful mood. "Of all the people we have lost in the past year, Licinius, do you know who I miss the most?"

Sura did not even wish to make a guess because the names were too many. "Tell me, Caesar. Who?"

"Our fellow countryman from Hispania. There will never be a wit like him again, I am afraid."

"Ah, you mean Martial. Yes, poor Marcus Valerius. Poet to three emperors. He will live forever through his epigrams, I am sure of it." Sura raised his wine cup. "As will you, Caesar, through your name and your accomplishments."

Trajan gave his friend a half smile. "And you, Licinius? Why so humble about yourself?"

Sura laughed. "No poets will ever sing my praises. I am but a blade of grass under the boot of Emperor Trajan."

"Ah! But that would be very unfair. Without Licinius Sura there would be no Emperor Trajan."

"Who said that history is fair, Caesar?"

Before Trajan could reply he was interrupted by the arrival of two familiar faces.

"Longinus! Titus Lucullus! Welcome. Come, you must have a cup of wine with us. This new vintage of red from the wineries of Mount Falernum is excellent."

"Greetings, Marcus. And when do you not have an excellent new vintage on hand?" asked the older man with a knowing grin.

Gnaeus Pompeius Longinus was one of the Emperor's generals, and like Sura he was also a longtime friend who had been a mentor to the younger Trajan. He was growing thicker around the middle with advancing age, and his brown hair was turning gray, but Longinus still had a very sharp mind. His blue eyes were always bright with good humor and intelligence.

Titus Lucullus was a simple soldier, not a friend. He greeted the Emperor with the Roman salute, standing straight at attention and extending his right arm stiffly in front of him. "Hail, Caesar!"

"Greetings, Lucullus. How was your trip from Dacia?"

"Very long and tedious, Caesar," Titus replied, sounding weary. "It did however give me a great deal of time to think."

"Good," Trajan proclaimed. "Then you will give us your report and tell us your thoughts. But first, have some wine. You too, Gnaeus."

"The reports we get from Dacia and Banat are not good," Sura told them once the men were served their wine and seated comfortably.

"Not good and getting worse," Trajan added. "Gnaeus, what do you know about these attacks in Banat?"

"Ah! You know how these barbarians are," Longinus replied. "The Dacians grow bolder and more aggressive. In the past they restricted themselves to raids in Iazygi lands and against Celtics aligned with Rome. This spring they began to attack Roman camps."

"Are Dacian troops attacking our Roman positions directly?" the Emperor asked with some surprise.

"Yes. That is what I read in reports from my officers in Banat," Longinus said. "Decebalus has broken the peace treaty."

"But why?" Sura asked. "What benefit is there for him?"

General Longinus gave a shrug. He took a long sip from his wine goblet. "This is an excellent Falernian, Marcus."

The Emperor turned to Lucullus. "What are your thoughts, Titus? You spent two years in Dacia and know Decebalus best. You have been doing some thinking about this, you say?"

"Yes, Caesar," Titus replied, expecting the question. "From what I have seen in Dacia, King Decebalus regarded the treaty as a mere formality. He still does what he wishes, when he wishes, if he believes it is in the interests of Dacia."

"Which, in all honesty," Longinus said with an ironic tone, "is not dissimilar from what we do."

Trajan gave his friend an irritated look. "It is the right of the ruler to make decisions as necessary, Gnaeus. It is the duty of the ruled to obey those decisions."

"Decebalus does not see himself as being ruled," Sura said. "He certainly does not act like it. Do you agree, Lucullus?"

Titus gave a nod. "Decebalus will never allow himself to be ruled. His pride of kings prevents it."

Trajan gave him an amused smile. "His pride of kings, Titus?"

"Yes," Lucullus said, feeling somewhat embarrassed that Caesar might take offense. "That is what the High Priest Vezina called it."

"Smart man!" Longinus exclaimed with a laugh.

"Damn his pride!" the Emperor said. "Decebalus has broken the treaty and now he attacks Roman troops! This cannot continue."

Sura raised his wine goblet in a toast to Trajan. "And once again, Caesar plans with brilliant foresight. We shall use the bridge in Moesia to launch an invasion into Dacia after all."

"Yes," Trajan agreed. "It was inevitable."

Lucullus cleared his throat. "I must tell you, Caesar, the Dacians believed the same."

"Explain, Lucullus. They believed what?"

"That it was inevitable. That Rome would use the stone bridge in Moesia to invade Dacia."

"Well, that is why we built the bridge," Sura explained in a mild tone. "It is meant to transport armies."

"I understand," Titus said. "And so do Decebalus and his advisors. This is what makes them aggressive now. They expect to be attacked by Rome, so they strike first."

Trajan waved his wine cup dismissively. "It makes no difference what they expect, Lucullus. It only matters what we do."

"Yes, Caesar," Titus conceded. The pride of kings is not limited to Dacians, he thought. Wisely he kept the thought to himself.

Gnaeus Longinus drained his wine and placed the silver goblet on the table. "One cup is enough for me. But now we have work to do. It is time I returned to Banat and put matters in order there."

"Do that, Gnaeus," the Emperor said. "Take one additional legion with you to strengthen our forts. And if you face Dacian aggression, crush it."

"I will do so with great satisfaction," Longinus said.

"And the invasion of Dacia?" Sura asked.

"We must begin now, Licinius. It is almost June and late in the season to start a campaign, but we cannot wait until next year. We march for Pontes and Drobeta within the week."

"A question, Caesar," Titus said with a tone of concern. "What are your orders for the garrison currently in Sarmizegetusa? My men there will be in a defenseless position when hostilities break out."

"Send a messenger, Lucullus. Order them to march south and join Longinus."

"Yes, Caesar," Titus acknowledged. "Do I have your permission to lead the men out myself?"

The Emperor shook his head, losing patience. "You will return to Sarmizegetusa as part of my invading army, and not before. You are too valuable now to risk being captured by Dacia."

Titus gave an unhappy nod. "Yes, Caesar."

Sura gave him a clasp on the shoulder. "Laberius Maximus will be happy to have you back on his staff. And Caesar just now saved your life. Be happy, Lucullus!"

"Of course," Titus said, but he was disappointed. The two hundred legionnaires in Sarmizegetusa, who now had no mission except to survive, were his responsibility. He did not wish to abandon them.

The Senate House was packed full to hear Caesar's address to the Senate of Rome on the subject of Dacia. This meeting was announced on very short notice only the day before, which made it clear that the matter to be addressed was of critical importance. Dacia had often been a topic of critical importance for the Senate of Rome for the past two decades, and now there was talk of new troubles there.

The ex-consul Licinius Sura spoke to the assembled senators about Rome's last war with Dacia, in which he was a key participant. He reminded them of the peace treaty that was agreed upon between Emperor Trajan and King Decebalus. He reminded them of the terms agreed to by King Decebalus. Finally he reminded them of Caesar's fairness and generosity towards the people of Dacia. He did not give them bad news or reasons for concern yet, but left that task in the capable hands of Caesar.

Once Trajan took the floor his audience was prepared to hear the worst about their old enemy Decebalus. They were never convinced that he could be trusted in any case. What treachery and crimes was this barbarian king guilty of now?

"King Decebalus of Dacia makes agreements with Rome that he does not intend to keep," Trajan began in an even tone. "He agrees to draw down his armies, but instead he builds up his armies. He agrees to destroy his artillery and engines of war, but instead he builds and buys more engines of war. He agrees to tear down the walls of his forts, but instead he re-builds what was damaged and destroyed in the last war with Rome."

Trajan paused to let the senators take in the information and build up their ire. Already angry voices erupted as senators shouted their displeasure with the Dacian king. Decebalus was like a stone in their shoe that could not be removed.

"Fathers of the nation, this treachery will not stand. But there is more," Trajan continued. He raised his voice and his level of passion and it was clear to the senators that his feelings were heartfelt, not an act. "When I last made war on Dacia I took the heads of two hundred traitors, deserters who betrayed their duty to Rome and dishonored themselves by accepting pay in the service of our enemies. Now I learn that once again Decebalus is paying Roman deserters!"

Many senators rose to their feet in angry protest. No assault was resented more than an attack on Rome's dignity and honor. Their reaction was the same as if Decebalus was standing there before them and spitting in their faces.

"But there is more!" the Emperor continued. "After accepting the clementia of Caesar, the mercy shown to his people, Decebalus now attacks our forts in Banat and spills more Roman blood!"

"Kill him!" a senator shouted, jumping to his feet in a fury. Angry shouts around him grew louder.

Trajan raised his arm for silence. When the senators took their seats he continued in a strong voice. "Fathers of the nation, the time has come when we must deal with this rebel king with finality. The Senate and people of Rome must declare King Decebalus of Dacia an Enemy of Rome!"

Every senator rose to his feet to express his loud and enthusiastic approval.

In the centuries long history of the Senate of Rome there were very few occasions on which the Senate agreed unanimously on a law or a proposal. This now became one of those rare occasions, as Trajan knew it would. Among the nobles who made up the Senate of Rome, resentment, indignation, and hostility towards King Decebalus was universal.

Being named an Enemy of Rome was a death sentence. Every man there, from the lowest ranked magistrate to Emperor Trajan himself, now shared a common conviction and a common duty. They would do everything in their power to put King Decebalus of Dacia to death.

# Chapter 5

# The Final Campaign

*Rome, June 105 AD*

"I must make war on Dacia one more time," the Emperor announced to the Empress Pompeia Plotina. "For the last time, if the gods are good and have any sense of justice." Caesar was preparing to march with his legions in a matter of days, before the first week of June passed. Before he left Rome however there were matters of family and business nature that also had to be attended. As usual Plotina was in charge of such matters while Trajan was on campaign. She was often in charge of family and business matters even while Trajan was in Rome.

"The gods are good when you sacrifice well to them, Husband," Pompeia replied. "Has your experience on successful campaigns not taught you that lesson yet?"

"Yes, yes, I know," he said. "I sacrifice well to Mars and Jupiter and they help me defeat my enemies. It has worked on every occasion in every one of my military campaigns."

"Then keep making good sacrifices and stop fretting about Dacia," Pompeia chided him. "Although in truth, I think that what bothers you now is all this rushing about. You have no patience for it."

"We are already three months into the campaign season, my dear," the Emperor said. "Time grows short. I will not reach Pontes until late summer."

"Ah! Yes, but remember this. When you do reach Pontes you will cross into Dacia on a stone bridge!" the Empress exclaimed. "Hadrian sends letters and sketches from Apollodorus. Those sketches look marvelous."

"I have seen the drawings and I agree. The bridge already carries traffic across the Danubius, Hadrianus says. It takes only hours for a legion to cross the river, not days."

"This bridge is a miracle, Marcus. Your miracle."

Trajan shook his head in modesty. "No, my dear. I only gave the order for the miracle and Apollodorus made it happen. He is a master designer and builder."

"Nonsense!" Pompeia insisted. "Your vision, and your orders, and your money made it happen. Without those things and without your backing Apollodorus would still be just another obscure designer of artillery."

Trajan laughed. "It is futile to argue with you when you insist on giving me all the credit. We must credit Apollodorus and Hadrian as well however. They learned to work together surprisingly well. Did I tell you that Sura was afraid they would kill each other?"

"Yes, dear. Apollodorus is much too arrogant and dismissive, and our Hadrianus takes it poorly. If anyone gets killed it will be the little Greek, I fear."

"It won't come to that, they would be disobeying my orders against bloodshed," the Emperor said with a smile. "Now, about those olive groves in Hispania. Have you hired a new farm manager yet?"

"Hang the olive groves in Hispania," Pompeia said. "Marciana and I will see to them. You have more important things to attend to. Get the army prepared to march and head back to Dacia."

"In short time, my dear." Trajan paused in thought for a moment. "I am wondering about our Dacian guest. Have you spoken with her about this campaign?"

"I have not yet had the occasion, but I will. Tanidela is friendly with Salonia and the girls and keeps their company for the most part. Vibia relies on her like an older sister in matters of the heart."

"Poor unfortunate Tanidela," the Emperor said. "She bears no blame for the actions of her brother but this cannot be easy for her to bear."

"I have found that she is not lacking for political sophistication, Husband," Pompeia said. "She understands that Decebalus is now your enemy again and that you must respond to his challenges to your authority."

Trajan gave a mild frown. "It might not become necessary, but should she become a difficult presence in the palace then find other living arrangements for her."

"Pah, she is no trouble at all," Pompeia said dismissively. "And if it becomes a problem then Marciana and Salonia will take care of it. Don't let it concern you."

"Very well, then. As always your judgments regarding matters of home and heart are impeccable, my dear."

"I am glad that you think so," the Empress replied with a smile. "But you have more urgent matters, so go. The sooner you put things in order in Dacia the sooner you will return home."

"This campaign will take some time. Dacia is a tough nut to crack. I will be gone for or least one year, perhaps two."

"Then I will count on two. Difficult campaigns always take longer than we expect."

*Sarmizegetusa, July 105 AD*

"New coinage from Rome," Vezina announced. He joined the King and Queen at their breakfast table and slid a shiny new silver coin in front of each of them.

Decebal picked up his coin and looked closely at each side. "Very freshly minted. Trajan is very eager to celebrate his stone bridge, it appears."

"It looks simply majestic," Andrada said. "This must be the largest bridge in the world."

"Yes, My Queen," Vezina agreed. "It is the longest and strongest bridge ever built, and now it connects Dacia and Moesia."

"It's hard to believe that it's real," she said.

"It is real," Decebal said. "And so are the Roman troops marching across it. Emperor Trajan marches from Rome with eight legions, we are told. In a few weeks he will arrive there to inspect it in person."

"Are we at war again?" the Queen asked.

"War is coming," Vezina replied. "Emperor Trajan ensured that when he declared Decebal to be an enemy of Rome."

"No, Vezina," Decebal said. "Trajan made war a certainty much earlier, two years ago when he started building his bridge to Dacia."

Andrada sighed. "Peace never lasts for long in this world."

Decebal sat back in his chair, lost in thought. These developments were not surprising but they were still troubling. They long expected this invasion from Rome and now it was finally heading their way.

Vezina waited patiently. Andrada was less patient.

"What are you thinking, Decebal? I know that your mind is racing like a Sarmatian stallion on the open prairie."

"We must capture the bridge," Decebal told them.

Vezina agreed with a nod. "Capture it and then hold it, before the Emperor gets there with his legions."

"Exactly. That means that we must strike first and strike quickly," the King continued. "The bridge is defended on each side of the river by a strong fort. We must capture both forts. Then we hold the fort on the Moesia side and deny the Romans use of the bridge."

"That sounds like a plan to steal Trajan's bridge," Andrada said.

That made Vezina smile. "In war it is not stealing, My Queen. We call it conquering."

"Ah! Thank you for that lesson in semantics, Your Holiness."

Decebal gave the Queen a patient look. "We must be serious about this. When Trajan declared me an enemy of Rome he declared a death struggle between us."

"Oh, I do understand," she replied. "You must destroy him before he destroys you. This time there is no turning back."

"We have to weaken them before Emperor Trajan arrives with his eight legions," Vezina said. "Destroying the garrison at Drobeta would be a good start."

"What do we know about their forces guarding the bridge?" the King asked.

"General Hadrian commands four legions, IV Flavia Felix, VII Claudia, V Macedonica, and XIII Gemina," Vezina replied. "These are all veteran legions and tested in battle. Plus of course he has auxiliary infantry, and a small cavalry force that is used primarily as scouts."

"That is a good sized army and they will give us a difficult fight," the King said. "Hadrian is very young, is he?"

"He is young, not yet thirty years of age. However he has served on Trajan's staff for many years. When he is given responsibility he manages it well."

Andrada turned to Decebal. "You were winning major battles as a general when you were his age. We should not think of Hadrian as too young to be capable."

"He is untested," the King said. "Then again, at Drobeta he will be fighting a defensive battle from inside a strong fort. That does not require a tactical genius to be effective."

"We shall soon find out how good a commander Hadrian is," Vezina said. "He was raised in Trajan's family since he was a young boy so Trajan knows him well. He trusted him with this command."

"Understood, Vezina. Now we must take our army to Drobeta, there is no time to waste," Decebal decided.

"Yes, Sire," Vezina agreed. "The attack at Drobeta must overwhelm their defenses quickly and capture the bridge. And it must be done on the first try, because there might not be a second try."

Andrada picked up the newly minted silver coin and examined it again. "I must stay behind and rule the city, but I wish that I could see this bridge. It must be a wonder of construction."

"It is a wonder," Decebal agreed. "Unfortunately it is a wonder that was built to pave the way for our destruction."

*Drobeta, July 105 AD*

General Hadrian crossed over the bridge from Pontes to Drobeta on horseback. A troop of cavalry rode after him, riding two abreast. The bridge was wide enough so that infantry could march six abreast in the center section, and cavalry could ride two abreast without fear that their horses would get spooked. Gone were the old days when the animals had to be walked very carefully across a narrow boat bridge, in single file, with a cloth draped over their heads.

From atop the bridge the view of the great Danubius River flowing into the distance towards the east was simply magnificent. Hadrian felt almost like a god, riding his horse across the sky. No one before them had ever built such a bridge or enjoyed such a view.

The north fort on the Drobeta side of the river was still not quite finished. The fort walls were in place, arranged in a square boxy shape and long enough around to house military quarters and also warehouses. The warehouses were still under construction. These were needed because Emperor Trajan expected large quantities of wealth to pass over the bridge. Grain, cattle, and slaves would flow from Dacia into Moesia, and the warehouses would hold them for transport by land and by river.

Hadrian rode through the fort at a leisurely pace, enjoying the cooling breeze as dusk approached. Everywhere men were busy with construction, sawing wood and hammering nails. They would work until nightfall because their work schedule was always sunrise to sunset with not one hour to waste. Emperor Trajan demanded results at a high level of quality and in a speedy fashion.

Hadrian was exceedingly proud of what he and Apollodorus, and their legions and army of workers, had been able to build in a little over two years. He was eager to show Caesar the results of their work. He was also impatient for Trajan to arrive with his legions for more important military reasons.

The barbarians had not launched any attacks on his bridge yet, but Hadrian was not confident that situation would continue for long. His scouts reported more frequent sightings of Dacian scouts and other troops beyond the flat ground bordering Drobeta. There could be only one reason, Hadrian judged, for the increased scouting and for Dacian troops to be gathering here.

The young general rode his horse just beyond the open gates of the fort. He sat high in the saddle and looked to his left, towards the west, where the setting sun turned the sky a blazing reddish orange. To the north were some low wooded hills. Hadrian looked closely but could see no movement among the trees. When the enemy comes, he thought, they will come through those trees.

*Roman province of Moesia, July 105 AD*

The army of Emperor Trajan reached the southern part of Moesia in good time, following a good Roman road towards the Danubius and Pontes. Following long established Roman military practice, which Trajan was much too smart to ignore, the army set up a full camp every day before nightfall and established a defensive perimeter. It increased travel time but more importantly it avoided disaster. This policy was based on painful and costly Roman military losses that occurred when army commanders foolishly grew overconfident and were not prepared for enemy attacks in the night.

*Peter Jaksa*

Trajan joined a group of infantry soldiers for a meal in their mess tent. Taking his meals with his legionnaires was a common practice for him and a carryover from his many years spent as a general. He did it because he enjoyed the company of the common soldiers and considered himself their comrade in arms. This close association with his men earned him the loyalty and love of his soldiers, as it had when he was a general.

The legionnaires stood respectfully to greet Caesar and his party. Trajan was accompanied by Tiberius Livianus, the Prefect of the Praetorian Guard, and also by his food taster. The Emperor shared the same plain food that was provided to his soldiers, but no food or drink reached Trajan's lips until it was first sampled and checked for poison by the imperial food taster. There were many people in the world who wished Caesar dead.

"Good day, my fellow soldiers," Trajan greeted them. "Sit, sit, and finish your meal."

"Good day, Caesar, and welcome," one of the legionnaires said in reply. He had shared a table with the Emperor before, and he also knew that Trajan did not want his soldiers to be overly formal with him in casual situations.

Tiberius sat on one side of Trajan and his taster on the other. Six Praetorian Guards stood watch behind them. Servants assigned to the Emperor brought plates of food and cups of drink. The taster sampled each item before presenting them to Trajan.

"How are the feet holding up, men?" Trajan wondered. It was a very practical question because on a long march the most common problem for the infantry was foot problems.

"We're holding up well, Caesar. We are Roman soldiers, we love a good march," a centurion replied with a grin.

"That is good to hear, Soldier. Remain stout because after Moesia we will continue the march all the way through Dacia."

That made the soldiers smile. Conquering Dacia meant bonuses and promotions for many of them.

"Lead us, Caesar, and we'll march all the way to Germania as long as our boots hold out."

Trajan gave a nod. "You'll get new boots. Take care of your feet, men, because those we can't replace."

"Yes, Caesar," the centurion said. The men understood that Trajan was not just making small talk. He genuinely cared about the health and well-being of his men. It was a quality of leadership that only the best commanders demonstrated, and it further earned Trajan the strong loyalty of his troops.

Livianus addressed the legionnaires around him with a stern look on his face. "Last time we were merciful with the Dacians and let them keep their holy city with its temple of gold. This time we will finish the job, and you men will share in the plunder."

"Is their temple really made of gold?" a young soldier asked, eyes wide with amazement at the very idea.

"Only the pillars," Tiberius replied. "But they are massive pillars."

The centurion cleared his throat. "Caesar, a question?"

Trajan pushed away his empty plate. He was a fast eater and took only a few minutes to finish a meal. There were always many more important things to do. "What is your question, Centurion?"

"The month is almost August. Do we have time enough to invade Dacia in this campaign season?"

Livianus glared at him. "You will know Caesar's plans at a time when Caesar gives the orders to execute his plans!"

Trajan held up a hand to still the Prefect's criticism. "There is no need for rancor. The centurion is only curious."

"Yes, Caesar," Livianus said. "I did not wish to sound rancorous."

"It comes naturally to your character, Tiberius," the Emperor said with a patient smile. He turned back to the soldier. "We shall invade Dacia in due time. Plans often change due to season, weather, and sometimes due to the actions of the enemy."

The centurion nodded his thanks. "Yes, Caesar. Please forgive my curiosity but we are all impatient for the Dacian campaign to begin."

"It has already begun! We are in the midst of it, Centurion. First things first, we march to Pontes and assess the situation there. I am very eager to see my bridge. It will be a sight to see, I promise you."

*Forests of southern Dacia, August 105 AD*

"General Hadrian is scouting the area well," chief of scouts Dadas reported to King Decebal, Diegis, Drilgisa, and Buri. "My scouts have not engaged his scouts so far because that might only put him on higher alert."

"That was a good tactical decision," the King said. "Starting now, however, keep the Roman scouts at even greater distance. Attack them and kill them if need be. Our army is nearly in place and we can't have our positions scouted now."

"Yes, Sire," Dadas acknowledged with a bow, then turned and left the tent where the officers were meeting. It was late evening and dark in the forest but no fires were lit. The Dacian army did not wish to reveal itself.

"Do we attack tomorrow?" Diegis asked.

"Yes, no reason to wait," Decebal replied. He looked from Diegis to Drilgisa, his most senior generals of infantry. "Position your men tonight. We attack tomorrow at first light."

"Good," Drilgisa said. "Let's catch the bastards sleeping."

Decebal laughed. "Oh, they'll wake up fast enough! The surprise attack will give us some advantage but it won't last very long. Attack the gates and scale the north wall. Overwhelm their defenses."

"That's what we will do," Diegis said, standing up to leave. "Let's get to work."

Buri waited until Drilgisa and Diegis left the tent, then turned to his friend the King. "Shall I call them in now?"

Decebal gave him a skeptical look. "Do you think these men are worth our time?"

The big man shrugged. "I don't know. But what we do know is that Trajan made a vow before the Senate of Rome to kill you. This is a battle for survival. You only win if you kill him first. If we can do that then it also blunts the Roman attack."

"Cut off the head of the snake, eh? This Roman army will prove very hard to kill even without Trajan leading it."

"You are far superior at strategy than I am, My King," Buri said in a respectful tone. "I thought perhaps we should listen to these men at least, after Marcu talked to me about them."

"Marcu? The son of Danillo?" Decebal asked doubtfully. "Marcu is only a child."

Cassius Danillo was a Roman deserter who lived in Sarmizegetusa for many years after his desertion from the army of Tettius Julianus. In time he became a very valuable trainer for Dacian troops in fighting against Roman legionnaires. He married a Dacian woman and made a new life for himself in Sarmizegetusa.

Cassius was one of the two hundred Roman deserters who were turned over to Emperor Trajan three years ago as part of Dacia's peace treaty with Rome. Trajan promptly had all the former deserters executed, Cassius among them.

"Marcu is seventeen," Buri said. "Not a child anymore."

"Very well," Decebal said. "Let's hear what they have to say. Call in the Romans only, not Marcu."

Buri stepped outside briefly. He returned with two men following after him. They were strangers to Decebal but from their appearance and bearing they were clearly Roman. The men stopped and stood at attention before the King.

"Your names?" Decebal asked.

"Atticus Falco, ex-legionnaire, Legio VI Victrix," said the slightly older man. He looked to be about thirty years of age, of medium height and athletic build, with very dark hair and eyes. Something in his manner gave him the look of a calculating and silent killer.

"Linus Spurius, ex-legionnaire, Legio VI Victrix," said the other man. He looked to be about five years younger than Falco. He was a big man with brown curly hair and a prominent Roman nose. The look in his eyes spoke of stubbornness and defiance.

The King took a moment to take the measure of both men. Falco was the more intelligent and disciplined of the two, he reasoned. He spoke first and was likely the leader. Spurius had the look of a more aggressive and less disciplined man.

"How did you come to talk with Marcu Danillo?" Decebal asked.

"He approached us, King Decebal," Falco replied. "He heard that we were veterans of VI Victrix, his father's old legion. He wanted to know more about that."

"Then we found out that we all had something else in common," Linus added with a look of amusement.

"Explain, Spurius."

"We all hate that bastard Trajan," Spurius said with a scowl. "He had us flogged for discipline. I still have the scars on my back if you want to see them. And he had the boy's father beheaded, of course."

"Tell King Decebal about your plan," Buri said impatiently.

"Our plan, King Decebal," Falco explained, "is to rejoin the Roman army. Then we'll find a way to get close enough to Caesar, and we'll kill him. Trajan likes to fraternize with his men."

Decebal gave the men a hard look. "Why do you think that is even possible? This sounds like foolishness."

Atticus gave the King a small bow. "It can be done, King, and we ask only for the opportunity to try. Emperor Trajan is very careless about being close to his soldiers. I myself have stood within five paces of Caesar."

Linus Spurius jumped in the conversation. "I am a natural killer. I can kill with any weapon or with my bare hands. Put me within five paces of any man and he's a dead man." He paused, catching himself and looking slightly embarrassed. "I don't mean you, King Decebal."

That made Buri laugh. "Don't try it. It would be the last move you ever make."

Decebal waved his hand dismissively. "We are not here to fight each other. You two are ambitious and daring, I will give you that. If you are able to assassinate Trajan, and if you escape with your lives, you will be rewarded generously."

"How generously?" Linus asked.

"You will bring me your helmet, Spurius, and I will fill it with gold. Dacian gold, not Roman."

Falco and Spurius looked at each other and smiled. Dacian gold coins were made of pure gold, and everyone knew they were worth more than most other gold coins. A helmet full of Dacian gold was more than they could earn in thirty years of military service. They would both be wealthy men.

"That would be very generous, King Decebal," Falco said and gave another bow. "Do we have your approval for this mission?"

"I will consider it," the King said. "Be prepared to leave promptly if I give you the command."

Spurius looked disappointed, but Falco kept his composure. "Yes, King Decebal. We'll be ready, just say the word."

Buri got the men's attention. "You both are smart enough to not say a word of this to anyone, right?"

"Of course!" Linus exclaimed. "We're not stupid."

"Good," Buri said, "because your lives depend on it."

"Of course, sir," Falco said. "You need not worry about that. I have one more request? If we get the go ahead, I mean, sir."

"What is it?" the King asked.

"Marcu Danillo wants to come with us," Atticus said. "I think he would help. It was him that first came up with the idea, and he looks and sounds Roman."

"Request denied," Decebal replied.

There was a commotion outside the tent and some loud words were exchanged. Buri frowned. "I think I know who that is."

Decebal turned to Falco, standing by the entrance. "Ask Marcu to come in. I will hear him out."

Marcu Danillo entered the tent, gave Buri a nod, and gave a bow before the King. "You wished to speak with me, Sire?"

The King calmly looked him in the eye. "I am told that you wish to kill Caesar. Is that so?"

"Yes, Sire. I made a vow to Zamolxis to kill Caesar on the day that Caesar executed my father."

"That is a noble vow, Marcu," Decebal said. "However you were but a child then, and you are little more than a child now. If you make a vow to kill, then do so when you are a man and a warrior."

Marcu's face reddened. "I am a warrior, Sire. My father was one of your best military trainers, you said so yourself. I trained with him since I was old enough to hold a sword."

"It is a difficult thing to kill a Caesar, Marcu. It is not like going in battle with your infantry unit."

"Emperors are often assassinated!" Marcu exclaimed. "My father taught me Roman history."

"Your father was correct about Roman history," Decebal told him. "It is not uncommon that Rome's emperors are assassinated. When it does happen however it is usually the work of other Roman nobles or military leaders."

"And with the help of the Praetorian Guard," Buri added. "You are brave and honorable, Marcu, but you are neither a Roman noble, nor a military leader, nor in the Praetorian Guard."

Danillo shook his head. "None of that matters to me. I made a vow and I shall keep it one way or another."

Buri glanced at Decebal and gave him a small shrug.

"May I speak, King Decebal?" Falco asked.

"Speak," the King said impatiently.

"Marcu is right, his swordsmanship is superior, in my estimate," Falco explained. "He speaks both Dacian and Latin at a high level. With his black hair and blue eyes, well, he looks Roman and he will fit in easily. He is crafty and fearless and I can always use a man like that on a mission."

"Will it take three men to kill Trajan?" Buri asked. "One man being sneaky and careful might have a better chance."

"Spurius will kill Caesar," Falco answered. "A dagger in the heart, or a fork in the throat to rip out his windpipe, or bare hands used to snap his neck. He will however need to be free for ten heartbeats to make the kill. We need at least one other man to give Linus assistance and then a third man to arrange our escape."

Decebal sat back for a few moments in thought. No one dared to interrupt. When the King addressed them again he turned to Falco, the obvious leader of the assassination party.

"I will consider your plan. In the meantime plan it well in detail as a military mission. Infiltration strategy, attack, and escape. Consider also that you might not survive."

"Yes, King Decebal," Falco said, and bowed again. Spurius did the same. Marcu looked pleased and also gave a small bow.

Buri showed the men out. When they were alone he sat quietly and allowed the King to gather his thoughts.

"It is very high risk," Decebal said. "But it might work. However we are likely sending young Danillo to his death, and that thought pains me."

"You could forbid him to go," Buri suggested.

"Do you think he would obey such an order?"

Buri shook his head. "No, he would not. He would sneak off and join the other two anyway."

"That is my thought as well, Buri. Marcu has his father's courage and also his independent nature. He will do what he thinks is right even if it kills him."

"He is brave but maybe too stubborn for his own good," Buri said. "He is right about Roman history however, their emperors are often assassinated. It is a Roman disease, I think."

"Yes. Romans are overly fond of assassinating their rulers, as my Uncle Duras used to say. Vezina tells me that of the last ten Roman emperors, nine of them died violent and unnatural deaths."

Buri raised an eyebrow. "Unnatural deaths?"

"Since the time of Tiberius, who was the adopted son of Augustus, nine of ten Roman emperors were either assassinated like Domitian or forced to commit suicide like Nero. So yes, unnatural deaths."

"Then perhaps we can help Trajan continue the tradition," Buri said with a grim smile.

Decebal laughed softly and shook his head. "That is one Roman tradition he would not appreciate."

"Have you decided, then?" Buri asked. "Order the mission, or turn it down?"

"Dacians are not good at assassinations, Buri. But you already know this. We have no tradition of it and no experience."

Buri nodded. "The assassination of King Burebista showed us that it only brings greater problems. And that was, when, about one hundred and fifty years ago?"

"Yes, almost exactly that."

"Well, here is some good news, My King. Falco and Spurius are not Dacians."

"Ah! That is correct. Perhaps they have some talent for it then."

"If it succeeds," Buri said, "it might well shorten the war. And if it fails, it will likely make Emperor Trajan even more angry."

Decebal gave him a half smile. "The man has already vowed to have me killed. How much more angry can he get?"

# Chapter 6

# The Battle Of The Bridge

*Drobeta, Dacia, August 105 AD*

D acian cavalry approached Drobeta from the west, in the dark, at a leisurely walking pace. The infantry approached from the wooded hills to the north. The attacking armies wanted to be within short and fast striking range when the first morning light came up over the eastern horizon. In a surprise attack timing was everything.

The main gate in the fort guarding the Drobeta side of the bridge faced north. The heavy wooden gate reinforced with iron was locked and bolted with a heavy crossbar during the night. The night sentries standing on top of the stone walls were tired, hungry, and drowsy as they waited to be relieved by the morning sentries. Over the past few months they had gotten used to the monotony of sentry watch.

As the eastern sky slowly turned from black to blue and the night shadows receded, the cavalry and the infantry both picked up their pace. There was no rushing, shouting, or beating of weapons against shields. By the time the first Roman sentries noticed movement in the field the invaders were within a short run from the walls. The first Roman bugler to notice pushed aside his sudden feelings of panic and sounded a loud alarm that reverberated through the fort.

"Attack!" General Drilgisa shouted to his infantry troops. "Rush the walls! Move in fast and kill the bastards!"

Most of the Dacian cavalry fought as horse archers. They reached the fort first, riding alongside the north wall and shooting up at the Roman defenders who showed themselves. They would kill some of those defenders on the wall, but their main job was to make them keep their heads down. The main assault would come on foot from the rapidly approaching infantry. Many of those carried long scaling ladders that would reach the top of the walls. A troop of soldiers pulled a heavy battering ram assembly towards the north gate.

Each of the forts guarding the bridge, in Drobeta and Pontes, had housing built for five hundred Roman troops whose job was to guard the forts and the bridge. The troops in the Drobeta fort woke up to the alarm bugle calls and scrambled in the near darkness to find their armor and weapons. They hurried to their defensive positions on the walls, where the Dacian invaders were already engaged in battle and positioning their ladders for assault.

The largest part of the Roman army was camped on the Pontes side of the river, along with most of the construction workers. The reason was simple logistics and convenience because the army and workers were supplied from Moesia, not Dacia. It took less time and work to supply the men and animals in Pontes without having to transport materials across the bridge.

General Publius Aelius Hadrianus was awakened by the loud banging of a closed fist on his door in the officers' quarters in Pontes. A moment later a senior tribune rushed into the room.

"We are under attack in Drobeta, General!" the man announced with urgency.

Hadrian tossed aside his blankets and stood up in a heartbeat. His servant, sleeping on a cot close by, also bolted to his feet and lit a torch to provide some light in the dim room. This servant was in charge of Hadrian's armor and weapons, which he now hurriedly fetched for his master.

"What scale of attack?" Hadrian asked.

"I do not know, General," the tribune replied. "We just now picked up the signals from Drobeta. The alarm is continuing so the attack must be large."

"Send in the reinforcement troops now, Tribune. Now!" Hadrian barked as his servant helped him don his armor.

"Sir!" the tribune acknowledged and quickly turned and went back outside to issue orders. Plans were immediately executed for sending support troops across the bridge.

Hadrian could hear faint bugle calls in the distance, three fourths of a mile away across the Danubius. This was the attack he feared and prepared for. It was not quite daylight yet, which told him that this was a well-planned strategic attack and not some minor raid.

Very well, then. If King Decebalus was coming to pay a visit he would find that General Hadrian was prepared with a very capable defense that would not give up the bridge.

"Hurry up, man!" the young general snapped at his servant, then reminded himself to keep calm. The servant was already working quickly and efficiently, but Hadrian was showing his impatience and perhaps his inexperience. The heavy metal plate armor, padded on the inside with leather, was heavy and cumbersome to position around his torso. There were numerous leather straps to secure for the armor to make a snug fit.

"Here you are, sir," the servant said patiently, providing Hadrian with his helmet and then his sword.

Hadrian rushed outside. Three of his officers waited there for him, one of them holding the bridle of the general's horse. An older man with short brown-gray hair approached them, walking briskly almost at a run.

"Are we under attack?" Apollodorus asked, short of breath.

"Obviously so," Hadrian replied with a hint of disdain. This little Greek architect had never tired of demonstrating his authority and arrogance during construction of the bridge and forts, but in this

Peter Jaksa

moment he was just a helpless old man. Hadrian took the bridle of his horse and bounded up unto the saddle in one swift motion.

"Stay here, Apollodorus," the general commanded. "You will only get in the way." He turned his horse towards the bridge, his three aides following close behind.

Apollodorus felt his ears burning with embarrassment but kept his tongue. He feared for his bridge, his masterpiece and by far his greatest creation. He knew that the barbarians saw it as a threat and might want to destroy it. Defending the bridge was the responsibility of General Hadrian however, as ordained by Emperor Trajan. The fate of the bridge was now in the hands of young Hadrian.

"To the top!" yelled Tarbus, a captain in the Dacian infantry. His unit carried four scaling ladders which his men quickly positioned at the base of the wall. He held his round shield, made of oakwood with a copper sheath, directly over his head for protection against Roman arrows and javelins. The man next to him took an arrow in the upper thigh and stumbled to the ground with a sharp cry of pain.

"Up the ladder! Go! Go!" Tarbus yelled again, more to encourage the men than to command them. The Dacian attackers were now in full battle cry and did not need to be told what to do.

The first men on the ladders climbed as fast as they could, their shields strapped on their backs and swords hanging from their belts so they could use both hands for climbing. There was no protection on the ladders because the Roman archers and javelin throwers could shoot straight down at them and also provide flanking fire from the sides. The best hope for these first climbers was speed and some luck. Most of them fell quickly, casualties of Roman arrows and spears. The men just behind them on the ladders continued their rapid climb.

Dacian foot archers and slingers following the infantry added their fire to that of the horse archers. Swarms of arrows and lead sling bullets aimed up at the defenders killed and wounded some and made others more reluctant to expose themselves. One big advantage for the Dacian army was the much greater numbers of archery units.

More Roman reserve troops arrived to reinforce the original night sentries. The line of defenders on top of the wall grew thicker, Tarbus saw, and the attacks on the Dacians scaling the ladders became more intense. The Roman defenders were determined and unafraid and now the battle was fully joined.

To the left of Tarbus' infantry unit the battering ram assembly rolled forward on its large wooden wheels and finally reached the gate on the northern wall. The infantry soldiers gave a loud cheer.

"Keep going! Attack!" Tarbus shouted. "Let the ram do its job! You do your job!"

The shed like structure of the battering ram was covered on top by a thick sloped roof. The soldiers manning the ram began to smash the large iron tipped oak timber against the gates, but they were taking flanking fire from the Roman archers on the wall. As some Dacians fell others quickly took their place.

More Dacian horse archers moved towards the gate to provide covering fire for the crew of the battering ram. Tarbus understood why that was necessary but he was not happy that his own men now received increased fire from the defenders. Some of his men were almost to the top of the ladders but faced fierce resistance and were beaten back.

The falling body of a Dacian soldier made Tarbus step quickly to his right to avoid becoming a casualty himself. The man hit the ground with a loud thud, bones breaking, but he was already dead from a spear wound through his throat.

Tarbus put a hand on the shoulder of the soldier waiting to climb the ladder next. "Wait, I will go first," he told the man. He strapped his shield on his back, placed his left foot on the first rung, and climbed in a hurry to catch up with the man above him.

General Hadrian stopped riding well short of the north gate in Drobeta and dismounted. He handed the bridle to a servant who worked in the fort as a groom.

"Stay close!" Hadrian commanded the man. He approached the wall on foot with his aides walking at his side. The sounds of battle were very loud all around him, shouts of anger, screams of pain, and the sharp clash of metal against metal. He knew that Drobeta was under a large scale attack but his men were holding their own.

The centurion in charge of the gate detail gave the general a smart salute. "Septimus Castorius, sir!"

"Report!" Hadrian said. "What scale of attack?"

"At least five thousand, sir! More infantry are approaching from the north and the east. The first attack at sunrise was a quick strike by cavalry and infantry. The infantry units coming up now also bring artillery with them, sir."

Hadrian gave a nod. "Very good, Castorius. How long has that ram been knocking on our gate?"

"Not long." Septimus flashed a grin. "It's just making a lot of noise for now, sir."

"Carry on, Castorius." Hadrian turned to his aides. "I am going up for a look. You may join me." It was an order, not a suggestion.

At the top of the wall two legionnaires stood holding a scutum, the large concave Roman shield. Hadrian stood behind them and peered out between the shields to survey the ground below. This attacking army was closer to ten thousand, not five thousand, he estimated. The enemy would be able to sustain a strong attack for a long time, several days if necessary. Hadrian suddenly had a feeling of dread in the pit of his stomach. He needed more reinforcements here and he would need time to bolster his defenses.

"General, you should not stay up here any longer," one of his aides said with worry in his voice. "The enemy is firing at us with scorpions and carrobalistae, sir."

At the rear of the Dacian infantry formations Hadrian could see a row of perhaps thirty pieces of light artillery. These could shoot large bolts from several hundred feet away that would penetrate any type of shield or armor.

"They are not shooting at us," Hadrian said. "They will not aim for the wall for fear of hitting their own men. They are shooting over the walls to hit the troops inside the fort."

"Yes, sir. We should get you off the wall and better protected in any case, sir."

"Very well," Hadrian agreed. "Give an order to the signal corps. Bring up all the troops in reserve in Pontes. All of them!"

King Decebal located his command post at the edge of the woods north of the Drobeta gate. He watched from the saddle of his big gray war stallion so that he would have a good view of the entire battlefield. Diegis and Buri watched with him, also from horseback. Drilgisa was directing the main attack against the gates.

"Apollodorus builds well with stone," Decebal said. "That is a very sturdy fort with very strong walls."

"Indeed," Diegis agreed. "I think that Emperor Trajan got tired of seeing how easily we destroyed so many Roman forts in the last war."

"You are likely correct, Brother. Trajan learns from his mistakes and he corrects them."

Buri nodded toward the fort gate. "The ram is doing no damage so far. We should not count on breaching the gate."

"I take nothing for granted, Buri," the King said. "The ram is only one part of the attack. This Apollodorus builds strong gates as well as strong walls. Very well, we will go over the walls."

Buri gave a grunt in agreement. "Unless we want to have a long siege we'll have to climb over the walls."

"We don't have time for a long siege," Decebal said. "I want those walls breached today. Trajan is marching here with eight legions."

"Exactly so," Diegis said with a nod. "Let's capture the bridge now, otherwise we will never again have enough troops to capture it or destroy it."

Buri looked at the bridge and shook his head in wonder. "How do you destroy something that big and solid? It would take weeks."

"Let us capture it first," Decebal said. "Diegis, join Drilgisa and press the attack. Assault the walls very aggressively."

"I will be happy to," Diegis replied, and guided his horse forward at a gallop towards the position of General Drilgisa.

Buri turned to Decebal with a quizzical expression. "Should we have attacked here sooner? I wonder whether we gave them too much time to strengthen their position."

"No, my friend," Decebal answered without a pause. "We were not strong enough to attack sooner. And had we destroyed the bridge earlier, before it was finished, Trajan would have simply tried again and defended it better. Let's capture it now and then fight to keep it."


The two men in front of Tarbus were the first to reach the top of the ladder. Dacian archers and slingers on the ground unleashed a flurry of projectiles that cleared the defenders above their ladder. The first man pulled himself up to the top of the wall, crouched defensively, and drew his sword. He took one step to his left when a Roman arrow sank deeply into the right side of his abdomen. The man groaned with pain and staggered to his right, then fell to the ground inside the fort.

The second Dacian soldier sprang up like a lion and effortlessly pulled himself up on the wall. He crouched very low and slid to his right, making room for Tarbus who came up right behind him. To his surprise Tarbus recognized him as Boian, the young man who lost the Messenger to Zamolxis competition to Tiati.

"Stay to the right, I will go left!" Tarbus told him. "Let's clear some room for the others!"

"Yes, sir," Boian grinned, excited to have reached the top without getting killed. He drew his sica, the light but razor sharp Dacian sword, and moved three steps down the wall while the Dacian foot archers kept up a withering fire on the Romans closing in. Boian had his shield on his left arm, facing towards the inner fort, and grimaced as a Roman arrow hit the copper sheath and glanced off.

On the left side of the ladder Tarbus took a few steps forward and braced himself to face a Roman spearman coming at him. He was also fighting with a sica. The spearman stabbed towards the Dacian's head, which Tarbus easily deflected by swinging his shield upwards. He lunged forward with the sica and slashed across the legionnaire's unprotected left leg. The Roman staggered backwards and was pulled away by another legionnaire.

"There! A breach!" Drilgisa yelled to the horse archers in front of him, pointing to the section on the wall where Tarbus and Boian were already being joined by other Dacian soldiers. A group of Romans streamed towards their position to drive them off the wall. The horse archers moved quickly to join the foot archers to attack the Roman defenders. A Dacian archer or slinger was deadly accurate from one hundred paces and the soldiers on top of the wall made easy targets.

"More ladders here!" Drilgisa shouted the order at the top of his lungs. "Climb, lads, climb! Go! Go!"

The attackers found a weak point not far from the gate and now were exploiting it rapidly and efficiently. Dacian archers used the new ladders to join the infantry streaming up to the top of the wall. Once at the top they had the Romans defending the gate within easy kill range.

"Sir, the gate will not hold," Centurion Septimus Castorius of the gate detail announced to his general.

"I am aware of that, Centurion," Hadrian said with a growl. It was only mid-morning but his defenders were being overwhelmed by too many Dacians attacking too quickly in too many locations. Reserve units from Pontes were still marching over the bridge to his aid, but not fast enough. The remaining reserve troops would not arrive in time to cut off this attack on the northern wall. Hadrian made a quick tactical decision.

"Sound retreat," he told his aide. "We will fight a retreating action to the bridge. We will make a stand there and deny them the bridge."

"Yes, sir!" the aide replied, hoping that his general was making the right decision. No one had ever expected that the strong Drobeta fort could fall to an attack so quickly.

"My horse!" Hadrian called to the groom, who promptly brought the horses for his staff. The General mounted quickly and headed back towards the southern end of the fort, towards the bridge. The bridge was a natural choke point. Hadrian was certain the enemy would not be able to fight their way through his massed forces and reach the bridge.

"We have them backed up, Sire," Drilgisa reported, "but they will fight like demons to keep us away from the bridge."

"I expect so," Decebal said in an even voice. He was on foot inside the fort, with Buri ever alert at his side. They reached the Dacian front line at the southern end of Drobeta. The Roman troops were a distance away, out of bowshot range. The high wooden arches of the bridge of Apollodorus rose majestically behind them.

"How many troops does General Hadrian have massed on this side of the bridge, General Drilgisa?" the King asked.

Drilgisa gave a small shrug. "At least a thousand, I would guess. Maybe more. The legionnaires will wait for us in testudo formations so that our archers cannot kill them, then face our infantry with a wall of shields and armor. Cutting through that wall will take some time and will cost us dearly."

"Then we should not attack them with infantry," Decebal said.

"How, then?"

"We have a better strategy," Buri said grimly, "for killing demons in armor packed closely together in testudo formations."

"Ah! I understand," Drilgisa exclaimed. "But do we have enough artillery?"

"We have twenty four carrobalistae that Diegis is bringing up even as we speak," the King explained. "A single well placed bolt will cut through shields and armor and take out two or three men."

Buri gestured down the street, where Dacian soldiers cleared the way for a string of mule drawn carts carrying the light artillery. "Here comes Diegis now."

"Good," Drilgisa said with relish. He walked up to greet Diegis and together they instructed the artillery teams where to line up. Within minutes the batteries were launching their oversized iron bolts at the tightly packed Roman formations.

Diegis and Drilgisa rejoined Decebal and Buri, who found a good spot from which to watch the carnage unfolding in the distance.

"Those poor dumb bastards. How long do we pound them with the artillery?" Diegis wondered.

"Most likely not very long," Decebal replied. "Young Hadrian will soon realize that he chose to defend the wrong end of the bridge. Here we have him pinned down and have the advantage."

Drilgisa gave a nod. "If he is smart he will withdraw across the bridge and defend the Pontes side. But is he willing to give us the bridge?"

"He will have to," Diegis said. "If not then his army is slaughtered."

By the middle of the afternoon the last of the Roman troops were across the bridge and positioned for defense on the Pontes side. Here they would not be under attack from the enemy artillery. The Dacian troops would have to come across the bridge, where they would be the ones tightly packed and at a disadvantage.

General Hadrian positioned his infantry up front, archery units behind them, and his artillery on the flanks to fight off the Dacian advance coming over the bridge. His men knew that if they lost this position the bridge and the forts would be lost. They had to hold the line here.

"General Hadrian, a word?" an anxious voice asked.

Hadrian turned to face Apollodorus, irritated with the architect for interrupting his thoughts. "Yes? What do you want?"

"You cannot fire artillery at the bridge, Hadrian. It will damage the wooden arches."

Hadrian gave him a mirthless smile. "If Decebalus drives us away from this position he will then be free to reduce your wooden arches to ashes."

Apollodorus swallowed hard. "He will not. Even a barbarian can see that this bridge is a wonder and must be preserved."

"I am in command here and I make all military decisions," the General said dismissively. "Do you wish to be helpful, Apollodorus? Then round up your workers and put some axes, shovels, and picks in their hands. We might need them before this fight is settled."

"Surely it will not come to that?"

Hadrian turned away without a reply and focused his attention on the bridge again. The first units of Dacian infantry were coming into artillery range.

"Commence artillery fire," Hadrian said calmly to his commander of artillery. Damage to the bridge could be repaired later. Losing this battle would be a much bigger disaster.

By late afternoon the Dacian infantry had suffered very heavy losses but were pushing the Roman lines further south and away from the bridge. A stream of horse archers made their way along one side of the wide bridge, and these now attacked the artillery on the Roman flanks. The artillery commander ordered his units to retreat before they could be captured or destroyed.

"Hold formation!" the Roman officers shouted to their men. They retreated slowly before the advancing Dacian infantry, fighting from house to house and defending the narrow streets inside the fort. The bridge was lost, Drobeta was lost, and it became a desperate fight for survival to save Pontes.

Tarbus and Boian found themselves fighting side by side on the front line. Both were strong and athletic warriors in their prime, highly trained and experienced in hand to hand combat. Each wore light chain mail armor and carried the round Dacian shield, much lighter and more maneuverable than the heavy Roman scutum. They darted in for quick strikes with the sica when they saw an opening, then swiftly backed away out of range of the shorter Roman gladius.

Tarbus walked past the corner of a house, Boian half a step behind and to his right, when he caught a flicker of movement out of the corner of his eye.

"Look out!" he yelled sharply to Boian.

The younger warrior bent his knees to crouch low and raised his shield up over his head. The instinctive defensive reflex saved his life as the heavy blade of a work shovel aimed for his head instead crashed down on his shield. The attacker, snarling with rage, was dressed in shabby work clothes. Boian straightened his knees and lunged forward, his sica plunging deep into the man's stomach. The attacker screamed with pain and dropped the shovel, then dropped down to his knees.

Tarbus turned to face a group of four more Roman workers armed with construction tools. One rushed forward and took a sideways swing with a long handled pick, aiming to hit Tarbus in the ribs. The Dacian knocked the pick aside with his shield, then stepped up and slashed with the sica to slice through the man's throat. A red spray of blood covered them both as the attacker stumbled and fell forward on his face.

Boian kicked away his attacker to free his sword from the man's guts. He also turned to face the remaining Romans. The three men froze, afraid and uncertain of what to do next. They were civilians, not used to the violence and bloodshed they just witnessed, and wary of the two blood-stained warriors before them.

Tarbus waved his shield and sword as if to shoo away pesky birds. "Run! I don't wish to kill you! Go!"

The three men glanced at each other, then turned and ran away.

Boian shook his head, amused but also impressed. "They don't give up easily, do they?"

"No, they don't," Tarbus answered. "They gave their sweat and blood to this place for years and they don't want to give it up."

"The battle is ours and the bridge is ours," Boian said. "They will die for nothing."

The south wall of Pontes was now within sight of the Dacian troops. The gates were opened wide and Romans were retreating, streaming out through the gates and leaving the fort. The sight of it made Tarbus glad. Good, he thought with satisfaction, leave the fort to us and the battle will end.

A loud series of trumpet calls made everyone pause, Romans and Dacians alike. The first trumpet calls were joined by more calls, from both inside the walls and from outside, some close by and some in the distance.

The Romans outside the gates began to cheer loudly. Those inside the fort picked up the cheers, which turned to laughter and shouts of joy. The battle had just turned.

The army of Emperor Trajan arrived at Pontes.


Hadrian happily welcomed Trajan just outside the gates of Pontes. The newly arrived legions from Trajan's army joined the battle and were already driving back the Dacian troops inside the fort. Dacian units were now retreating across the bridge to the Drobeta side of the river. It seemed like a miracle to the Roman defenders who were on the verge of collapse, but Caesar and his army arrived just in time and saved the day.

"Hail, Cesar!" Hadrian gave him a sharp and enthusiastic Roman salute. He was exhausted but at the same time exhilarated that Trajan was there to prevent a disastrous military defeat and the loss of the bridge.

"Greetings, Hadrianus. It appears that you had a very eventful day today," Trajan said with a wry smile. Licinius Sura, standing beside the Emperor, gave Hadrian a sympathetic smile as well.

"Indeed, Caesar, long and eventful. The Dacians attacked at first light and we have been fighting them off ever since."

Trajan placed a hand on Hadrian's shoulder. "Well done, General Hadrian, and Rome is grateful. You protected the bridge and that was paramount."

"Yes, the bridge is everything," Sura added. "I am very eager to see it myself, Hadrian. You must show it to us later."

"Ah! And here comes the bridge master himself," Trajan said as Apollodorus approached them. The architect looked very relieved to see them.

"Welcome, Caesar! I am extremely happy to see you." Apollodorus gave him a small bow. "Once these barbarians are cleared out I would be very honored to show you your bridge."

"In due time, Apollodorus. I wish to know everything about this marvel of architecture and you will show me in due time," Trajan said. He turned back to Hadrian. "But first, Hadrianus, let us talk about King Decebalus. He is the reason I am here."

King Decebal watched from the saddle atop his gray stallion on the edge of the woods north of Drobeta, as he had done earlier that morning. This time however he watched the last of his troops retreat from Drobeta. The Dacian army was too small in numbers to fight the legions of Emperor Trajan head on, and there was nothing more to be done. Trajan had his bridge and he would keep it.

"Will he march after us today, do you think?" Diegis wondered.

"No, not immediately," Decebal replied. "He will want to rest his troops. He will also make his plans because Trajan does nothing without a plan."

"That much we know from experience," Drilgisa said. "And what is our plan? Do we fight them in the mountains again?"

"Again and always, Drilgisa. We must make them fight our fight. We fight them in the mountains."

Diegis looked back at the bridge and scowled. "We should have put a torch to it earlier. Trajan can now march legions across it at his leisure."

"It would take a hundred torches setting fires for two days," Buri said. "And that would still leave the stone structures in place."

"It should be taken down," Diegis repeated stubbornly.

Buri shook his head. "No one will take down this bridge any time soon. It will stand for a hundred years, long after we are gone."

"No matter now, what's done is done," King Decebal declared. "We need to position our troops in the mountain forts and ensure that supplies are in place. Diegis and Drilgisa, you are in command of planning all matters of the infantry."

Diegis gave a nod. "It will be done. It sounds like you have other plans, Brother?"

"Yes, Diegis, I do. I will travel back to Sarmizegetusa and work on diplomacy with Vezina. Trajan is back with a very large army and we must rally all our allies to oppose him."

"We will need them again," Drilgisa said. "We can slow down and bleed this Roman army but we can't kill it. Our allies will fight with us because their necks are also on the line."

"If Zamolxis wills it, it will be so," the King declared.

# Chapter 7

# Assassins

*Drobeta, September 105 AD*

Caesar began his day in the early morning by sacrificing a white ram to Mars, the god of war. He stood patiently and reverently along with his officer staff and watched while the sacrifice was being burned on the sacrificial altar.

This ritual sacrifice to the gods was followed every single morning for two reasons. First, because Emperor Trajan was a highly religious and pious man. And second, because Emperor Trajan knew very well from many years of experience that sacrificing to the gods brought him boundless good fortune. He did not need his wife to remind him of this, although of course Pompeia's advice was ever welcome.

Other soldiers in the vicinity milled around to pay homage to Mars and watch the sacrifice beneath the walls of Drobeta. They were kept a distance away from Caesar and his officers by a unit of the Praetorian Guard. The Praetorians were quick to scowl at anyone not behaving in a sufficiently deferential manner or getting too close to Caesar's group.

Two of the watchers on the sidelines were auxiliary infantry. One was a man of medium height with very dark hair and eyes. The other soldier was a large and muscular man with curly brown hair who looked like he had been in more than his share of rough fights. A third watcher of the sacrifice was a recently hired stable boy who looked to be perhaps sixteen or seventeen years of age. Around the stables he was known as Marcus, but his mother called him Marcu.

"The campaign season will be over soon, Caesar," remarked Licinius Sura. He knew that he was stating the obvious but simply wished to nudge Trajan into discussion. Thus far Caesar had not announced any details at all regarding Dacia.

"I am well aware of that," Trajan replied. "What is your question?"

"Have you decided on strategy and timing yet, Marcus. We have been here for some weeks now and the officers are waiting to hear your thoughts on the matter."

"Ah! Of course they are," Trajan said with a smile. He refilled his goblet with wine from the new shipment just arrived from Rome, an excellent red Caecuban. "Patience is a virtue, Licinius, as you well know. We will not follow the same strategy as in the last war. New strategies require thought and development."

Sura gave him a patient smile. "Indulge me, Marcus. Is there some strategy emerging?"

"Very well, stop nagging me and I shall tell you." Trajan took a long sip from his silver goblet and savored the wine. It was widely known that good wine was one of his three passions in life. "It is too late in the season to initiate a full scale invasion now, would you agree?"

"Yes, of course. Hence my statement of a minute ago."

"The full scale invasion of Dacia will begin in the spring, after the snows melt and we have enough new greenery to feed the animals while marching through enemy lands."

"That sounds eminently reasonable," Sura agreed, helping himself to more wine. A Roman army on the march depended heavily on mules, oxen, and horses to pull the transport wagons and move the vast quantities of supplies an army needed. For that reason the ideal time to start a new campaign was in the spring, when there would be sufficient new grass and foliage to feed the animals on the road.

"However, before we have the final confrontation with Decebalus we must weaken him," the Emperor said in a serious tone. "We must weaken him considerably. I will not accept the high losses in Roman casualties again that we suffered three years ago."

Sura gave a nod. He understood now why his friend gave so much time and thought to planning. "How do you propose that we make Decebalus weaker, Caesar?"

"In two ways. Via military attacks, but also via diplomacy. For the next several months we will attack their forts and villages in eastern and western Dacia and either pacify or destroy them. We must be ruthless to reduce the manpower available to Decebalus."

"I see. And I trust that my role will involve diplomacy?" Sura asked with a half-smile. "Laberius Maximus and Lusius Quietus can attack the forts and villages."

"Yes, Licinius, diplomacy! Since the days of Emperor Domitian, Decebalus has been greatly superior to Rome in forming alliances," Trajan said in a sour tone. "This has always caused great problems for Rome, and it cannot continue."

Sura nodded again. "I understand and I agree with you. We must turn Dacia's allies into Rome's allies."

"Precisely. I want you to bribe, threaten, or kill, use any means necessary to separate Decebalus from his allies. Those whom you cannot persuade, bring them to me."

"I see the plan now, Marcus. It is an excellent strategy." Sura raised his wine goblet in a toast. "This is why Caesar plans strategy and we mere mortals must be patient."

Trajan put his wine goblet on the table and clasped his friend on the shoulder. "Come, Licinius. I am hungry. Let's go have a meal with our soldiers."

Sura winced. "In all honesty I wish that you would not do that so frequently, Marcus."

"And why not? I enjoy the company of my soldiers, and it helps to earn their trust and loyalty."

"It places you at greater risk. You know this."

"Nonsense!" the Emperor exclaimed. "No harm will come to me from my own legionnaires. And besides, what man is better protected than Caesar?"

Atticus Falco always explored all his options. Once that was done he took decisive action. Experience taught him that it was better to have more options than fewer.

Falco carried a small vial of very potent poison that he made on his own, a skill learned when he was growing up in the Roman province of Syria. Linus Spurius was not very bright but he was very strong, fearless, and aggressive. That made him a useful companion for a soldier in the Roman army, not to mention a soldier wishing to work as an assassin. Between the poison and Linus, Falco considered, he had two highly lethal options for delivering death.

The boy Marcu was clever and had a way with people. Falco brought him along as another option, which paid off when Marcu was able to easily get hired as a stable boy. Now they had access to horses at any time of day or night.

The final options for Falco to consider involved making decisions on the time, location, and method for killing the Emperor of Rome. For method he preferred using the poison if the opportunity arose. If not then his attack dog, Spurius, might be able to get close to Trajan for the several seconds it would take to kill him.

The two best options for location were in the infantry mess hall when Trajan sat down for a meal with the soldiers, or at the morning sacrifice ceremony. The issue of timing was often a matter of pure chance and luck. One never knew when the goddess Fortuna would smile on you.

"I could sneak into his sleeping quarters very late at night," Linus Spurius said, keeping his voice low. "It would take me ten seconds to wring his neck, then sneak out."

The assassins talked while sitting under a leafy shade tree near the stables. Falco wanted to get a report from Marcu Danillo and talk briefly with the boy. If they needed to get away quickly Danillo would have to do his job well. At the moment however the boy was losing patience with Linus and his bad ideas.

"You could never sneak into his sleeping quarters," Marcu said. "He is surrounded by Praetorian Guards all night. That is simply a dumb idea."

Spurius' face reddened as it always did when he felt offended. "Don't call me dumb, Marcu!"

"I am Marcus in this camp," Danillo reminded him. "Marcus. Do not call me anything else."

"Quiet, both of you," Falco said in a quiet but firm tone. "The boy is right, Linus. It would be too dangerous for you to try."

"How do you know? I know how to move under cover in the night," Linus said in protest. He recalled a fond memory and broke into a grin. "Back in my village there was this woman - ."

Falco silenced him with a hard look. Spurius frowned and looked away. Falco never showed him the respect to take him seriously, it seemed.

Marcu turned to the older man. "So, my job is mostly shoveling horse manure but my new duty sometimes is grooming the scouts' horses. They are smaller horses but fast, and don't tire as quickly. They are bred for stamina."

"Smart boy," Falco said. "Pick out which are the better ones and always be aware of their location when they are in the stables and not out on patrol."

"I am already doing that," Marcu said. "When the time comes I will be ready."

"Do you see?" Falco asked Spurius with a smile. "The boy is always planning ahead. This is what you must do also."

"But I am planning ahead! I am telling you, Atticus, in the night I move silent as a Dacian strigoi. Perhaps I should scout the sleeping quarters at least?"

"You will not," Atticus growled in a low voice. "If the Praetorians catch you they will turn you into a real strigoi. Stay close by in the mess hall when he is there. I will cause some commotion and give you a chance to attack. It is our best option."

"How long do you think it will take us to create that opportunity?" Marcu wondered.

"I don't know, boy. It will take as long as it takes. You do your job and be ready when I need you." Falco turned to Spurius. "And you do your job as I tell you. No skulking in the night."

Linus acknowledged him with a grunt.

Spurius walked very casually down the narrow street in Drobeta. He was anonymous here, just another common soldier walking in the early evening. He would walk close by the officers' quarters but not too close. Perhaps there was some way to get to Trajan while he was sleeping.

Perhaps Falco was right and it was too risky, Linus told himself. Even so it would be worthwhile to take a look. Didn't Falco say more than once that fortune favors the bold? Also everyone knew that the best opportunities come along when you least expect it. Smile on me, Fortuna, Linus prayed.

Spurius was deep in thought and all his thoughts led to the death of Caesar. The quickest and surest kill blows were those that attacked the head and neck. A sharp blade across the throat. A heavy blow with any type of hard object to cave in the skull. A quick sharp twist that broke the neck. Most men lacked the strength and aggression for such kills, but he was not like most men.

Linus passed the corner of a house, lost in thought, and carelessly ran into one of the two legionnaires who just turned the corner. The smaller man was caught off guard, and he stumbled and almost fell.

"Watch where you walk, you oaf!" the legionnaire complained.

"Don't call me names," Linus said irritably. He knew instantly that was a mistake because auxiliary troops were required at all times to show deference to legionnaires.

"Oaf is the kindest name I would call you," the man replied in a cold and superior tone. He glanced at his friend, who simply shook his head dismissively.

"He's not worth your trouble, Vibius. Come on, we are already running late."

"Right." The man gave Linus a scornful look. "Next time I won't be so forgiving with you, oaf."

The men laughed, then turned and walked away. They did not have time to bother with a fool below their social status.

"Asinus!" Spurius called after them, then silently cursed himself for losing his temper again. He hated legionnaires, but losing one's temper with people of a higher social class was dangerous.

Linus turned to walk away, face red with anger, and found himself facing an officer of obvious high rank who was accompanied by four Praetorian Guards. This officer heard his altercation with the two legionnaires and now gave Spurius a curious look.

"Who are you?" Titus Lucullus asked. "You look familiar to me for some reason."

"I never saw you before," Spurius said. "But maybe you saw me somewhere, sir. I served in many places with the legions over the years. Did you ever serve in Germania, sir?"

"No," said Lucullus, shaking his head. "I never served in Germania. But I have seen you before, I am certain. You were on a road work detail."

"Never worked on no road work detail, sir."

Peter Jaksa

Titus took a step closer for a better look at Linus' face. "Yes you did. It was on the road outside Sarmizegetusa."

"I never been to Sarmi-tusa," Linus protested.

Lucullus gave him a hard look. Spurius returned the look.

"You are a liar, and a bad liar at that," Titus said in an even voice. He turned to the Praetorian Guards. "Arrest him."

Spurius got a wild and panicked look in his eyes. He turned to his left and took a running step. One of the Praetorians deftly reached out with his spear shaft and tripped him. Linus fell forward hard on his face, stirring up a small cloud of dust.

Titus leaned down slightly to address him. "It was Sarmizegetusa. You taunted my men when they were marching past your work detail. I am happy to see you again, traitor."


Interrogation of suspicious prisoners was managed by the torture detail. Effective torture saved time and always produced answers. All men broke under torture sooner or later. The Romans perfected a wide variety of torture techniques, and were considered to have no equals except for perhaps the Egyptians.

Titus Lucullus arrested Linus Spurius because he knew that the man had been a deserter from the Roman army. That by itself was reason enough for Spurius to be executed. The mystery for Lucullus was why Linus had returned to the Roman army. His answers were not convincing and only created more confusion, and that earned Spurius the attention of the torture detail.

Linus was tied securely to a post, standing upright, his hands tied behind his back, his feet in leg irons. The interrogator was an older man with cold eyes and no signs of emotion on his hard face. He was very experienced in his job and took pride in being good at it. His most basic tools were a variety of sharp knives and hot irons. For the most difficult prisoners, or those enemies who Caesar wanted to punish most severely, he had more ingenious and hellish methods.

After a half hour of cuts and burns Spurius howled out in agony and resignation that he had enough. Lucullus, who did not enjoy watching men tortured but fulfilled his duty to question the prisoner, resumed his interrogation. After only three more brief questions an astonished Titus urgently sent one of the Praetorian Guards to go and summon Caesar.

Emperor Trajan arrived within minutes, accompanied by Licinius Sura and a large detail of Praetorian Guards who formed a perimeter around the interrogation site. Sura and Lucullus looked more upset and angry than Trajan. The Emperor remained calm as he examined the bloodied prisoner with curiosity.

"Who sent you?" Trajan asked in an even voice.

"We come on our own," Linus groaned.

Trajan glanced at the torture detail specialist, who applied a hot iron to the prisoner's ribs. Spurius shuddered from the intense pain but refused to cry out again.

"Who hired you?" the Emperor asked again. "Who promised to pay you? We know that you were a defector to Dacia so do not lie to me."

"All right, sir, I won't lie to you. King Decebalus promised to pay each of us a helmet full of Dacian gold."

Trajan gave a small nod. "As I suspected. Your greed made you a deserter so why not also an assassin, eh? You miserable wretch."

"Us, you say?" Sura interrupted. "You have companions?"

Linus hesitated. He grew alarmed as his torturer took another red hot iron from the fire and approached him. "No! Wait! I'll tell you. Don't burn me any more."

"How many companions? Who are they?" Sura continued.

"There are three of us, sir. One is auxiliary infantry like me. His name is Atticus Falco. The other is a boy, I don't know him well."

"What boy? What is his name?"

"His name is Marcus," Linus groaned, spitting out blood. "I don't know his other names."

Licinius Sura laughed. "One in twenty men in this army is named Marcus." He turned to Trajan with an amused look. "Is that not so, Marcus?"

The Emperor frowned at Sura's joke. "You are a dead man already, Spurius. Tell me something useful and make your death easier. Or do not, and die in great agony."

Linus spat out more blood. "He works in the stables."

"Yes?" Sura asked. "What does he look like?"

"Young, maybe sixteen or seventeen. Black hair. Very blue eyes. He looks very Roman."

Trajan turned to one of the Praetorian officers. "Lock down the fort immediately. Find this Falco and bring him to me. The same for the stable boy."

"Yes, Caesar!" The Praetorian hurried off to give orders. There were assassins in Drobeta and the fort was now on high crisis alert.

Trajan turned away and motioned for Titus to follow. "Well done, Lucullus. This foolish plot by Decebalus will not go unpunished."

"Yes, Caesar," Lucullus said. He paused for a moment. "I must say however that this took me by surprise. Dacians are not known for assassination plots."

"The man must be desperate," Sura added. "Imagine it, a plot to kill Caesar! Not even the Parthians are so reckless."

"Perhaps he is desperate," Trajan said. "But Decebalus must also know that acts of desperation are rarely successful."

"The man is known to take some gambles, Caesar," Titus said. "More often than not his gambles worked out for him."

"Very well. So now we are in agreement, Titus. You keep telling me to expect the unexpected from Decebalus, and once again you are proven right."

"Yes, Caesar," Lucullus replied. "The history of King Decebalus is doing the unpredictable."

Trajan's face turned grim. "I will deal with Decebalus later, but first let us deal with these traitors and assassins."

Atticus Falco knew there was trouble when Linus Spurius did not show up to meet him. Linus often showed poor judgment but he was usually punctual. If he did not show up to meet Atticus it was because something or someone prevented him from doing so. Falco also knew that if Spurius was detained it would not take long for him to reveal their plot.

Falco headed for the stables, which were located just inside the fort gates. He would warn the boy to be on alert and ready to leave in a hurry if he so decided. They would not be able to fight their way out, so stealth and fast horses were the only options. Dreams of Dacian gold had to be put aside if their necks were on the line.

Most of all Falco knew that he must avoid capture at any price. He knew what Roman torture details did to prisoners. Any fate would be better than that. As he walked Atticus put his hand inside his tunic and was comforted by the solid feel of the stone vial of poison resting there. The poison was very fast acting, and if he took it there would be no question of suffering the agonies of interrogation and torture.

Falco found Marcu Danillo waiting for him near the front of the stables, standing by himself in the dark. He knew instantly that something was amiss because the boy had a tense and anxious look on his face. Falco motioned with his eyes and directed Marcu in the direction of the shade tree.

"What is wrong?" Falco asked. "You look like you're ready to piss your britches."

"We got word just now that the stables are locked down," Marcu replied in a hushed voice. "The gates are shut and the fort is locked down. No one is allowed to leave or enter."

Falco grimaced as if in pain. "That fool Linus got caught. I was a fool to bring him along."

"What do we do now, Atticus?"

"We go our separate ways, boy. I am certain that Linus named me but perhaps not you." Falco took a quick look around them, where soldiers were rushing to their posts with urgency. "Sneak away, boy, if you can. It's your only chance."

"I came here to kill Trajan," Marcu said stubbornly. To Falco's astonishment he was reacting with anger and frustration, not fear.

"That is over," Atticus declared. "We failed."

A unit of Praetorian Guards approached the stables at a brisk marching pace, some carrying torches. The officer in charge of the stables greeted them, and after a very brief exchange looked to where Marcu and Atticus were standing. He pointed the soldiers there.

Falco groaned with despair and sat down on the ground. "You may run if you wish. I am finished."

"There is nowhere to run," Marcu replied, watching the soldiers approach at a fast walk. In the corner of his eye he saw Atticus reach inside his tunic, bring out a small stone vial, raise it to his lips, and drink the contents. Falco closed his eyes and the empty vial fell from his hand.

The Praetorians approached with drawn swords and made a circle around them. They avoided the fallen Atticus, whose body began to twitch in a strange manner.

"Marcus the stable boy?" the officer asked. "You are under arrest by order of Caesar."

"What's wrong with him?" one of the soldiers asked, looking at Falco.

"Don't touch him!" the officer ordered. "He is poisoned."

Marcu Danillo allowed himself to be escorted away quietly and without resistance. He was sad that his mission to kill Trajan failed. In the back of his mind he had a memory from many years ago of his father Cassius Danillo also being led away by Roman soldiers to his execution. His father had been resigned, stoical, and brave. In a way he was now following in his father's footsteps. That thought gave Marcu a feeling of pride.

"You are not like those other two. Why do you wish to kill Caesar?" the Emperor asked Marcu after the young man had been questioned. He had answered all the questions freely and there was no need for any kind of coercion or torture. Indeed there was no sign of any bruise or mark on his body.

Marcu was resigned to his fate, as his father had been. He looked Trajan in the eye and answered in a calm voice.

"You killed my father at Aquae. His name was Cassius Danillo."

"Your father was a deserter?" Trajan asked.

"Yes. He lived in Dacia for many years. You took him away from my mother and my brothers and sisters. Then you took his head off by executioner's axe."

Trajan leaned back easily in his chair. Somewhat to his surprise he found himself becoming impressed with the honesty and passion of this young man. Impressed, but not entirely sympathetic.

Licinius Sura cut in. "The punishment for desertion in the Roman army is death. Your father knew that."

"Yes, he knew that," Marcu replied. "But no matter, my father made his decisions and I will not judge him. I don't know the reasons for his decisions."

"Ah! Your loyalty to your father is commendable," Trajan said. "But you see, Caesar must also make decision. And the punishment for desertion for a Roman soldier is death."

Marcu took a deep breath, fighting painful memories. "I was also at Aquae that day. I watched from far away. I was hiding in the branches of a tree when you had my father executed. That day I made a vow to kill you."

"I see. And so you did what you believed was honorable. Did King Decebalus also persuade you to join these assassins?"

The question took Marcu by surprise. "He did not. King Decebal was reluctant to allow me to join this mission." He paused and gave a small shrug. "I would have carried out my vow with or without the permission of the King."

"I see. Your father Cassius, were he alive, would be proud of you, boy," the Emperor said. "In truth I too would be proud of you if you were my son. You have all the qualities of a fine Roman."

Marcu gave him a grim smile. "My father was a Roman but I am a Dacian. And I do not seek the approval of my father's killer."

"The blood of Rome and Dacia runs in you, Marcu," Trajan said. "Your father was a deserter but his crime is not your crime. So it pains me to make this decision."

"Let's be done with it," Marcu said calmly. "I know how Roman justice works."

Trajan paused for a moment, then hardened his face. "You tried to kill Caesar. The penalty for that crime is death."

Two guards took Marcu by his arms and led him to the execution ground. He went quietly, without protest. When they told him to kneel on the ground he did so obediently and calmly laid his neck across the log that served as a chopping block.

Marcu Danillo had long ago prepared himself for a proud and honorable death. He pursued his mission to fulfill the oath to avenge his father with no fear or self-doubt. He did not achieve his highest goal because his father's killer still lived. He took satisfaction in knowing that he did the right thing. That honored the memory of his father, and it was enough.

# Chapter 8

# Fata Padurii

*Sarmizegetusa, October 105 AD*

N ews of the assassination plot against Emperor Trajan first reached Sarmizegetusa through Vezina's large network of informers and spies. There was not much that happened within the world of Rome that did not eventually reach the ears of the High Priest of Zamolxis. This bit of information however caught him by complete surprise.

In the long history of Rome assassination attempts on the lives of Roman rulers was accepted as a fact of life. Usually these threats came from rivals among the Roman nobility and military. What was surprising to Vezina was that this attempt against Trajan was made by a foreign power. What shocked him was that the news struck too close to home.

Vezina went to the royal palace for a talk with the King and Queen. He found them in their dining room and interrupted their mid-day meal. This was not a problem because the High Priest had a standing invitation to join the royal couple at their table.

King Decebal's first reaction to the news was not surprise but a mild look of disappointment. Queen Andrada on the other hand looked very perplexed. Their very different reactions told Vezina all that he needed to know.

"But how can that be, that the assassins were sent by Dacia?" the Queen asked Vezina. "We sent no such assassins."

Rather than answering her Vezina turned to King Decebal. "Is there some truth to these stories, Sire? They say that there were three assassins, that they were captured, and that they confessed under torture they were sent by Dacia."

Decebal calmly looked from his High Priest to the Queen. "It was better that you were not informed until later, after the plot either succeeded or failed. The only two people who knew of it were Buri and me."

Vezina paused for a heartbeat, and then acknowledged the King with a small nod. "I understand, My King. This was a risky business and the fewer people involved the better."

Andrada, feeling less understanding, threw up her hands. "How could you send Dacians to kill the Emperor of Rome and not tell me of such a thing? You could not trust me with a secret?"

The King shook his head. "It was a matter of strategy, not trust. As Vezina said, the fewer people involved the better. As it turned out they were discovered and caught anyway."

"Were they Dacians?" the Queen asked. "How could they disguise themselves as Romans well enough to reach Emperor Trajan?"

"One was Dacian, the son of Cassius Danillo. Marcu spoke Latin better than most Romans. He insisted on going because he wanted to avenge the execution of his father. The other two men were Roman deserters who wanted to be showered with gold."

"Am I interrupting?" asked Adila, having just entered the dining room. "I was working in the garden and got hungry."

"It is all right, Daughter," said the King. "You may join us. We are discussing matters that soon everyone will know about."

"Come sit by me," Andrada invited her. "You knew Marcu Danillo, did you not?"

"Not well, Mama. He was a few years younger than me." Adila looked to her father. "Did you send him to kill Emperor Trajan?"

"I did not stop him from going and doing what he wished. So yes, you can say that I sent him."

"What he wished for most of all," said Adila with a sigh, "was to kill Emperor Trajan. That much I know because he talked about it to all of his friends."

"What a shame it is that he was caught," said Andrada. "Such a sad loss of a young life."

"Yes, I agree," Decebal said. "I had regrets from the start that he got involved."

Vezina was also understanding. "It is impossible to stop young men with a passion."

Adila banged her water cup down on the table with a loud noise that filled the room. "I cannot believe what I am hearing from all of you right now!"

"Do you wish to say something, Adila?" her mother asked.

"Yes! The only shame, Mama, is that Marcu failed to kill Trajan. We are in a war of survival with Rome! And the decision to try was his decision entirely, Tata, and not one for you to regret. And what is so wrong, Your Holiness, for young people with a passion to pursue our passion in defense of our people?"

A moment of silence followed, then Vezina gave her a smile filled with pride. "There is nothing wrong with that at all."

"You are in the right, Adila," the King agreed. "Everything you said is true."

Andrada placed her hand on her daughter's shoulder. "Four years ago you asked for my blessing to go and fight at Tapae. You were only sixteen years old then, and I worried."

"Yes, I remember," Adila said. "I was too young to fight then."

"You were, and I could not convince you otherwise. But now, my daughter, you have the skills and clearly also the heart of a warrior."

"Thank you for saying so," Adila said. "But do I now have your blessing? And will you still worry about me?"

"I will worry about you, but not quite as much," Andrada replied honestly. "And yes, you have my blessing. You are as ready as any warrior in Dacia."

"And I will fight like any warrior in Dacia," Adila said. "Marcu fought Rome for his father, but not only for his father. He fought for his family and for all of us. I can do no less."

Zia was just finishing feeding her young son when her sister came to visit. At ten months old Brasus was growing at a healthy pace and taking his first baby steps. Her husband Tarbus was with the army in eastern Dacia. Zia was sad to know that both her sister and her father were soon leaving to join the army as well.

"Oh, just look at him," Adila said, leaning down to give her nephew a kiss on the cheek. "With that curly hair he looks more and more like Tarbus every day."

"Yes he does. But with the big blue eyes he looks more like us," Zia said with a laugh.

"No matter, he is a very handsome little boy."

Zia turned to her sister with a worried look on her face. "So you are leaving tomorrow, then?"

"Yes, we leave at first light. Tata will travel to inspect some of our forts. I am going to join the army of General Drilgisa."

"Oh, good!" Zia exclaimed. "That means you will be close to Tarbus then?"

"That is my plan, Zia. Actually my unit of archers will be assigned to the infantry units that Tarbus commands."

"I am glad. Then you can look after each other."

Adila smiled and gave a small shrug. "When the fighting starts, Sister, it's hard enough to look after yourself. But don't worry, Tarbus can take care of himself."

Zia gave her a somber look. "And what about you? Can you take care of yourself?"

"Oh, quit worrying about me. Any Roman that tries to get within thirty paces of me gets an arrow right between the eyes."

"Ha!" Zia replied with a soft laugh. "My sister, the archer. I still can't get used to the idea, but I know that this is what you wanted for a long time."

"No, Zia," Adila said, her voice turned serious. "This is not really what I wanted, but it is what I must do. What I most want is very simple, to have a family like yours and a happy life." She paused and gave a sigh. "I cannot have that however until we are at peace again."

Zia put her arms around her sister and drew her into an embrace. She held her tightly for a few heartbeats as her eyes grew misty with emotion. When she pulled away Zia gave her sister a warm smile.

"You will have that, Adila. I know it in my heart that you will. Just come back safely to me. I will be at your wedding, and at the birth of your children. We will raise our families together."

"Thank you, Sister. I will come back, and when I do I will expect you to keep every one of your promises."

"If Zamolxis wills it, it will be so," Zia said in a solemn tone.

Adila smiled again. "I will make it so."

*Mountains of eastern Dacia, October 105 AD*

The season was drifting into late fall. The night air in the mountains was chilly and leaves were turning red, orange, yellow, and brown. The heavy snows were perhaps still two months away, and the Roman armies pressed their attacks against Dacian forts and villages.

Emperor Trajan found that, somewhat surprisingly, his second war against the Dacian mountain forts was even more difficult than the previous war of three and four years ago. Fort walls were made stronger and defenders were better protected behind stone ramparts. Even the heavy Roman artillery, the catapults and large ballistae, could not breach the walls or gates. That meant that the forts had to be defeated with a siege if the invaders had the time and patience to do so. If the Romans wanted faster results, which was most often the case, then the walls had to be scaled with ladders. There were simply too many forts to conquer to make long sieges practical.

A frontal attack against well defended stone walls always caused large numbers of casualties for the attackers. The defenders, fighting mainly as archers and spearmen, put up a ferocious and desperate resistance. They were less willing to retreat in the face of defeat than in the previous war, a fact that also caught the Roman commanders by surprise.

"Decebalus already has a severe manpower shortage," General Laberius Maximus stated, watching from horseback while Roman troops assaulted the fort. He was speaking to Emperor Trajan and General Hadrian. "Why then does he sacrifice his soldiers to defend mountain forts when he knows that we will overwhelm them and kill his men every time?"

"Perhaps he cares more about causing Roman casualties than about his Dacian casualties," Hadrian replied. "I saw that firsthand when he attacked Drobeta and Pontes."

"No doubt he wants to make our invasion as costly as possible by inflicting heavy casualties," Trajan said. "However there is something much more important to Decebalus."

"What is that, Caesar?" Hadrian asked.

"Time, Hadrianus," Trajan replied. "He is sacrificing casualties for time. He needs to rally his allies to put up a united front again, and that is proving very difficult for him."

Maximus gave a snort. "Good. All the more reason for us to attack more aggressively. Don't give him any room to breathe."

"Patience!" the Emperor declared. "We must have patience and follow our strategy as planned. Impatience and rash decisions always cost Rome dearly in the wars with Decebalus."

"That is true, Caesar," Maximus conceded with a curt tone. "I am not questioning your strategy, but I am very eager to see the head of Decebalus on a pike."

Trajan turned to him and raised an eyebrow. "Laberius, your lack of political sense shocks me!"

"How so, Caesar?"

"I do not wish to see the head of Decebalus on a pike. That would be a terrible lost opportunity," Trajan explained. "I profoundly wish to see King Decebalus, very much alive and well, marching in chains down the Via Sacra in my triumph parade."

"Ah, of course," Maximus replied.

"We must humiliate him before we kill him," Hadrian said.

"Precisely, Hadrianus," Trajan agreed. "You are learning to think like a politician."

The Roman cavalry patrol was not Roman cavalry, Adila could see even from a distance. Only a small number of cavalry in the Roman army were actually Romans, and these were used for messages and communications and not for fighting. The riders now approaching were auxiliary cavalry recruited from the tribes in the region who were friendly with Rome. In the wars against Dacia these were most likely Gauls or Iazygis.

Adila hoped they were Iazygis. Many years ago she was attacked and almost kidnapped by Iazygis. That assault persuaded her to ask her brother Cotiso to train her in using the army bow. She became an archer because of that Iazygi attack.

Boian was the captain of the forty Dacians in the ambush squad, twenty archers and the same number of spearmen and swordsmen. Close to twenty enemy cavalry now approached their well-hidden positions on the mountain slope just above the road. Spearmen were most effective against cavalry in close combat but the archers always struck first. The first sign the cavalry would have of the Dacian attack would be a hail of arrows from the trees and shrubbery up the slope.

"Iazygis," the archer next to Adila whispered to her. "I hate the damn Iazygis."

*Peter Jaksa*

His comment made Adila smile to herself. After all these years it was time for payback. She smoothly and silently notched an arrow on her bowstring and waited for the enemy to come within range. The Dacians would attack when Boian gave the signal.

The Iazygis were riding two abreast in a column on the narrow mountain road. It was not a long column and the Dacians would hit them hard with archers positioned just above them. At the same time they would cut off the riders in front and back of the column with spearmen and swordsmen.

The Dacian captain Boian stepped forward from behind cover and silently pointed his spear towards the column of Iazygis. The archers were only half a step behind him, bows at the ready, and they unleashed a wave of arrows from twenty to thirty paces away. At such close range they were deadly accurate. Within three heartbeats they notched, aimed, and shot again.

Adila was positioned towards the left of the Dacian line, which was the rear of the Iazygi column. She stepped out from behind her shrubbery cover and found herself twenty paces away from the rider at the rear of the line. She fixed her eye on the rider's unprotected neck that became her target, drew the bowstring back to her ear, and loosed. The Iazygi rider never even saw his attacker before her arrow pierced his throat.

Almost half the cavalry riders were down from the archery attack, and the rest frantically urged their screaming and panicked horses to sprint away. They were met by Dacian infantry on either end of the road who formed a wall of spears to cut off their escape. Some of the Iazygis carried lances, which they threw to take down a number of the enemy infantry. The riders then drew their swords and charged the Dacian line that formed at the back of their column.

Adila anticipated that some riders might break through. She ran further to her left, staying on the mountain slope some ten paces above the road. She turned sideways to make herself a smaller target and

> 104

became completely hidden behind a tree. She notched another arrow on her bowstring and waited.

Moments later the pounding of hoof beats came in her direction. There was no time to think. Adila stepped out from behind the tree, a scant ten paces away from the road, and was almost face to face with a Iazygi rider and another rider following right behind. The rider's eyes widened for an instant as he caught a glimpse of the archer just above him, then shut tightly in pain as an arrow pierced deeply into his stomach. He slumped forward in the saddle and his horse sped by his attacker.

Adila notched another arrow on her string and looked towards the second rider, now almost parallel to her position. Something bright and metallic flashed by very close to the left side of her face and with a loud noise imbedded itself in the tree trunk. The shock of it made Adila hesitate, and in that moment the second Iazygi sped by and was quickly out of sight. She turned her head and saw that the metallic object that just missed her face was a sword. The second Iazygi rider had thrown his sword at her as he sped by.

Dacian soldiers led by Boian came running down the road in her direction. The rider Adila shot in the stomach was lying on the side of the road, but the second rider had escaped. Boian looked at Adila, then at the sword sticking out from the tree trunk beside her head, and slowly shook his head.

"Two things, Adila," the captain said.

"And what are those, sir?" she asked, her voice surprisingly calm.

"First, good job of killing that escaping rider. And second," Boian paused and gave her a grin, "when an archer is close enough to allow an enemy to almost take her head off by throwing his sword at her, it means that her fighting position is much too close to the enemy."

"Yes, sir," she replied. "Things happened very quickly and I was not thinking of the danger."

"Next time, think first," Boian chided her, concerned rather than critical. "It would have been an offense against the gods if that sword scarred your beautiful face."

"Do you say that to all your soldiers, Captain?" Adila asked in an even tone.

Boian grinned again. "Only those who warrant it." He turned away to issue orders.

"Strip them of weapons and armor! Take the horses to camp! Hop to it, quickly now!"

Adila was an experienced rider and so was one of the soldiers to ride one of the captured horses to the Dacian camp further down the road. What surprised her the most, she thought as she rode, was how calm she felt during the fight. Her heart beat fast for a few moments from the shock of seeing the Iazygi sword that narrowly missed her head, but otherwise she felt no fear.

The enemy were only targets to her and she felt no remorse for killing them. They would kill her without remorse if given the chance. This was very different from the battle at Tapae, where she knew that she did not belong. Now she belonged.

*Marcedava, Dacia, October 105 AD*

The four Dacian village chiefs welcomed Lucius Licinius Sura as an honored guest. They prepared a feast for him and his Praetorian Guard unit, along with entertainment that included singers and dancers. As the main Dacian army retreated further to the west these chieftains chose to stay behind and keep their people at home.

Licinius Sura, envoy of Emperor Trajan, brought small gifts and even more importantly he brought offers of peace. His messengers rode ahead and arranged such meetings with several Dacian village chiefs each day. Sura was an excellent diplomat, and to his pleasant surprise he found that he had a willing audience for his diplomatic efforts. Many of these tribal chiefs were simply exhausted from war.

"We do not ask that you fight against King Decebalus or any other of your fellow Dacians," Sura assured them. "Caesar has enough men to defeat Decebalus. We ask only that you remain in your villages and do not fight against Caesar."

A wizened old village chief with a long white beard nodded his head in assent. "We are tired of war, and we have so few young men left in our village. Leave us in peace and we will leave you in peace."

"Yes, exactly so," Sura agreed in a pleasant voice. "Tend to your fields and your cattle. Allow your young men to get married and start their own families. Caesar only wishes for you to live in peace."

"We have sacrificed much for King Decebal but now have nothing left to sacrifice," another chieftain added in a sour tone.

"King Decebalus acts without honor and does not deserve your loyalty further," Sura explained. "He broke the peace treaty with Rome by acting dishonorably. He sent three paid assassins to kill Caesar, which is a stench in the nostrils of the gods. Surely you good Dacians do not consider that honorable?"

"No," a third chieftain shook his head. "That was not honorable."

"Then we are agreed, my friends. You will stay in your villages and live in peace, and you will have no cause to fear Rome."

The first chieftain stroked his beard and cleared his throat, a nervous habit. "Will Caesar impose taxes on our people?"

Sura paused briefly as if in thought. This was an important point for all the chieftains and required a diplomatic answer. "That is yet to be determined. If however Caesar decides to tax you it will be with a fair and just tax, no different than other taxes in the Roman Empire."

The four chieftains exchanged glances with each other. A few words were murmured between them. The eldest, who appeared to be their leader, looked Sura in the eye.

"We wish to make peace with Rome, Senator Sura. We accept the terms that you offer."

"Very good," Sura replied with a broad smile. These men did not require threats but only reason and a little coaxing. "I am very pleased.

I will tell Caesar of your decision, and I know that he will be pleased also."

*Mountains of eastern Dacia, October 105 AD*

Tarbus found Adila by the small cooking fire, examining her arrows to make certain that none had damage or irregularities. One white goose feather out of alignment would make the arrow go off target. One arrow head not sharpened to a needle point would fail to pierce its target and leave the enemy still able to fight. That kind of common carelessness got archers killed.

"Hello, Adila," Tarbus said as he sat down to join her. "Boian told me of your daring against the Iazygi cavalry."

Adila gave a small casual shrug. "I did my job, that's all. I killed two of them. The third one got away."

"The third one, I am told, almost killed you with a thrown sword," Tarbus said with a small frown on his face.

"Boian exaggerates," she said dismissively. "I was not in any more peril than any other soldier in that fight."

"He is not known for exaggerating," Tarbus said. "He is concerned for your safety if you take unnecessary risks. And for that matter, Adila, so am I. You are very brave but bravery must be tempered with sound judgment. You know this."

She turned to face him, eyes blazing. "Why can't everyone just treat me like any other soldier? I take the same risks as everyone else."

Tarbus slowly shook his head. "You are not like any other soldier. You are a princess of Dacia, which everyone knows and so will treat you accordingly."

"I wish it were not so."

"That is something that will never change, Adila." Tarbus paused, gathering his thoughts. "And there is one more thing I must mention. You hate Romans with a strong passion, and I understand the reason why. Unfortunately that carries a risk, and sometimes it makes you more daring than you ought to be."

"Now you sound like my father."

"I hope so, Adila," Tarbus replied. "I would feel proud if that is true and my judgment agrees with the King's." He paused to watch the flames of the fire, giving time for their tempers to cool down.

"Very well. I promise to not take foolish risks," Adila said. She looked up and gave Tarbus an amused smile. "I promised Zia that I would return home, and that we would raise our babies together."

Tarbus laughed. "Good! I know both of you well enough to know that kind of promise between sisters is sacred."

"I will do all that I can to keep my promise, Tarbus. But first we must defeat this Roman army so that we can live in peace again. See how simple life is?"

"Ah! Life is never simple. However, when it comes to defeating the Roman army there is one simple thing that you must remember."

Adila raised an eyebrow. "What might that be?"

"It is not necessary that you defeat them all by yourself, Adila," he replied with a grin.

"I understand," Adila said. "I will do my part, and you will stop nagging me about it. Do we have a deal?"

Tarbus gave a nod. "We have a deal."


On days when Adila's archery unit was given a rest she often grew restless and impatient with camp life. On days like that, whether in good weather or bad, she sometimes took a long solitary walk in the forest. She felt most at home in the woods. Indeed, she felt more at home when she was walking in the forest than when she was in her rooms in the royal palace.

Like all other Dacian children, when Adila was a little girl she learned the many stories of Fata Padurii. This was the Dacian female spirit of the forest, capable of endless mischief towards the humans who wandered around her forest kingdom. Depending on her mood

Fata Padurii was the bringer of laughter and joy, or sorrow and tears, and sometimes danger and death.

At certain times when she was walking in the woods, alone with her thoughts, Adila's imagination drifted to the forest spirit. She felt a natural kinship with Fata Padurii. Perhaps the forest spirit entered her body at those times, she wondered. Or perhaps the forest spirit lived within her. If she had the choice of being a god or goddess, Adila decided, she would rather be Fata Padurii than the unpredictable and capricious Zamolxis. Such thoughts were heresy for a Dacian and she kept them to herself.

On this particular late afternoon Adila was hiking in the forest looking to collect medicinal plants. She learned from her mother and from Zelma about the many plants that reduced pain, or calmed the nerves, or helped to induce sleep. She dispensed them to the other soldiers as needed.

Adila's peace of mind was interrupted by the sounds of horses nearby. They were stationary, not on the move. Soon she also picked up the low murmuring sounds of men's voices. Neither Dacian nor Roman troops were stationed in this area, which meant that this was a travelling party. A very small travelling party based on the sounds of their voices.

In the forest Adila blended in with the trees and shrubbery. She moved noiselessly from one place of cover to another until she had the group of travelers in sight.

A distinguished looking Roman in his middle years was in charge, accompanied by two soldiers and a boy who watched their horses. The older man was likely a noble, perhaps a lower level senator. The boy of thirteen or fourteen was dressed in the simple and inexpensive clothes befitting a servant or a slave. The two soldiers wore the lighter leather armor of the cavalry, not the heavy metal armor of infantry.

In an instant Adila had a plan in mind. Whatever the mission of this Roman might be it would be better to end it here. She had to kill the two guards first, then deal with the older man and the boy as the situation called for. Dusk was approaching and she could get closer without being seen.

The first soldier never knew that he was being stalked until the moment when the arrow slammed into his torso just below the arm pit and pierced into his lungs and heart. He groaned with pain and dropped to the ground, where he remained unmoving.

The second soldier stood up in alarm and drew his sword, and frantically scanned the woods around them for a sign of attackers.

"Senator, to horse!" he shouted.

He expected at any moment to see a swarm of wild and screaming barbarians rushing out of the trees to overwhelm them. There was however no sight or sound of any attackers. The woods were silent.

The soldier also backed away towards the horses, his eyes on the spot from which the attack came. The second arrow came from the trees to his right and hit him just underneath the rib cage. It was shot from close range and with enough force to knock him down. The pain in his side was searing and he dropped his sword. He fell to the ground, gasping for breath, and knew that he would die.

The senator was already in the saddle and urging his frightened horse forward. The servant boy scrambled to mount his own horse. Out of the corner of his eye he saw a figure emerge from the trees, a young woman who raised her bow and shot an arrow in his direction. Before he could scream in terror the arrow shot past him and hit the fleeing senator in the middle of his back, cutting through the spine. The Roman fell like a sack of stones as his horse galloped away.

Adila had another arrow notched on her string but did not aim it as she approached the servant boy. She calmly motioned for him to dismount. He obeyed without hesitation and stood beside his horse, expecting that he would die. He watched this female archer with a growing sense of awe. She had just killed three men very quickly and ruthlessly, and still had not uttered a word.

"Are you a slave to the Romans?" Adila finally spoke.

"No," the boy shook his head, his voice shaking. "I am a servant. Senator Caepio hired me. I am from Moesia."

"Don't be afraid, I will not harm you. Take your horse and ride home to Moesia."

Adila lowered her bow and turned to walk away. The servant boy stood transfixed to the spot.

"Wait!" he blurted.

Adila stopped and turned back to face him. "What is it?"

"I want to thank you for my life," he said. He paused, and then asked the question that was burning on his mind. "Who are you?"

Adila was surprised by the tone of wonderment in his voice. He was looking at her and addressing her as if she was some kind of goddess. The thought brought a smile to her face.

"Tell your people in Moesia that your life was spared in the forest of Dacia by Fata Padurii. Will you remember that?"

"Yes, I will," the boy replied with a nod. Even in Moesia people knew the legend of Fata Padurii.

"Tell them that I guard the forests of Dacia with a fierce pride and an all seeing eye. Tell your people, and also tell the Romans, what you saw here today."

The boy had no words so simply nodded again. The young woman turned away and with a few swift steps vanished into the trees and the haze of twilight. He took a deep breath to calm himself. He had just seen the most beautiful woman he ever saw in his life, who was also perhaps a goddess. To his surprise he was still alive while the Roman senator and his guards were all dead. Sometimes the gods were unpredictable. Sometimes the gods were good.

# Chapter 9

# The Hostage

*Banat, Dacia, November 105 AD*

General Gnaeus Pompeius Longinus, the former mentor and current close friend of Emperor Trajan, was under siege by a large and determined force of Dacian infantry. In some parts of Dacia the Dacian armies were retreating, and in some parts they were attacking and harassing Roman camps and fortifications. The fort commanded by General Longinus was one of the locations under attack.

After several days of repulsing the attackers Longinus knew to his dismay that he was fighting a losing battle. Almost half of his men were dead or wounded. The remaining defenders were getting more battered by the day. His own army was the largest Roman army in the region, and Longinus knew there were no other troops in the vicinity to come to his aid.

On the morning of the sixth day a lone and unarmed Dacian rider approached the fort gates carrying a flag of truce. He was allowed to reach the gates, dismount, and approach on foot to within speaking distance of Longinus.

The Dacian was Osan, a captain of horse archers. He gave a small respectful bow towards the famous general before addressing the Roman commander.

"General Longinus, I bring terms from General Drilgisa."

"Speak," Longinus said impatiently. "What terms?"

"You will surrender the fort, sir, and prevent the massacre of your soldiers. You will then ride with General Drilgisa to Sarmizegetusa for discussions with King Decebal, sir."

Longinus laughed, taken by surprise. "Discussions with your King Decebalus? These are the most unusual surrender terms I have ever heard. Why does King Decebalus wish to talk to me?"

Osan gave a shrug. "I do not know, sir. I was not told."

"Ah, the follies of war," Gnaeus said with a shake of his head. "Very well. Tell General Drilgisa that I accept his terms."

*Sarmizegetusa, November 105 AD*

Gnaeus Longinus and a small group of his men were escorted to the Dacian capital on horseback. The general understood that Decebalus wished to speak with him because he was a high level military officer and also a confidant of the Emperor. Longinus had information that, to Decebalus, was more valuable than gold.

After his men were quartered in the city and placed under guard, four Dacian soldiers took Longinus to the royal palace. He was led to the throne room, where two men sat in discussion around a long and brilliantly polished table. Longinus needed no introductions to know who these two men were.

One of the guards announced him. "Sire, here stands General Gnaeus Longinus!"

"King Decebal and High Priest Vezina, I trust," Longinus said in greeting and gave them a curt bow.

Vezina stood and motioned to a chair on the opposite side of the table. "That is correct. Have a seat, General, so that we may talk."

Decebal gave the Roman a good look, taking the measure of the man. Longinus was almost sixty years old, with graying brown hair and blue eyes. He had the prominent long Roman nose so common among the Roman nobility. Trajan also had such a nose, King Decebal remembered. Unlike Trajan however Gnaeus Longinus did not stay in fighting trim and was growing paunchy around the middle.

"You have been a friend of Emperor Trajan since he was a young man, I am told," Decebal addressed him.

"That is so, King Decebal," Gnaeus replied in a polite tone. "I have been fortunate to call Caesar a friend since he was very young."

"Then perhaps you can be helpful in reasoning with the Emperor. That is why you are here, Longinus."

"I shall be helpful in any way that does not betray Caesar or betray Rome, King Decebal. Those are my terms for discussion."

The King ignored the comment. "What does Trajan want? Why is he waging war on Dacia a second time?"

Longinus paused to gather his thoughts. "That is a complicated question. In part he is here because of destiny. In part he is here to punish Dacia for breaking your treaty with Rome."

Vezina raised an eyebrow. "What does destiny have to do with it?"

"Ah, that is not difficult to understand if you have a Roman mind," the general said. "It is the destiny of Rome to rule the world. It is the will of Jupiter, Mars, and all the gods."

Vezina waved his hand dismissively. "That is superstitious rubbish and nothing more than an excuse for theft and aggression."

Longinus looked almost offended. "I will not deny that Rome uses aggression when necessary to keep the peace in the empire."

"Do you mean to say that Trajan invades Dacia because he wants peace?" The King asked the question in a mocking tone.

"Indeed, King Decebal. Caesar wants peace. He invades Dacia again because you broke the treaty with Rome. I do not – "

Decebal turned on him with a fury. "Romans are the robbers of the world! You plunder, butcher, and enslave, and you call that building an empire. Wherever you go you create destruction, and you call that destruction peace. Peace!" the King shouted with scorn. "Dacia will not accept your sham ideas of peace. What you call Roman peace is nothing more than a different name for enslavement."

Longinus remained silent. He had no good reply to Decebal's harsh words and did not wish to provoke further confrontation.

After a tense silence Vezina intervened. "A just peace can be agreed upon, General Longinus. However Rome must set aside its ideas of destiny and treat with Dacia as a trading partner, not as a target for conquest."

"What kind of agreement do you propose, Vezina?" Gnaeus asked in an even tone.

Vezina turned to the King. "Sire, do you wish to explain the terms that will be asked of Emperor Trajan?"

"I will," Decebal replied, his tone calmer. "Rome will remove all troops from Dacian territory. And Rome will return to Dacia all of the captured lands north of the Ister River, which you Romans call the Danubius."

"Those terms are negotiable. Anything else?"

"Yes. Rome will use the stone bridge at Drobeta only for moving grain, cattle, timber, and other trade goods. The bridge will not be used for transporting troops or for any other military purpose."

"Ah! That will be a difficult concession for Caesar to make. He takes great pride in his bridge and will not wish to see limits placed on its use."

"And lastly," Decebal continued, "as a show of Rome's goodwill Emperor Trajan will free my sister Tanidela and her daughter and provide safe passage for them to return home."

Longinus gave a respectful nod. "I would like to see that arranged as well, King Decebal. I had chance to see and talk with your sister while I was in Rome. She is treated well but would prefer to return to her own people, of course."

"Will Caesar consider these terms, in your opinion?" Vezina asked. "You know Trajan as well or better than any other man."

"Reasonable people can always discuss reasonable terms," Gnaeus replied. "However I cannot say what Emperor Trajan might think of these terms until I propose them to him."

Decebal shook his head. "No, it will not be you who presents this proposal to Trajan. I will send a Dacian envoy, along with one of your men who will vouch that you are unharmed and are treated well."

"Surely I could be more persuasive than a Dacian envoy?"

Vezina gave him a patient smile. "Come now, Gnaeus. You are much too valuable to be used as a messenger."

"Ah, I see. Am I your prisoner then?"

"For now, you are," the King answered. "Until we receive Emperor Trajan's reply consider yourself a prisoner of Dacia. We do not have prisons with iron bars nor do we have torture details, but you will be kept under guard here in the palace."

"I see. And what of my men?"

"They will also be under guard," Vezina answered him. "We will talk often, so make yourself comfortable here in Sarmizegetusa."

*Roman camp, southern Dacia, November 105 AD*

"Gnaeus is a tough old bird and a clever one," Licinius Sura said to Trajan and Titus Lucullus. "He won't betray Rome. Dacians don't even use torture with prisoners, although I fail to see why not."

Trajan frowned. "Even if they torture him there is nothing of such critical importance that he could tell them. He has been in Banat for months now, not planning strategy here with us."

"Then he is merely a prize that Decebalus wishes to dangle in front of us to get concessions from Rome," Sura added.

The Emperor turned to Lucullus. "What is your opinion of Dacian intentions, Titus? You spent time with them. You know Vezina, who advises Decebalus."

"I agree with Sura, Caesar," Titus replied. "King Decebalus knows that General Longinus is your friend. He is most valuable to him as a hostage to be used to persuade you."

"I will not agree to unreasonable demands," Trajan said. "Draw back my army, when we have a knife at his throat? Such nonsense."

"Of course, Marcus," Sura agreed. "We have not travelled this far to turn back now."

Trajan paused to refill his wine goblet with an excellent Sabine white wine. Longinus being captured took him by surprise.

"What do you propose that we do?" Sura asked.

"We must send Decebalus a reply to turn down his proposed terms. And yet I do not wish to place Gnaeus in peril."

"A very delicate situation," said Licinius. "If we show too much concern for Gnaeus then Decebalus will expect more concessions. Too little concern and Gnaeus will lose value as a hostage in their eyes and perhaps be in more danger."

Lucullus cleared his throat. "General Longinus is not in immediate danger. He has no value to Decebalus as a dead man, and the Dacians have no reason to wish him dead."

Trajan gave a nod. "Your judgment is sound, Lucullus. For now we should not give any clear or decisive reply. Let's keep Decebalus guessing, bide our time, and see how things develop."

Sura raised an eyebrow. "And how do we keep him guessing?"

"Cleverly, Licinius," Trajan replied. "We must be clever in this or it may cost Gnaeus his life."

*Sarmizegetusa, December 105 AD*

Gnaeus Longinus was guarded day and night by soldiers stationed outside his door. He was visited often by Vezina, who engaged him in a variety of talks related to Roman life and Roman and Dacian goals. Both were intelligent and well informed men of mature years with a natural curiosity about each other's people.

Longinus was treated well, even being assigned a palace servant to look after his needs. The servant, a young man named Orola, brought Gnaeus his meals, fetched reading materials, and carried messages for him. Gnaeus often claimed a poor appetite and gave his meals to

Orola instead. Over time the servant came to like and even admire this old general.

At times Longinus was summoned to the throne room for talks with King Decebal. Those discussions were mostly about military matters, about which Gnaeus was less forthcoming. He would not provide military information, he resolved, even under pain of death.

Three weeks after his capture Longinus was brought before the King's council. This council included Vezina, Queen Andrada, and Decebal's friend and confidant Buri. Gnaeus could tell from the King's expression that he received unpleasant news.

"Emperor Trajan offers nothing to bargain for your freedom, and yet he also does not flatly refuse my proposal," Decebal told Gnaeus. "I was told that he values you highly as a friend and would consider terms to set you free."

Longinus gave a casual shrug. "I am an old general ready to be put to pasture. Yes we are friends, but friendship has limits."

"It depends on the friendship," Andrada said with a sympathetic smile. "You are an old and dear friend to Caesar."

The Roman acknowledged her with a polite nod.

"I do not wish you harm, General," Decebal continued. "I wish to ransom you, but in exchange I must receive equal value from you."

"Of course. However I have given you all the information that I can, King Decebal."

"Provide some information that we can use," Vezina said. "What are Trajan's intentions for the coming year? Who commands what troops, and what are the commanders like? Specific information."

"If I provide that information then I am a traitor to Rome." The general paused and shook his head. "I can no more betray Rome than you can betray Dacia, King Decebal."

The Queen cut in. "What would convince Emperor Trajan to seek peace? Killing each other in endless wars is not the solution."

"In truth, Queen Andrada, I believe that this time Caesar will seek Dacia's surrender." He turned to the King. "As you know, Emperor

Trajan is a very intelligent man. It makes him a very capable general and a good emperor."

"I have never thought otherwise, Longinus. Your point?"

"Besides intelligence he also has vision," Longinus continued. "He plans far ahead, as you have seen. But other men also have vision. What makes Caesar very different from other men is that he always makes his visions and his plans come true."

Decebal gave him an indulgent smile. "And what plans do you now see in the Emperor's vision? You know him well."

Longinus kept his tone even. "He sees a Dacia, King Decebal, without you as its inspiration."

Vezina frowned. "Many men have wished that. Wishing does not make it so."

"Indeed it does not," the Roman agreed. "But can we agree that Caesar is no simple dreamer? He makes plans and takes action."

"Tell me this, General Longinus," Queen Andrada interjected again. "What does Dacia without King Decebal look like to Trajan?"

"A Dacia pacified," Longinus replied. He saw a look of indignation on every face and said no more.

"Do you mean a Dacia ruled as a Roman province?" Vezina asked.

Longinus gave a shrug. "I do not know. Caesar has not told me his plans for the future of Dacia."

"The future of Dacia," Decebal said in a calm but firm tone, "is not for Emperor Trajan to decide."

Longinus gave him a respectful nod.

Buri, who had been sitting and listening quietly with his arms folded across his chest, had heard enough. "You are right, Sire. And Dacia will never be pacified." He turned to Longinus. "And do you know why, Roman?"

"I can think of many reasons, Buri. But tell me your reason why?"

"No, not because of many reasons," Buri replied with a shake of his head. "Because of one main reason. And that reason is that we never stop fighting. Defeat us with superior forces and we still come back and fight you. Defeat us again, and we come back and fight you again. We do that as many times as necessary, even if it takes one hundred years."

"Well put, Buri," Vezina said. "That has been the history between Dacia and Rome."

"So what now?" Andrada asked.

Decebal addressed Longinus. "Write a letter to Caesar, General. Be more persuasive and convince Trajan to be more agreeable. You will bring this letter to me tomorrow."

"Very well, King Decebal. I shall give it my best effort."

"Do so, Longinus. We'll talk again tomorrow."


Gnaeus spent the day with parchment and ink writing to Trajan. He did not believe that Trajan could be persuaded but he gave his word to make an effort. He stopped only when the servant Orola brought his evening meal. His dinner was roasted duck with vegetables and freshly baked bread. The delicious smell of hot food and spices filled the room, and Orola watched him hungrily as he ate.

Longinus ate a small portion of the meal then pushed the plate towards his servant. "You may have the rest, Orola," he offered with a smile. "I am sated, and you look hungry."

"Oh, thank you, General," Orola said happily. "You are very kind."

Gnaeus watched the man dig into his food with gusto. "Orola, I shall ask you for a favor. No, two favors, when I think of it."

"Yes, General?"

"This letter that I am writing I will give to King Decebal tomorrow. He will want it sent to Emperor Trajan. Orola, I want you to carry the letter to Caesar personally."

The servant looked up between bites of food. "But why me?"

"Because I will tell you what to say to Caesar, so that he knows the message came from me and that he should take it seriously."

"I see. And you ask a second favor, you said?"

Longinus gave him a calm look. "Yes. This one is a small job, and Caesar will pay you twelve gold coins when you tell him of it."

Orola's eyes grew wide. Twelve gold coins were the wages of a Roman legionnaire for a full year of service. It was more money than he could hope to make in ten years.

"Tell me, General, and I will obey."

"I want you to purchase for me a pouch of herbal medicine for sleep and bring it to me. This must be a secret between us, Orola. If the guards find it they will take it from you."

Orola gave a nod. "I understand. What kind of sleep medicine?"

"You call it wolfsbane, I believe," Gnaeus said in a casual tone. "It is a purple flower. Do you know it?"

The man paused, surprise showing on his face. "Yes, I know it. But it is not a sleep medicine, General."

"It is a medicine for me." Longinus put a firm hand on the man's shoulder. "Do these things for me and you will be very well rewarded. Twelve gold coins. This I swear to you, on my honor."

Orola could think of nothing more to say and so he simply nodded his head. He left the remainder of his meal on the plate because his appetite deserted him.


Orola left the next morning accompanied by a small troop of Dacian cavalry, carrying the letter from Gnaeus Longinus and King Decebal to Emperor Trajan. He also carried a message from General Longinus to ensure Caesar that the General was in good health and was being treated well by his Dacian captors.

An additional message, which the servant carried only in his head but which Caesar would know came from his friend Longinus, wished Caesar good health and freedom in his actions. The private message also asked Trajan to pay the messenger Orola twelve gold coins and to grant him the protection of Rome.

Three days later Gnaeus Longinus was again visited by Vezina for one of their ongoing discussions. The talks were civil and friendly and never treated as interrogations. In his long years of experience Vezina found that information was best gathered through reward and cooperation rather than through coercion.

"The attacks on our forts have almost ceased since the winter cold set in," Vezina informed the general. "Emperor Trajan will keep his army sheltered in winter camps."

"He will," Longinus agreed. "You Dacians are more fond of winter attacks, but we Romans prefer to fight in warmer weather. It is not a matter of comfort Vezina, but of tactics."

"I understand the tactical reasons," Vezina said. "We attack in small groups so that we are mobile and move quickly. You Romans fight in large groups. You are loaded down with baggage carts and the animals needed to pull them." He paused and smiled. "We move like a pack of wolves. You move like a herd of cattle."

"Ha! But you have a point. Our war season is spring and summer because we cannot feed our pack animals on the road in winter."

"Then I expect that Trajan's main attack will come in the spring."

Longinus gave him a small smile. "You know that as well as I do, Vezina. There are no secrets here."

"Do you expect that this letter just sent will get a different reaction than your first letter, Gnaeus?"

"Perhaps, but the gods only know. Caesar is a proud and stubborn man, as is your King Decebal. Such pride seldom bends."

"It never bends," Vezina said. "I call it the pride of kings."

"That is a very astute observation, and very true." Longinus turned to look Vezina in the eye. "What is to be my fate then, when Caesar does not bend?"

"That will be determined by the King. In truth, Gnaeus, I cannot see that future yet. Much may happen in the coming months."

"Nothing to my benefit, I expect."

"We shall see. It would be to your benefit to be more forthcoming about military matters. You know a great deal and say nothing."

"I am surprised to not be under torture yet," Longinus said with a grim smile. "It is curious that you Dacians don't believe in torture."

Vezina could not help but laugh. "Do you wish to be tortured?"

"Of course not. I am only saying that if I were a prisoner of Rome I would be under torture and forced to provide information."

"At times we torture prisoners as a punishment," Vezina said. "We do not torture to obtain information. It is inhumane and irreligious and Zamolxis does not allow it."

"Ah! I should be grateful to Zamolxis then."

"It is always wise to be grateful to Zamolxis," Vezina said as he stood up to leave. "Farewell, Gnaeus. We shall talk again tomorrow."

After Vezina left Gnaeus Longinus prayed not to Zamolxis but to Mars the god of war and to Jupiter Optimus Maximus. He would now determine his own fate and not leave it in the hands of the Dacians. Most importantly he would untie Caesar's hands and free him from the burden of difficult decisions on his behalf. He would eliminate all risk of being forced to betray Rome.

The general searched underneath his tunic for the small cloth pouch that was delivered to him in secret by Orola. Loyal and greedy Orola, well on his way to Trajan's camp and out of the reach of King Decebalus. When he received the message Caesar would no doubt understand the action that Gnaeus took, and he would be grateful.

Longinus opened the pouch and smelled the pungent smell of the wolfsbane. He put a small handful into his mouth and chewed it, then washed it down with a cup of water. He laid down on his bed. The strong poison worked quickly. He felt drowsy, then paralyzed, then fell into a sleep from which he would never awaken.

# Chapter 10

# Strategies

*Sarmizegetusa, December 105 AD*

Perhaps the very last thing Vezina expected to see the next morning when he went to talk with Gnaeus Longinus was the cold dead body of his Roman prisoner. He liked and respected the man. Gnaeus could be stubborn and unbending but he was also very intelligent and knowledgeable. He had a quick wit and often a twinkle in his eye. Vezina had been looking forward to their next conversation.

After questioning the guards Vezina was satisfied that no one had entered the prisoner's room during the night. Indeed the last person to see Longinus alive was Vezina himself. A guard searched the body and found the medicine pouch. A quick look and a sniff told Vezina what the poison was.

King Decebal was summoned immediately. He arrived in an angry and unforgiving mood. Buri came with him, and he simply shook his head sadly at the sight.

"How could this happen?" the King demanded, fury in his eyes. "How did Longinus obtain poison?"

"I questioned the guards, Sire," Vezina said. "I am certain this was not their doing."

"The servant! What is his name? He brought his meals and looked after him."

"Orola," Vezina answered with distaste. "He was the only one who saw Gnaeus in this room besides me."

"Damn him," Decebal cursed. "Find him and bring him to me."

"He has been on the road for four days now," Buri said. "We won't catch him before he reaches the Romans."

Vezina agreed. "Buri is right. He is out of our reach."

"Longinus planned it this way, no doubt," Decebal said. "Clever bastard outsmarted us."

"He was afraid that we would force him to betray Rome," Vezina added. "He feared that more than death."

Decebal turned to him. "Send a messenger to Trajan. Demand that the traitor Orola be returned here."

"Yes, Sire," Vezina acknowledged.

Buri glanced at the body of Longinus again. "Poor old man. He died an unusual death for a Roman noble."

"How do you mean?" Vezina asked.

"Roman nobles do not sacrifice themselves through death," Buri explained. "If they are taken prisoner they expect to be ransomed, but Longinus preferred death to imprisonment."

"He knew that Trajan could not ransom him," Decebal said. "In the end he died to protect Trajan. He stayed a great and loyal friend even unto death."

*Roman camp, southern Dacia, December 105 AD*

Licinius Sura read the letter for his audience of Trajan, Hadrian, and Titus Lucullus. "Decebalus offers us the body of Gnaeus, along with the release of ten Roman soldiers who are still held captive." He paused and raised an eyebrow in surprise, then continued. "And all that he asks from Caesar is the return of the freedman Orola who was Gnaeus' servant while he was captive."

"That seems like a favorable exchange," Hadrian said. "Ten of ours for one of theirs, and we can honor Gnaeus with a proper funeral."

Trajan shook his head. "It is not so simple, Hadrianus."

"To begin with," Sura cut in, "this Orola is now one of ours and not one of theirs. Gnaeus promised him gold and also the protection of Rome. We must honor that promise."

"Exactly so," the Emperor agreed. "He was promised protection by a general of Rome. That makes it a matter of honor for Rome."

"I see," Hadrian said. "Forgive me, I spoke too quickly."

"A word, Caesar?" Lucullus asked.

"Speak, Titus."

"King Decebalus is certain to view Orola in the same manner that Caesar regarded the Roman deserters who went to the Dacian side."

"Do you mean the deserters I executed in front of the legions?"

"Yes, Caesar. This is a matter of honor for Decebalus as much as it is for Caesar."

Sura laughed, amused. "Shall we now worry about Dacia's honor? Dacia's honor means nothing."

"Come now, you are too harsh," Trajan chided him. "Rome's honor supersedes all but Decebalus has a strong sense of honor as well."

"Perhaps so," Sura conceded sourly.

The Emperor turned to his young general. "Tell us Hadrianus, how would you decide this matter?"

Hadrian did not hesitate. "I agree with Caesar that Rome's honor supersedes all. We must refuse the terms from Dacia."

"That is the correct decision," Trajan proclaimed. "Lucullus, send the messengers back to Dacia. Tell them Rome does not accept the offer from King Decebalus."

"Yes, Caesar," Titus said. "Are there any additional messages?"

"No," Trajan replied. "That is all that need be said."

"What now, Caesar?" Hadrian asked. "The snows are getting deep and the mountain passes difficult to navigate."

"Now we go to winter camp. My two new legions II Traiana Fortis and XXX Ulpia Victrix are in Moesia. I wish to get them settled in and prepare them for the battle ahead. In the spring we will attack Dacia with twelve legions."

"Yes, Caesar," Hadrian acknowledged. "May I ask, will you grant me a command for the attack?"

"Patience, General Hadrian. Our strategy is still being formed."

Patience, Hadrian thought, was the one thing that he lacked. He was the youngest general on Trajan's staff and for the most part still unproven. The spring campaign would be his best opportunity to prove himself to Caesar and the senior officers. Although he was part of Trajan's family by marriage to Vibia Sabina, there was only one thing that won Caesar's favor. Emperor Trajan rewarded results.

*Sarmizegetusa, January 106 AD*

Most days Queen Andrada spent her mornings dealing with the civic matters of running the city. She spent her afternoons working at her free clinic serving the citizens of Sarmizegetusa. She was trained in herbal medicine and nutrition medicine, which was helpful for most of the ailments people complained about. The body heals itself, as Zamolxis taught his people five hundred years ago, but the right medicine made healing easier and faster.

Andrada was ably assisted by Zelma, a Christian refugee from Rome. They cultivated the medicinal herbs in the clinic's very large garden. Zia hoped to follow in her mother's footsteps, and was an eager student when not running around to keep the rambunctious Brasus from getting into mischief. Ana along with Lia, Zelma's daughter, also kept an eye on the little boy.

"Lia, don't let him put anything in his mouth!" Zelma called to her daughter.

"I know, Mama," the girl said. She shook her head and smiled. "But can't you give him something to calm him down so he doesn't run around so much?"

Ana laughed. "Yes! He's running us ragged."

"Hush, now," Andrada said. "He is just an energetic little boy. This is good practice for you for when you have children of your own."

"I find that a little chamomile tea helps him slow down and go to sleep at night," Zia said. "It works well for me too, especially if I start thinking and worrying about Tarbus." Her husband was fighting with the army of General Drilgisa.

"Tarbus will be fine," the Queen said. "The Romans are in their winter camps. There will be no more big battles for the next two or three months."

"I understand, but I worry still," Zia said.

"Oh, we have visitors," Zelma announced, glancing at the couple across the large room near the front door. She recognized them as the nobleman Bicilis and his wife Zena. The visitors saw the Queen and headed in their direction.

Bicilis was a middle aged man of medium height, stocky build, and graying brown hair. His hooked nose and bushy eyebrows made him look a bit like a bird of prey. His wife was ten years younger, a thin woman with a haughty air about her. She had a preference for wearing green eye shade that gave her a vaguely Egyptian look.

"My Queen," Bicilis greeted Andrada with a small bow. Zena also bowed but remained silent. She was a woman of few words when out in public.

"Lord Bicilis, it is good to see you again," Andrada said. "And how are you, Zena?"

"I am well, My Queen," Zena replied politely.

"Ah! Most days she is well." Bicilis gave his wife a sympathetic smile. "But her nerves trouble her. That is why we are here."

"Your nerves trouble you, my dear?" Andrada asked. "How so?"

"She gets melancholy and irritable," Bicilis answered for her. "It is always worse when winter arrives."

Zena gave him a sharp look. "I can speak for myself, Husband."

"Of course you can, my flower. I was simply trying to help."

Andrada turned to her daughter. "Is there anything you would suggest for feelings of melancholy and irritable temper, Zia?"

"Yes, many things," Zia replied, pleased with this little test her mother just offered her. "Many people feel more melancholy in the winter, Lady Zena. Perhaps it would help to spend more time outside particularly on sunny days. Also might you go for a walk with your husband every day?"

"Yes, we could do that," Zena said without enthusiasm. "But do you have any medicines for me?"

"Well, saffron and chamomile produce feelings of relaxation. Also holy basil and water hyssop."

"I tried chamomile tea," Zena said. "I disliked the taste and it does not help me."

"Oh, but it works wonderfully for me!" Zia said cheerfully.

"You must try different remedies," Andrada suggested in a patient tone. "Nothing works for everyone. Perhaps Zia can show you some medicines that might help you?"

"I would be happy to," Zia said. "Would you please come this way, Lady Zena?"

Andrada turned to Bicilis. "These are common problems that we see every day."

"She worries too much," he said with a small shrug. "Sunshine and saffron are all well and good, but what troubles my wife most severely is this war with Rome."

"Unfortunately, Lord Bicilis, we have no remedy for the war in my clinic." The Queen turned to face him. "We all worry about the war. And we all do what we can to help our soldiers end it."

"But are we doing all that we can, My Queen?"

"What do you mean by that?" she asked, surprised by the question. "Speak plainly Bicilis, I have no patience for riddles."

"I mean that perhaps we should try harder to make a peace with Rome," he replied in a hushed tone. "Many of our nobles believe this. They no longer believe that our weakened army can defend Dacia."

"I see," Andrada said with a sigh. "Tell your friends in the nobility this, Bicilis. If we do not remain united then Rome will most certainly defeat us. Those who don't stay strong and remain loyal are traitors to our people."

Bicilis felt the sting of her words. "As you say, My Queen."

"Also tell your friends this," the Queen continued. "The day may come when we must defend Sarmizegetusa. They can either show bravery and defend against the enemy, or they can show cowardice and capitulate. Those are the only two choices."

"I understand," Bicilis said as his wife and Zia walked back to join them. "Thank you, My Queen. We shall try the saffron."

*Fort of Piatra Rosie, south central Dacia, February 106 AD*

"How are the spirits of the men?" King Decebal asked the officers gathered in the dining hall of Piatra Rosie. Some troops found shelter in the houses inside the fort but others were living in tents outside. The soldiers sometimes complained but they always endured.

Drilgisa, Diegis, and Buri joined Decebal for the officers' meeting. Vezina was in Sarmizegetusa and would not be travelling. No one knew exactly how old Vezina was, but he was the oldest man any of them knew. Long travels in harsh winter weather no longer suited him.

"The men are in good spirits," Diegis answered. "They have plenty of food and are too proud to complain about the cold."

"The only complaints I hear is that they sit around too much," Drilgisa added. "They are bored. They want to go out and raid."

Buri frowned. "If they are bored with sitting around too much they need to spend more time training, and train harder. That worked well in my time."

"Of course, Buri," Drilgisa agreed. "We'll keep them active, but they still want to go out on raids."

"There will be plenty of fighting soon enough," Decebal said. "For now let them train and sit around and be bored. That is no different from what the Romans are doing."

"Have you heard from the Bastarnae or the Scythians?" Diegis asked, changing the subject. "We need their armies to fight with us in the spring."

Decebal shook his head. "No word yet. We should not count on them at this time. Not the Marcomanni either, they just made a treaty with Rome."

"Peace treaties between the Germans and Rome don't last very long," Drilgisa said with a laugh. "We shall see about this one."

King Decebal agreed with a nod. "The Sarmatians as always are loyal allies but I have yet to hear from Prince Davi."

"Davi will arrive soon, the messenger from Vezina says," Buri told them. "The Roxolani never lose heart."

The King frowned. "Unfortunately that is more than can be said for some of our own Dacian nobles."

Diegis raised an eyebrow in surprise. "What do you mean? What Dacian nobles?"

"The usual greedy and ungrateful bastards," Buri growled. "They don't want to lose what they have, so they always think of saving themselves first."

"Many of the chiefs in the east have agreed to peace terms with Rome," the King said. "Now I hear from Vezina and Andrada that some nobles in Sarmizegetusa have lost the will to fight. They argue among themselves about whether they should fight or surrender."

"Traitors!" Drilgisa spat. "Surrender, they say? Find these traitors and cowards and take their heads off!"

"I agree," Diegis said, angered by the selfishness and disloyalty. "These traitors are a danger to Dacia."

"Before we summon the executioner let as talk to these noblemen first," Decebal said in a calm tone. "We must not act rashly or treat our own people unjustly. If we find any who betray Dacia, then yes they will be executed."

"I cannot fathom that Dacians would betray Dacia," Diegis said. "I cannot believe that any would betray you, Brother. For more than twenty years you have been the heart and spirit of Dacia."

Decebal gave an indifferent shrug. "Remember that Dacian nobles once betrayed King Burebista. They had him assassinated because they craved more power and wealth. Am I greater than Burebista?"

"That happened in a time of peace," Diegis replied. "They were driven by jealousy and greed. This is different."

Buri frowned. "Jealousy and greed, fear and greed. It makes no difference, traitors act for many reasons. What we must do is make sure they do not succeed."

"I do not fear for my life," Decebal said. "And neither should you fear for my life. The people of Sarmizegetusa will remain loyal when they face Roman aggression."

"Very well," Buri shrugged. "I will not worry about it. But I am sworn to protect your life and so I will keep my eyes open. I will not be understanding or merciful with traitors."

*Drobeta, Dacia, March 106 AD*

"The winter snows are melting away by the day, gentlemen," Emperor Trajan told his officers. "It is time to resume the Dacian campaign."

His words were met with looks of relief and grins of approval from Licinius Sura, Laberius Maximus, the cavalry general Lusius Quietus, General Hadrian, and Titus Lucullus. This was what they waited to hear through the long winter months. Twelve legions of soldiers were growing impatient to go on the attack again.

"We will attack with three armies from three directions," Trajan told them, reviewing the general strategy again that had already been discussed and agreed upon. "General Maximus will pacify the west of Dacia, then march east to Sarmizegetusa. General Hadrian will lead the army from here in Drobeta and march north. I will lead my army of five legions from the east, through Bumbesti. By early summer we shall have the lower portion of Dacia pacified and then march with our combined armies on their capital."

"It is about time," Maximus declared.

"A major campaign takes a great deal of preparation and planning to be successful, Laberius."

"Of course, Caesar," the general agreed. "We are all impatient, is my meaning. I want to march west now, within the week."

"And so you shall," the Emperor said. "Ready your troops, all of you. There will be no more delays."

"Caesar, when we finish here, there are men waiting to see you," Sura announced. "I already spoke with them but they wish to pledge their loyalty to Caesar in person. You know how tedious they can be."

"What men are these?"

"Chiefs from the Marcomanni. And more pileati, Dacian nobles."

Lusius Quietus frowned. "I don't like seeing so many Dacians make peace, damn them."

Sura laughed. "Why is that, Lusius?"

"Because once they make peace we can no longer raid their cities. That means fewer slaves, less wealth."

"Ah, you will have ample opportunity for plunder, Lusius," Trajan assured him. "These are the local Dacian nobles and chiefs. Venture some distance west or north and you will find plenty of wealth. Take as many slaves as you wish."

"When this campaign is over we will all be very wealthy," Sura said matter of factly. "The streets of Sarmizegetusa are paved with gold. Is that not so, Lucullus?"

This was a joke that Titus heard many times before. "No they are not. However we know that the Dacian reserves of gold and silver are vast. If we capture those it would be to great benefit for Rome."

"We will capture them," Trajan declared with certainty. "It will pay for the war and much more. "

The Emperor turned to Sura and Hadrian. "Licinius, see to your guests and I will join you shortly. Hadrianus, stay. I wish to speak with you."

As the others left the room Hadrian stood quietly and waited for Trajan to speak first. Although he was raised in the Trajanus family since he was a ten year old boy, Hadrian never felt particularly close to his guardian who was now Emperor of Rome. He had been raised primarily by the women in the family, Pompeia Plotina and Trajan's older sister Marciana, while Trajan was away on military campaigns for years at a time.

"Sit, Hadrianus," the Emperor said with a relaxed and pleasant smile. "Have some wine."

"Thank you, I will." Hadrian poured himself a cup from the silver wine container and took a small sip. "This is an excellent wine."

"It is, isn't it? Another fine Caecuban red. I find that I now prefer it to Falernian."

Hadrian acknowledged him with a nod. It was widely accepted that Caesar's taste for fine wines was unmatched.

"Let me get to the point," Trajan said. "You are part of my family, Hadrianus. I have not however shown you any favoritism on account of that, would you agree?"

"Yes, I agree, Caesar. You have not shown me any favoritism nor would I seek it."

"Good. I reward only ability and achievement. That way I promote only the best men, not those who think themselves highly privileged and entitled. Military officers understand this best, and now so do many of the politicians in Rome."

"Of course, Caesar. I understand perfectly."

Trajan paused to refill his wine goblet. He had thought carefully about his next message.

"Not showing you favoritism, Hadrianus, does not mean that I will not offer you opportunities for which you are suited. You have one of the three major commands in this campaign, along with me and Maximus."

Hadrian acknowledged with another nod. "I am honored, Caesar. I will not let you down."

"If I thought that you would let me down I would not have offered you the command in the first place," Trajan said with a smile.

Hadrian returned the smile. He was not used to compliments or jokes from Caesar so this was a pleasant surprise.

"I have a gift for you, Hadrianus, to show my appreciation," Trajan continued. He glanced towards a small box on the table near the wine container. "It is there. Take it."

The box was very small, of the type used to hold jewelry. Hadrian opened it and took out a ring with a large and dazzling stone. His eyes grew wide.

"Do you remember it?" Trajan asked.

"Yes, of course I remember it," Hadrian replied. His voice was thick with emotion. "This is the diamond ring that Emperor Nerva sent to you when he adopted you as his son. He sent me to personally deliver the ring to you, when you were serving in Germania."

"You have a good memory," Trajan said. "Emperor Nerva gave me this ring as a sign of his affection and esteem. Now I give it to you, as a sign of my affection and esteem."

"You honor me beyond words, Caesar."

"Honor my trust in you by excelling in your command, Hadrianus. That is all I ask in return."

Hadrian gave him a bow, an expression of profound gratitude and respect. "On my life, Marcus. I will not fail you."

# Chapter 11

# The Road Home

*Bumbesti, Dacia, March 106 AD*

B efore the armies of Emperor Trajan could invade the lush mountain valleys that formed the heart of Dacia they first had to destroy the mountain forts guarding the path into the valleys. The Dacians built more than one hundred such forts on Dacian soil. Fortunately for the Romans it was not necessary for their armies to destroy every single one of them. They needed only to destroy the forts blocking the attack routes, which in itself was a daunting and costly campaign.

Bumbesti was one of the largest and most powerful fortresses blocking the eastern pass to the Dacian plains. As soon as the March snows melted Emperor Trajan led his five legions to attack this key fort. He knew that taking Bumbesti might require a siege of two weeks or longer, and there was no time to waste.

Like all Dacian mountain forts the walls and terraces of Bumbesti followed the natural contours of the land. Steep mountain slopes and cliffs provided natural defensive advantages. Approaches to the gates were narrow and whenever possible built on an incline to make it difficult for attackers to approach. Thick stone walls with fighting platforms built on top gave the defenders a big advantage in fighting off assaults on the walls.

After the first week of the attack Roman artillery and assaults on the walls were thinning out the Dacian defenders. Dozens of siege machines including catapults and the large ballistae hurled boulders and iron bolts at the fort. They could not bring down the sturdy walls but killed and injured many defenders on the walls and wrecked buildings inside the fort.

As always Emperor Trajan kept a close eye on developments in the fighting from an observation post not too far from the front line fighting. He wanted to be close to the fighting without actually taking part in it. This provided both tactical and motivational advantages.

Being close to the fighting allowed him to direct a very aggressive attack and marshal his forces as needed. Trajan always preferred to initiate action to create the situations he wanted, and not to passively react to the enemy's moves. And second, being close to the front let his men doing the fighting know that Caesar himself was watching them fight. Every man in the army knew that Trajan rewarded great bravery and daring feats. This pushed the men to give their greatest efforts and try to outdo each other in battle. For Caesar the most highly prized soldierly virtue was courage.

In the end the siege of Bumbesti took only ten days. The Dacian soldiers refused to surrender so very few prisoners were taken. They either fought to the death or, if they were incapacitated or sure to be captured, they took their own lives.

The civilian population of Bumbesti had already been evacuated to camps in the mountains long before the Roman army arrived. People fleeing from the Roman invaders migrated to the northern parts of Dacia where the Costoboci tribes lived, and towards the northeast to the lands of the Carpi tribes. Emperor Trajan had neither the troops nor the incentive to go after them. The prize was Sarmizegetusa and the gold and silver mines in the mountains surrounding it.

After Bumbesti was put to the torch Trajan gathered his legions in the mountain valley beyond it. Here there was plenty of new forage for the animals, ample fresh water, and grain and cattle to be taken from the villages and farms to stock up their food supplies. Once the armies reached Sarmizegetusa they needed to be well supplied for a long siege of several months if that became necessary.

At dusk Emperor Trajan watched his men settle into camp and took time to review developments with Licinius Sura, the Praetorian general Tiberius Livianus, and Titus Lucullus. Sura was his closest friend and confidant. Livianus was in charge of his personal safety. Based on his experience in dealing with the Dacians, Lucullus was the expert on his staff on matters related to Dacia and King Decebalus.

"In the morning I will address the legions," Trajan informed his officers. "Speak with the centurions and select for me ten men who showed the most boldness and aggression."

"Of course, Caesar," Sura acknowledged. "Will a promotion in rank and ten gold coins for each soldier suffice?"

"That would suffice for me," Livianus said with a laugh.

"Earn the reward first, Tiberius, and you shall not lack for either rank or gold."

Livianus gave a smug grin, an expression that some took as a sign of arrogance. "There is no higher rank that you may promote me to now, Marcus. Although when we return to Rome I would be pleased to be elected consul of Rome."

"All things are possible," Trajan said. "They must first be earned however, not demanded."

"Tiberius is speaking in jest, I think," Sura offered with a sarcastic tone. He was one of those people who found Livianus imperious and unpleasant. "He would not be arrogant and demanding."

Titus Lucullus interjected diplomatically. "The scouts have seen no Dacian troops at all in the valley. That is not surprising however because they will not attack us on open ground in the valley."

"I expect not," the Emperor said. "We will march west and then north and gather food supplies along the way. Guard forage parties and supply wagons against Dacian attacks."

"Yes, Caesar," Titus said. "For now they will only skirmish with our troops if they see an easy target. When we are back on the mountain roads they will attack us in ambush attacks."

Trajan agreed. "We know the enemy well, and they know us well. Now it is a simple matter of imposing our will on them."

*Costesti, central Dacia, April 106 AD*

The army of King Decebal defended the Dacian forts by fighting to the death on a few occasions. At other times however they inflicted as much damage as they could on the Roman attackers, then retreated further into the interior of Dacia to consolidate their strength. Their aim was to slow down the armies of Emperor Trajan. This strategy was, by simple necessity, similar to the strategy they followed in the last war with Rome that ended four years ago.

Decebal's army was reduced to less than twenty-five thousand troops. They were being attacked by a Roman army five times larger. The tribes in the northern part of Dacia had more warriors, but even if those joined King Decebal's army there would still not be nearly enough troops to match the Roman invaders.

In the fort of Costesti King Decebal reviewed strategy with Buri, Diegis, and Drilgisa. Their main strategy was one of small groups of fighters carrying out hit and run raids on Roman troops. The targets were often auxiliary troops and cavalry. Roman legionnaires fought as heavy infantry and were too well armored and disciplined to be attacked effectively by skirmishers.

"General Maximus is putting our villages and forts in the west to the torch," the King informed his generals. "Ziridava is burned to the ground."

This was grave news. The fort of Ziridava was the largest and strongest fort in the western part of Dacia.

Diegis shook his head. "I understand taking the fortress, but why burn it down? The Romans might want it for their own use."

"Emperor Trajan is making it clear that he wants no more Dacian forts in Dacia," said Decebal. "Bumbesti is destroyed, also Blidaru, and now Ziridava."

"Trajan's nephew Hadrian is marching to Piatra Rosie," Buri said. "At least I think that's his nephew."

"It does not matter what he is to Trajan. All that matters is that he is marching at the head of three legions," Decebal said.

"We gave the little bastard a beating at Drobeta before Trajan showed up," Drilgisa said. "Now Hadrian has us outmanned and he's got the upper hand."

"How long can Piatra Rosie hold out?" Diegis wondered.

"Two weeks perhaps," the King replied.

"And after Piatra Rosie he will march north to Costesti," Diegis continued.

"Most likely so, Brother."

"We should not stay here long," Buri said. "This is not the place to make a stand."

The King shook his head. "No, we will not make a stand here. The only place where we will make a final stand is Sarmizegetusa."

"Why not go now and prepare our defenses there?" Drilgisa asked impatiently. "We are bleeding strength here and we can't afford to lose more men."

"Perhaps you are right, we should return to Sarmizegetusa now," Decebal said. "We are hurting Trajan but he can afford his loses. We can't afford ours."

The men paused as Tarbus entered the room. He was escorting a familiar figure whom they were all glad to see. The man walked with a slight limp in his left leg, the result of a severe wound from a spear suffered years ago fighting the Romans near Adamclisi in Moesia.

"Look who came looking for you," Tarbus said with a grin.

"Greetings to you all," said Prince Davi of the Roxolani tribe of Sarmatians. The Sarmatians had long been Dacia's most dependable allies in the wars against Rome. Prince Davi was related to the Dacian royal family by marriage, although his wife Tanidela was still being held prisoner in Rome. He was greeted warmly by the Dacians.

"You look like you're still in fighting trim," King Decebal observed. "You can still ride a horse as well as ever, no doubt."

"Ah, I almost lost the leg but it's fine now," Davi said. "It's just a limp and it doesn't stop me from fighting on horseback."

"Good!" Diegis said. "We can use you and a few thousand more Roxolani cavalry besides."

Davi shook his head sadly. "I would gladly fight with you Diegis, but I cannot vouch for any other Sarmatian troops."

"The chieftains decline to fight?" Decebal asked. He did not sound surprised.

"That is so, King Decebal. I regret to say the chieftains decline to fight Rome again so soon after the last war. Our armies are depleted, just as yours are."

Decebal waved his hand dismissively. "That is what I hear from almost everyone in these times."

"I am sorry to bring bad news, my friend," Davi said. "Will you make peace with Trajan again?"

"We shall see, Davi. Trajan is in a vengeful mood. He burns down our forts with a passion."

"Ah. It makes strategic sense for him, I suppose," Davi said.

"How do you mean?" Buri asked.

Davi's tone became very serious. "In the past twenty years, Buri, how many times has Rome invaded Dacia?"

"This is the fourth time."

"Yes, the fourth invasion," Davi continued. "And each one has been very costly and painful for Rome. Invading Dacia is like running through a thorn bush for them. Who wants to do that four times, much less five?"

Buri gave a nod. "I see. So Trajan is removing the thorn bushes, you are saying?"

"That is precisely what he is saying," King Decebal said. "And your point is well made, Davi. We refuse to take down our forts so Trajan takes it upon himself to destroy them."

Drilgisa laughed bitterly. "Then Trajan can go to whatever hell he believes in! Dacia will always be a thorn in the side of Rome."

Davi acknowledged him with a smile. "You in particular will be a thorn in the side of Rome."

"Thank you for your visit, Davi," Decebal told him. "You will always be a friend to Dacia and a brother to me."

"Of course, and you will always be like brothers to me," Davi said. He paused for a moment. "I have no word from Tanidela. It has been four years now. My little Tyra is growing up without me."

"No, no word," Decebal said. "We know only that they live and are treated well in Rome."

Davi's face grew dark. "I fear that I shall never see them again. If you make peace with Trajan again, Decebal, will you insist that my wife and daughter be freed?"

"I will do all that I can," Decebal promised in a solemn voice. "They are safe for now, and who knows what the future holds."

*Piatra Rosie, central Dacia, April 106 AD*

General Hadrian left from Drobeta, the site of Emperor Trajan's now famous stone bridge across the Danubius, and marched north into Dacia at the head of three full legions. He was deeply gratified that he finally had the command he longed for, and the respect of Caesar and the senior staff that came with it. His days of shame, when he felt treated like Trajan's messenger boy, were over.

The army marched along the Cerna River and Timis River valleys. Everywhere one looked the land was green and lush with new grass, shrubbery, trees, and all forms of spring vegetation. Dacia was famed for its fertile soil that every year produced abundant crops of wheat and other grains. The rich dark soil and plentiful river waters of the valleys was ideal for growing farm crops and orchards.

Emperor Trajan wanted Dacia's gold and silver, which of course was understandable. General Hadrian also saw Roman colonists building Roman settlements and taking over this rich land for their own use. But first, however, the Dacians had to be pacified or driven out from this part of Dacia. They were a very proud and troublesome people, and unfortunately would always be a troublesome people.

The objective of Hadrian's army was to destroy the large fort of Piatra Rosie. From there they would march farther north to the fort of Costesti. From there they would march east to Sarmizegetusa and combine their army with that of Emperor Trajan. The army now in western Dacia, commanded by General Laberius Maximus, would also join them there.

The armies were not in a hurry. They had the full war season of spring and summer to pacify the countryside, destroy any pockets of resistance in their way, and still wage a long siege at Sarmizegetusa if a long siege became necessary. Be very thorough in your work, Caesar commanded his generals, because we are not coming this way again.

Hadrian's army was met with very sporadic but fierce resistance. Cavalry attacked his scouts and occasionally launched hit and run raids against his supply trains. Small bands of skirmishers attacked in the night but were never able to get past the outer defenses of his camps. By first light of the next day they were nowhere to be found.

What surprised General Hadrian when they finally reached the walls of Piatra Rosie was how sparsely manned the walls appeared to be. Typically the Romans would find the parapets swarming with archers and spearmen determined to put up a strong resistance. The defenders guarding Piatra Rosie were perhaps half the number he would normally expect to see.

Hadrian wasted no time in giving orders to his three legates for preparing the attack. Artillery was positioned and began firing as soon as the siege machines were in place. Men set to work quickly and efficiently building ladders.

"We will take the fort within the week," Hadrian told his officers. "We shall be aggressive and overwhelm their weakened defenses. Once we put this place to the torch we will march to Costesti and take that fort as well. And following that conquest, gentlemen, we march to meet Caesar at Sarmizegetusa."

*Sarmizegetusa, May 106 AD*

King Decebal and the major portion of the Dacian army returned home to the holy city in the middle of May. Other smaller units from other regions would drift in after them in the days that followed. Weak defensive positions in the region were abandoned because the Dacian army was needed to defend Sarmizegetusa.

The King and Queen met with their council that evening. Other than Queen Andrada and their children, the person most happy to see King Decebal was Vezina. The elderly High Priest was no longer fit for travel with the army and missed his consultations with the King when Decebal was away on campaign.

Vezina had served as a mentor and advisor from the time Decebal was a young man, the nephew of King Duras. Decebal had been only fifteen years old when his father King Scorilo died. The man who stepped in to provide fatherly guidance then was not his uncle King Duras, but the High Priest Vezina. Over the years, as Decebal grew and matured into a warrior, then a general, and then as the monarch of Dacia, Vezina was always at his side.

Also gathered around the council table in the throne room were Buri, the generals Diegis and Drilgisa, and the nobleman Sorin. The elderly Sorin was one of the leading nobles of Dacia and also father in law to Diegis and grandfather to Ana. In past years he had travelled to Rome as an envoy of King Decebal, and had direct talks with the

Emperor and his closest advisors. He had just returned earlier that day from an envoy mission to the Roman commanders.

"So Emperor Trajan was gracious enough to receive you?" Decebal asked. "I will credit him that."

"He received me politely, Sire," Sorin replied. "But not with any enthusiasm certainly. He was not in a talkative mood."

"What does he ask for, if we are to have a peace agreement?" Queen Andrada asked.

"Emperor Trajan asks for the surrender of King Decebal along with the surrender of Sarmizegetusa, My Queen. He does not offer any concessions on his part."

Andrada frowned. "That is a demand, not a negotiation."

"The Romans excel at making demands," Drilgisa said. "It works for them because more often than not people give in."

Diegis shook his head. "He must know that we will never accept those terms. He asks for the surrender and subjugation of Dacia. It would mean the end of Dacia."

"Exactly right," Decebal agreed. "That is what he seeks now."

Drilgisa growled. "If he wants Dacia let him come and take it. We do not surrender."

"What are your thoughts, Vezina?" King Decebal asked. Everyone turned to the High Priest attentively. They all valued his judgment very highly.

"I agree with Diegis and with you," Vezina replied. His somber tone gave his words a sense of weight and dignity. "Your surrender and the surrender of Sarmizegetusa will be seen by nations as the capitulation of Dacia. There will be no more Dacia. Trajan will want to rule us as one of his Roman provinces, no different from Moesia or Pannonia."

Andrada shook her head emphatically. "That can never happen."

"No, it will not happen," said Decebal. "We fight for our freedom as we always have."

"There is one critical difference in the nature of this fight, Sire," Vezina said.

"How do you mean?"

"This is a fight that we must win, there is no choice otherwise," Vezina continued. "There is no place to retreat further and nowhere else for us to go. This is the true battle for survival."

They all knew that he was right. The room grew silent.

After a moment Buri broke the silence. "Emperor Trajan and his army are about to learn something very unpleasant."

"What is that, Buri?" Decebal asked.

"They are about to discover how a wolf fights when it is trapped and cornered."

*West of Sarmizegetusa, June 106 AD*

As the month of May turned into June the armies of Emperor Trajan, General Maximus, and General Hadrian arrived and gathered in a valley west of Sarmizegetusa. Their combined forces made for a vast army of over one hundred twenty thousand fighting men including legionnaires and auxiliary troops. Simply camping such a large army required a great deal of logistical planning and organization.

Trajan invited his generals and advisors to his command tent. It was early evening so the Emperor had the servants fill silver pitchers with his best wine. Trajan found that wine made the officers more talkative and more agreeable, and that made their discussions more productive.

"This is the final stage of the campaign," Trajan told them in a pleasant tone. "All planning and strategy will now be executed exactly to my specifications."

"Of course, Caesar," Maximus assured him. "You have brought us all this far and we are at your command. Under the leadership of Caesar we cannot fail."

"It is not a question of winning or losing, Laberius. It is a question of winning a difficult battle ahead without suffering severe losses to our troops." Trajan paused and looked around at his officers. "Make no mistake, gentlemen, this will be the most difficult battle any of us has ever fought."

"We understand, Marcus," Maximus said. "I have never seen city walls like these before. And the steep mountain terrain makes our approach difficult. However we have one very decisive advantage."

"Which advantage do you mean, Laberius?"

Maximus flashed an imperious smile. "We are Rome. Our tactics are superior, our arms and machinery are the best in the world, and the men are eager to go. Unleash them and they will bring us victory."

"Those things are true but it is still not as simple as that." Trajan turned to Lucullus. "Titus, is it true that Sarmizegetusa has never been attacked before?"

"Yes, Caesar. That is true."

"And why is that, do you think?"

Titus paused and cleared his throat, choosing his words carefully. "I can only surmise, Caesar, that before us no one else had the daring or the strength to risk such an attack."

"Ah! I surmise that you are correct, Titus." Trajan paused to pour himself another cup of wine. "Well, we Romans have the daring and the military strength to finally conquer Sarmizegetusa."

"We are all in agreement about that," Hadrian said.

"Nonetheless," Trajan continued, "we will engage them smartly, never recklessly. History teaches us to respect our adversaries. This particular enemy must never be taken lightly because in all instances taking them lightly led to a disaster for Rome." Trajan paused to let his words sink in. "That is why our strategy will be executed precisely as I planned it."

"It will be done, Caesar," Sura assured him. "And do you realize, Marcus, that it was exactly one year ago when we left Rome on this campaign?"

Trajan gave a nod. "Yes, I know. I count every day as it passes. Now the time has come for us to make history."

"Excellent!" Sura exclaimed. He raised his wine cup to give Trajan a toast. "Making history is what you do well, Marcus."

"It is expected of Caesar, Licinius, which is why I labor so hard to make it happen."

"How may we assist you now, Caesar?" Hadrian asked.

Trajan clasped him on the shoulder. "I wish to address the army. Prepare the legions to assemble in the morning."

"All the men?" Sura asked.

"Yes, all the legions. Let us make it clear to them why we are here."


"Soldiers of Rome!" Trajan shouted in a loud and clear voice. He sat up very straight in the saddle so that he could fully expand his chest and make his voice carry out over the assembled legions.

"We are in the first week of June! Exactly one year ago in the first week of June we left Rome to march here! To march through Dacia! To conquer this place, the holy city of Sarmizegetusa!"

The Emperor paused briefly so that his words could be repeated through the ranks to the men towards the rear of the formations. No single voice was powerful enough to reach the back sections of such a vast army.

"Soldiers of Rome!" Trajan continued, pacing his horse slowly along the front lines so that more of the men could see him. "Our march is over! We are here today before the walls of Sarmizegetusa! The citadel of Dacia and King Decebalus, the hated enemy of Rome!"

Enthusiastic shouting and cheering went up among the troops, celebrating the journey's end and the prize in sight.

"Soldiers of Rome! The time for marching is over and the time for fighting is here!"

Caesar's call to battle was welcomed heartily and the cheering and shouting grew louder and more aggressive.

"Sarmizegetusa has strong walls! Walls do not stop an army of Rome! We will invade their city! We will capture King Decebalus and march him in chains in Caesar's triumph parade!"

Men beat their spear shafts against their shields, adding to the clamor of the cheers and shouts.

"Soldiers of Rome!" Trajan continued. "You all heard the stories that the streets of Sarmizegetusa are paved with gold!"

Shouting turned to laughter and more cheering. They all heard the stories.

"Some say the stories are true! Some say the stories are not true! Soldiers of Rome! Who will go into Sarmizegetusa with me and find out for ourselves?"

The exuberant cheering and shouting erupted from every man in the field. It became louder and grew into a roar that swelled out across the valley. It echoed up the mountainsides and touched the walls of Sarmizegetusa.

# Chapter 12

# Siege at Sarmizegetusa

*Sarmizegetusa, June 106 AD*

N othing more could be done that had not already been done to prepare Sarmizegetusa for the coming Roman attack. The city was well supplied to withstand a siege that might last for months. The city defenders were well trained and already in position to respond rapidly to an assault at any hour of the day or night. Large stocks of arrows, javelins, spears, and other weapons essential for the defenders on the wall were positioned in place. More weapons were produced around the clock. There was nothing left to be done except to wait for the attack and then respond to it.

In the meantime it was better for everyone in Sarmizegetusa to go on with their lives, the royal family no less than the common people. Queen Andrada decreed that nothing would be allowed to delay or disrupt the routine of her family sitting down for their evening meal. Everyone understood this and complied. The servants went about their regular duties and were as efficient as always in preparing and serving the meals.

As usual the King and Queen sat at the head of the long table. Zia and Tarbus sat near the Queen, along with a nursemaid holding the toddler Brasus. Buri kept an eye on his energetic grandson as well. Adila and Dorin sat further down the table. Diegis was there with Ana, who sat next to her grandfather Sorin. Dacian family meals by tradition were large affairs.

Adila had less patience and ate less than most of the other family members. She finished half a bowl of the thick lentil soup, then pushed her bowl away.

"I should go help with sentry duty on the wall," she announced to her parents.

Dorin looked up from his food. "Can I go with you?" he asked her eagerly. He was sixteen years of age, not yet a warrior but no longer a boy, and he wished to be helpful.

King Decebal addressed his daughter first. "Have patience, Adila. You will go on sentry duty when you are scheduled to be on sentry duty. When are you next scheduled?"

"In the morning," she replied. "But I will go on the wall now to have a look around. I don't want to sit around doing nothing."

"May I go with her, Tata?" Dorin asked the King.

"You may, but only as an observer. If any fighting starts you will immediately return to the palace," Decebal instructed. "Your duty is here with your mother and Zia and Ana, to give them protection. You will not fight on the front lines."

Dorin's expression turned stubborn. "I can fight. General Drilgisa says that my swordsmanship is passable with both sica and falx."

Diegis gave his nephew a patient smile. "Passable swordsmanship gets you killed quickly. You are not ready for front line fighting."

"But I am ready," Dorin insisted.

Adila shook her head. "No, you are not. When I was your age I was impatient too and went to join the army at Tapae. I learned there that I was not even close to ready for combat."

"But happily you survived, Zamolxis be thanked," Andrada said.

"Do you agree then, Brother?" Adila asked. "You may come with me but only as an observer, and you will do exactly as I say if I give you any orders."

"Yes, I agree," Dorin conceded.

"Keep practicing your swordsmanship, Dorin," Buri said. "And eat plenty of good food to put more muscle on your frame. This siege might last a long time and you might need to use your sword."

"How long will the siege last?" Ana wondered.

The table grew quiet. They all wondered the same thing.

King Decebal broke the brief silence. "We cannot know that right now, Ana. But we will fight the enemy for as long as we must, even if it takes a year."

"A year?" The girl asked in surprise, then turned to her father. "Do we have enough food to last for a whole year?"

"Yes, Ana," Diegis reassured her. "We have enough food and we can grow more. The Romans will run out of food before we do."

"And speaking of food, Ana, I have many apples and pears to pick," Buri said. "Will you come by tomorrow with your friend Lia and help me out at the orchard? You may invite as many of your friends as you wish, the more the better."

"Yes, we'll be happy to help," Ana said. "There is nothing better than a juicy apple picked fresh from the tree!"

Tarbus chuckled and looked at Buri. "I think perhaps you have found your new apprentice for tending the orchard. I know that you once hoped that would be me, but alas."

"Alas, nothing," Buri replied. "Some people have farming in their blood and some don't. Now, Ana here would make a fine orchard steward. You on the other hand are better at killing Romans."

"First things first, my father," Tarbus said. "Let's fight off these Romans, then we can talk about tending pear and apple trees."


Emperor Trajan surveyed the walls of Sarmizegetusa from the saddle of his horse while the Roman artillery was being positioned in place for the attack. The approach to the city gates was narrow and on an incline, so strategic placement of the artillery was essential. Trajan had more artillery than he could use at any one time on this narrow battlefield, however that provided the opportunity to rotate his crews and bombard the city with artillery fire from sunrise to sundown.

Simply hearing about the formidable walls of Sarmizegetusa did not do them proper justice, the Emperor decided. Looking at them in person now, the stone walls rose up like a mountain cliff and looked just as insurmountable.

The city walls were thirty feet high and nine feet thick. The outer shell of the wall and the inner shell were made of thick blocks of stone. The middle section of the wall was filled with gravel and dirt, reinforced with thick timbers. This ingenious building method was designed by the Dacians specifically for military fortifications, and it became known as the murus dacicus method. It made the city walls very resilient against attacks from artillery and battering rams. These walls could not be breached with artillery and rams.

The battlements on top of the walls included stone towers from which archers could attack invaders climbing ladders with crossfire as well as direct fire on those below them. The towers were made of limestone and andesite, a very dense and hard volcanic rock. The wide ramparts on top of the walls provided plenty of fighting room for archers, spearmen, slingers, and the light artillery on the wall.

Sarmizegetusa had one main gate. This was a massive structure made of heavy timbers reinforced with iron, which made it nearly as strong as the walls. This gate would not be breached by artillery or battering rams either. Towers built on the ramparts above the gate meant that any attackers going directly against the gate would face heavy and murderous fire.

"Lucullus!" Trajan called for his aide.

Titus Lucullus urged his horse forward until he was alongside the Emperor. "Yes, Caesar?"

"Tell me again, Titus. What will I find just behind those walls? The short description will do just fine at this time."

"Yes, Caesar," Titus replied with a smile. He was the only man on Trajan's staff who had been inside the city, and Trajan never tired of asking him questions about it. Every detail was important to Caesar.

"Behind the gates are the military barracks, armories, warehouses, and workshops. The city is built on terraces carved into the side of the mountain, and this is the lowest terrace. On the terraces just above is mostly civilian housing. Higher terraces are for growing and storing food, and pastures and pens for livestock. Above that are the royal palace and government buildings. On the highest terrace is the Holy Temple of Zamolxis, which is the highest point in the city."

"I see. And how much of that is within range of our artillery?"

"The military sections certainly, and also some areas of civilian housing. The palace and the temple are well beyond artillery range. Keep in mind, Caesar, that this is not a fort but a very large fortified city that is much better defended than any fort."

"Well described, Titus," Trajan said. "Your knowledge of the city is invaluable. Stay close for when I need you."

"Of course, Caesar."

Licinius Sura pulled up beside them. "We fought our way through the mountains for three long months to reach this place. Shall we launch our attack?"

"Yes, Licinius. Open with artillery fire. Sound the attack."


Each Roman legion was equipped with thirty pieces of heavy and light artillery. Heavy artillery including catapults and ballistae were most often used in sieges, and these became the first to open fire on the city. The large catapults threw one hundred pound stones and large burning projectiles over the city walls, some from distances as far as four hundred yards away. These caused damage to buildings and started fires that had to be put out quickly.

The smaller ballistae, two-armed torsion catapults, fired stones or iron bolts but with greater accuracy. These could be used to target the defenders on the walls. The light artillery including scorpions and carrobalistae were primarily field weapons but could also be used in a siege. Scorpions shot large iron bolts at long range with accuracy. These were capable of penetrating shields and any form of armor. The smaller carrobalistae, very mobile in carts drawn by mules, fired large arrows from a distance of three hundred yards.

When the artillery bombardment began Dacian defenders took shelter behind the stone parapets and sturdy towers on the walls. They would not come out from behind their shelter until the Roman infantry came to attack the walls directly. In the early stages of the siege the artillery fire killed more civilians huddling in their homes than it injured or killed Dacian troops on the walls.

"Get the people on the lower terraces to higher ground, Diegis," King Decebal ordered. "There is no reason for them to stay in range of the artillery."

"Yes, right away. I'll send a few companies of infantry to knock on doors and tell the people still in their homes to leave. They should have left sooner, stubborn fools." Diegis left briskly to issue orders.

"Civilians don't know what artillery can do," Vezina said. "It will make the infantry's job easier to also send a hundred priests to help them knock on doors."

Decebal looked up. "You would place your priests in harm's way?"

"We are all in harm's way, Sire." Vezina turned to his assistant priest. "Mircea, kindly go and give them the order? We must all serve the people of Zamolxis in every way that we can."

"Yes, Your Holiness," Mircea replied. "I shall go with them, and gladly." He gave a small bow and rushed out the door.

"You're right Vezina, we are all in harm's way. Ah! I tell you, it makes me want to strap on my sword and go up on the wall with them," Decebal said.

"But of course you will do no such thing," Vezina said. "If we lose you the people will lose hope. Never forget that, Decebal."

The sound of trumpets from outside the palace came in through the windows. It was a call to arms to inform the Dacian troops that the city walls were under infantry assault.

Decebal stood up and strapped on his sword. "Don't worry Vezina, I won't join the fight now and neither will you. I need to get closer however and see how the battle develops."

"Let them get closer, don't waste your arrows," Tarbus told the troop of archers assigned to his section of the wall. Veteran archers knew this but the inexperienced ones needed reminders. Inexperienced fighters reacting under pressure made hasty decisions.

Hundreds of legionnaires approached in testudo formations, tightly packed units of men carrying their shields raised over their heads. The large rectangular shields overlapped both in front and on top of the formation, which made the soldiers almost invulnerable to arrows, javelins, and spears. The testudo formation provided a tough outer shell like the turtle shell that gave it its name.

The Dacians had two dozen scorpions and carrobalistae on the walls, and these now opened fire on the approaching infantry. They were lethal but too few in number to stop or even slow down the very large scale attack. The Roman army on the ground fired back with hundreds of heavy and light artillery.

"They bring ladders," said Adila, standing next to Tarbus. "They will not reach the top with ladders. All of them will die."

"Many will die, Adila. But enough men on enough ladders will reach the top of the wall over time."

A bolt from a scorpion struck the wall nearby and sent splinters of stone flying in all directions. The bolt travelled so fast they never saw it coming.

"Keep your heads down!" Tarbus shouted, crouching lower.

Adila dropped down to one knee so that she was shielded behind the stone parapet. "I wish they would start climbing their ladders so the artillery targeting the wall will stop," she said.

"You are about to get your wish," Tarbus replied. "But even so, keep your head down!"

The legionnaires at the base of the wall came out of the testudo formation and went into attack formation. Dozens of the very long ladders went up propped against the wall. Men climbed as fast as they could because speed gave them the best chance for survival. They could not use their shields when climbing and were protected only by their helmets and the metal armor that covered their torsos.

"Now! Kill them!" the captains of archery units shouted. The men and women on the wall needed no directions or encouragement. This was what they trained for since they were young boys and girls. The women of Dacia fought with bows and spears and as determined and fierce as the men.

Dacian archers stood shoulder to shoulder on top of the wall. They gave each other just enough room to shoot their bows. The Roman infantry assaulting the walls came under a withering fire of arrows and thrown javelins and spears.

Adila did not shoot directly down at the soldiers scrambling up the ladder closest to her because their heads and shoulders were very well protected by their armor. She aimed instead at the soldiers climbing the ladder to her left. Unprotected faces, necks, and legs made easy targets.

At that short distance Adila could hit a stationary target the size of an apple and a moving target the size of a pigeon. She fixed her eye on the soldier highest on the ladder, pulled the string back to her ear, and loosed. As the legionnaire lunged up for the next rung the arrow bounced off his shoulder armor and made a glancing cut on his neck. That was enough to make the soldier hesitate very briefly and Adila put another arrow into his unprotected left leg.

The Roman stopped moving and that was his doom. An arrow from the other side of the ladder pierced his lower face. He let go of the ladder and fell heavily to the ground. The soldier behind him moved up and was immediately hit with two arrows that found their targets. He also fell and made way for the soldier behind him.

Adila knew that neck shots were usually the surest kill shots when fighting well armored men. Legs were bigger and easier targets, and a leg wound for a man climbing a ladder would debilitate him and leave him helpless. An armored soldier falling from a ladder twenty or thirty feet up was a dead man when he hit the ground regardless of the nature of his wound.

Tarbus carried a falx, the two-handed Dacian weapon with a long handle and long blade and a curved tip like a scythe. This was the fearsome weapon that legionnaires learned to dread, so much so that Emperor Trajan ordered changes in the design of Roman armor to better protect his troops. In the past wars with Dacia far too many legionnaires lost arms, legs, and necks to the falx.

Three hours into the Roman attack however Tarbus still had not faced even a single enemy with his falx, for the simple reason that no Romans in his area were reaching the top of the wall. In some other sections the legionnaires who reached the top were quickly beaten back and thrown off the wall.

The Roman attack was floundering and suffering heavy casualties. The Dacian advantage would not last forever, Tarbus knew, and this long battle had only just begun. So far however the Dacian defenders were holding their own. The Dacian draco flag flew high and defiant in the breeze and mocked the assembled might of the Roman army.

Adila sat down wearily near Tarbus, shielded behind the parapet. Her face was glistening with perspiration and she needed a rest. A boy carrying a bucket of water walked up and handed her a drinking gourd filled to the brim. Adila drank it down thirstily. She thanked the boy with a smile and handed back the gourd. Seeing that he was not needed elsewhere, Tarbus sat down beside her.

"How is your arm?" he asked. "You have been fighting up here since morning."

"Tired," Adila replied with a small grimace. "I've never shot this many arrows in one day before. My arm and shoulder burn like they are on fire."

"Some rest will fix that. You have done a magnificent job today, Adila. Now let others take your place for a while."

"No, there is no time for rest," she protested.

"You will rest for one hour and that is an order," Tarbus said in a calm but firm voice. He was the officer in charge of that section of the wall and he knew that she would respect a direct order. Respect for military authority was something that King Decebal instilled in all his children, because those officers made decision in situations of life and death.

"Yes, sir. I will rest for a while."

"Good. The Romans outnumber us five to one. They rotate in fresh troops whenever they like. Over time fatigue becomes our enemy so we must fight smartly as well as aggressively."

"I understand." Adila gave him a smile. "You are thinking like a smart officer, Tarbus, sir."

Tarbus laughed. "You can think like an officer too if you put your mind to it. You have courage beyond measure but you must couple that with wisdom. Do that and you will be the equal of any queen."

Adila gave a small shake of her head. "No, thank you, we already have a queen. I am an archer and that is enough."

"Very well," Tarbus said. "This is a time for archers. Rest for a bit and regain your strength. There is a great deal of fighting still to be done."


Evening brought an end to the Roman attack that was welcomed by both sides. The Romans retired to their camps for meals and rest. The Dacian defenders did the same except for the sentry details on the walls. Other than occasional minor skirmishes a siege was not carried out in darkness.

King Decebal's council was held in the throne room. The Queen and Vezina attended along with the generals Diegis and Drilgisa.

"Our losses today?" the King asked.

"Less than four hundred," Diegis replied. "Half of the casualties are wounded and most will live. Our medics are very good, they fix all except for the most severe wounds."

"And the Roman losses? Drilgisa?"

"Three times higher than ours, and most of their casualties are dead," General Drilgisa reported. "Attacking well defended walls is more dangerous than defending them. That goes double for these high walls of Sarmizegetusa."

"Yes, and that is our biggest advantage," Decebal agreed. "The Romans have the advantage in numbers but they are easier to kill when they storm our walls."

"How many Romans are out there?" Queen Andrada asked.

Decebal directed the question to the High Priest, also the King's primary military advisor. "Vezina has the latest information. What do you hear from our scouts?"

"Emperor Trajan commands twelve legions. That is about sixty thousand legionnaires. He has an equal number of auxiliary infantry and some auxiliary cavalry. So, in total, we face an army of perhaps one hundred and twenty thousand fighting men," Vezina said.

Drilgisa shook his head. "How does he feed an army that large? Bastards must eat like sparrows."

"On their march here they have been pillaging Dacian villages and farms for three months now," Vezina replied. "They gathered a great deal of grain and large numbers of cattle on the way. And we know that Rome never lacks for supply wagons and oxen and mules. So they have enough food to last them a while."

Andrada was not interested in hearing about food. "And how many warriors do we have defending the city?"

"Close to nineteen thousand," Decebal answered.

"Will that suffice?"

"Yes, it will suffice," Decebal said in a firm tone. "We must keep them outside the walls through the summer and fall. Their supplies of food won't last through the winter, even if they eat their oxen and pack mules and even the leather of their boots. Trajan will be forced to withdraw his army down to the plains to find food and shelter."

Vezina looked at Andrada and gave her an affirming nod. "It may well be a very long and difficult siege, but we can survive it."

"I understand," the Queen said. "Truthfully, I do not wish to sound discouraging even though I worry. Our people must never lose hope, and as their Queen I must give them hope."

"Exactly so, My Queen," Vezina said.

Andrada turned to Decebal with a determined look on her face. "On the day we believe in our hearts that we will be defeated, on that day we are already defeated. You said that to me many years ago."

"Yes, of course," Decebal replied without hesitation. "It was true then, it is true now, and it will always be true."

"Then we must keep fighting, come what may."

Two days later the infantry attack against the city walls was greatly intensified. The Roman commanders knew that the only way to breach the Dacian defenses was with a massive assault that would overwhelm the defenders on the walls. They committed the bulk of two legions, ten thousand fighting men, to the next attack. Emperor Trajan did not wish to fight a long and protracted siege.

By early afternoon the attackers were reaching the top in some sections of the wall. They fought desperately to gain a foothold and take the battle to the Dacians in hand to hand fighting on top of the wall. While climbing the siege ladders they were helpless targets. On the wall they would be the aggressors, well-armed and well armored.

"Reinforcements here!" a Dacian captain of archers shouted to a group of infantry to his right. He retreated two steps, paused to notch an arrow on his bow, and shot the arrow into the face of a Roman soldier coming up over the top of the ladder. The man screamed and fell back to the ground.

An instant later another legionnaire came up behind him and pulled himself up onto the wall. The Dacian archer retreated another two steps because he had no chance of survival against this armored legionnaire in hand to hand combat.

"Reinforce that position!" General Drilgisa ordered a group of thirty infantry, pointing with his falx. "Get the Romans off the wall!"

Dacian spearmen engaged with attackers at several points in this area of the wall. His men were growing more and more fatigued while the Romans sent up fresh troops to press the attack. It was common for a large battle to follow a pattern of ebb and flow, Drilgisa knew, with first one side and then the other side gaining a temporary advantage. However, at this fast pace of attack the enemy's numbers would soon prevail unless he found additional troops to reinforce his weakest positions.

General Diegis was the commander on the ground directing the Dacian troops held back as reinforcements. He sent units of archers and infantry to where they were most needed when the need was most acute. The pace of battle was frantic. Romans were making gains in certain areas but there were not enough Dacian troops to strengthen all positions.

"General, behind you!" a spearman shouted the warning.

Drilgisa turned swiftly to see a legionnaire climbing on the wall and another right behind him at the top of the ladder. The first man crouched low, wary of the Dacian archery fire. He drew his gladius and turned toward the Dacian general.

Drilgisa shouted a battle cry and charged him. The falx had a much longer reach than the Roman short sword, and that gave Drilgisa a big advantage. He was confident fighting with a falx against any Roman soldier, even a fully armored legionnaire fighting behind a shield. This soldier on the wall wore the most modern plate armor but did not have a shield.

The falx basically gave Drilgisa a sword with the reach of a spear. He stabbed at the Roman's legs, the most unprotected areas and the easiest target for a falx attack. The soldier deftly parried with the gladius from left to right and pushed the falx aside.

Drilgisa was out of reach of the short sword and would remain so. He continued the attack by pushing the falx past the man's right leg and then very quickly pulling the falx back. The razor sharp curved tip caught the Roman on the lower leg, just below the knee, and sliced through muscle and tendons to the bone.

The Roman groaned with pain and fell down on his left knee, still near the outer edge of the wall. Drilgisa raised the falx high and swung it like a club against the left side of the soldier's head. The man toppled over the edge and fell down to the ground.

Dacian spearmen rushed around Drilgisa to meet the incoming attackers and repulse them off the wall. The reserves from Diegis had arrived.

"I have this section secure, General," a young captain of infantry said. "You don't need to be in peril on the front line, sir!"

Drilgisa laughed. "I was not the one in peril, that Roman was. But carry on, Captain. Keep these bastards off the wall!"


"Legio VI Ferrata is bloodied, Caesar," General Hadrian said. "We should relieve them soon."

"You are correct, General Hadrian," Trajan said. "Follow the battle plan. What troops are in line?"

"IV Flavia Felix."

"Then give the order, General. Send them in."

"Yes, Caesar." Hadrian promptly turned his horse to go and issue fresh orders.

Licinius Sura watched the battle with his usual calm disposition. "Well, Marcus. So far this is not quite Julius Caesar at Alesia."

"Nor should we expect it to be," Trajan said evenly. "You recall that Vercingetorix and the Gauls defended Alesia with trenches, earthen works, and wooden palisades. Decebalus puts up stone walls thirty feet tall and defended by cliffs."

"Yes, you are right of course. But what have we learned from this battle thus far?"

"We have tested the Dacians," Trajan answered. "We know their capabilities and now we adjust our strategies. A direct assault on these walls is murderous and works very greatly to their advantage, even more so than I expected. Decebalus' men are well trained, their defensive fire is well coordinated, and they fight like demons."

"Preparations for building the ramp will be complete within a week," Licinius said. "That might swing the advantage in our favor."

"It is a strategy worth the try, Licinius. We shall have to see how well it works," Trajan continued. "There is no end to strategies. Do you know what defeated Vercingetorix in the end?"

"Hunger," Sura replied.

"Yes, hunger. But it was a hunger directly caused by Julius, his strategy that starved and weakened the Gauls into submission."

Sura agreed with a nod. "Many sieges are decided by hunger in the end. That will be difficult to accomplish here, so says Titus Lucullus. The Dacians are well supplied and have the means to produce more food."

"Licinius, have faith," Trajan chided him. "Julius was inventive, and so are we. If one strategy fails we find another. In the end we will take Sarmizegetusa by whatever means necessary and however long it takes."

"Of course, Caesar. In a week we build the ramp, then."

"Yes, next week we build the ramp. See to it that all materials and the engineers are in place."

"Brother, you should come and see this," Diegis told the King one late morning during the third week of the siege. Roman infantry attacks against the city walls were now more sporadic, although the artillery continued their murderous barrage. The worst damage caused by artillery was from the flaming projectiles that set warehouses and other buildings on fire.

"What is it you want me to see?" Decebal asked curiously.

The King was busy going over reports with Vezina. Many scouts were still operating outside the city, coming and going through the elaborate and extensive tunnel system built underneath the city. The tunnels came out in various parts of the mountain far beyond enemy lines. Dacians were expert miners of gold, silver, and other minerals, which made them expert diggers of tunnels as well.

"The Romans are building some kind of structure outside the wall, out of timbers and dirt," Diegis told them. "You should take a look and see what you think of it." He looked at Vezina and gave him a relaxed grin. "You too, Vezina, if you think that you can climb to the top of the wall. And if not, I would be honored to carry you up."

Vezina was used to the casual teasing and bantering from Diegis. This had been going on for years and neither was ever offended.

"Ha! While you are so nimbly climbing up and down stairs, young pup, I am doing something useful and sending messengers to the tribal chiefs in the north. They need persuading to send more troops."

"That would certainly be helpful if they would send more men," Diegis replied in a serious and respectful tone.

"We are almost finished here," Decebal said. "We will come with you shortly. Your curiosity now has me curious, Diegis."

The Roman structure outside the wall, not far from the city gate, was made of logs nailed together and increasing in height as it neared the wall. As it was slowly taking shape its purpose became clear.

"They wish to build a ramp that goes from ground level to the top of the wall," Vezina said. "That is very ambitious of them."

"Ambitious and very ingenious if it is ever completed," Decebal agreed. "They could send ten or twelve men walking abreast, in their beloved testudo formation with shields overlapping, up the ramp and right to the top of our ramparts. We might as well open our gates for them to march through."

"Does Trajan think he's at Masada?" Vezina wondered with a small laugh. "That trick will not work here."

"What is Masada?" Diegis asked.

"It was a stone fortress on top of a tall hill in Judea," Decebal told him. "The Romans finally defeated it by building a large ramp that reached the top of the wall. It is a tragic story."

Diegis scoffed. 'These Romans will not get within thirty paces of the wall."

"It appears that they certainly intend to try," Vezina said.

Decebal turned to Diegis. "Make it difficult for them. Concentrate artillery and archery fire on the structure. Kill their workers."

Two days later more than half of the Roman construction crew had been killed. The losses were accepted, the men replaced, and the ramp construction continued. The structure now stood twenty feet high and came within forty paces of the wall. The incline of the ramp was decreasing by design, so that the Roman attackers at the top would not be attacking uphill when they reached the city wall.

In the very late hours of the night, no more than two hours before daybreak, a group of sixty Dacian cavalry streamed out of the partly opened city gate. They rode in the moonlight along the city wall and in less than a minute reached the Roman construction site. One in three horsemen was armed with bows and lances, but the rest carried buckets of oils and pitch sealed at the top with a cloth cover. The armed riders quickly dispatched the half asleep soldiers guarding the ramp and set up a defensive perimeter.

The other forty riders trotted their horses around the construction site and hurled their buckets over the timbers around the base and on the sides of the ramp, then headed straight back to the gate. Within a few short minutes all the riders were back inside the gates, having fought off the small number of Romans who were not sleeping. More legionnaires stirred awake but the damage was done and the Roman construction was already doomed.

As soon as the city gate was shut and bolted a troop of Dacian archers appeared on the wall opposite the Roman ramp. They notched extra-long arrows with a thick wrapping of wool just behind the arrow head, then dipped the arrow heads and wool in buckets of pitch. Fire bearers held torches for the archers to set their arrows alight. A swarm of fire arrows arched gracefully through the night sky and fell on the Roman construction site. Then another. Then another.

Emperor Trajan was awakened by the distant cheering and shouting coming from Dacians on the city wall. This was followed by alarmed calls and shouts from Roman soldiers in his camp.

"What is happening?" asked Licinius Sura, who shared Caesar's tent. He was groggy and confused and trying to get his bearings.

"I do not know, Licinius. Let's go and find out."

Once they stepped out of the tent and saw the bright glow of fire reflecting off the city walls they quickly understood the cause of all this commotion. The construction site for their ramp was a tall pillar of fire burning fiercely and bright.

"Damn them!" Sura exclaimed. "They set fire to it."

"So they did," Trajan said, stifling a yawn. "It would have been too easy a solution for us."

"Shall we try it again? We can gather more materials."

"No," Trajan decided. "Now we change strategy."

"Circumvallatio?" Sura asked.

"Yes, circumvallatio," Trajan replied. "It worked well for Julius at Alesia and it will work for us."

# Chapter 13

# Survival

*Sarmizegetusa, June 106 AD*

R omans built circumvallatio walls during a major siege battle as both a defensive and offensive strategy. The walls fully encircled the enemy fort or city and protected the Roman troops from skirmish attacks from inside the besieged city. Even more importantly it formed a complete blockade to keep the enemy from leaving or entering the city, and it prevented any supplies and reinforcements reaching the city from the outside. It was a blockade meant to starve the besieged enemy into submission.

The sections of Sarmizegetusa that could be blockaded were the western and southern areas of the city. The areas protected by cliffs were not accessible to either the Romans or the Dacians. In the areas that were accessible the circumvallatio walls were built to face the city walls. The Romans waited behind their blockade walls made of soil and timber and bombarded the city with artillery.

"They are doing us a favor," Vezina said to the council meeting of the King, Drilgisa, and Diegis.

"How so?" Diegis asked.

"Their wall is more of a hindrance to them than it is to us," the High Priest explained. "We have no wish to go out and attack them because they outnumber us five to one. The supplies that we need are already in the city and we do not depend on outside help. Emperor Trajan is only making it more difficult for him to attack the city."

"Romans value the protection of walls," Drilgisa said. "When their army is on the march they build a defensive wall around their camp every single night, even when there is no enemy anywhere in sight."

"It is a smart thing to do," said King Decebal. "It takes some time to put up but it protects them from surprise attacks in the night."

"It does. However let's not rule that out, Sire," Drilgisa said. He was met with questioning looks from the men around the table. "A surprise attack in the night, I mean."

"What do you have in mind?" Decebal asked. "A large scale attack is out of the question."

"Small raids. Thirty or forty men going out by tunnel. Hit them in the night, or where they are weak or sloppy, or out on patrol."

Diegis gave a nod. "I like the idea. Let's make sure they don't sleep too well at night."

"Very well," Decebal said. "You two plan the missions and choose your men carefully. Security must be tight, we cannot have any men captured or tunnels discovered."

"Security won't be at risk," Drilgisa promised. "Our men know the forest and they know how to evade capture. And if they are at risk of being captured, they won't allow themselves to be captured alive."

"The tunnels we use are far from enemy positions," Diegis added. "We know where they patrol."

Vezina approved of their plan. "Good, this will help the men stay hungry and aggressive."

Diegis laughed. "Yes, we don't want them getting bored playing Trajan's waiting games."

"A poor choice of words perhaps, Diegis," Decebal said evenly. "Trajan is too smart to play games. We should never assume that we know what he thinks or what his next strategy will be."

"Ah, you are right," Diegis conceded. "Those who underestimate the enemy usually pay a big price for their foolishness."

The King looked at each of the men around him. "Take nothing for granted. Trajan could muster his army tomorrow and assault the city with three or four legions."

"He could, Sire," Vezina agreed. "Our men know this and they stay vigilant. We will not be caught unprepared."

"Any word from the chiefs in the north?" Drilgisa asked.

Vezina shook his head. "Not yet. I should hear back something within a week."

"They will want their men to stay home and harvest the summer crops," King Decebal said matter of factly.

"That is very likely, Sire," the High Priest acknowledged.

Drilgisa scowled. "Cowards. Sarmizegetusa is in peril. Dacia is in peril. This is no time to worry about their damn wheat crops!"

"They are not cowards, Drilgisa," Decebal said patiently. "We do not have an army of professional soldiers like Rome. Our soldiers are farmers and herdsmen first, soldiers second. You know this."

"Yes, I know," Drilgisa replied. "But they should also understand that this is a time for hard choices. We either win this battle or we perish, and Dacia will perish with us."

"I need no convincing of that," the King said. "Perhaps I should send you north to convince the chiefs?"

Drilgisa waved the question away. "If I go talk to them I would show up with a club in my hand, and that makes for poor diplomacy."

Titus Lucullus found it helpful now and then to walk around the camp and engage groups of soldiers in casual conversation. That was when the men were most at ease and the most open and honest while talking with an officer. It also helped that he did not carry himself with an air of arrogance or superiority, a rare quality that the soldiers in the ranks appreciated and found easy to like.

Some of the soldiers camped on the outskirts were uneasy because of sporadic Dacian raids in the night. These were quick hit and run strikes that lasted only minutes, following which the raiders melted back into the forest. The Dacian archers in particular preferred to kill Roman officers and artillery crews when they could reach them.

Titus was drawn to a carrobalista crew engaged in a lively and heated conversation. Six of the men were sitting around a small cooking fire, while the other two tended to the mules that were used to draw this small but deadly efficient piece of field artillery.

"I don't believe in spirits," one man said dismissively.

"But he saw her! He said that he talked to her."

"Pah! He says that he saw her. He was probably pissing himself when Senator Caepio was killed, so who knows what he saw?"

Titus greeted the men with a friendly nod. "What is this I hear about spirits?"

"We were talking about Dacian snipers killing our officers, sir," the first man replied. "Servius here believes the Dacians can turn themselves into wolves at night. That is how they sneak past our guards."

"They can," Servius declared to Lucullus. "Isn't that right, sir?"

Titus gave a casual shrug. "That is a legend but I don't know that it is true. Most likely it is just a legend."

The first man nodded. "They kill us with archers and I have never seen a wolf carry an army bow. Have you, Servius? No, I believe it is the forest spirit that Dimu saw kill Senator Caepio and his guards."

"Enlighten me, please," Titus said. "Who is Dimu and what is this forest spirit?"

"Sorry, sir," the first man said. "Dimu is a boy who used to work with us for a while as a mule tender. He got tired of army life and went back to Moesia. The forest spirit takes the form of a female archer. She is called Fata Padurii."

"Ah, is that so?" Lucullus asked. "That is another Dacian legend. Fata Padurii means the girl of the forest."

"Dimu swears that he saw her and talked to her, sir. He was there when she attacked and killed Senator Caepio and four of his guards.

She uses magic to make herself invisible and conceal herself in the woods."

"Pure nonsense!" said the second man, the spirit doubter. "It was only two guards, not four. And she used a bow, not magic."

Titus raised an eyebrow. "A single Dacian female archer killed two Roman soldiers and a senator? That sounds very unusual, would you not agree."

"Very unusual, sir," said the first man. "We know for a fact that Senator Caepio and his guards were killed. I do not believe that was done by any ordinary Dacian woman. She told Dimu that her name was Fata Padurii."

"That is a very interesting story," Titus said. He got up to leave. "Keep your eyes open for Dacian raiders, men. I hear that they seek out artillery crews."

"Yes, sir," the first man replied. "You keep your eyes peeled too, I hear that they seek out officers also, sir."

General Laberius Maximus had a good laugh when Titus told him the story. "Come now, Lucullus! You know that I don't believe in magic."

"Yes, I know that, General. Some of the men are a little spooked, so they spread tales about wolves, ghosts, and goblins."

"Senator Caepio was ambushed and killed by a band of Dacian raiders. They overwhelmed the guards and killed the senator. We can be quite certain there were no Dacian spirit women involved."

"Yes, sir, that was the report." Titus paused and could not suppress a wry smile. "Although if the killer was indeed a single Dacian female, would we ever admit it?"

"I don't know and hardly care about that, Titus. What I do know is that I have lost some fine officers and I want it stopped. Post extra sentries and send out more patrols to catch these Dacian archers."

"Have any been caught, sir?"

Maximus scowled. "No, not yet. We cornered a few but they kill themselves before we can grab them. Some even laugh at us as they die. Madmen!"

"No, sir, that is not correct. They are not laughing at us as they die. They are laughing because they are happy."

"Happy?" Maximus asked with a snort, puzzled.

"Yes, they are happy because in their moment of death they are joining their god Zamolxis. It is what Dacian soldiers believe and it explains why they do not fear death. Emperor Trajan himself has seen this behavior and remarked on it."

Maximus shook his head. "I will never understand these people. I don't believe in spirits or magic. Do you know what I do believe in?"

"What is that, sir?"

"Dead Dacians. Find these archers and snipers. If this Fata Padurii exists, in spirit or in the flesh, find her and bring her to me."

"Yes, sir," Lucullus said. "We will double our patrols tomorrow."


Adila walked by herself through a tunnel wide enough for four people to walk abreast. She carried a torch that gave enough light so that she could see her way forward. The tunnel was wide enough and tall enough so that a small group of people could walk through it in a hurry if they so wished. There were hidden air vents after a distance that allowed fresh air to circulate so that people could breathe and torches could burn.

This was the hidden tunnel built into the cliff side on the east side of Sarmizegetusa, on the highest terrace near the Holy Temple of Zamolxis. It was intended as the escape route for the High Priest and the other priests, and any other people of Sarmizegetusa who wished to use it if they were in danger. It had never been used as an escape tunnel before because the city had never been threatened before.

The walking was slow because the tunnel inclined upward so that those escaping would emerge high on the mountain and far away from the city, where they were unlikely to meet any enemy troops. From there they could travel north or east. The safest passage for any refugees seeking escape from Sarmizegetusa would be northeast.

When Adila came out of the tunnel, higher up on the mountain and well east of the city and the Roman camps, the farthest thing on her mind was fleeing as a refugee. She was the hunter, not the prey.

On two previous occasions she joined the Dacian raiding parties attacking the Roman camps. She greatly preferred going out on her own, however. She was a lone wolf. The forest on the mountain was her home and her hunting ground.

Even walking downhill and keeping to a southwesterly direction, it took over an hour to approach the outer reaches of the Roman camp. She moved carefully, stealthily, silently, at all times keeping to cover. She paid attention to the singing and chatter of the birds in the trees, and the movements of small animals on the ground, because if there were intruders in the forest their behavior would change. She was not an intruder. She behaved as a part of the forest.

Adila heard the sounds of metal studded sandals on the rocky ground long before she saw any sign of the Roman patrol. The birds in the trees became quieter as the men approached. This was further out to the east and higher up the mountain slope than the patrols she encountered in the past, but that did not matter. Her strategy would remain the same.

The terrain here was much too steep and rocky for use by cavalry, so the patrol would be on foot. She would attack from above, then escape by going up the slope to distance herself from any pursuers. She would then head straight east for a while to lead them away from the tunnel. No Roman soldier was fast enough or fit enough to keep up with her for long on the mountain. This was even truer if they wore the heavy legionnaire plate armor.

Adila chose her attack position behind an outcrop of rock that gave her a clear view of the mountain slope below. She would have time enough to fire three or four arrows at selected targets, then take off uphill and use cover to hide herself. With practiced ease she took her war bow off her shoulder and notched an arrow on the string.

The front of the Roman patrol came into view. The soldiers were legionnaires in full armor because the Romans learned from bloody experience that poorly armored auxiliary infantry were near helpless against Dacian ambush attacks in the mountains. Fifty soldiers were in view with more following. This size unit was most likely led by a centurion.

Adila's eyes scanned the column to pick out the top three targets that she would attack as soon as she came out of hiding. She locked in on an officer in the middle of the line, then another close behind. She was focused so intensely on picking her targets that she was much too slow to pick up the danger signals. Her blood ran cold at the sound of fast moving footsteps rapidly approaching her from behind.

Adila spun around in one swift motion, her heart beating in her chest like a trapped animal, and in that same motion raised her bow and pulled back the string to her ear. She hesitated for the briefest moment before letting the arrow fly and in that brief instant her mind registered the long brown hair and hazel eyes of Boian. She lowered her bow, still in mild shock but very relieved that she did not shoot.

They were still out of sight of the Roman column, hidden by the boulder. What are you doing here, Adila mouthed the words with her lips, soundlessly. Boian touched his finger to his lips for silence. He notched an arrow on his bow, then nodded to Adila and her bow. They would attack together. The marching Roman column was now directly below them.

Adila stepped to the left side of the boulder and Boian to the right. She picked out her targets on the left side of the column, he on the right. Each shot an arrow and had a second one on the way before the Romans realized they were under attack. They launched a third arrow as the Romans began to scramble, raising their shields up and getting into defensive formation. Four of the six arrows found their targets and men went down. Adila and Boian ducked behind the boulder again.

"Fata Padurii!" one of the legionnaires shouted out.

An officer near the front echoed the call. "It's the woman Fata Padurii! Take her alive!"

Boian turned to Adila. "What are they yelling?"

"They are calling me Fata Padurii," she said, laughing softly.

"They are calling you the girl of the forest?"

"Yes! Now we have to go!" Adila said urgently.

"Just one moment," Boian said. He stepped out from behind the boulder to face the Roman soldiers who were spread out and moving up the slope after them. Boian raised his bow over his head and used his right fist to beat his chest.

"I am not a fata! Go home or die, Roman pigs!"

One of the soldiers threw a pilum that fell just short.

"Let's go!" Adila shouted at him and took off running up the slope. Boian followed a step behind her. They were both athletic and fit young warriors who grew up and lived in these mountains. Within minutes they were out of sight and out of hearing of their armored pursuers. Adila followed her preplanned escape route, heading east.

After an hour of moving fast, and no sign of pursuit, they stopped for a rest and a drink from their water skins.

"So, you never answered my question," Adila said. "What are you doing here? Did you follow me?"

"Yes, I followed you," he replied.

"I almost killed you!"

"That part about catching you by surprise like that was not part of my plan," Boian said. "But when I saw that you were about to attack the column I could not let you do it alone."

"That was brave but reckless, Boian. I don't know why I hesitated to shoot but luckily for you that I did."

"Thank you for hesitating," he said with a grin.

"Why are you following me? Was this your idea, or someone else?"

"Tarbus believes that you take excessive risks, and so do I," Boian explained. "It was my idea to keep an eye on you."

"My risks are my business."

Boian shook his head. "No, they are not. Not entirely. You are not a simple archer, you are a princess of Dacia. There are things you must do that are more important than killing Romans."

"What must I do that is more important than that?"

"You must survive," Boian said. "You must stay alive and survive, Adila. You are too important for Dacia to take reckless risks."

Adila laughed. "I am not so important."

"Many people think you are." Boian paused and gave her a puzzled look. "Why were the Romans calling you Fata Padurii?"

"Oh, haven't you heard? Besides being a princess I am now also a goddess." She gave him a mocking bow. "The spirit of the forest, at your service."

"You must tell me sometime how you earned that title. It must be quite a story."

"And what of you being reckless? Taunting the Romans as they came after us?" Adila broke into a smile. "I am not a fata! Ha!"

"That was just a show of pride," Boian said. "It did not put us at greater risk at the moment."

"We should go," Adila said, standing up to leave. "Let us not invite greater risk."

"Will you consider what I said to you? In seriousness?"

"Yes, I will consider what you said seriously. I must survive. Such is the burden of princesses and goddesses."

"Indeed, my lady. Let's get back to Sarmizegetusa. Your people need to see that their princess is well and safe."

# Betrayal

*Sarmizegetusa, July 106 AD*

Clouds rolling in on a hot summer evening often signaled that a rainstorm was on the way during the night. Most of the people of Sarmizegetusa considered it to be a bad sign for religious reasons, because the rainclouds might also bring a storm of thunder and lightning. A lightning storm was regarded as a bad omen from Zamolxis, an indication that their god was displeased with his people.

It was the second week of July and the weather turned scorching hot. Three people in the city welcomed the rain clouds however, for three different reasons. Buri hoped for rain because his orchards were very dry, and without rain the fruit harvest would be poor. King Decebal was concerned that large sections of the pasture land were drying up, which meant poor grazing for the farm animal that would in time affect the city's food supply.

Queen Andrada appreciated the benefits of rain for the orchards and pasture land, but she was also very grateful for the cool evening breeze that came in through the windows of their sleeping chamber. Rainfall on a summer night provided respite from the day's heat and perhaps would allow for a rare good night's sleep.

"The heat will be with us for another two months," Decebal told her. "Let's be thankful at least that we have water for drinking and bathing. They are worse off."

Andrada gave a mild frown. They, of course, were the Romans. Most conversations these days touched on the subject of they sooner or later. For the most part they seemed content to wait behind their circumvallatio walls, but they were always on the minds of the royal couple and of every other person in the city.

"At least they stopped the assaults on the city walls," the Queen said. "Is it worthwhile, I wonder, to send envoys again and try to make a peace? We are at a stalemate."

"Every siege is a stalemate, Andrada, until one side or the other gets the upper hand." He paused briefly in thought. "Trajan will not want to discuss peace terms unless we surrender the city. Right now he believes that he has the upper hand."

The soothing sounds of rainfall came through the windows, and with it came a fresh breeze of cooler air. Andrada got up from the bed and walked over to stand by the window and watch the rain.

"How peaceful it is to watch a gentle rain," she said. "It makes me want to forget about them for a while."

Decebal gave her a small smile. "Unfortunately, kings of Dacia do not have the simple comfort of forgetting about the enemies of Dacia. It is a responsibility that never goes away."

She turned back to face him. "What a strange thing it is, the power and responsibility of a king. At least you wanted the crown, Decebal." Andrada paused and smiled. "I only came by it through marriage."

"Ha! And yet you became a splendid queen, whether by fate or by choice. And now we share the responsibility. It is who we are whether we wish it or not."

"Do you wish it still? Or not?"

"King Duras would ask me that question at times, just to test me I think," Decebal said. "It was a test of my conviction to serve as king."

"Yes, your uncle Duras tested you. He was clever, and he was also completely devoted to Dacia when he wore the crown. He would want to know if you were as devoted. But this is a question that I have also asked you before. How do you answer the question now, Decebal?"

The King's expression became serious. "Being the king of Dacia is not fate, it is a matter of duty. I understand that now. When King Duras gave me the crown on the field outside of Tapae he passed on that duty to me. It is a sacred duty and I must honor it to my last breath."

Andrada walked back to bed. "Spoken like a monarch, truly. The people know this about you, which is why they obey and follow you. It is why you are the hope of Dacia."

"Who am I to doubt your wisdom?" Decebal said with a small smile. "But not all the people obey and follow me. Many of our chiefs and nobles betray Dacia and make their own peace with Trajan."

Andrada rested her head on his shoulder. "So what happens now? Do we simply wait the Romans out?"

"We do not have enough troops to attack an army this size. So for now, yes, we wait them out."

"I wish I had your patience," Andrada said with a sigh. "But in war patience is a virtue, you keep telling me."

Decebal turned to look into her eyes. "The fortunes of war can change very quickly, towards the good or the bad. Until such a thing happens we have to wait the Romans out."

"There is a Dacian taraboste who wishes to speak with Caesar on a matter of urgency," Licinius Sura announced as soon as he entered. It was stifling hot inside the Emperor's command tent but amazingly Trajan seemed not to notice such things.

The Emperor frowned at being interrupted. He was reviewing scouting reports and maps with General Hadrian. "I do not have time for any more Dacian nobility. They all beg for favors and mercy and it is always a matter of urgency."

"Ah, but this one is intriguing. He is being interrogated by Titus Lucullus right now, and Lucullus also finds him very intriguing."

Trajan looked up from his maps. "What are you talking about? I told you I don't have time for beggars."

"Marcus, listen," Sura continued. "If what this man says is true you will drop all else and listen to his every word as if he were Jupiter Optimus Maximus in the flesh."

Trajan shook his head, then laughed and gave in. "All right, you have my curiosity."

"You have my full attention as well," Hadrian said with a grin.

Sura motioned to one of the Praetorian Guards, who quickly stepped outside Trajan's tent. Moments later Titus Lucullus entered, leading a portly middle aged man who was dressed in the fine clothes of Dacian nobility. The man looked tense and nervous, his face sweaty from nerves as well as from the heat.

Before the nobleman could speak Trajan held up a hand to stop him and turned to Lucullus instead. "Give me a summary, Titus, if you think it worthwhile."

"Yes, Caesar. This man calls himself Zoutula and he offers critical information. To be brief, as you know Sarmizegetusa is supplied with water from streams higher up the mountain. It is brought in via pipes hidden beneath the ground."

Trajan's eyes widened. "Yes? Continue."

"This man Zoutula claims that he knows the locations where the Dacian water pipes draw their water from the streams."

Trajan turned to the taraboste and gave him a curious look. "Why would you betray your people and give us this information, if it is true information?"

Zoutula cleared his throat nervously before he spoke. "Because King Decebal is leading us to destruction. He is too proud and will not listen to reason, so he must be made to surrender and end this ruinous war with Rome."

"Ah! So you are a patriot then, who only wishes to save Dacia from destruction?" Trajan asked with a trace of scorn in his voice.

Zoutula gave a small shrug. "I have no grand ambitions, Caesar. I ask only for my freedom and that I am allowed to keep my lands."

"Where are these water pipes located?" Sura asked eagerly.

"They are well concealed at the bottom of a stream. You will never find them unless I show you."

"Very well, Zoutula," Trajan said. "If what you say is true you may keep your freedom and your lands. You will now go outside and wait for instructions."

The Dacian gave him a stiff and formal bow. "Thank you, Caesar." The Praetorian Guard escorted him out.

"Is he credible, Titus?" the Emperor asked.

"I believe so. What he says makes sense, and he puts his life in our hands by coming here. Also I don't think that he is brave enough to make a good liar."

"By the gods!" Sura exclaimed. "This will change the course of the war, and quickly!"

Trajan gave a nod. "This is a gift from the goddess Fortuna and we must take full advantage. Hadrian and Lucullus, go with this man and find the water pipes. Take as many infantry with you as you wish. Take construction crews with their equipment for digging."

"Yes, Caesar," Hadrian acknowledged. "What is to be done with the water pipes when we find them?"

"Destroy them, Hadrianus. Bury them. We will cut off the water supply to Sarmizegetusa."

It took half a day for Zoutula to lead General Hadrian, his troops, and his construction crews on a march up the mountain slope. The water in the large stream was cool and crystal clear. They found four water pipes at the bottom of the stream, hidden by boulders that provided concealment but still allowed water flow.

"How ingenious," Hadrian declared. "This was the work of master builders. Apollodorus himself would be proud of this."

"The Dacians know how to dig, we must credit them that," Titus said. He kneeled down beside the stream, scooped water in his cupped hands, and drank thirstily. "I drank this water for two years while I was stationed in Sarmizegetusa. It is very good water."

"I'm sure it is, Titus, but now we must do what we came here to do." Hadrian waved to summon the boss of the construction crew.

"Yes, General? Do you want us to proceed?"

"Yes, get your men to work. Destroy these pipes. I don't want a single drop of water to go through these pipes again."

The water pipes of Sarmizegetusa led to public wells to provide water for drinking and cooking, and also fed water to the public baths. Over the course of one afternoon water levels in the wells dropped lower and lower, until finally the wells went dry as the water supply already in the pipes was used up. For the people of Sarmizegetusa confusion turned to concern and then to panic.

"The Romans have blocked the pipes in some way," Vezina said. "There can be no other explanation."

"But how could this happen?" Andrada asked. She learned of the water stoppage from her kitchen staff and sounded the alarm to the King and the High Priest.

"Someone betrayed their location," Decebal said.

"Yes," Vezina agreed, his face tense and angry. "A person with a working knowledge of the water system, and that means a Dacian of high position."

Decebal pushed his anger aside. "Nothing can be done about that now so let us deal with the problem at hand."

"Our water tanks will provide drinking water for about two weeks," Vezina said. "Nothing for the animals."

"Meaning that animals will begin to die within a week," Decebal said grimly. "And then in two weeks people begin to suffer."

"No, that can't happen," Andrada said with a shake of her head. "We can't let our people die of thirst. They must leave the city through the tunnels unless we find another solution."

"Pray to Zamolxis for a heavy rain, Vezina," the King said. "I see no other solution to increase our water supply."

"There will be no rain," Andrada said with a tone of resignation. "We had one evening rain shower the entire past month, and that lasted barely two hours."

Decebal sat back for a few moments. "Our strategy must change, but first let's deal with the immediate crisis. There will be panic in the streets soon."

The Queen turned to the High Priest. "Will you ask the priests of Zamolxis to go out and talk to the people?"

"Yes, My Queen. We can provide comfort if nothing more."

Decebal pounded his fist on the table. "There must be more! We cannot simply wait to wither away and die."

"Yes, Sire. Sadly our choices are limited and none are very good."

"Tell me your thoughts, Vezina."

"We cannot attack because we lack the necessary troops. We will not surrender. We will not sit here to wither away and die. In the end, when our water supply runs out, we must leave the city."

"It is the only choice," Andrada said. She turned to look Decebal in the face. "We must ask the people to leave the city. The tunnels will take them out of reach of the Romans."

"You are both right," Decebal agreed. His face grew dark and grim. "This is why we built the tunnels, although I never dreamed even in my darkest dreams that this day would ever come."

"How long can we hold off the Romans?" Andrada wondered. "We must give people time to escape."

"We can fight for as long as the water lasts," Decebal said. "Once people start to leave however many of the soldiers will leave with their families, to provide protection for them in the mountains. Our defenses will thin out fast."

"The city may fall in a short time, then," Andrada said.

Decebal acknowledged what she already knew. "We cannot save the city. We must save the people, and we don't have much time."

Five days later the Dacian defenders on the city walls were thinning out noticeably. More and more families decided to leave through the tunnels and escape a hopeless situation. They would travel north and east and provide their children with a chance to live a new life in a new location. The soldiers who were heads of families left with their families and no one would even consider questioning their decision.

General Drilgisa looked out towards the Roman camp from his position on the wall. He saw no change in the Roman positions or any signs of an impending attack. The Romans were in no hurry, nor did they have any reason to be. Time was completely on their side. It was the Dacians who were running out of time.

"When do you expect they will attack, Drilgisa?"

He turned to see Diegis walking up, carrying a water skin in one hand. Drilgisa greeted him with a nod, took the offered water skin, drank barely a mouthful, and handed the water skin back. Water was precious and strictly rationed even among the troops on the walls.

"I expect they will attack when they decide that we are too weak to beat them back," Drilgisa answered the question.

"I expect that you are right," Diegis agreed.

Drilgisa's face turned into a frown. "I am having some dark thoughts, Diegis. Some might call it sacrilege."

"Oh? Tell me."

"I think that Zamolxis has abandoned us. The city cannot be saved when we lack the water to stay alive. And I wonder," Drilgisa paused and turned to look Diegis in the eye, "why don't we just put a torch to it now and leave?"

"Put the city to the torch?" Diegis asked with surprise. It was a shocking idea for any Dacian.

"And why not? If we don't, the Romans will. I don't want to give those bastards the satisfaction."

Diegis shook his head. "I could never do that, my friend. I would rather fight to the end."

"Fight for what? You would die for nothing. For a city of corpses and ashes."

"I will fight for pride." Diegis gave a shrug. "I am not as practical minded as you, Drilgisa."

"Not true. You are sound and practical minded when you don't let your pride and stubbornness get in your way."

Diegis conceded the point. "Ah, perhaps you are right."

"When the Romans attack," Drilgisa continued, "resist when you can but don't stay here long enough to die."

"I will keep that in mind," Diegis said in a serious tone. After a moment he smiled and chuckled to himself.

"What seems funny to you now?" Drilgisa asked.

"You talk of committing sacrilege and burning the city, yet here you stand still living and breathing."

Drilgisa shook his head. "I still do not see the humor."

"I am saying that Zamolxis is not listening," Diegis continued. "Perhaps you are right, Drilgisa. Zamolxis has abandoned us."


"Their reserves of water must be close to nil, Caesar," said General Maximus. "We shut down their water supply two weeks ago."

"I am aware of that, Laberius. What is your point?"

"An attack now would meet little resistance."

"How long do we wait, Caesar?" Hadrian asked impatiently.

The Emperor smiled and looked at the men around him. "We will attack in two days. Will that make you happy?"

"If Caesar is happy then I am happy," Maximus said.

"And what of prisoners, Caesar?" asked General Lusius Quietus. "We have no Dacians for the slave markets."

"Take all the prisoners you want," Trajan replied, "except of course the members of the royal family. They belong to me."

"Also the High Priest Vezina, Caesar," Titus Lucullus said. "He is almost as valuable a prisoner as King Decebalus himself."

"Yes, of course. Give orders to every soldier. King Decebalus and the High Priest Vezina must be taken alive and delivered to Caesar. Disobeying this order will be punished by death."

"Will we find them in the city, I wonder?" Licinius Sura asked. "They have multiple escape tunnels from what we are told."

"We will find them," Trajan declared. "Hadrian and Lucullus, you are in charge of seeking out and capturing the high level prisoners. Titus will know best where to look for them."

"Of course, Caesar," Lucullus acknowledged. "I know what they look like and where most likely to find them."

Hadrian also acknowledged with a nod. "Decebalus will be at your feet in chains before the week is out, Caesar."

"A fitting end for a barbarian and rebellious king," Sura declared gleefully. "And a most satisfying end to this infernal siege that has taken too long in these godforsaken mountains."

"Ha! I think you will be much happier when you are back in Rome, Licinius. The Senate suits you better than army life."

"Indeed," Sura agreed. "Even so, I can say that I was here with Caesar when history was made."

"And what will history say about this siege, Licinius?"

"Ah, that question is easy to answer. History will record that whereas Julius Caesar conquered Alesia with hunger, Emperor Trajan conquered Sarmizegetusa with thirst."

Trajan laughed. "Whatever strategy works, Licinius. Whatever strategy works."

# Chapter 15

# Collapse

*Sarmizegetusa, July 106 AD*

**M**any of the people of Sarmizegetusa had already fled the city by the time the month of July was drawing to a close. They streamed out in small groups, sometimes only one family at a time, through the tunnels that took them out to locations on the north and the east side of the mountain. From there they walked through the vast mountain forests to join the Dacian tribes in the northern part of the country.

The summer weather stayed very hot and that made the water shortage more deadly. There was a stench in the air coming from the carcasses of many dead animals, combined with a haze of smoke coming from the many fires that could no longer be put out due to lack of water.

Feelings of panic and despair among the people of the city turned to sad resignation that the city was lost and they must find a new place to call home. There were some among them, the very old, the infirm, and the very stubborn who resolved that they would not leave come what may.

Queen Andrada gathered the royal family together in the family quarters to prepare them for leaving the city. King Decebal treated this like a high risk military operation. Plans and resources were in place, everyone was in agreement about the plans and procedures, and all were clear on what their role would be.

"We must leave today," Decebal said. "There is nothing more to be done, and when the Romans attack there will be chaos."

"Not everyone wishes to leave," Andrada said with a sad voice. "Some people are staying. Some are preparing poison."

"We are not taking poison, Mama," Adila said in a tone of disgust.

Zia shuddered and picked up Brasus in her arms. "I don't want to hear such talk. It is horrible."

Decebal placed a reassuring hand on his daughter's shoulder. "No one here is taking poison, Zia. Everyone will leave as soon as Buri tells us all preparations are in place."

"Yes, Tata. I understand."

"Buri is preparing the escorts and the wagons on the north road," Decebal continued. "Take only what you need for travel on the road. Take only clothes that you will wear for travel."

"Our servants are preparing those things," Andrada explained. "Only essentials because we must travel fast. Buri will come for us in the afternoon, and then we go. We will travel through the night and all day tomorrow."

"Tarbus is still on the wall," Zia said. "Does he know our plans?"

"Don't worry, Zia," Adila told her. "I'll go and collect him and bring him here before the afternoon."

"Thank you, Sister. Make sure that he comes."

"Oh, he will come," Adila said with a smile. "He will not let you and Brasus leave without him."

The Queen turned to her son, who was pouring a small amount of water into a wooden bowl for his dog Toma. The dog was panting from the heat but he could only be allowed enough water to keep him alive. Toma was one of the few animals in the city to be so fortunate.

"Dorin, will you take a message to the clinic?" Andrada requested. "Zelma and her family are there. Tell them to come back here with you immediately because they are travelling with us."

Zelma was Andrada's chief medical assistant for herbal medicine, who over the years also became a trusted friend. Her daughter Lia and Dorin had grown up together.

"Of course," the boy said. "Will you need any medicines?"

"Zelma will know what to bring. Just tell them to come."

King Decebal turned to Diegis. "We should go and see Vezina now, Brother."

Diegis gave a nod. "Yes, we should."

"What does Vezina plan to do?" Andrada asked.

"He has not yet said," Decebal answered with a small shrug. "I cannot order him to leave. Vezina is happy to advise kings but he bends only to the will of Zamolxis."

"I can guess what he decides," Diegis said with a small smile. "But let's go talk to him and find out."


The Holy Temple of Zamolxis was built on the highest ground of the city so that it would always be the closest to the heaven of Zamolxis. It was built in a round shape to symbolize the sun. The temple roof was supported by eight great pillars of stone, each covered in an outer layer made of a sheet of gold. The gold covered pillars dazzled all who looked at them over the years.

"It is a shame to leave this for the Romans to pillage," Diegis said as they approached the temple. "What do you think they will do with these golden pillars?"

"I do not know, Diegis. Not worship them, certainly."

They found Vezina finishing a conversation with his assistant priest, Mircea. Surprisingly Vezina was dressed in the simple plain blue robes of a priest of Zamolxis, something that Decebal and Diegis had never seen before in their lifetimes. The deep blue robes of the High Priest of Zamolxis, richly embroidered with thread of gold and silver, were folded neatly and in the hands of Mircea.

"Go with the King, my son," Vezina said to Mircea in a gentle and solemn tone. "The mantle of Zamolxis is now yours."

"Are you certain this is what you want to do?" the King asked him. "I hoped that you would come with us and continue as my advisor."

Vezina shook his head. "I would be honored still to serve you, Sire, but this temple of Zamolxis is where I belong. My heart is here. My soul is here. My fate is here, Decebal. Where else can I go?"

"But what good can you do here now?" Diegis asked.

"I must try to save the temple from destruction. The Romans have a respect for the gods, this we know. Not only for their gods but for other gods as well."

"Then we must part ways here, Vezina," Decebal said. "It saddens me greatly to do so because you are the wisest and also the kindest man I have ever known. You are a treasure to our people. You are the spirit of Dacia."

"Thank you, Sire," Vezina replied, deeply touched. "Mircea will serve you well as High Priest and advisor to the king. Place your trust in him the way you placed your trust in me."

Decebal gave a silent nod of acknowledgement. He hoped that Vezina was right. Mircea was a good man and a good priest, but Vezina was past advisor to three kings and a legend of Dacia. His name was spoken with respect in the royal halls of all neighboring countries and even in the halls of the nobility of Rome.

"Well, Vezina," Diegis turned to him with a smile. "Now that you are no longer the High Priest is it allowed to touch you?" He gave Vezina a clasp on the shoulder, his eyes bright with affection. "I shall miss you, old man."

Vezina returned the good natured smile. "I am certain there will be plenty of other old men where you are going, Diegis. In time you will replace me."

"Ha! None like you, Vezina."

A frantic trumpet call from the direction of the city wall caught their attention. It was followed by three more similar calls.

"The Romans are inside the walls," Decebal said gravely.

"I must go and see to the infantry troops," Diegis said urgently. He turned to walk away but very briefly looked back over his shoulder. "Stay alive, Vezina! You do that better than any of us!"

From his command position on the wall atop the city gate General Drilgisa watched the Roman troops approaching the wall. They were at least one full legion in strength, spread out on a wide front and carrying scaling ladders. This was the final attack that the Dacian high command anticipated and dreaded, the attack that would finally break the backs of the Dacian defenders.

To Drilgisa's great surprise however, even before the Roman troops outside the walls came within bow range of his archers he was distracted by shouts of alarm coming from inside the city walls.

"Romans inside the walls! Guard the gates! Guard the gates!"

"Tarbus, take command here!" Drilgisa ordered, then briskly moved to have a look over the inside edge of the wall. He watched with disbelief as a group of legionnaires, he guessed no more than forty, fought their way along the inside wall toward the gates below him. If they reached and opened the gates the battle would quickly turn into a massacre of Dacians.

"Archers, attack there!" Drilgisa yelled, pointing with his falx. He turned to the infantry standing near him. "You men, follow me!"

Once on the ground Drilgisa saw that groups of Dacian infantry already moved in to block the legionnaires' path to the gates. Other infantry came down from the walls to join them. The Roman troops, suddenly under overwhelming attack from archers and infantry, stopped their advance and got into a defensive formation.

Drilgisa stopped an infantry officer with a face streaked with sweat and blood who had already engaged the legionnaires. "Where did these damn Romans come from?"

The soldier pointed back along the wall. "They drilled a hole through the wall during the night, sir! These troops snuck in!"

"Drilled a hole through the wall?" the General asked.

"They have a machine for that, sir!" the soldier explained.

"Never mind. Carry on, Captain," Drilgisa told him. He turned to a newly arrived group of infantry. "You men! Go in that direction and make sure no other Romans are inside the city!"

From above him Tarbus peered down over the edge of the wall. "General! We need reinforcements in this section immediately, sir! We cannot hold for long!"

Adila's head appeared next to him, also peering down at Drilgisa. "More arrows! We need resupply!"

"Fight them off best you can!" Drilgisa shouted back. He had no more resources to send them.

Diegis approached, his face shiny with perspiration from rushing in the heat. "How did Romans get inside the walls?"

"They drilled a hole in the wall. Over there somewhere," Drilgisa pointed in the general direction.

"Ah! One of their infernal machines," Diegis said. He looked up at the wall where defenders in some sections were fighting Romans in hand to hand combat. "We cannot stop them this time, Drilgisa."

"No, we cannot. We'll fight a delaying action to give people more time to leave."

Diegis gave a nod. "When the walls are breached we should make a withdrawal towards the palace. Just slow them down, as you said."

"Right," Drilgisa agreed.

"Oh, one more thing Drilgisa," Diegis said, his face harsh and fierce. "As we retreat, burn the place down."


"It is time to leave, My Queen," Buri said. "There are Roman soldiers inside the city and in time they will find their way here."

"We are almost ready to leave," Andrada said. "With all our family and some of the servants there are thirty people total. Do we have enough wagons and horses?"

"Yes, more than enough. We have passenger wagons and supply wagons. There are twenty cavalry and sixty infantry from the palace guard for your protection."

"Decebal and Diegis should be here shortly, then we can leave. Perhaps we should send the servants ahead, Buri? They will need to store away the few possessions we are taking and settle themselves into the wagons."

Buri agreed with a nod. Andrada left to give orders to the servants who would be travelling with them. On the Queen's instructions most of the servants had already left the city.

"Tarbus and Adila are also not back yet," Zia said.

Buri stooped down to pick up his one and a half year old grandson who dashed to him, wanting to be picked up. Brasus liked being held up high in the air by this giant of a man who was his grandfather.

"Tarbus will know where to find us. And so will Adila," Buri said.

"Good. The sooner we leave the better. This is the only home I have ever known, Buri, but now it just feels like a place of death."


The retreating Dacian forces numbered only in the hundreds and were spread out thin. The city walls were indefensible and had to be abandoned. The fighting was now on the city streets in the civilian sections of the city. Many of the houses and building were on fire, most set by the Dacians themselves, which added more smoke and confusion to the fighting and slowed the Roman advance.

There were people still escaping through tunnels located on the upper terraces of the city. The Dacian defenders now fought to give them time. Many of those who stayed behind, including the old and infirm, had no value in the slave markets and were killed by Romans on the spot. The prize captives were children and young women but unhappily for the invaders few of those were left in the city.

Adila was fighting from the rear of the Dacian lines along with the other archers. They could shoot with great accuracy at enemy soldiers scarcely fifty paces away. Shoot, retreat. Shoot, retreat.

"Will you spare me some of your arrows?" came a familiar voice from behind her.

Adila turned to see Boian grinning at her. His leather quiver was empty, whereas she had been resourceful and picked up two extra quivers from Dacian archers who had fallen in battle.

"Of course," she replied, quickly removing one quiver from around her shoulder and handing it to him.

"Thank you, Adila," he said hurriedly. Romans were advancing and there was no time to talk. Boian was an expert archer who finished second only to Tiati in the Messenger to Zamolxis competition. Adila was very glad to have him fighting by her side.

Diegis was directing infantry troops when a group of legionnaires broke through a section of the Dacian line and headed straight for him. They recognized that he was a commander and that made him an important target.

The legionnaires were well armed and well armored. Diegis had the round Dacian shield and fought with a sica. He knew that he was badly overmatched against three armored legionnaires. He retreated cautiously before them.

"Get back, sir!" a Dacian spearman shouted and stepped up in front of Diegis. He lunged with his spear at the legs of the soldier on the right. The legionnaire easily swept the spear aside with his shield and in the same move took a quick step forward and plunged his gladius into the spearman's stomach.

The other two Romans stepped forward also and Diegis was again faced with the wall of three overlapped shields. He retreated again.

The savage battle cry came from his left and suddenly Drilgisa was beside him, menacing the legionnaires with his falx. He was a big, fast, and agile warrior, and the falx gave him a very significant reach advantage over the short gladius. The Romans paused their advance. They knew what a falx could do to their legs and arms.

"Get back behind the line! Or get a falx!" Drilgisa cried.

As Diegis stepped back a young Roman, sword arm and lower body stained red with enemy blood, came around the side of the three legionnaires. He took a quick look at Diegis, seeing an easy target in the retreating older man, and rushed at him.

"Fool!" Drilgisa said with a hiss. The falx flashed out low, quick as a snake, and caught the rushing soldier just above the ankle. The man screamed with pain from his half severed lower leg. He fell forward and landed at the feet of Diegis, his intended target.

Diegis went down to one knee and plunged the sharp blade of the sica into his attacker's neck to finish him. As he straightened up he noticed, too late, that one of the legionnaires was charging him. The Roman parried Drilgisa's falx with his gladius and used his heavy shield to deliver a shattering blow to Diegis' left knee.

Drilgisa forced the Roman to retreat with a series of short and fast stabbing moves with the falx. Tarbus joined him, also fighting with a falx, along with two Dacian spearmen.

Diegis heard the bones in his knee shatter even before he felt the pain and staggered back a step. He went down on his good right knee and knew that he would not rise to his feet again. Now immobile and helpless, he also knew that this was how warriors died. The very next Roman to come at him would take his life.

"Tarbus, take him!" Drilgisa yelled. He took hold of one of Diegis' shoulders with his left hand, was quickly joined by Tarbus who grabbed hold of the other shoulder, and together they dragged the wounded man away from the fighting.

Diegis protested. "My knee is shattered, I cannot walk. Leave me."

Drilgisa ignored him. He saw the familiar face of Boian looking in their direction and summoned him to come over. Adila also saw them and ran to her uncle's side.

"Tarbus, you and Boian will carry Diegis back to the palace," Drilgisa commanded. "Adila, go with them and provide cover. If an enemy approaches put an arrow in his face. Go quickly. Now!"

"Yes, sir," Adila replied. No one argued with a direct order from General Drilgisa on a battlefield. She stood up and notched an arrow on her string, scanning the grounds around them. She would be their lookout and bodyguard.

Tarbus and Boian picked up Diegis to carry him. Drilgisa gave him a farewell nod. "I will see you back at the palace, Diegis. Now go!"

Diegis returned the nod, then grimaced with pain again as the two young warriors carried him away at a fast walk. Adila looked down at him and gave him a grin. "We'll have to get you a walking stick, Uncle."

Diegis laughed despite the pain. He was still alive. He knew that he would never fight again. He wondered if he would ever walk again. Walking stick, indeed.

The terrace in Sarmizegetusa just below the royal palace was where some of the wealthiest Dacian nobles built their large houses. Lord Sorin lived there, father of Mirela who died young but first married Diegis and gave birth to Ana. His neighbors were Lord Bicilis and his pinched-faced wife Zena. This terrace also housed the finest bath house in the city, made with marble and equal to many of the finest bath houses in Rome. Members of the nobility gathered there for conversation as well as for the heated bath waters.

On the day the Romans breached the city walls the bath house did not offer soothing waters, because there had been no water for weeks now. Neither did it offer on that day particularly lively conversation. What the bath house had to offer, for those who wished it, was a large pot of boiled liquid, very thick and somewhat sweet smelling. It was a poison that brought a quick and painless death.

Bicilis and Zena were not the type of people to take their own lives. They enjoyed their wealth and privileges too much and the many life pleasures that they bought. They were leaving the city but first wished to say farewell to some of their friends staying behind.

They found Sorin there, calm and composed as ever. Bicilis had been jealous at times of the silver haired and distinguished looking man, so unlike his own portly build and big bushy eyebrows that made him look like a peasant.

Sorin saw and greeted them first. "Ah! I was just about to leave. But I am glad to see you before I go."

"You are leaving?" Bicilis asked, surprised. "I thought you came for that," he continued, gesturing at the pot of liquid that was placed on a table against the wall.

Sorin held up a stone medicine vial that was tightly wrapped in his hand. "I did, and I have it. However it would be in bad taste to die in such a public place. I prefer to die in my own home."

"But why die at all, my friend? You have wealth. You are related to the royal family."

Sorin shook his head. "This is my home. My wife is buried here, and also my dear Mirela. And besides I am too old and too ill for a long journey. I don't wish to die on some road in northern Dacia."

"I can understand that," Bicilis said. Zena kept her silence. She did not like this aristocratic but foolish old man.

"Go, Bicilis. Find a new home," Sorin told him.

"Yes. Farewell, my friend."

"Farewell. Now go while you still can."

There was nothing more for them to do. Bicilis and Zena walked away from the bath house towards the Holy Temple of Zamolxis, where one of the larger tunnels was located. All the wealth Bicilis now had was in gold coins in a thick money belt tied around his waist. It hurt him greatly to leave his lands behind. It hurt Zena even more.

"We should stay and bargain with the Romans, Husband," she told him again as they walked. It was an old argument repeated too often. "You are a wealthy and important man. They will listen to you."

"Do be silent, Wife," Bicilis snapped, his patience at an end. "I am not a traitor to Dacia."

At the royal palace Diegis' broken knee was wrapped in wet cloths soaked with medicines that would ease the pain and reduce swelling. Zelma and her husband Nicolae made a stretcher for him so that he could be carried more easily. They owed their lives to him and were devoted to his care.

The escape tunnel for the royal family was built under the royal palace. It was designed to be used only by the royal family. It led to a secluded road on the mountain separate from all the other roads.

"Every fourth person carries a torch," Buri instructed. "We can walk two abreast and not bump into each other. There is plenty of air to breathe so do not be afraid that you will suffocate."

No one in the royal family had ever used this tunnel before. The younger people were not even aware that it existed. It was a secret saved for a day of crisis. That day was now upon them.

"Buri will lead the way," King Decebal told them. "Tarbus and Boian, you will carry Diegis on the stretcher. I will bring up the rear along with the palace guard in case we are followed."

"Will the Romans find the entrance and follow us?" Adila asked.

"They will not find the entrance unless they tear the palace apart," Decebal answered. "Which they may do anyway, but not today."

Decebal and the royal guardsmen turned towards the door on alert at the sound of fast approaching footsteps. The figure who rushed in through the door looked like a bloody horror. They were all very happy to see him.

"The city is lost," Drilgisa said. "Some of our soldiers are escaping but some will fight to the end."

"We leave now, Drilgisa," said King Decebal. "We will fight again, but not today."

"Come this way," Buri said loud enough for everyone to hear. "Every fourth person carries a torch. Walk briskly but do not run. The Romans will not catch us now."

After a long siege is broken what follows most often is a massacre. The people still alive in the besieged city are among the most weak and defenseless. The attackers take out their built up frustration and anger in an orgy of destruction.

Vezina watched the battle move slowly and gradually from the lowest levels of the city to the upper terraces. A great many houses and buildings were on fire now and the air was thick with smoke even at a distance. Eventually Romans would reach the royal palace, just one terrace below, and then finally come to the temple.

Throughout the day people had been streaming past Vezina on their way to the escape tunnel. Many noticed him standing in front of the temple and stopped briefly to talk. Some tried to persuade him to leave, but he simply gave them his blessing and sent them on their way. Now, in late afternoon, the stream of people finally stopped.

Vezina stood alone in front of the empty temple. He felt a deep calmness and resolve that came from knowing he was fulfilling his fate and his life's mission. Vezina was nothing more than the hand of Zamolxis. His task now was to protect the temple of Zamolxis from destruction. It was the only task left that mattered.

He could see groups of Roman soldiers approaching. Some went to the royal palace but many headed for the temple, as he knew they would be. Like all visitors to Sarmizegetusa they were dazzled even from a distance by the magnificent sight of the great pillars covered in gold. Unlike all other past visitors however, these Roman invaders believed they had the right to defile and pillage his temple.

A group of thirty legionnaires approached the temple. They gaped at the golden pillars with excitement and greed. They did not even notice the solitary old man standing in front of the temple doors.

"Are they solid gold?" one soldier asked, transfixed by the sight.

"No, you fool," answered another. "Nobody has that much gold, not even Decebalus."

A grizzled veteran soldier walked in the lead. He paused in front of Vezina, surprised to find his path blocked. His gladius was stained red to the hilt and his shield and boots were spattered with blood.

"What do you think you're doing, old man?" the legionnaire asked irritably. "Will you stop us from going in and taking your gold?"

"The priests of Zamolxis do not keep gold, soldier," Vezina told him in a calm tone. "We have no gold here."

One of the legionnaires laughed. "I see plenty of gold here!" Other soldiers joined in the laughter with him.

Vezina looked out over the group. "Soldiers of Rome, you stand before the Holy Temple of Zamolxis! I ask in the name of all the gods that you do not defile this temple!"

"Get out of the way, old man," the veteran growled.

Vezina calmly held up both hands. "This temple is sacred ground. You must not –"

The legionnaire raised his gladius and lunged forward, a smooth stabbing motion practiced hundreds of times. The sword cut easily through Vezina's priestly robe and pierced into his upper stomach and then up into his chest.

The High Priest of Zamolxis gave a soft gasp. He put his hands to his chest, then fell to the ground.

# Chapter 16

# Escape

*Sarmizegetusa, July 106 AD*

H adrian had the unpleasant responsibility of informing Emperor Trajan that the Dacian King and his family were not captured and their bodies were not found in the city. A Dacian captive repeated a rumor that the royal family took poison and died. That rumor was quickly proved to be false. Hadrian and Titus Lucullus found a bath house near the royal palace littered with the bodies of Dacian nobles dead from poison, but no royal family members were among them.

"Dacians build escape tunnels in their forts, as we discovered," General Hadrian explained. "The tunnel system here under the city is much more elaborate and extensive."

"Send out cavalry patrols in all directions," Trajan ordered. "In truth I did not expect to find Decebalus in the city but we will still capture him."

"There is nowhere he can run," Licinius Sura declared.

Cavalry General Lusius Quietus provided reassurance. "My men are already on patrols. We'll catch him on the roads."

"Find Decebalus!" Trajan demanded. "This war is not over while he still runs free."

"I will bring him to you in chains, Caesar," Quietus promised again. His cavalry had the best chance to catch the refugee king.

The Emperor turned to Lucullus with a frown. "You found Vezina, I am told."

"We found his body," Titus said with disappointment. "He was killed on the steps of his temple."

"I gave orders!" Trajan said angrily. "He was not to be harmed!"

"We have the man who killed him, Caesar," Hadrian said. "He is a veteran legionnaire with long years of service. He was rash and used poor judgment in the moment."

"Vezina was dressed in a plain priest's robe, not the robes of the High Priest," Titus added. "Our man mistook him for a simple priest."

Trajan was not in a forgiving mood. "He should have been more careful. He disobeyed orders, damn him."

"Do you want him executed?" Sura asked. "Orders are orders, and who will respect orders if men are allowed to break them?"

"Yes, that is the point." Trajan turned back to Hadrian. "Have him executed. Gather the men so they can all watch and learn from his mistake."

"As you command, Caesar."

"Titus, are you familiar with Dacian funeral rites?" the Emperor wondered.

The question took Lucullus by surprise. "Yes, Caesar. In a general kind of way."

"All I know is that they do not burn their dead as we do," Trajan said. "Would Vezina expect a burial?"

"I believe so. He believed that when he died his soul would join his god Zamolxis, but he would wish his earthly body to have a burial."

"Then give him one," Trajan said in a respectful tone. "He was a worthy enemy of Rome. We should honor our enemies when they merit the honor."

"Yes, Caesar," Titus said. "It will give me great satisfaction to carry out this order. I came to know Vezina well during my years in Dacia. He was as fine a man as any Roman I have known."

The high praise of being compared to a Roman made Trajan smile. "You are a very honest judge of character, Lucullus. You never stoop to flattery, not even with Caesar. I know that your opinion of Vezina is correct."

The next day Titus Lucullus found three Dacian female prisoners and enlisted their help in a very sacred rite. The women washed the body of the High Priest Vezina and prepared him for burial. They wrapped his body in a simple burial shroud. Following Dacian tradition he was buried with his head pointing to the east. There was no headstone or monument. The gravesite was not far from the Temple of Zamolxis, where long ago King Scorilo and King Duras were also buried.

After the funeral ceremony was completed Lucullus stayed for a while to think and reflect. He turned his face up to the bright blue sky and smiled. I hope that you are happy in the heaven of Zamolxis, my friend, Titus thought to himself. And I am happy that you are not here today, and not witness to what you would consider the worst sacrilege you could imagine.

As Titus walked back towards the Holy Temple of Zamolxis he no longer saw a temple but a scene of devastation. The magnificent stone pillars were being cut and brought to the ground. Once on the ground they were cut into smaller pieces, because that made it much easier for the construction crews to strip off the outer layer of gold.

*Mountains north of Sarmizegetusa, July 106 AD*

The column of passenger wagons and supply wagons, and the escorts of cavalry and infantry guarding it, finally stopped for a rest at sunset on the second day. After leaving the fallen city of Sarmizegetusa they travelled through the previous night and all of the following day.

King Decebal and Queen Andrada would be parting ways in the morning. The Queen was leading the group of refugees to safety in Dacian territory far to the north where no enemy troops would reach them. After the conquest of Sarmizegetusa the armies of Emperor Trajan occupied the lower third of Dacia. The territory north of that was still under Dacian control.

Buri was in charge of leading this group of refugees on the road. He was assisted by the wounded General Diegis and by Mircea, the new High Priest of Zamolxis.

King Decebal, Drilgisa, and Tarbus would stay behind to organize the remaining Dacian troops and lead the ongoing resistance against the invaders. Thousands of Dacian troops escaped during the long siege of Sarmizegetusa before the city was captured. Many others still manned forts that were not attacked by the Romans on their marches to Sarmizegetusa. The Dacians could not hope to defeat this large Roman army, but they would attack and harass their enemies and provide protection for the civilian population travelling north.

After a sparse evening meal the royal couple and high command of Dacia gathered for planning and discussion. There would be no time to talk in the morning because the two groups would be leaving and travelling in separate directions at sunrise.

"How long do you plan to fight them, Brother?" Diegis asked. His broken knee was swollen and painful but there was nothing more to be done for it. It would take many weeks for it to heal.

"For as long as necessary, as long as we can," Decebal replied. "I will put together an army from the forts in the east and carry on the fight from there."

"The summer crops are harvested now so we'll get some troops from the northern tribes," Drilgisa said. "As they say, better late than never, eh?"

"Be thankful for their help, Drilgisa," Buri said. "Those men are not professional soldiers, and if they don't harvest the wheat in July their children go hungry."

Drilgisa conceded with no argument. "Yes, you are right. And had they joined us in the city they would have left anyway when we lost the water."

"They were better off staying in the north," Andrada said. She turned to look at Decebal. "We would all be better off in the north."

"I will join you there before the winter snows fall," Decebal told her. "For now we must continue resistance and protect the people who are leaving."

Diegis gave him a sorrowful look. "I wish that I could join you."

"No, Brother, you have done enough. You must now heal and be a leader for our people even though you can no longer fight."

"My leg will heal," Diegis said stubbornly. "I will fight again."

Andrada shook her head. "No, Diegis. Decebal is right. Your skills as a leader are more important now than your skills with a sword."

The travel column for the refugees was in line on the mountain road before the first rays of the morning sun turned the eastern sky blue. Farewells were emotional but of necessity brief.

King Decebal walked to the front of the column where the royal family would travel in their passenger wagons. In the second wagon Diegis was seated with his daughter Ana. His nurse Zelma and her husband Nicolae and daughter Lia accompanied them. Mircea sat with them because he enjoyed their lively conversation.

"Look for us with the Carpi or the Costoboci," Diegis said.

"I will find you," Decebal assured him as he shook his hand. He turned to Ana for an embrace. "Take good care of your Tata."

"I will, Uncle. Good-bye until I see you again." Ana bid farewell with one of her sweet smiles.

The royal family travelled in the lead wagon with Buri. Zia was talking softly to Tarbus. She knew that this would be their longest separation yet. Buri stood patiently next to them holding Brasus.

"Watch after Tarbus, Tata," Zia said to her father when he gave her a warm embrace.

"Tarbus will be fine," Decebal replied, then gave her a smile. "And besides, he is supposed to watch after me."

Tarbus laughed. "Exactly! Now I have the job that my father had for thirty years."

The King turned to Buri, who was holding their grandson. The boy was still sleeping and Decebal gently ruffled his hair. "We have grown to be old men, Buri. Brasus is the future of Dacia. Take him to safety."

"I will guard him with my life," Buri said. "And Zia too."

"I know you will. I will see you in three months, perhaps four."

"Look for us with the Carpi first," Buri told him.

Dorin gave his father a mild frown. "I wish that I could come with you but I know that you will say no."

"Your job is to protect your mother and your sisters, Dorin, as we discussed. That is more important than fighting with me."

The boy extended a hand and gave him a firm handshake. "I will see you soon."

"Stay healthy, my son."

"End this war soon, Tata," Adila said to him in a somber voice. "It will not end as long as you keep fighting."

"I understand, my dear brave daughter," Decebal replied. "Do you no longer hate the Romans?"

She gave a small shrug. "I am just tired of all the killing, I think."

Decebal embraced her then looked her in the eye. "You most of all must protect your mother. Be her champion when she needs you."

"I will, I promise," Adila replied, her eyes moist with emotion.

Andrada was used to saying farewell to her husband as he went off to war. It happened so often over the years that it seemed common, yet each time it felt even more difficult.

This farewell was anything but typical. Her entire family was now at risk for their lives. She could no longer expect to wait at the royal palace and welcome Decebal back from the war, because there was no more royal palace. Everything in their world was changed.

Decebal embraced her and she held him close. Everything that was important to be said was said wordlessly in that embrace. Each knew intimately the hopes, fears, love, and affection of the other. Sometimes just a look was enough, and an embrace spoke volumes.

"Travel safely, my love," he told her.

"Come back to me, my love," she replied.

*Sarmizegetusa, July 106 AD*

Emperor Trajan walked through the smoky ruins of Sarmizegetusa knowing that his mission was not yet complete. King Decebalus was still free somewhere in the Dacian mountains. Very little gold had been found in the city, and to the Emperor's surprise none was found in the royal palace. The King of Dacia was known to be very wealthy. He was also very clearly good at hiding his wealth.

The city was a strong citadel but Trajan did not consider it a prize. For defensive purposes it was built high up in the mountains. That made it inconvenient and difficult to reach, which in turn made it a poor location for a Roman governor to live in. Trajan had a different vision for what the Roman province of Dacia would look like.

There had been no fighting inside the royal palace and no damage to the structure. Roman troops found the palace empty and deserted. Trajan gathered inside the throne room with his high command to interrogate a number of Dacian noblemen who were either captured or willingly surrendered themselves. The more patriotic nobles had either fled the city or were dead. The ones who remained were most interested in their own welfare.

Trajan looked at the ten nobles standing meekly in front of him and came straight to the point. "Where is King Decebalus?"

Some Dacians stirred uncomfortably and some remained still as statues. When none replied Trajan pointed to the man in front.

"You. Give me an answer."

"In truth, Caesar, I do not know. None but his closest advisors would have that information."

"Where would you go if you were King Decebalus?" the Emperor persisted.

One of the men cleared his throat nervously. "Most people seeking refuge would do so with some of the northern chieftains, Caesar."

"Which chieftains in particular?" asked Sura. "There are two or three hundred of them. Are there any who are close allies with King Decebalus that he would prefer to see?"

The man in front shook his head. "All of them are allies of the King, sir. He did not favor any particular ones."

"If you seek mercy or favor from Caesar," Sura addressed them in a cold tone of voice, "then you must provide more information."

The Dacians remained mute. It was clear that they did not know.

"Where did Decebalus hide his gold?" the Emperor asked. "He has vast reserves, and yet we find nothing in the city."

The nobles again grew uncomfortable. None had an answer.

"I should have you all tortured, one by one, until somebody tells me," Trajan said in an even voice. Some of the men blanched at the threat but nobody spoke up.

Trajan turned to the Praetorian Guards guarding the Dacians and waved a hand dismissively. "Take them away and hold them until I decide what to do with them."

"They are either exceptionally brave or simply ill informed," said Licinius Sura as the prisoners were led away.

Trajan turned to Lucullus. "What is your opinion, Titus?"

"I think that their profession of ignorance is sincere, Caesar."

"I believe that as well," Trajan said with a frown.

"We should expand our cavalry patrols further to the north and do it quickly," Sura offered. "If we don't catch Decebalus within a week then we never will."

"Yes we should," Trajan agreed. "Get word to Quietus now."

"It is possible, Caesar," Titus Lucullus said with some reluctance, "that King Decebalus is not travelling north with the refugees."

"Explain, Lucullus."

"He is a very proud and stubborn man. His army is shattered but there are still Dacian troops in the mountains, a few hundred here and there." Titus gave a small shrug. "It is possible that he will try to organize them and continue the war."

"You have a point," Trajan said. "We have learned to expect the unexpected from Decebalus."

"We should expand our cavalry patrols further north regardless." Sura persisted.

"Yes, do that," Trajan said calmly. "You never know what you might catch next in your fishing nets."

*Road in central Dacia, August 106 AD*

The summer heat wave continued in the first week of August as the travelling party of Queen Andrada continued on its way north. The roads now went through farmland and forest. It was very dry and the horses' hooves kicked up clouds of dust even going at a moderate pace. Most of the cavalry rode in the back of the column, guarding against pursuit, which helped to reduce the clouds of dust up front.

They passed through a village every hour or so now. The farming villages were small, no more than a few hundred people each. They could not stop at each one but the people still came out to greet them as they passed through. They happily offered them many baskets of food and other supplies. The supply wagons and even the passenger wagons were soon filled with baskets of fresh fruits and vegetables, smoked sausages and other dried meats, fresh and smoked cheeses, and breads and baked goods of all kinds.

"Another week of travel and we should be clear of Roman patrols," Diegis said. He was in the lead wagon with Andrada and Buri.

"Good. I am surprised we have not seen any yet," the Queen said.

"The army of Rome is an army of infantry, not cavalry," Diegis continued. "A legion of five thousand men has barely over a hundred cavalry assigned to it."

"True, but they also have auxiliary cavalry who do the fighting for them," Buri said. He was in the driver's seat and holding the reins. "Infantry will never catch us but cavalry pursuit still might."

A rider from the back of the column pulled up with the wagon. Adila looked down from her saddle with a grin.

"Boian says we should start saying no to all these people bringing us food. It's too much!"

That made Andrada smile. "Tell Boian that no, we will not refuse their gifts. The people have plenty of food and will not go hungry. We should accept and honor their generosity to us."

"Yes, Mama. I am happy to hear you say that." Adila turned her horse to ride back to the cavalry at the rear. "And save some of the good cheese pastries for me!"

"There are no such things as bad cheese pastries!" Diegis shouted after her with a laugh.

"Do you know what surprises me?" Zia asked no one in particular.

"Tell us," her mother replied, curious.

"Yes, the people are very generous to us as they have always been," Zia continued in a pleasant voice. "But what surprises me is that they also seem as happy as they have always been. Sarmizegetusa fell but they still go on happily with their lives."

"That's a very good observation," Buri said from his perch in the driver's seat. "But you should understand, people are made happy or unhappy mostly by the events in their daily lives."

"You are right, Buri," Andrada said. "And there is one more thing that we should understand."

"What is that, Mama?"

"Sarmizegetusa fell, but Sarmizegetusa is not Dacia," Andrada said. "The people in these villages are Dacia. We are Dacia."

# Chapter 17

# Resistance

*Mountains of eastern Dacia, August 106 AD*

A fter the fall of Sarmizegetusa the war in the eastern mountains of Dacia still raged on. There were many Dacian forts that were never attacked by the Roman army, and King Decebal now travelled between them gathering troops. Many soldiers who escaped from the siege of Sarmizegetusa made their way to these forts and joined the King's army again. The fight against the Romans would continue.

The Roman forts and camps east of Sarmizegetusa were guarded primarily by auxiliary infantry. Emperor Trajan wanted his legions to be stationed near him and fighting in strength when needed, not fighting bands of Dacian rebels in skirmishes and ambush attacks in the mountains.

"Another two hundred infantry came in today," Tarbus announced as he joined King Decebal and General Drilgisa. They were meeting in the King's quarters inside the fort.

"That will help," Drilgisa said. "A drob here and a drob there, and soon you have a full bucket of water."

"We need many buckets more," said Decebal. "This gives us four thousand fighters at most."

"Enough to attack the forts to the south and west of here, Sire?" asked Tarbus.

"Yes. Two forts. We hit them quickly and overwhelm them in the first attack. No long battles and no sieges."

"Good, two attacks will not spread our forces too thin," Drilgisa said. "I will lead one attack. Will you lead the other?"

"I will," said the King. "Tarbus, you will come with me. It is time that you were properly trained to become a general for Dacia."

"I am honored, Sire," Tarbus replied in a grateful tone. This was not a responsibility he expected at his young age.

"You earned the honor," Drilgisa told him with a clasp on the shoulder. "You are a very capable second in command and you will do well with higher responsibilities."

"Thank you, sir," Tarbus replied. "I will not let you down."

"We will travel through the night and attack at daybreak," Decebal told them. "Hit them hard, Drilgisa. No mercy. Destroy the fort, then return here no later than two days from now."

"As you command," Drilgisa said, then gave them a grin. "That was exactly my plan all along."


King Decebal watched and waited while Tarbus directed the attack. He would not join in the fighting because it would be a great victory for Emperor Trajan if King Decebal was captured or killed. Worse, it would deal a serious blow to the spirit of the Dacian troops. After thirty years Decebal still remained the inspirational leader for the soldiers of Dacia.

As planned the attack was sudden, fast, and brutal. A large force of two thousand Dacian infantry assaulted the walls of a fort manned by five hundred Roman troops. After two hours the gates were breached and the slaughter of the defenders began. No men of fighting age would be spared. All the servants were women and they were allowed to go free, along with all the other women and children in the fort. The Dacians had neither time nor interest to deal with prisoners.

Within three hours of the initial attack the fort was burning. The Dacian troops prepared to leave and return to base. They were not concerned about any Roman pursuit because there were no large forces of Roman troops stationed in the area. To fight these attacks more effectively Trajan would need to send additional troops east.

"We caught them by surprise," Tarbus said when he rejoined the King. "They think they won the war so they no longer fear us."

"They did win the war," Decebal said. "Their mistake is to believe that the fighting is over."

"Yes, Sire," Tarbus said. He had a cut on his right leg from a spear. He appeared not to notice and ignored it. The bleeding was slow but steady and stained the leg of his white woolen breeches.

"We are no longer fighting to win the war but only to keep the Romans in place," the King continued. "And you had better bandage that wound before we leave."

"It's not bad," Tarbus said. "I can walk on it just fine."

The King stopped him with a stern look. "Tarbus, there is one quality above all others that a good leader must demonstrate. Do you know which quality I mean?"

"Bravery," the young man replied without hesitation. "A leader of men who does not show bravery does not earn respect or obedience."

"Yes, bravery is important. But more important than bravery is good judgment. Bad judgment not only gets you killed but it also gets your men killed."

"Ah, you are right, Sire," Tarbus said with a groan. "I need to show sound judgment and not give in to foolish pride." He sat down on a log and motioned to one of the Dacian medics nearby.

"Spoken like a general," the King said to him.

*Road in north central Dacia, August 106 AD*

"There is a large village a short distance up the road, My Queen," the cavalry scout reported. The bulk of the cavalry escort guarded the rear of the column but some riders always scouted ahead.

"A good place to rest for the night," Buri suggested from his front seat in the carriage.

"Yes, let's do that," Andrada agreed. It was almost dusk and the horses were tired after another day of travel in the heat. The village would have water and food and would provide extra protection.

Within a few short minutes the alarm calls came from the rear of the column. "Cavalry! Roman cavalry!"

"Damn them," Diegis swore with disgust. "I didn't think they would follow this far north."

"Buri, can we reach the village in time?" Andrada asked.

Buri stood up in the driver's seat to get a better look up the road. "No, it's too far. We cannot outrun cavalry."

"Then we have to fight," Diegis said. He could not stand on his wounded leg but still kept a falx next to him in the passenger wagon.

Buri reined in the horses, handed the reins to a servant, and went to stand at the side of the wagon near Andrada and Zia. He was also armed with a falx. The long two handed weapon was deadly against riders and their horses.

Adila rode to the lead wagon in a hurry, dismounted, and tethered her horse to the back of the wagon. She climbed into the wagon to stand beside her mother and sister, her bow and full leather quiver of arrows on her shoulders. Dorin also stood on the wagon bed armed with a sica and holding a shield. He and his sister would be the last line of defense to protect Queen Andrada.

"I fight better as a foot archer than a horse archer," Adila told her family. She turned to her sister and flashed a grin. "Don't worry, Zia. Any Roman that comes within twenty paces of us is a dead man."

"How many cavalry?" Diegis asked Adila.

"A large group. From what I could see, maybe fifty or sixty."

"They are here to fight, not to scout," Buri growled.

The twenty Dacian cavalry and sixty infantry deployed urgently to form a circle around the passenger wagons as the Roman cavalry closed in. The supply wagons did not matter and the Romans had no interest in those whatsoever. They were looking for King Decebal and the royal family.

The Romans were auxiliary cavalry, a mixture of Gauls, Iazygis, and Spaniards. They fought with spears and lances, and with cavalry swords that were longer than the gladius. The gladius was a short stabbing weapon for the infantry and had limited use for fighting on horseback.

Dacian foot archers opened fire when the attackers were within two hundred feet of the travelling column. The horse archers, fighting with a lighter and less powerful bow, fired when the Romans were within one hundred and fifty feet. The Roman cavalry were fast moving targets and difficult to hit, and only a few attackers and their horses went down.

"Kill their horses!" Boian shouted. Some archers re-directed their fire and more horses went down. Still the cavalry closed in with frightening speed, horses' hooves pounding the dry soil and sending up a thick cloud of dust. They threw their javelins at the defenders, then charged forward fighting with swords and spears.

Some thirty Dacian spearmen formed a line in front of the Queen's wagon. They knelt down on one knee and planted the butts of theirs spears firmly into the ground, with the spear blades pointed up and forward to meet the chest of a charging horse. They knew that horses would not charge into a line of spears and the cavalry charge would stall and go in a different direction.

"Stand firm!" Buri shouted. "Hold your ground!"

The front line of cavalry approached the spear wall and veered to the sides, looking for openings in the Dacian lines. The unprotected sides of the Roman horses made easy targets for the Dacian archers, impossible to miss. Once his horse went down the lightly armored rider of the auxiliary cavalry was an easy kill for Dacian infantry.

Adila stood firmly on the bed of the wagon next to her crouching mother and sister. She chose her targets swiftly and strategically. She shot not at the closest riders but at those who were the greatest risk to break through. She was guided by instinct more than by deliberate thought. Target, notch, pull, loose. Shoot again. Her instincts were quicker than thinking and she trusted them implicitly.

"Look out!" Dorin yelled and jumped in front of her, raising his shield to protect his sister. The round shield blocked a spear thrown at Adila's chest. The spear deflected to the side and fell with a clatter on the wagon bed to land at the feet of Zia and Brasus. Zia cried out in alarm and crouched down even lower to cover and protect Brasus. Andrada leaned her body over to protect Zia.

"Thank you, Brother!" Adila shouted and immediately returned to shooting her bow. A rider paused in front of their wagon to hack at a defender and Adila put an arrow into his chest.

In the frenzy of battle Buri was the equal of any three other men. He centered the line of Dacians guarding the Queen's wagon and used the long reach of the falx to keep enemy riders at bay. The ground around him was littered with the bodies of dead and dying men, and of horses thrashing on the ground with mortal wounds. Other riders veered to the sides to find easier targets.

The Roman attack created some openings, and once inside the Dacian lines they attacked with savage fury. Dacian infantry armed with spears and falxes beat them back at the points of attack. Dacians were taking heavy losses however and their line was shrinking. Most of their horse archers were down. The infantry retreated slowly to the lead wagon that held the royal family.

Diegis stood up on his one good leg and used the other leg lightly for balance, leaning against the inner side of the wagon. If an enemy came close he would be good for one solid blow, but one good blow from a falx could slice off a leg or arm or mortally wound a horse with a neck wound.

"Uncle, look!" Dorin cried to get his attention, pointing to the north.

Diegis took a quick glance up the road and his face broke into a grin. He whooped with glee. "Ha! We have the bastards now!"

"What is it?" Buri called up to Diegis from the ground.

"Help from the village, men on horses! A big group! Hold them off for a little while longer, Buri!"

Buri bellowed out a ferocious war cry. "You heard him, men! No Roman gets through! Fight for your Queen!"

The captain of the Roman cavalry also noticed the approaching group of Dacian horsemen. Few of these villagers would be trained cavalry but they were armed with spears, swords, and axes, and they greatly outnumbered his men. Combined with the Dacian forces on the ground they would be enough to overwhelm his troops. He cursed his bad luck and knew that the fight was lost.

"Retreat!" the Roman officer called out. "Retreat!"

The cavalry stopped fighting and regrouped. They turned their horses to ride south, back in the direction from which they came. The commanding officer took one last look at the lead passenger wagon. He did not know exactly what the Dacian queen looked like, but he knew for certain that the dark haired middle aged woman with the regal bearing must be Queen Andrada. He cursed again, knowing bitterly that the prize had just slipped through his fingers.

The horsemen from the village pulled up when they reached the wagons. They had no interest in chasing after Roman cavalry and little chance of catching them in any case. Their only interest was to protect the travelers.

One of the older villagers rode up to the lead wagon, then stopped abruptly in surprise. He promptly dismounted, walked over to the wagon, and gave a deep bow before Queen Andrada. The others from the village followed him and did the same.

"Welcome to Uzdin, My Queen," the man said. He once made a trip to Sarmizegetusa for a festival, and no Dacian ever forgot the face of Queen Andrada.

Andrada stepped down from the wagon to greet the villagers. Buri and Dorin stood by her side, her bodyguards.

"What is your name?" Andrada asked their leader.

"I am Dotos, My Queen," the man replied in a very respectful tone. "I am the elder of Uzdin. Please do us the honor to stay as a guest in our village."

"Thank you, Dotos, to you and your people," Andrada said. "We are very grateful for your military aid and for your kind hospitality."

Diegis walked up, limping, with the aid of a walking stick. "Have you seen any other Roman troops in this area, Dotos?"

The man shook his head. "No, sir. In truth these are the first and only Roman troops we have seen near our village. They do not come this far north, sir."

"They were on a mission to capture us," Diegis explained. "Your men arrived just in time to turn the battle, Dotos. Well done."

Dotos gave him a big grin. "I fought with you, General, and with King Decebal at the first battle of Tapae. Romans do not scare us. If they come this way again we will fight them."

"Will you help us see to our wounded, and help bury our dead?" Queen Andrada asked. "Those Romans are not coming back, but we should stay in your village for the night."

"Of course, My Queen," Dotos replied, bowing again. "Anything that you wish for, all you need do is command and we obey."

The Dacian wounded were taken to the village in wagons. Their dead would be buried in the village in the coming days. The horses taken from fallen Roman cavalry were given to the villagers for their own use. Roman dead were stripped of weapons and armor. Their bodies were left for the carrion of the field.

*Ranisstorum, Dacia, August 106 AD*

"We chase after Decebalus for a month now," Licinius Sura said with a tone of exasperation. "I had eels served at my dinners in Rome that were not as slippery as this man."

"Why does he continue to fight?" asked General Hadrian. "Rome's war with Dacia is over. He has no hope for victory."

"An excellent question, Hadrian," Emperor Trajan said. He turned to his expert on Dacia. "Decebalus has his reasons. What are your thoughts on that, Titus?"

"I have given it thought, Caesar," Lucullus said to begin his reply. In fact he had given the question a great deal of thought because it defied all conventional wisdom. "Of course he knows that he has no hope for a military victory over Rome. He might however view victory in a different way than we do."

Sura waved his hand dismissively. "Nonsense. In every war there can only be one winner. What other type of victory can Decebalus hope for?"

"Let's hear him out, Licinius," Trajan said. "Continue, Titus."

"Yes, Caesar. From the very start Decebalus has always fought a defensive war against Rome. He never dreamed to conquer Rome and surely never even considered it a possibility. He wished only to defend and preserve Dacia."

Hadrian gave him a very skeptical look. "But is that really true? Last year when the Dacians made the surprise attack on Drobeta without any provocation from us, was Decebalus fighting a defensive battle then?"

"Yes. That was an eminently defensive battle, General," Titus said. "The Dacians viewed the bridge at Drobeta as a provocation in itself. They saw it as an open road for Rome to invade Dacia."

Trajan laughed softly. "And that is exactly how things happened in the end. Decebalus was right to have those fears about my bridge."

"Very well," Sura acknowledged the point. "That still does not tell us why he keeps on fighting Rome now."

"Don't you see?" Lucullus continued. "Decebalus still fights the same battle as ever, only on a smaller scale now. He fights to protect Dacia and those areas to the north that remain in Dacian hands."

Hadrian gave Lucullus a grin. "Perhaps you should go and have a talk with King Decebalus? Tell him the war is over. You were always a very good envoy to the Dacians, Titus."

"No thank you, not me," Titus said with a shake of his head. "The people that I knew well in Sarmizegetusa are either dead or else they have vanished. No one will listen to me now."

"The time for talking with Decebalus is over so we have no need for more envoys," Trajan declared. "Titus, you said that perhaps he views victory in a different way than we do. What do you mean?"

Lucullus continued. "The second reason why King Decebalus still fights is a matter of pride. He fights to preserve the pride and spirit of Dacia. Refusing to capitulate to Rome is a victory for Dacia in their view."

"That is no victory," Sura scoffed. "That is only foolish pride."

Trajan disagreed. "No, it is not foolish pride. It is the soul of the man and what drives him to continue fighting even when the odds of winning are impossible. But it is bigger than that now. This pride of Decebalus has now become the pride of his people."

"Yes, Caesar," Titus agreed. "This is why he will never surrender and Dacia will not end their resistance to Rome."

"What shall we do about Decebalus, then?" Hadrian asked.

"Continue to search for him aggressively. He must be found and captured and put in chains," Trajan told them in a serious tone. "We must humble him before the people of Rome and Dacia, because that is the only way to crush his spirit and the spirit of his people."

# Chapter 18

# I Will Not Be A Slave

*Eastern mountains of Dacia, September 106 AD*

D ecebal ordered fewer ambush attacks and raids on the Roman camps as August turned to September. This was a tactical decision driven by necessity. His troops in the mountains were only a few thousand men scattered in various locations. Emperor Trajan increased the number of infantry and cavalry stationed in the eastern mountains and the search for King Decebalus intensified.

Having a small army and no reserves also meant that Decebal had to push the same groups of soldiers harder. Many were asked to go on missions with little rest, and to fight with minor wounds and injuries that had no time to heal. The soldiers obeyed and persisted because that is what soldiers do. Refugees were still streaming north and were thankful to not be harassed by Roman patrols.

Near the top of the King's present concerns about his troops was the health of his son in law and infantry general in training. He had taken a surprising turn for the worse.

"What makes Tarbus so ill?" Decebal asked the Dacian doctor. "The spear wound to his leg did not look to be very serious."

"No, Sire, the cut on his leg was not severe," the doctor answered. "I believe the weapon was coated with some kind of substance, and that is what makes him ill. He has weakness, vomiting, and difficulty with his breathing. These are the effects of some type of poison."

The King frowned, disgusted by the thought of his soldiers being poisoned. "Will he recover? This is not a death worthy of a warrior."

The doctor paused to choose his words carefully. He knew that the King demanded absolute truth at all times. "I cannot say for certain, My King. Many soldiers would have died by now, but Tarbus is a strong and healthy young man."

"Are you hopeful that he will recover?" Decebal persisted.

"I am hopeful," the doctor replied. "We should know within the week whether he lives or dies. It is in the hands of the gods."

"I understand," Decebal said. "Do all that you can for him. He is the husband of my daughter and dear family to me."

"Yes, Sire. I will do everything that I can."

Decebal walked over to a corner of the medical tent where Tarbus was stretched out on a cot. General Drilgisa was already there talking to him. Tarbus looked tired and drawn. His pallor was pale and his skin was sweaty.

"I just spoke with the doctor," the King told him. "He says that you are stronger than most men and will recover soon. While you rest here make certain that you eat well and sleep well."

"Yes, Sire," Tarbus acknowledged. His breathing was very shallow and his voice raspy.

"The King has spoken, get more rest and you will be well," Drilgisa said. He turned to Decebal. "Do we make a raid tomorrow?"

"No, no more raids in this territory," Decebal replied. "We only have two hundred men in fighting shape in this camp. The Roman forts are reinforced and their cavalry patrols are more active."

"Then we should move further east," Drilgisa said.

"Yes. In the morning we'll take half our infantry and travel east." The King paused and looked down at Tarbus on his cot. "You will stay here in camp until you are healthy again."

"I hoped to travel with you," Tarbus said, disappointed.

Decebal gave him a patient smile. "You are barely strong enough to stand on your feet and walk to the latrine. When you are healthy again find a horse and join us then."

"I understand," Tarbus acknowledged the order. "I will do as you command."

"Good," the King said. "Your mission now is to get healthy. We shall see you in a few weeks."

*Village of Giura, northeastern Dacia, September 106 AD*

Queen Andrada and a group of two hundred refugees received a very warm welcome in the large farming village of Giura in the northern part of Dacia. The village was located in the territory of the Carpi, a large and powerful group of Dacian tribes. To the north were the Costoboci, another large collection of tribes. Farther east and to the north were the Bastarnae tribes. Still further east were the Roxolani Sarmatian tribes.

Queen Andrada, Diegis, and Buri made the decision that this was the location where the royal refugees from Sarmizegetusa would end their journey and make a new home. The area was surrounded by friendly allies whose military was not depleted compared to the tribes in southern and central Dacia. This territory had never even been scouted by the armies of Rome, much less invaded by the Romans.

The decision to settle in the village was aided by the unexpected presence of Prince Davi of the Roxolani. By chance Davi was in the village visiting his ally Mucatra, the chief of Giura. Mucatra was a tall and garrulous man who was overjoyed to see Queen Andrada and her travelling party stop at his village.

After the evening meal in the chief's dining hall Andrada asked Prince Davi to stay so they could talk. Diegis, Buri, and the High Priest Mircea also gathered around the table. There was a great deal to talk about.

"Mucatra is very happy to have you stay here," Davi told them. "This is a fine location with plenty of rich farmland for the village to grow. The Romans never venture this far north, and if they come they will meet strong resistance."

"I am so very tired of travel," Andrada said. The fatigue showed in her voice. "Perhaps it is an omen that we found you here, Davi."

"I thought the same, My Queen," Mircea said reassuringly. "This is a good omen from Zamolxis."

"This is good land," Buri said. "We will not find any better, I don't think. The soil is very fertile for crops, and I even saw a spot by the river that would grow a fine orchard."

"Well, that settles that!" Diegis said with a laugh. "We are staying and planting an orchard."

"I am glad for it," Davi said. "It will make it much easier for me to visit you than travelling to Sarmizegetusa."

Andrada's mood became very somber. "What do people say of Sarmizegetusa, Davi?"

"That you were betrayed," Davi answered in an even tone. "Thirst kills much faster than hunger. Once you lost your water supply the city was doomed."

"Oh, how I wish I could find the traitor who betrayed us," Diegis said with cold anger.

"Me too," Buri added. "One day we will find out and then justice will be done."

"We must forget about that now," Andrada said. "We have so much work to do here. We must look ahead and not behind."

Davi cleared his throat and turned to the Queen. "A question for you? Although it might be that perhaps I already know the answer."

Andrada gave him a sad smile. "Because his pride will not let him do what most men in his situation would do. He will not give in. Does that answer your question, Davi?"

Davi acknowledged with a small nod. "Yes, it does."

"In matters of pride and stubbornness my brother has few peers," Diegis said. "But without those qualities he would not be Decebal."

"It is a stubbornness driven by honor, Diegis," said Prince Davi. "You were there with me, along with Chief Fynn and Chief Attalu, when he made his vow to us on the training field in Sarmizegetusa. Do you remember?"

"That was many years ago, but of course I remember," Diegis said.

Andrada gave them a questioning look. "Now, this is something I don't know about. What vow, Diegis?"

"Decebal took a vow that he would always lead the fight against Rome. It was a promise made to our allies gathered there."

"He also took a personal vow," Davi continued. "He vowed that for as long as his heart is beating and he has the strength to fight, he will never stop fighting."

"And as we all know well," Andrada said with a soft sigh, "Decebal is a man of his word."

"He will join us here before the winter snows fall," Buri declared with a strong voice. "That is also a promise he made. I will send a messenger to let him know where to find us."

"He will find us when he is ready, Buri," the Queen said. "But yes, it won't hurt to send the messenger anyway."

*Eastern mountains of Dacia, September 106 AD*

King Decebal and General Drilgisa stayed towards the middle of the infantry troop as they moved along the narrow mountain paths. A group of almost a hundred archers, swordsmen, and spearmen were tightly packed in a fast moving column. This group of Dacians had no cavalry scouts of their own and had to rely on stealth and quick movement to avoid attack in enemy territory.

The infantry scout leading the march guided them on a detour around a long and steep rocky ledge. That took them along a path lower on the mountain slope where the timber and vegetation was more sparse and provided less cover.

"I don't like it," Drilgisa said impatiently. "We are too close to the valley here."

"The scout knows the mountain, Drilgisa," Decebal said. "He has traveled this route hundreds of times."

"I don't doubt that he knows the mountain," Drilgisa replied. "What he does not know is where the Roman cavalry are patrolling, and we are exposed here on the lower slopes."

"There is thicker forest just ahead," Decebal pointed out. "We'll climb higher up the slope there."

One of the archers marching next to them turned to the King with a grin. "Does Emperor Trajan march with his men like this, Sire? Or would he rather be carried on a litter?"

"Before he became Caesar, General Trajan used to march with his men exactly like this, soldier," Decebal explained. "He was famous for it because it was not typical for a Roman general."

"Now he prefers a horse, no doubt," Drilgisa said. "They are very sensible men, these Roman nobles."

Three hundred paces in front of the tree line the leading scout suddenly stopped and raised his left arm. The men following stopped also, instantly on alert. Decebal and Drilgisa walked to the front.

"A glint of metal shining among the trees, Sire," the scout reported before he was asked. "Now it is gone."

"Ambush attack," Drilgisa growled.

"You could be right," Decebal said. He turned to the men behind him. "Pass the word, march up the slope. Stay in formation."

The column moved as a unit and began to walk at a brisk pace up the mountain slope. They would forsake the shelter of the trees in order to avoid walking into a likely trap.

Within a minute the column of Roman auxiliary cavalry emerged from the trees at a fast trot. As they approached the group of Dacians the riders fanned out into a line in attack formation.

"Forty or maybe a few more," Drilgisa said.

"Spear line in front!" the King ordered. His archers were already firing at the Romans who closed in rapidly.

This low on the mountain the slope was not steep and not difficult for horses to maneuver. The Romans skirted the front spear line for easier attacks on the Dacian flanks and tried to get behind them to attack the rear. Archers standing in the center of the formation took their shots from close range and more riders and horses went down.

The soldiers fighting with falxes and spears fought with a savage determination to keep the horsemen from breaking through their line. They fought for their lives, but they also fought with the fierce desperation of knowing that in the center of their formation the life of King Decebal was at risk.

Two spearmen fell side by side and a rider shot through the gap. He slashed down with his sword and cut deeply into the neck of an archer. He urged his horse forward two paces and slashed another archer across the back. Archers were near defenseless against cavalry. Other archers near the horseman hurriedly backed away.

Drilgisa fought with a falx. He approached the cavalryman from behind but had no shot at reaching the rider. He lashed out with the long two handed weapon and caught the rider's horse across the left hind leg. The falx hit with the force of a scythe and sliced almost clean through the horse's leg. The panicked animal cried out in pain and fell heavily on its side, trapping the leg of the cavalryman underneath it. An instant later one of the infantrymen drove a spear blade through the helpless rider's neck.

For the first time in many years King Decebal found himself with a falx in his hands fighting for his life. He was a very experienced warrior and a veteran of many battles since he joined the military at the young age of sixteen. He had not been involved in hand to hand fighting, however, since he took the crown of Dacia twenty years ago.

Decebal rushed at a horseman who was slashing down at a Dacian soldier with his cavalry sword. The falx could be used as a slashing weapon or a stabbing weapon with equal effectiveness. Decebal lunged at the Roman and drove the falx deep into the man's side. As he pulled the weapon back he also pulled the rider off his horse. The man fell hard and stayed on the ground unmoving.

The battle was fought at a furious pace and with savage intensity. Twenty of the Roman cavalry were down along with some thirty of the Dacian infantry. This pace favored the Dacians because they were the much larger group.

The captain of cavalry made the decision to stop fighting a losing battle of attrition. He called for a retreat. The horsemen promptly disengaged from the Dacians and moved back close to their original position. For the time being the battle was paused.

"Up the mountain!" King Decebal ordered. "Carry the wounded. The Romans will follow but they will not fight us now."

"They will fight us later," Drilgisa said. "Two riders rode off to the west. They will fetch reinforcements, no doubt."

"No doubt," Decebal agreed. "We'll deal with that later but first let's move higher up the mountain. We'll have better cover and make it more difficult for their horses."

Drilgisa glanced up at the sun overhead. "It is near mid-day. We'll have to fight one more battle today, I think. Then we can lose them in the night."

Decebal gave a nod. "If Zamolxis wills it, let it be so."

In the mid-afternoon the Dacian troops stopped for a brief rest. Climbing up the side of a mountain was very strenuous work even for men trained for battle who were used to travelling and fighting on mountainous terrain. The summer heat of August gave way to the cooler weather of September, but even so the climb was draining.

"Water and small rations only," Drilgisa told the soldiers. "We are being pursued so we must stay on the move. Stay on the alert."

King Decebal gave field command of the troops to General Drilgisa. The General knew the men better and they knew what he expected of them. Decebal also knew, from long years of experience fighting together, that when it came to battlefield instincts there was no one better than Drilgisa.

"There is cavalry following," Decebal said. "They will attack again as soon as they are reinforced."

"I think so too," Drilgisa agreed. "And we have no idea how many more cavalry patrols they have in the area."

"No matter. We'll fight them off one more time."

Drilgisa took a look down the mountain slope, satisfied that no enemy was in close pursuit. He turned to catch the King's eye. "This may be a poor time to ask, Decebal, but how long are we going to do this? We should not put your life at risk this way."

"I ask myself the same question," Decebal replied. "And I always come to the same answer."

"Which is?"

"That we must fight for as long as necessary to give our people hope for as long as necessary."

"I see," Drilgisa said. "But even so there must be an end sometime. Do you agree?"

Decebal gave him a grim smile. "Everything comes to an end sometime, Drilgisa. Nothing lasts forever."

"Very well. Then you must tell me when that time comes, Sire. At this moment I cannot see it." Drilgisa raised himself to stand up. "We should get the men moving."

"Yes, let's keep moving. Two more hours of climbing and they will have to leave their horses behind."

Within half an hour Roman cavalry were spotted behind the Dacian troops and also along the flanks of their position. The riders stayed out of bow range but moved faster than the infantry and would soon outflank them. This would be the decisive battle.

"We must fight them here," King Decebal said.

Drilgisa nodded his agreement and turned to address the men. "Form a circle! Defensive formation! Wounded men in the center!"

The infantry moved quickly but maintained discipline. They formed a tight circle, two rows of spearmen and swordsmen in front with archers behind them. They had a dozen wounded. The men still capable of fighting were almost half the number that fought off the first attack hours before. They did not know how many cavalry they faced now because many riders were still shielded by the trees.

The Dacian archers opened fire first when the riders came into view. The cavalry charged them and initiated their attack by throwing their javelins and spears. The defending spearmen and swordsmen carried shields, but the archers did not. The tightly packed Dacian infantry made easy targets and many fell in the initial onslaught.

"Hold steady!" King Decebal encouraged his troops.

"Kill the bastards!" Drilgisa shouted. "No one gets through!"

The cavalry attacked from all sides. Once more the battle turned into a furious and savage struggle. Archers fired their bows at the poorly armored auxiliary cavalry from close range and hit torsos, necks, and faces. Spearmen killed horses and then the riders who fell with them. The ground around the Dacian circle became littered with bodies and slick with blood.

In the early stages of the fight the slaughter was even sided. There were not enough horsemen to overwhelm the defenders completely but the Dacians took heavy casualties. As more front line Dacian fighters went down their defensive circle pulled back and became smaller. Some Roman attackers were finding gaps.

Drilgisa met attackers head on with his falx. He was bleeding from a cut on his shoulder, and his face and chest were splashed with the blood of dead Roman cavalry and horses. For a while he found himself fighting next to Decebal, back to back. Both men were tall, powerfully built, skilled warriors. In past battles both had killed fully armored legionnaires with their falxes, and auxiliary cavalry were a much easier kill.

Two spearmen moved closer to flank the King and provide him some protection. "Leave me, protect the archers!" Decebal shouted at them. The men obeyed and moved away although, as Decebal saw unhappily, there were not many archers left to protect. There were no more than thirty Dacian troops still standing and able to fight. There were also many fewer Romans still in the fight. The battle was taking a heavy toll on both sides.

Decebal lunged with his falx at a Roman fighting with a spear and made a slashing cut across the man's upper leg. Smartly the rider backed away, then kept his distance out of reach of Decebal's falx while looking for an opening to attack.

The King waited in a defensive posture, falx leveled out in front of him. A javelin thrown from somewhere to his right pierced deeply into Decebal's upper leg. He grunted from the sharp pain and turned swiftly to meet the horseman who threw the javelin and was now rushing at him with drawn sword.

Decebal would have met the horseman head on with the tip of his falx but Drilgisa reached the rider first. The General swung his falx in a high sweeping arc to meet the torso of the rider, just underneath the rib cage. The blade sliced through his stomach and dragged him off his horse. The rider fell heavily to the ground as his panicked horse galloped away.

Drilgisa moved quickly past Decebal to head off the Roman horseman with the spear. A Dacian spearman joined him as well to defend the King. The cavalryman backed off two paces, then listened as a bugle call signaled a Roman retreat. The dwindling number of cavalry broke off the fight again and rode back down the slope, still within sight but out of bow range.

Decebal found that his right leg gave away and would no longer support his weight. He slowly lowered himself to his knees, planting the long handle of the falx on the ground for balance. The Roman javelin was still deeply imbedded in his upper leg.

"We have to take that out," Drilgisa told him. "It looks deep enough to have hit bone."

Decebal agreed with a nod. "Yes, take the damn thing out."

The Dacian medic was dead so Drilgisa took over medical duties. He used both hands to pull the lance out slowly, careful not to inflict more damage to the King's leg. The wound bled steadily and stained the leg of the woolen pants.

Decebal sat on the ground while another soldier wrapped a strip of cloth around his upper leg to bandage the wound and reduce the bleeding. The ground all around them was littered with the bodies of dead and dying men and horses.

Drilgisa took a knee beside Decebal. His face was sweaty and streaked with blood, his expression grim. They were both looking down the mountain side where the Romans were gathering.

"They will be back," the King said. The pain in his leg was sharp but still bearable. What hurt worse was the terrible gut-wrenching knowledge that he could no longer fight on one good leg.

"Yes, they will," Drilgisa agreed. "They wait for reinforcements."

"The reinforcements will come," Decebal said. "We cannot lose them now, so we'll make our final stand here."

"No, My King," declared a nearby voice in a strong tone.

The man who spoke walked over to stand in front of Decebal and Drilgisa. He was one of the older veterans. The man was stained with sweat and blood and looked exhausted.

"Forgive me, Sire, but I must speak," the man continued. "Those of us who are left will stay and hold off the Romans for as long as we can. My King, you must leave now and escape before the next attack."

Decebal looked the soldier in the eye and shook his head. "I will not desert you."

"This man is right," Drilgisa said, giving the veteran a respectful nod. "You must not fall into the hands of the Romans."

The soldier turned to Drilgisa, his voice urgent. "General, you must leave with the King immediately. Go, we beg you. Only you can guide our King to safety. We will give you as much time as we can."

Decebal grimaced with frustration but he knew the soldier was right. The King of Dacia could not be allowed to be taken prisoner.

"Here, soldier, take my falx," Decebal said. "Fight well. You honor me greatly with your loyalty and your sacrifice."

"All Dacia is honored by your service for all these years, My King. Now go, I beg you. There is nothing more you can do for us here."

Tiberius Claudius Maximus arrived late to the cavalry's pursuit of the Dacian troops. The Roman auxiliary cavalry were already repelled twice in attacks against the enemy, but they still maintained close pursuit and kept the Dacians in sight. Now it would be up to Tiberius Maximus, leading the one hundred and twenty cavalry of the ala II Pannoniorum, to finish the Dacians.

Maximus was a highly respected and highly decorated veteran of the Roman cavalry. He fought under Emperor Domitian in the first Dacian wars as a member of the cavalry of Legio VII Claudia. As he got older and his regular term of military service expired, he took the very unusual step for a Roman citizen of signing up to serve with a unit of auxiliary cavalry made up of foreigners.

Now well over forty years of age, also very unusual for the cavalry, Tiberius had served as a leader of auxiliary cavalry in both of Trajan's wars with Dacia. His authority was never questioned, and when he arrived at the site of battle on the mountainside he took immediate charge of the fight.

"Sir, we think that King Decebalus is with these Dacian troops," one of the horsemen told Maximus when he arrived. "One of our men thought he recognized the King, but he was uncertain. The man was killed in the last attack unfortunately."

"If that is true then we are all rich men!" Maximus exclaimed. "Caesar will be very generous to the men who capture Decebalus."

"How will we know if it's him?"

"I saw Decebalus at Aquae when he came to make the peace treaty with Caesar. He is a tall man and broadly built, like Caesar. I will know him when I see him."

"Yes, sir. What are your orders?"

"We'll attack from all sides," Tiberius ordered. "Cut off escape in all directions. Take prisoners! I want Decebalus taken alive."

The cavalry attack overwhelmed the Dacian troops in quick order. After inspecting the Dacian dead and the few prisoners who were taken alive, Tiberius Maximus found to his great disappointment that King Decebalus was not among them.

"Spread out and search the forest," Maximus ordered. "He is on foot and could not have gone very far."

One of his scouts ran over, excited by his news. "We found a blood trail, sir." He pointed uphill. "Over there, heading up the mountain."

"Very good! I would also be heading up the mountain if I was him. Scouts, with me! Let's go find Decebalus."

After half an hour of walking up the mountainside King Decebal knew that he was near the point of exhaustion. He lost a considerable amount of blood from the deep wound in his leg. Even with one arm draped around the shoulder of Drilgisa for support he struggled to keep moving forward.

"Wait," the King said. "Stop here."

Decebal sat down on the ground and leaned back against the trunk of a large oak tree. Drilgisa knelt on one knee beside him. They listened to the sounds of the Roman cavalry below, still some distance away but slowly gaining ground on them.

Drilgisa took a look higher up the slope. "We should move higher. The cavalry will reach us here soon."

"No," Decebal said in a calm but firm voice. "I can go no further. My leg will not carry me, and you cannot carry me."

Drilgisa gave him a pained look. "I will not leave you here. We stay and fight then."

"I cannot fight on one leg," the King said. He spoke in a tone of resignation and acceptance, not sadness. "Earlier today you asked me, when will the end come? Well, this is my end."

Drilgisa cursed, angry and frustrated. He took a quick look down the mountain slope again. There were no enemy troops yet in sight but he could hear them.

"I will stay with you, then."

"No. You cannot fight them all, so you at least must escape and continue the resistance." The King paused and looked Drilgisa in the eye. "The wise man knows when to fight and when to retreat. You will not sacrifice yourself needlessly, Drilgisa. I command you to escape."

Drilgisa looked away. When he turned back and spoke again his voice was thick with emotion. "Do not let them capture you, Sire."

"I will not be a slave," Decebal said. "No one will capture me. It is not my fate to be paraded in chains through the streets of Rome."

Drilgisa gave him a small silent nod. "Then we will meet again in the kingdom of Zamolxis."

Drilgisa held out his right hand. Decebal gripped his friend's hand and shook it firmly, not as a monarch but as a brother in arms. The two men had fought many battles side by side, too many to count. They knew this one was the last.

A horse neighed not far away, pricked by a thorn bush.

Decebal let go of Drilgisa's hand. He drew his sica and laid it flat across his thigh. He looked Drilgisa in the eye again. "This is my fate and I accept it. Your fate is not to die here today. Go north and find my family. Protect them."

Drilgisa gave him a small smile as he stood up to leave. "Then let that be your final command, King Decebal."

"I will see you again in the kingdom of Zamolxis," Decebal said.

"Farewell, my friend."

Drilgisa turned and walked away up the mountain slope. He was quickly lost out of sight among the trees.

The forest was quiet now. The birds in the trees went silent with the approach of men and horses. Some among the Roman cavalry shouted questions and directions to each other.

Decebal looked up at the sky, clear and blue beyond the treetops. A single white cloud floated lazily by. His thoughts drifted to his family. They would be safe now in the northern part of Dacia, led there by Buri and Diegis. His lovely wife Queen Andrada, so wise and strong. His beautiful daughters now grown into young women. Zia with her son Brasus, a family of her own. Adila such a fearless warrior. Dorin, his last son, growing into a young man. They would be safe because Trajan would not carry the war that far north.

A small movement to his right caught Decebal's eye and made him turn his head in that direction. Twenty paces away, half hidden in the thick shrubbery, a lone grey wolf stood unmoving and stared at him. It showed no trace of fear or aggression, only curiosity at the sight of this lone injured man. For a moment man and wolf stared at each other in silence.

Decebal laughed softly to himself. "Zamolxis, do you send a sign? Have you come for me?"

The sound of horses drawing near startled the wolf. It turned swiftly and silently and vanished into the forest.

"Over there!" a voice yelled. Riders urged their horses to go faster.

"Take him alive!" Tiberius Maximus shouted.

Decebal raised the sica to his throat, the wooden handle gripped firmly in his right hand. That morning, the same as every morning, he sharpened the blade to a razor's edge. He took in a slow deep breath, inhaling the sweet pine smell of the forest. His arm drew the sica from left to right, swift and hard.

# Chapter 19

# Vae Victis

*Ranisstorum, Dacia, September 106 AD*

Plans for organizing the new Roman province of Dacia would start with building a new capital city, the Emperor declared. Sarmizegetusa was now a charred ruin. It was also located too high up in the mountains to serve as a convenient location for a Roman governor.

Trajan moved his command center and his staff to the Dacian plains, twenty miles south of Sarmizegetusa. His legions needed easy access to large amounts of food and water and grazing land for the animals. The Dacian plains were abundant in those resources.

"The new capital will be called Ulpia Traiana Sarmizegetusa," the Emperor told his friend Licinius Sura. "It will be home to my veterans who serve in Dacia. When they retire they will be given farmland to settle on and raise their families."

"A reward well deserved," Sura said. "There is plenty of farmland here for Roman colonies."

"Dacia is still the land of wheat and honey, as Alexander called it four hundred years ago," Trajan said. "To our great benefit that has not changed."

Sura gave the Emperor a small bow. "All the more to your credit. No one else has accomplished what you have accomplished here."

Trajan waved his hand dismissively. "I have no need for flattery, Licinius. We have a great deal of work to do here before I return to Rome. We have a new province of Dacia to build."

"Indeed. There are many more Dacian nobles now coming to us to surrender, and many offer their assistance in the new Dacia. Some even bring a few ingots of gold."

"Ah, I don't care about a few ingots of gold!" Trajan said irritably. "We must find the royal treasury of Decebalus. That is where the real gold and silver will be."

Sura was about to reply when he was interrupted by three men who entered the room in some haste. Hadrian had a serious look on his face. Titus Lucullus looked somber and strangely subdued. Trajan recognized the third man as Tiberius Maximus, the officer of cavalry that he once personally rewarded for meritorious service. Maximus carried a bundle wrapped in a red officer's cape.

"Caesar," Hadrian announced, "on this momentous day Tiberius Maximus brings a gift for you."

Trajan pointed Tiberius to a table. "Show me," he instructed. Based on the behavior and tone of the men he already knew what the prize was.

Maximus gave a bow and very reverently placed his bundle, wrapped in a Roman cape stained reddish brown with dried blood, on the Emperor's table.

"Remove the cloth," the Emperor ordered.

Maximus did so. "Caesar, I bring you the head of the former King Decebalus of Dacia."

Trajan stared for a long silent moment at the face of his most formidable enemy. The eyes were closed in death and the expression on the face was calm and peaceful. Even in death Decebalus carried the same sense of dignity and majesty that he showed when the two leaders faced each other in Aquae.

Trajan's first reaction of relief and satisfaction was also tinged with sadness and regret that his most capable enemy should end up like this. He hoped for one more confrontation, perhaps one last conversation with this man. Now the opportunity was lost and he felt cheated.

"I wished that he be captured, not killed," the Emperor said to Maximus. "Was that not possible?"

"No, Caesar. I gave the order to take him alive but Decebalus was dead when I reached him. He took his own life with his own blade."

Trajan glanced around at his advisors, a small smile on his face. "The man had a talent for defying my wishes, to the very end."

Sura was thinking more pragmatically. "The outcome is the same, Marcus. With Decebalus gone the threat of Dacia is diminished."

"Diminished perhaps, but not gone," the Emperor said. "He leaves a legacy that will inspire others. He died in his own way, the Dacian way, and that now becomes part of his legacy."

"My deep apologies for having failed you, Caesar," Maximus said. "It would have been better to capture him alive."

Trajan turned to face the cavalryman. "No need for apologies, Maximus. You did well to find Decebalus even if you could not take him alive. You will be decorated in front of the legions for this."

"I am greatly honored, Caesar," Tiberius replied. He saluted, then turned and briskly walked away. His mission was done.

Titus Lucullus gave a nod towards the table. "What is to be done with the remains of King Decebalus, Caesar?"

"Take them to Rome," Trajan replied. "Display them before the Senate and the people. That is your mission, Lucullus."

"Yes, Caesar. And following that?"

Trajan paused for only a brief moment. "Let his head be tossed down the Gemonian stairs, as befits a great enemy of Rome."

Hadrian agreed. "The Senate will rejoice and celebrate, and so will the people."

The Emperor turned to his young general. "You will also travel to Rome along with Lucullus. Inform the Senate of the end of the war and of our work in Dacia now."

"Yes, Caesar. I am always happy to be the bearer of good news," Hadrian replied with a smile.

News of the death of King Decebal spread quickly across Dacia. The common people met the news with sadness and went into a period of mourning. The people in the territory occupied by Rome resigned themselves to the reality that the Romans were there to stay. Dacians in the unoccupied territories reacted with a mix of sadness and also defiant anger. Although the Romans managed to kill King Decebal they would never kill his spirit. His legacy of resistance lived on and many people vowed to fight on against Rome.

The reaction of some of the nobility of Dacia was less combative. They had more to lose and thus more reason to work with Rome. A number of Dacian nobles found their way to Trajan's headquarters.

"Caesar, there is a man who just arrived who might be a great help to us," Licinius Sura announced. "A Dacian noble."

"What Dacian noble?"

"I don't know details, he just surrendered to Maximus. I sent word to Laberius to bring him here. Ah, here he comes now."

Laberius Maximus entered, followed by two well-dressed Dacians who appeared to be man and wife. The man was middle aged, of stocky build and florid appearance. He had a hooked nose and bushy eyebrows that looked vaguely familiar to Trajan. The woman was younger, of medium height and very thin. Her heavy use of green eye shadow gave her an exotic foreign appearance.

The Dacians bowed low before Trajan as Maximus introduced them. "Caesar, this man calls himself Lord Bicilis. He claims that he spoke with you once, at Aquae. His wife is Lady Zena."

Trajan's curiosity and attention perked up. "Bicilis. I do not recall the name but I remember your nervous eyebrows when you kneeled before me at Aquae. You were an envoy from King Decebalus?"

"Yes, Caesar," Bicilis said and bowed again. "I brought a message from King Decebal regarding the peace terms with Rome."

"I remember now. And what message do you have for me now?"

Bicilis shot a nervous glance at Zena. She gestured with her eyes, encouraging him to proceed.

"Caesar, I can lead you to where King Decebal buried his gold."

*Sargetia River, Dacia, September 106 AD*

The narrow Sargetia River was not very far from Sarmizegetusa. It ran swift and cold, fed by mountain streams. The river bottom was covered with pebbles and rocks worn smooth by the running water over centuries of time.

Bicilis led General Maximus, accompanied by several construction crews and a cohort of legionnaires for security, to a location where there was a small bend in the river. It was a peaceful and remote area distant from any roads or villages.

"It is here," Bicilis told Maximus, gesturing at a spot on the river. "King Decebal had soldiers dig a small canal and divert the river here. After they buried the gold and silver under the riverbed they directed the river back on its original course."

"Very clever," Maximus said with admiration. He gave Bicilis a hard look. "If you are right then Caesar will make you a very wealthy man. But if you are wrong and we find no gold, you will be torn to pieces by wild horses. Do you understand this?"

Bicilis gave a nod, looking grim. "I understand, General. The royal treasury is here, it has not been moved. King Decebal believed that it was safer to keep it buried here than to move it."

"Very well. Let's find out, shall we." Maximus turned to the chief of the construction crews. "You heard the Dacian. We must dig another canal and divert the river here to expose the riverbed. I want this completed by tomorrow, no later. Get to work!"

Emperor Trajan arrived three days later with the Praetorian Guard, more workers, and a long line of empty transport wagons drawn by oxen and mules. What he found on the bank of the Sargetia River at first astonished him, then filled him with great joy.

Long rows of sturdy wood and metal storage chests were neatly lined up along the near side of the river. They stretched out into the distance. Maximus greeted the Emperor with a grin on his face.

"What is inside them?" Trajan asked.

"One in three of these chests are filled with gold, Caesar," Laberius told him. "The others are filled with silver. Some of it is coin, most of it is bullion."

"How much of it is there, in your estimation?"

"Tons. From what we have dug up so far, easily one hundred tons of gold and double that in silver." Maximus gestured at the muddy, dug up river bed. "And as you can see, we are still digging."

Licinius Sura gave a low whistle of amazement. "It's no wonder they were able to cover the pillars of their temple with a sheath of gold. That was a mere pittance for them."

Trajan clasped Maximus on the shoulder. "Make sure to find all of it, Laberius. Do not leave any behind."

"Of course, Caesar. Our boys know what they're doing."

"Good. Also find more wagons for transport. We will need many more wagons, and a great many oxen and mules."

*Rome, November 106 AD*

The Senate of Rome became accustomed over the years to receiving first hand reports about developments in Dacia from Publius Aelius Hadrianus. They knew that the Emperor counted on him to be his envoy to the Senate. Hadrian was respected by the Roman nobility because he was an accomplished general in his own right, but also because he was a member of Trajan's family. It would be foolish and dangerous to show a lack of respect towards a man who might one day become Trajan's heir and the next Caesar.

Hadrian stood in the middle of the floor of the packed Senate House knowing that he had their full attention. He was an imposing physical presence, built so tall and muscular that some referred to him as Young Hercules. Beyond that he showed a confidence that came from knowing that he spoke for Caesar.

Hadrian addressed the assembled senators in a clear and loud voice. "Fathers of the nation! I bring greetings and news from Caesar. The campaign in Dacia is over. Caesar has won a great victory."

This was not news to them, but still every single senator rose to his feet to applaud and cheer Hadrian's historic announcement. This final victory over Dacia was twenty years in the making.

"After a majestic siege Caesar captured and destroyed their holy city of Sarmizegetusa. Now Caesar makes plans and arrangements for governing Rome's newest and wealthiest province, the province of Dacia Traiana!"

The senators rose again with cheering and applause. He allowed them a short while to express their approval.

"As the newly elected praetor for next year it will be my honor and my happy duty to plan the festivals celebrating Caesar's victories in Dacia. We shall surpass the generosity of Emperor Titus, who gave the people of Rome one hundred days of games. Caesar's festivals to celebrate the conquest of Dacia will be unmatched!"

This grand ambition impressed even Trajan's closest supporters. Hadrian basked in their applause.

"Fathers of the nation, now we go to perform a sacred ceremony before Jupiter and Mars and the people of Rome. Come with me to the Scalae Gemoniae!"

The Gemonian stairs, also known as the Stairs of Mourning, were a steep flight of stairs in the Forum built into the side of a hill. They led from an execution site at the top down to the street level below. The heads of executed criminals and enemies of Rome were tossed down the stone steps to shouts of approval from the cheering crowds. The ritual was both a demonstration of Roman justice and also a warning to all who dared oppose the might of Rome.

On a gray afternoon the ceremony was repeated one more time, on this occasion with the hated King Decebalus of Dacia. A large crowd gathered in the Forum to bear witness to this eagerly awaited event. Decebalus of Dacia was a name known to most Romans and hated by many Romans because he was the cause of Rome losing so many of her sons.

At the end of the ceremony a Roman officer walked with a calm dignity through the large crowd in the Forum. He carried a plain wooden box under his arm. The man walked to the bottom of the Gemonian stairs, bent down to retrieve the head of the former king from the ground, wrapped it in a cloth, placed it inside the box, and turned and walked away.

Few people in the crowd recognized the officer as Titus Lucullus, current advisor on Dacia to Emperor Trajan, past envoy of Emperor Domitian, traveler to Sarmizegetusa to negotiate peace terns with King Decebalus of Dacia.

Tanidela, sister of Decebal, was very aware of the scheduled public ceremony at the Stairs of Mourning. She had no wish to be anywhere near it and discouraged her two servants from mentioning it. She thought it better to keep her daughter Tyra unaware of the fate of her royal uncle. The girl had no memories of her Dacian relatives. She knew however that she was the niece of King Decebal and she would find the events now taking place in the city troubling.

Tanidela was still treated as a guest of Emperor Trajan. She was generously provided with all that she and Tyra needed. She no longer felt comfortable living in the royal palace with Trajan's family and moved into a house in the city that was owned by her friend Salonia Matidia. Salonia was the niece of Emperor Trajan. She remained a loyal friend and kept Tanidela and Tyra under her protection.

Tanidela was provided with two slaves to be her servants, one male and one female. They were there to keep watch on her as much as to look after her, Tanidela thought. She did not mind and did not consider it to be a problem now. She had no hopes of being set free unless Emperor Trajan had a change of heart to set her free.

Tyra was growing up Roman. She played Roman games with her Roman friends, learned Roman stories and songs, and learned to like Roman foods. Tanidela insisted still that she learn to speak and to write in both Latin and Dacian. Like most young children Tyra was a sponge for learning languages and the lessons came easy to her.

Tanidela was giving her daughter a lesson in writing the Dacian alphabet when the teaching was interrupted by their male servant.

"Domina, a visitor at the door," the man announced.

That took Tanidela by surprise. "Who would be visiting now?"

"An officer, Domina," the servant replied. "He did not give his name but says that you know him."

"Very well, show him in." Tanidela caught Tyra's attention. "We will finish your lesson later. We have a visitor now."

"Yes, Mama," Tyra replied. A moment later she looked up curiously at the powerfully built but kind looking man in military uniform who just entered the room. He walked with the somewhat stiff and formal bearing of a lifelong soldier of officer rank. Her mother seemed not to be concerned or afraid, so Tyra was not afraid.

"Titus Lucullus," Tanidela greeted the man politely. "I am very surprised to see you here."

"It is good to see you again, Lady Tanidela," Titus said in return. "I am sorry however to see you on such an unhappy occasion."

Tanidela smiled grimly. "It is dreadful. I try to keep it to myself and not talk about it." Her eyes flicked briefly in the direction of Tyra.

"Mama, who is this man?" the girl asked. Along with her mother's green eyes she also inherited qualities of character that would make her honest and bold in dealing with people.

"His name is Titus and he is a soldier of Rome. A very long time ago, when you were just a baby, he rescued us and possibly saved our lives when we were attacked by angry soldiers."

"You are Tyra, I remember you," Lucullus said with a smile. "I found you and your mother then only because you were crying so loudly I could hear you from a long distance away."

"I don't remember that," Tyra said.

Tanidela crouched down and looked into her daughter's eyes. "No, you were too young then to remember what happened. Will you go to the kitchen now and ask Valentina to fix you a snack? I wish to speak with Titus for a while."

"Yes, Mama." Tyra gave her mother a kiss on the cheek and walked obediently away to find the woman who prepared their meals.

Once her daughter left the room Tanidela allowed herself to show the sorrow that she felt. She kept her dignity and physical composure but slow tears rolled down her cheeks.

"What they did," Tanidela began, then stopped and slowly shook her head. "He did not deserve that."

"It is the custom in Rome," Lucullus explained. "In some ways the ceremony recognizes Decebal as a worthy enemy of Rome."

"It seems to me like a ritual to humiliate a defeated enemy. What is that saying you Romans have about the vanquished?"

"Vae victis," Titus said. "It means – "

"Woe to the vanquished," Tanidela answered for him. "Ah, yes. I heard it said to me already in reference to my brother's death."

Lucullus frowned. "I apologize for that, Tanidela. It was callous and undignified to say that to you."

"I am beyond any pain caused by words," she replied. "But tell me, Titus, why are you here now? Surely not to tell me about how my brother was humiliated."

Lucullus gave her a kind smile. "No, my lady, I am not here to cause you pain. I am here to grieve with you. And I am here to help you arrange a funeral."

Tanidela and Titus Lucullus buried the remains of King Decebal wrapped in a plain funeral shroud, in the Dacian tradition. They chose a burial site in the middle of an isolated grove of trees on the banks of the Tiber River. On the advice of Lucullus they went during the night when there were no other people around, to avoid the gaze or suspicion of the curious.

After the grave was covered Tanidela softly murmured a Dacian funeral prayer. She knew that Decebal's spirit was in the heaven of Zamolxis, but her brother had also been fastidious about following religious ceremonies such as funeral rites. She was also disappointed that her knowledge of the prayers and ceremonies was so limited.

"I am sorry, Brother, that I could not do better," she said to the grave. "I would not find a priest of Zamolxis in Rome."

"Priest or no priest, I think that your brother would be pleased by what you have done for him," Lucullus said.

"Thank you for helping me in this," Tanidela said with heartfelt gratitude. "I will rest easier knowing that my brother had a proper burial."

"You are most welcome. I did this for both of you. King Decebal deserved a respectful funeral."

"I am grateful for your show of respect, truly."

Titus looked out over the dark waters of the Tiber, lost in thought. "When I was in Sarmizegetusa I paid the same respects to Vezina. That was done at the request of Caesar."

"Oh? I was not aware," said Tanidela. "Poor old Vezina. How did he die?"

"He was killed by a legionnaire who mistook him for a simple priest. The soldier was executed for his mistake."

"Vezina would have been offended to know that. Death upon death, and to what end?"

Titus gave a small shrug. "Caesar was angry that Vezina was not captured alive."

"Did Caesar request that you bury Decebal as well?" she wondered.

Titus shook his head. "No, Caesar has no notion that I helped you in this funeral. He would not be as forgiving about Decebal as he was about Vezina, I think."

Tanidela turned away with a sigh. "How strange you men are sometimes when it comes to war. Such ungovernable pride. Such foolishness that only leads to more death."

Lucullus allowed her comment to rest in the air between them for a moment before he replied. "That is perhaps the nature of men. But know this, my lady. Your brother Decebal was the most proud man I ever knew. He gave Caesar his greatest challenge and he cost Rome the lives of many thousands of men."

"I know this," Tanidela replied. "I am glad that the killing is over."

"So am I," Titus agreed. "At least for now the killing is over."

She glanced up at him with mild surprise. "Do you think the war will continue? Who would still fight it?"

"The pride of King Decebal is the pride of Dacia. Some Dacians will continue to fight Rome."

"It must end sometime, Titus. If not then we will kill each other forever."

"It is in the hands of the gods," Lucullus said. "Isn't that how you Dacians say it?"

"No," Tanidela replied. "It is not in the hands of the gods. It is in the hands of men."

# Chapter 20

# In Free Dacia

*Village of Giura, northeast Dacia, November 106 AD*

Dacians from the central regions and the eastern mountains migrated to the northern parts of the kingdom. The lower one third of Dacia was now occupied by Roman armies and being re-made by Emperor Trajan into the Roman province of Dacia Traiana. The upper two thirds of Decebal's kingdom was not attacked or occupied by Rome and never would be. The people living in the northern territories still called their ancestral land Dacia. Some called it Free Dacia.

Queen Andrada settled into a modest house of five rooms that she shared with her children Zia, Adila, and Dorin. It lacked the opulence and certainly the spaciousness of the royal palace in Sarmizegetusa, but this house was cozy and comfortable. In the back was ample room for a large garden to grow vegetables, herbs, and flowers.

Next door was a similar house where Diegis lived with his young daughter Ana and with Buri. Next to them was a modest dwelling that housed the Christian family of Zelma, Nicolae, and Lia. The High Priest Mircea and many of the Priests of Zamolxis settled into the village temple. All of the city Dacians were slowly getting used to the simple and relaxed routines of village life. The winter crops were planted and the village settled in to wait for the arrival of winter.

Mircea and the village chief Mucatra called on Queen Andrada for a visit. They found her with her children, all seated together at the table in the large room that served as their sitting room and dining room. A single female servant lived with them to help with cooking and other household chores. The woman was clearing the table as the family finished their noonday meal.

"Join us," Andrada invited the newcomers. "There is just enough room around the table for all of us."

"Thank you, My Queen," Mircea said. "Chief Mucatra has a request for you and the royal family."

The Chief gave a small bow towards the Queen but shyly remained standing. "It is a request from all the people in the village, if we may have your permission and your blessing."

"Please don't hesitate to speak," Andrada encouraged him. "What is it that you seek permission for?"

"We wish to give a pomana for King Decebal to honor his spirit and his memory. There will be people coming from other villages nearby who also wish to attend."

Andrada looked around the table at the faces of her children. Each reacted to the Chief's words with expressions of sadness and pain, but each also seemed pleased with the idea.

"Of course you have our blessing, Chief Mucatra," Andrada told him graciously. "You honor Decebal and us with the ceremony."

"Dacia can never repay the debt it owes to the King and to your family, my lady," Mucatra replied. "This funeral service is a small way to show our gratitude and to join with you in grieving for our King."

"All of Dacia grieves," Mircea said. "I will instruct the priests of Zamolxis to hold funeral services in other villages."

"When shall we have this service?" Zia wondered. She took Brasus from her lap and put him down on the floor so the restless boy could run around.

"A week from today," Mucatra said. "There will be many hundreds of people attending and we'll need time to prepare all the food."

"Very well, a week from now," Andrada agreed. "Traditions must be respected, as my husband always said."

"Decebal will look down on us from the heaven of Zamolxis," the High Priest assured them. "He will be pleased."

The rider approaching the village from the south road had a grim and intense look on his face. This gave him a fearsome appearance that made others hurry to clear out of his path. He was the lead rider in a column of twenty men, some horse archers and some infantry who simply wanted to reach their destination quicker. The rider rode a big stallion that was captured from the Roman cavalry, not one of the smaller Dacian or Scythian horses that were preferred by the horse archers. To be captured by the Romans in possession of such a horse would earn him an immediate execution.

Adila and Boian were out exercising their horses and thus were the first to meet the column of riders. They rode up to greet them and the column stopped in the middle of the street.

"General Drilgisa, welcome to the village of Giura," Boian said and gave him a salute.

"Greetings Boian and Adila," Drilgisa replied. "So I must be in the right place, eh?"

"You are in the right place," Adila told him. "Your men will find the stables at the other end of town. You however should come with me. Mother will be very anxious to talk with you."

"Of course, Adila," Drilgisa said in a gentle voice. "Lead the away and I will follow."

"Were you with him at the end?" Andrada asked. She found that she had no more tears, only sad and numb acceptance.

"No, not to the very end. He ordered me to leave and not sacrifice my life in vain," Drilgisa told her in a somber voice. "Decebal's last words to me were that I should come here and find you to give you my protection."

She gave him a small smile. "That's what I would expect him to say. And you were right to obey the order. You could not save him then and sacrificing your life needlessly would have been a sin."

"He died the way he wished to die, with a sword in his hand and never surrendering to Rome."

"That is not the way I wished for him to die," Andrada said. "My wish would have been that he died at a very old age, on his deathbed, while holding my hand."

"Yes, my lady," Drilgisa said. "That is how many ordinary men die if they are fortunate. Decebal was not an ordinary man and his fate was not to live an ordinary life."

"I know all this, Drilgisa," she said with a heavy sigh. "It still does not make it any easier to bear the loss."

"How are you faring, my lady?" he asked.

"I am resigned to living a new life here, as we all must," the Queen replied. "The Dacia that we knew no longer exists."

Drilgisa agreed with a small nod. "And will you carry on with your duties as monarch from here?"

"No, there is no longer a need for that," Andrada replied. "When we lived in Sarmizegetusa Dacia needed a king and queen to keep the nation unified. That Dacia, as I said, is no more."

Drilgisa frowned. "Do our people no longer need a queen?"

"The people here don't need a queen, General Drilgisa. They are governed well enough by their village chiefs as they have been for hundreds of years."

"I understand. When it comes to knowing what is best for our people I will not question your wisdom, my lady."

"And what do you do now, General? Will you carry on the fight?"

Drilgisa paused for a moment. "It is now a very different fight. The Romans have ceased all aggression and will not come any further north. And if they do the Carpi and the Costoboci will kill a great many Romans. The Sarmatians are now feeling threatened and are putting up resistance to Roman aggression."

"Are we at stalemate again?" Andrada asked.

"They will not advance further and we cannot drive them out. So it is a kind of stalemate, I suppose."

"Then let us accept that as a kind of peace," the Queen declared. "It means that most Dacians will live free. We will not be ruled by Rome or any other outside power."

"I don't know if peace is ever possible between Dacia and Rome, Andrada," Drilgisa said. "Perhaps the best we can hope for is to cease fighting for a while."

Buri enlisted the help of Dorin and some of the other village youths to gather dry wood for a large bonfire in the village square. The village was hosting General Drilgisa and his men for the next week. In the evening the men of the village and their guests gathered around the bonfire to drink wine and tell stories. Dacians loved the light from a big bonfire. The wood for this bonfire was piled high and would burn through the night.

"I was fighting further to the south in the pass at Tapae," General Drilgisa told the men gathered around him, "so I did not see the fight with my own eyes."

"The same for me," Diegis said. "I was at the south end of the pass attacking the rear of the Roman column. However Buri was there with Decebal. Isn't that right, Buri?"

"I was," Buri replied. "I was standing no more than twenty paces away from them the entire fight."

"Tell us!" Chief Mucatra urged him. "Describe for us how the fight went. Do you still remember it well?"

"It was twenty years ago but I remember it like it was yesterday," Buri said, making himself comfortable and taking a long sip of wine. "General Decebal, he was not yet King then, offered General Fuscus the chance to surrender. By that point in the battle it was obvious that the Romans were losing badly and their entire army would be destroyed if Fuscus did not surrender. They were trapped in the mountain pass and surrounded by our troops."

"Fuscus declined the offer, of course," Mucatra said.

"Ah, you know how those Roman generals are!" Drilgisa added with a grin. "More proud than a peacock and more stubborn than a mule."

"Fuscus was more proud than most," Buri continued. "Keep in mind that he was leading Legio V Alaudae, the Praetorian legion. They were the Emperor's legion and the pride of the Roman military. It would have killed General Fuscus with shame to surrender them."

"It killed him anyway," Boian said with a laugh.

"Please continue, Buri," another man said impatiently. "What happened then?"

"So, yes, Fuscus refused to surrender. Decebal challenged him to a personal duel and Fuscus accepted."

"I wish I could have seen it!" a third villager exclaimed. "Just the two army commanders fighting a duel of honor!"

"Soldiers on both sides stopped fighting so they could watch the generals fight," Buri said. "It was indeed a battle for honor, ours and theirs. It was not a very long fight. Fuscus was a very skilled fighter but Decebal was better."

"Describe what happened, Buri," Mucatra said.

"Decebal was in his prime as a warrior then. He was faster than General Fuscus. Also he fought with a sica and a Dacian shield, which made him much more mobile. Fuscus was weighed down with plate armor and a heavy scutum. They went back and forth for a while and then Decebal wounded him twice, once on the sword hand and once on the left leg."

"Decebal offered Fuscus the chance to surrender again, he told me later," Diegis cut in. "And still Fuscus refused."

"Fuscus was a fool," Drilgisa said scornfully. "Not only did he get himself killed but he also killed his legion. That is the mark of a bad general."

"How did the fight end?" the first villager asked.

"After suffering the leg wound Fuscus was doomed and he knew it," Buri told them. "He gave Decebal a bull rush and tried to gut him with his gladius. For Decebal it was like fighting against a drunken bull. He let Fuscus lunge past him, then gave him a whack across the back of the neck with his sica." Buri paused and drained his wine cup. "And that was the end of General Fuscus."

"I will tell my children this story," one of the village men declared. "And one day they will tell their children."

"Good," Chief Mucatra said. "We must all do that."

Diegis gave him a smile. "My brother would never have asked for that nor ever expected it, but I think that it would please him."


The pomana included religious services followed by a large public feast. The gathering was much larger than expected because people from neighboring villages travelled for two and three days by horse to attend the funeral ceremony. The streets of Giura overflowed with visitors, many of whom found themselves invited by the local people into their homes. The village square could hold at most one thousand people but would not accommodate the five thousand visitors.

The religious ceremonies were held in the village square. Mircea, High Priest of Zamolxis, performed the prayer services along with several of his priests. Funeral songs were sung by the priests and the crowd in solemn and mournful tones.

Andrada and her daughters were seated on chairs close by the group of priests. Dorin stood behind his mother, keeping his dog Toma at his side. Diegis, walking slowly with the aid of a walking stick, was accompanied by Ana to sit beside the royal family. Buri and Drilgisa stood close by.

After the religious ceremony concluded Diegis stood up in front of the assembled crowd to say some words. He knew that the people gathered there were grieving just as his own family was grieving.

They needed comforting just as his own family needed comforting. That was the purpose of the pomana.

"Today King Decebal stands at the right hand of Zamolxis," Diegis began. "He stands alongside his father King Scorilo and his uncle King Duras. He stands alongside King Burebista."

"We will build no monuments to King Decebal, for that is not the Dacian way. It would be highly irreligious and my brother was ever strict about following our religious traditions. We honor his spirit, not his image. We will remember most his character, his heart, and his many sacrifices for the people of Dacia."

"We will remember King Decebal in our songs and in our stories that we teach our children. They will teach these to their children, from one generation to the next. This is how King Decebal will be remembered. His name and his legend shall live after him, and he will be remembered for all time."

Three days later the visitors had all departed and village life returned to normal. Andrada worked with Zelma on plans to develop several gardens of medicinal plants in the spring. The village needed a clinic for herbal medicine, which would also serve as a school for teaching doctors of herbal medicine from other surrounding villages.

Zia also continued to study with them, along with keeping her eye on Brasus throughout the day. The boy was a loving child but always active and curious about all things. Although hostilities with Rome were largely ended Adila kept up with her archery practice and horse riding. She and Boian were training Dorin in the use of the army bow along with his training with falx and sica.

Adila picked up her bow and two leather quivers filled with arrows and bid farewell to her mother and sister. "I will be at the practice field with Boian. I will take Dorin along."

Andrada looked up from her embroidery and gave her daughter a curious look. "You are spending a great deal of time with Boian. Are you growing fond of him?"

"Perhaps so," Adila replied in a mild tone. "We like each other."

"That's a good start," Zia said, looking up with a smile. She was playing a game with Brasus on a rug on the floor.

Adila returned the smile but did not reply as she headed for the door. The sisters communicated very well even without words.

"Don't forget your promise!" Zia called after her.

Adila looked back over her shoulder on her way out the door. "How could I ever forget when you keep reminding me?"

"What promise?" their mother asked.

"Before Adila left for war we made a promise to each other, Mama. We promised that we would raise our babies together."

"Ah!" Andrada exclaimed. "Then it's time to consider marriage perhaps. I should have a motherly talk with her about that."

"Be patient with her," Zia said. "This war has made her question everything. Even her own future, I think."

"I am not impatient with her. Adila is stronger than any of us so do not worry about her. She will be fine."

A commotion from outside the house made them both stop and look towards the door. Even Brasus stopped playing with his toys and paid attention. Outside on the street Toma was barking excitedly and Dorin and Adila shouted greetings.

Moments later Dorin opened the door and walked in with a big smile on his face. One step behind him came the tall thin figure of Tarbus.

"Oh!" Zia cried. "Brasus, look who is here!"

The two year old jumped up and ran to his father. Tarbus went down on one knee and wrapped his son in his arms, giving him a fierce hug. He picked him up and walked over to give Zia an embrace.

"I am overjoyed to see you," she said, touching his face. "You are so thin! What happened to you?"

"I am overjoyed to see you, all of you," Tarbus said with a happy smile. "I was wounded with a poisoned spear and was very sick for many weeks."

"How terrible!" Zia exclaimed. "Do you feel well now?"

"Yes, I am healthy now, but I lost a lot of weight because I could not eat. The poison was very strong. It would have killed a lesser man, the doctor said."

"No Roman spear can kill you," Adila said with a grin. "Not even one with poison."

"Welcome back to us," Andrada said and gave him an embrace. "All that matters is that you are safe. You will regain your strength in short time."

"Yes, I will," Tarbus agreed, then his face turned to anguish. "I am sorry that I failed King Decebal. I was not there to protect him."

Andrada shook her head. "You must not say that, Tarbus. You did not fail Decebal. He was beyond your protection."

Tarbus looked unconvinced but did not argue the point. "You at least escaped to safety and for that I am glad, My Queen. You are now the future of Dacia."

"We shall have time later to discuss these things," Andrada said. She bent down to pick up the boy tugging at her skirt. "For now I only wish to say one thing. You, my children, are the future of Dacia."

Andrada turned to the little boy hugging her neck and gave him a gentle kiss on the cheek.

"Brasus is the future of Dacia."

> Chapter 21

# 123 Days of Games

*Rome, June 107 AD*

Rome welcomed back Emperor Trajan with all the euphoria and adulation that befitted the most beloved Caesar since the Divine Augustus. He defeated at long last the hated King Decebalus of Dacia. He brought home to Rome a vast treasure from Dacia that included tons of precious metals and many thousands of slaves. The treasure of gold and silver alone would pay for building projects in Rome on a grand scale, including new public buildings that would forever change the face of the Forum.

It took almost a year after the fall of Sarmizegetusa for Emperor Trajan to set things right in Dacia before he travelled back to Rome. The stubborn resistance of some of the Dacian tribes and Sarmatian tribes had to be dealt with. Forts were built on the northern borders and the Roman army was now in a strong defensive position. Attacks on the occupying Roman troops were reduced to minor skirmishes.

After auspices were taken and the proper invocation prayer and sacrificial offering were made, the Senate of Rome convened to hear from Caesar. Since the days of Augustus the true power and authority in Rome lay with the Emperor, not with the Senate. Being a member of the Senate of Rome was a position of prestige and high social standing and not a position of authority. The Senators understood that their primary role was to listen and to carry out Caesar's wishes.

Emperor Trajan took his chair on the Senate floor, sitting between the two consuls. He listened with patience as Licinius Sura addressed the assembly and reviewed the events of the Dacian campaign.

Trajan took the floor with the supreme confidence of the ruler of the world. That came from the knowledge that he was acknowledged by all present as the supreme authority in Rome, and that his every wish would become law.

What made Emperor Trajan the good ruler that he wished to be was not only the glory earned from his military conquests, but also the grandeur of his generosity towards his people. Caesar would now astonish them with his generosity.

"The province of Dacia Traiana is fortified and secure," Trajan told them. "It is ably governed from the new capital city of Ulpia Traiana Sarmizegetusa, which is built on the Dacian plain to replace their remote mountain fortress of Sarmizegetusa."

This was not news to the Senators but they applauded respectfully to acknowledge Caesar's victory.

"Rome's victory over Dacia accomplishes three things," Trajan continued. "First, it removes the wolf from our borders in the north. The Empire of Rome will never again be troubled by the threat that was King Decebalus of Dacia."

"Second, the pacification of Dacia restores the pride and glory of Rome that was tarnished in past conflicts with Dacia. Mars Ultor is pleased with his sons of Rome today."

"And third, the conquest of Dacia brings a bountiful harvest of treasures that is unmatched in the history of Rome." Trajan paused for a moment to let his words sink in. "The precious metals wealth alone amounts to over thirty million aurei in gold and one hundred and sixty million denarii in silver."

These monetary figures were news to the assembled Senators. Their first reaction was stunned silence. These were enormous sums of money for the treasury of Rome.

The Emperor continued. "These treasures will be shared with the people of Rome in many different ways and for a long time to come. Apollodorus is at work even now designing plans for grand building projects, including public buildings, temples, and aqueducts that will benefit all the people of Rome."

"All the debts of the state treasury will be paid off. From Caesar's generosity, all citizens of Rome shall receive a gift of five hundred denarii. And from Caesar's generosity, all citizens of Rome shall be exempt from paying taxes for one year."

Now the applause erupted with enthusiasm. Five hundred denarii was a substantial sum for the common people of Rome, but the tax exemptions for a full year was a tremendous financial boon for the nobles who made up the Senate of Rome. This kind of generosity won Trajan unmatched approval and loyalty. No one knew that better than the Emperor himself.

As the applause decreased Trajan raised his arm for silence. Like every good showman he saved the best for last.

"In his elected role as praetor Publius Hadrianus has performed heroic work in planning Caesar's games to celebrate Rome's victory over Dacia. The games will require the participation of ten thousand gladiators and over ten thousand animals."

"The games and celebrations will be scheduled over the course of the next two years. Emperor Titus famously presented the people of Rome with one hundred days of games. In his generosity Caesar will present the people of Rome with one hundred and twenty three days of games. Such an august celebration has never been presented in the history of Rome, but it is warranted now."

"Fathers of the nation, the victory over Dacia is complete. Let us now celebrate it in the Roman way!"

After the Senate meeting concluded Sura walked up to his old friend, his face glowing with pride and satisfaction. "Superbly done, Caesar.

Watching you on the floor addressing the Senate was like watching the Divine Augustus in the flesh."

"Ah, Augustus," Trajan said with a sad smile. "Gnaeus Longinus would be happy to hear you make that comparison."

"Gnaeus? What do you mean?"

Trajan gave a small shake of his head. "Never mind, it is a small matter. Gnaeus had a premonition many years ago, at the time when Emperor Nerva proclaimed me as his adopted son. He thought that I would become the next Augustus."

Sura laughed, delighted. "Gnaeus was right in most things. I do miss his wit and his wisdom."

"As do I, Licinius," Trajan replied in a sad tone. "I very much regret that he became another casualty in the Dacian wars."

"Come, we must turn to other things that require your attention, Caesar. Your triumph is only five days away. Hadrian is working out the details for your parade and needs your assistance."

The Emperor gave a groan. "You know that I have no patience for such things. It would be better for Hadrian to consult with Pompeia and Marciana on details for the triumph."

"Your indifference is most unusual," Sura replied with a raised eyebrow. "Most men would be thrilled to plan their own triumph."

"My satisfaction comes from gaining the victory, Licinius, not from celebrating it. I have better things to do than plan a parade."

"Hah! Will you allow yourself to enjoy the triumph, at least?"

"Of course! Caesar must share the joy of victory with the people. Augustus once celebrated three triumphs on three consecutive days."

"Old Octavian knew how to polish his image," Sura said with a smile. "When it comes to vanity, Marcus, you are no Augustus."


The Empress Pompeia Plotina very often took charge of important projects for the simple reason that she wanted them to be done right. She was also very good at managing complicated things, which helped considerably. Trajan's sister Ulpia Marciana was the same way. When

Hadrian showed them the map and the schedule for the triumph parade they immediately took it over.

"The parade route looks fine Hadrianus dear, that is a pretty standard route," Plotina assured him. "Allow an extra hour on the parade schedule to reach the Temple of Jupiter. That would provide ample time for the animal sacrifices with no need to rush, and for the banquet after. Are the sacrificial animals pure?"

"Yes, my lady," Hadrian assured her. "The oxen are pure white and unblemished. I examined them myself this morning."

Marciana clucked her tongue. "The horse medicines should be administered two hours earlier, unless you want Trajan's quadriga rolling over horse droppings on the parade route."

Hadrian looked doubtful. "The veterinarian chose this schedule."

Marciana laughed. "The veterinarian may know animal health but I know parade schedules. The horse dung will be on your head, so to speak, Hadrianus."

"Very well, two hours earlier then," Hadrian conceded.

"The food preparation schedules and menus look to be in order," Plotina said. "You did a good job with this."

Hadrian smiled with satisfaction. He had been raised by these two strong women of the Trajanus household since he was a boy. Over the years he thrived under their guidance and basked in their approval. He married into the Trajanus family due to their influence, and took Marciana's lovely granddaughter Vibia Sabina as his bride. Although the marriage was not a happy one it raised Hadrian's social status within Rome's cultural elite to very high levels.

"Hello, my dears," Trajan greeted his wife and sister as he entered the room. "You are directing Hadrianus to the right course of action, I trust?"

"The only threat to your parade will be horse dung," Marciana said lightly, "and then only if Hadrianus rejects my advice."

Trajan clasped a friendly hand on Hadrian's shoulder. "Tell me that you would not do something as foolish as that?"

"I would never do such a thing," Hadrian replied, happy to play along with the teasing. The Trajanus family was very casual at home.

Pompeia Plotina took her husband by the arm and led him away to a side couch.

"Sit with me so that we may talk. You are hardly ever home since your return," she said. "Is everything in order?"

"Yes, my dear. A great deal of work had to be done after my two year absence from Rome, but everything is as we wish it now."

"Is the Senate compliant?"

"As docile as a flock of lambs on a sunny spring day," Trajan said with a smile. "The Dacian campaign is a historic victory for Rome. They all understand that and there is no cause for complaints. There is no dissent, imagine that."

"Nor should there be, Marcus. I also imagine that cancelling all their taxes for a year made even the worst ingrates happy!"

Trajan laughed. "I should think so. That took them by surprise."

"And what now, Husband? No more campaigns?"

"Now we celebrate for two years, so no campaigns. In truth, after Dacia I need a rest from campaigning. After two years we shall see."

"You will get impatient," Plotina said with a smile. "The invasion of Parthia is still in the back of your mind, I think."

"Perhaps so, but it will wait," Trajan said. "Now if you will excuse me, my dear, I must tend to one more task and then I will return."

"More work?" she asked with a mild frown.

"A small matter of state. It will not take long but it is important. And when I return I am yours to do with as you wish."

Emperor Trajan gave Tanidela the courtesy of visiting her at her house rather than having her summoned to the imperial palace. He wished to treat the visit as a social call more than a matter of politics, although the issue at hand also involved matters of state. He did not fear for his safety and instructed his lictors to wait outside the house.

"Your daughter is growing fast," Trajan remarked in a casual tone after Tanidela welcomed him inside. They sat on two facing dining couches. "How old are you now, my dear girl?"

"I am six years old," Tyra replied. Trajan was just another Roman man to her.

"Ah, six! When I was six years old I lived in a village in Hispania. That summer I learned how to fish, and I spent the entire summer just fishing in the river near my home."

"Sometimes we go to fish in the Tiber," Tyra said. "But Mama says we cannot eat the fish we catch there."

Trajan laughed softly. "Yes, I know. Never eat a fish caught in the Tiber, although many people do because they are hungry."

"You honor us with your visit, Caesar," Tanidela said politely. "Might this have to do with your triumph parade? I must tell you that I could not bear being put on display like that again."

Trajan heard the pain in her voice and slowly shook his head. "No, you are not asked to march in my triumph. That is not the purpose of my visit."

"Thank you, Caesar," Tanidela said with relief. "May I ask then what is the purpose of your visit?"

Trajan leaned back into the soft back cushion of the couch. He was in a thoughtful mood.

"Your relation to your brother is no longer of any concern to me. Rome's war with Dacia is over."

Tanidela looked him in the eye. "If that is no longer a concern then why not set me free, Caesar?"

"What concerns me now," Trajan continued, smiling once again at her fearless attitude, "is that you are the wife of Prince Davi of the Roxolani tribe of Sarmatians. And Tyra is his daughter. Is this not so?"

"Yes, Caesar. It is so."

"The purpose of this visit, my dear, is to tell you that I will set you and Tyra free. You are my gift to Prince Davi to build goodwill with the Roxolani."

For a moment Tanidela found that she had no words. "Thank you, Caesar. It is the only thing I have wished for, nothing else."

Trajan gave her a sympathetic smile. "You will be provided with an escort to the border of Sarmatia. Tell Prince Davi and the Roxolani that Caesar is not such a complete ogre, eh?"

Tanidela returned his smile. "I will tell him that. And if it helps to reduce bloodshed between our people that will be a good thing."

Trajan sat up from the couch. "You may leave at any time you wish. Make arrangements with Salonia, she will provide whatever you need and probably more. Have a pleasant journey, Tanidela. You too, little Tyra. Grow up healthy and strong, child."

"Farewell, Caesar. Thank you again," Tanidela said and escorted the Emperor to the door with a grateful smile on her face.

"Are we leaving Rome, Mama?" Tyra asked. She looked uncertain and confused.

Tanidela placed her hands on her daughter's shoulders and looked into her eyes. Her face beamed with happiness.

"We are going home to Sarmatia. You are going to see your father, my darling girl."

Her mother's happiness made Tyra happy. "Yes! And will I see my cousins also?"

Tanidela laughed. "You will see all your cousins in both Sarmatia and Dacia. And oh, they will be happy to see you!"

# Chapter 22

# Life Endures

*Free Dacia, September 107 AD*

P running the apple, pear, and quince fruit trees should only be done in the winter, Buri explained patiently to his assistant orchard stewards Ana and Lia. Then the tree will produce more buds and flowers in the spring and thus more fruit in the summer. Now, in the fall season, trees were preparing for winter and pruning them would only stunt their growth.

Over the past few months Buri enlisted the help of several of the young villagers, along with his two teenaged assistants, to plant an orchard of three dozen fruit trees on a patch of land by the river. It was rich soil and would never lack for water.

Ana and Lia were attentive students and eager to learn. They were best friends as well as assistant orchard stewards, so later they would get together and discuss what Buri taught them in order to better understand the lessons.

"What is Tarbus doing?" Lia asked and started laughing. Recently Tarbus began to show interest in helping his father, who was past fifty years of age and would soon start to slow down in his work. He pushed a hand cart filled with dried manure and was dumping the fertilizer around the trunks of several apple trees.

Buri shook his head with amusement. "He is trying to be helpful. Ana, will you go and teach him?"

"Yes, sir," Ana replied. At sixteen years of age she felt responsible for doing the job well. She was also no longer afraid to challenge adults and talk to them as equals.

"Tarbus, stop! You don't dump the fertilizer around the tree trunks, silly."

"Oh, is that right? Well, silly me," Tarbus said with a grin. "And I suppose that you know the proper way?"

"Yes! Start near the trunk and spread it out until you are one foot past the drip line. That way when it rains the fertilizer will best reach the roots and feed the tree."

"Ah, thank you for the lesson," Tarbus said, but he was looking up the hill at the road leading into the village. "We have visitors, Ana. And I think you will want to see them."

Prince Davi rode at the head of eighty Roxolani cavalry. They escorted two passenger wagons, one of which carried his wife and daughter. The travelers headed straight for the house of Queen Andrada.

When the wagons finally came to a halt the first person Tanidela saw coming to meet them was her brother Diegis. He used a stout walking stick and limped noticeably on his left leg. Tanidela jumped down from the wagon and hurried to her brother.

"You look well, Sister," he told her after she pulled back from her tight embrace. "Six years of captivity in Rome have not changed you."

"It was a mild captivity, but thank you for saying so," she replied. "I am sorry about your leg. A shattered knee, Davi said?"

"Shattered completely. Damned legionnaire hit me with a scutum and I never saw him coming."

Tanidela took him by the arm and led him to the wagon. "Come, there is someone else you have not seen in six years. She was only an infant then."

"Hello Tyra, I am your Uncle Diegis," he said with a smile.

"Yes, I know you!" Tyra said brightly.

"You know me? How can that be?"

"You're Uncle Diegis with the walking stick! That is what Papa calls you."

Diegis threw back his head and laughed.

Davi picked up his daughter from the wagon and set her feet on the ground. "Just call him Uncle Diegis, Tyra." He turned to Diegis and gave him a firm handshake. "I am sorry for that, brother. I only called you that once, and she remembered!"

"Don't be sorry," Diegis said, still smiling. "I don't care what she calls me, I am overjoyed to see her and Tanidela again."

"I am overjoyed as well," Andrada said, approaching with Zia and Brasus at her side. The women exchanged embraces and tears of joy.

"Hi, my name is Tyra," the girl said to Brasus.

"Hi, my name is Brasus," the little boy replied.

Diegis turned to Davi and gave a nod towards his cavalry. "You bring a strong escort. That is an excellent idea, brother."

Prince Davi's eyes flashed hot with anger. "I took an oath, Diegis. Never again will any Roman come near my wife or daughter. Never again."

The women sat around the dining table with cups of hot lemon water and honey. There were years of events to discuss and profound changes in all their lives.

"We knew that you and Tyra were alive but worried for your safety still," Andrada said. "So you were kept in the imperial palace?"

"For the first few years, yes," Tanidela replied. "I was both a royal guest and a prisoner, so they treated us well."

"Did the Romans not hate you?" Zia wondered. "You are the sister of King Decebal."

Tanidela gave a small shake of the head. "No, Zia, they did not hate me and I did not hate them. They are people just like us. Some good and some bad."

Andrada's face darkened. "Trajan sent Decebal's remains to Rome, we were told."

"Yes, sister." Tanidela reached out and touched the Queen's arm. "I gave Decebal a funeral in Rome."

Andrada's eyes widened. "You saw him? You gave him a burial?"

"I only saw the box and the funeral shroud that held my brother's remains. Diegis' friend Titus Lucullus was exceptionally honorable and kind and brought the remains to me. We buried Decebal in a grove of trees on the banks of the Tiber River."

This was news to the royal family and they sat in silence for a moment. Andrada and Zia wiped slow tears from their cheeks.

"I thought I had no tears left," Andrada said. "But that is not so."

Tanidela gave her a brave smile. "There is never an end to tears, sister. We must bear them as best we can."

"It has been a year since Tata died," Zia said. "To me it does not seem so long ago."

Tanidela agreed. "Time passes quickly. Ana and Dorin look so grown up now. And here you are Zia with a child almost three years old. And where is Adila? I have not seen her."

"Adila went to her farm to see her horses," Andrada answered. "Although she can't ride now, in her condition. She should be back soon."

"In her condition?"

"Ah, here she comes now," Zia announced brightly as Adila and Boian came through the door. "You have excellent timing, Sister."

"Oh, my," Tanidela exclaimed with a smile as she sat up to greet them. "Just look at you, my dear niece. Did you swallow a melon or are you expecting in three or four months?"

Adila gave her a warm embrace. "In about three months, Aunt Tanidela. And this is my husband Boian."

"I am very pleased to meet you, Boian. I am sorry that I missed your wedding in March but unfortunately I was detained."

Boian gave her a grin. "You are forgiven, Lady Tanidela. Welcome back to Dacia."

Zia sat up and offered her chair to her sister. "Come, sit! There is so much that you missed hearing."

"We have plenty of time to talk, Zia," Andrada said. "Village life in the winter is mostly sitting around and talking."

"Are you getting used to your new life here?" Tanidela wondered.

Adila gave a casual shrug. "I miss the mountains. This is much better horse country, however. Boian and I will raise horses and that never gets tiring."

"Life is calm and peaceful here," Zia said. "I like it. I was so tired of the endless wars with Rome."

"This is the new Dacia," Andrada said. "Some people call it Free Dacia, but to me it is just Dacia. We are making a new home here and life will go on. Life endures."

In the evening the men sat around the bonfire and talked. Some drank wine, and some drank ale that was brought in by Chief Fynn of the Bastarnae. The Bastarnae were tribes of Germans who over the centuries somehow migrated to territories northeast of Dacia.

"The Romans are finding the Carpi and the Sarmatians to be prickly neighbors," Prince Davi told the men around him. "They maintain defensive positions and mostly stay in their forts."

"They won't come into Carpi territory," Chief Mucatra declared. "There are too many of us and we defend our lands aggressively."

"That might change, Mucatra," Drilgisa said with a wry grin. "If you suddenly discover vast deposits of gold and silver you might see a few legions on your doorstep."

"No, the Romans won't come this far," Diegis said with conviction. "They are already stretched out too far north of the Ister River. This is a mistake that Rome will come to regret."

"I agree with Diegis," Fynn offered. "They will be hard pressed just to keep their gains in Dacia while fighting off attacks from the

Carpi, the Sarmatians, and my Bastarnae. We all hate Rome. Decebal is dead but his spirit of resistance still unites us."

"We should attack them more," Boian argued. "Let's take the fight to them and punish them for their invasion."

"I agree! We should attack them," Dorin declared. He was training as a military assistant to General Drilgisa and was eager to see action.

"Patience, youngsters," Drilgisa calmly advised. "In war patience is a virtue. Now is not the right time for an offensive."

"How will we know when the time is right?" Dorin asked.

Tarbus gave him a good natured grin. "The time will be right when the older and wiser heads tell us that it is right."

"Dorin, by nature I am not the most patient of men," Drilgisa told the boy. "But I learned patience from your father the King. It is an indispensable quality for a leader. You must learn to value it also."

"Yes, sir," Dorin replied in a respectful tone.

Buri had kept to his quiet nature, but now he stirred and looked around at his companions. "The war with Rome has changed. This is not a war that will last for five or ten years. No, it will last for fifty years or even one hundred years. In the end Rome will be driven out because our people will never accept Roman occupation."

"You are exactly right," Diegis said. "We will fight them for the next one hundred years if need be because this is what free people must do. Tyranny prevails for a time, but it does not last. In time Rome will be cast out of Dacia."

The men grew quiet, each lost in his own thoughts. They watched the hot embers from the bonfire swirl up in the updraft and vanish into the dark sky. They contemplated hopes, dreams, life, death, courage, loyalty, and sacrifice. They contemplated the price that free men must pay to live a life of freedom.

# Epilogue

Dacia was the last significant province added to the Roman Empire. It later became the first significant province to be lost to the Roman Empire, when in the year 274 AD Emperor Aurelian withdrew all the Roman troops and settlers from Dacia and moved them south across the Danube. A brilliant military strategist who saved the Empire when it was on the brink of collapse, Aurelian made the momentous decision that the province of Dacia was simply too difficult to defend.

Decebal is considered to be the last and greatest king of Dacia. In his time he was described as an ingenious military tactician and leader of men, but he was equally adept at diplomacy in forming and maintaining alliances in the fight against the Roman Empire. In his time he made Dacia the center of resistance to Roman conquest in that part of the world. His legacy made an impact beyond his death.

Cassius Dio described Decebal with considerable admiration as "skilled in war and skilled at deed; knowing when to sail and when to retire in time, valiant in battle, knowing how to use a victory and get away with a defeat; for which things he has long been for the Romans a fearsome opponent."

Unfortunately we know little about Decebal's personal life beyond the little that is provided by Roman sources. We know that he had children. His brother Diegis was a historical figure. However even the circumstance and details of his death are in dispute. The famous panel from Trajan's Column showing Decebal taking his own life is an artistic interpretation that is often accepted as historical fact.

Peter Jaksa

Emperor Trajan's conquest of Dacia in 106 AD is considered by historians as the last great conquest of the Roman Empire before it eventually went into its decline. By occupying approximately one third of Decebal's kingdom of Dacia, Trajan expanded the borders of the empire beyond the Ister/Danubius/Danube River to as far north as it would ever reach.

Trajan achieved all his major objectives. He defeated Decebal and removed Dacia as a military threat to Rome. He took possession of the most valuable territory in Dacia where the largest deposits of gold, silver, iron, and copper mines were located. Finally, he captured the vast wealth of Decebal's royal treasure that Emperor Domitian had only dreamed about but never got close to.

It has been estimated based on various sources of information, including notes (now lost) from Trajan's personal physician Statilius Crito, that Trajan brought back from Dacia treasure worth thirty one million *aurei* in gold and another one hundred sixty million *denarii* in silver. That approximates to 165 tons of gold and 300 tons of silver.

With this immense hoard of captured wealth it is no wonder that Trajan set a new Imperial record for celebrations with 123 days of games, the longest and most expensive celebration in history. The games stretched from June 107 to November 109.

The Emperor also put his brilliant master architect Apollodorus of Damascus to work on building projects that forever changed the face of the Forum and of Rome. Some of their works stand to this day, including most famously Trajan's Column.

Trajan's conquest of Dacia was the great achievement of his life. It increased his popularity with the Senate and people of Rome to levels not seen since the days of Augustus Caesar. Later generations would call him the *optimus princeps*, the greatest of all emperors.

In the year 113 Trajan launched an invasion of Parthia. His health grew worse with advancing age, likely not helped by his heavy wine drinking, and deteriorated significantly in 117. He died in August of that year while he was travelling back to Rome.

Hadrian was named Caesar following the death of Trajan, which apparently involved some mystery wherein the Empress Pompeia Plotina "discovered" some documents naming Hadrian as Trajan's heir. Hadrian always, it appears, was looked after well by the women of the Trajanus family.

Hadrian went on to enjoy his own illustrious career as Emperor of Rome. Apollodorus of Damascus stayed on as Hadrian's architect for a number of years, but their relationship remained prickly. After what apparently proved to be one too many disagreements or insults, Emperor Hadrian had Apollodorus executed.

Trajan's Bridge at Pontes and Drobeta, a wonder of the ancient world that was built by Apollodorus and Hadrian, lasted only about 170 years. Ironically it was destroyed by the Romans because they wanted to stop invasions across the bridge by tribes from the north. Perhaps Decebal and his fellow Dacians, looking down from the heaven of Zamolxis, had a good laugh at the irony of it all.

The new Roman province of Dacia Traiana prospered for a time but military resistance from the tribes in Free Dacia never ended. Large and powerful Dacian tribes including the Carpi and Costoboci continued their military hostilities, with help from their allies the Sarmatians. A major rebellion against Roman occupation occurred after the death of Trajan in 117 AD.

Lucius Domitius Aurelianus, also known as Emperor Aurelian, was the savior of Rome when the Empire was on the verge of ruin. One of his major decisions in managing the Empire was to evacuate the last Roman troops and settlers from Dacia in 274 AD. In effect Emperor Aurelian reversed the military actions of Emperor Trajan, and Dacia would not be under Roman occupation again.

Over the next several centuries the people and the land of Dacia went through tumultuous changes along with the rest of that part of the ancient world. It is a historical fallacy and logical absurdity to claim as some do that the people of Dacia were somehow eradicated by the Roman Empire when the Romans only occupied perhaps one third of the country to begin with.

Dacians built houses and most other structures of wood and clay and unfortunately left few archeological finds that survived for two thousand years. What survived of their temples are the foundations and pillars made of stone. They did not create statues of their gods, leaders, or heroes, most likely because that was considered irreligious to the followers of Zamolxis. One worshiped the spirit, not the image.

Nonetheless archeological evidence found in caves and graves provides evidence of an advanced civilization and complex culture that existed for thousands of years. The Dacians developed a 360 day calendar long before the Egyptians or Romans. Dacian doctors were highly prized for their expertise in herbal medicine and surgery even among the Roman legions.

Today Dacia is considered to be one of the many lost civilizations of the ancient world. Certainly we have better records of ancient Rome, while we have oral history and folk tales about ancient Dacia. It would also be accurate to say that the civilization evolved over the centuries and millennia. Its influence is seen most prominently in the culture and language of modern day Romania. It could be argued that at the population level Dacia is no more a "lost" culture because it evolved into Romania than ancient Rome is a "lost" culture because it evolved into Italy. But perhaps this is just semantics.

The author is indebted to a multitude of books, articles, and other resources relating to the history of ancient Dacia and ancient Rome, too many to list here. Readers wishing to learn more about Dacia may find interest in the excellent history book *Dacia: Land of Transylvania, Cornerstone of Ancient Eastern Europe* by Ion Grumeza. Readers looking for additional biographical information about Emperor Trajan may find interest in the book *Trajan: Optimus Princeps* by Julian Bennett.

# Historical Note

*Decebal Defiant* is a novel. As in the first two novels in this series, the author strives to present historical events and historical figures from that ancient time in a manner that is as fair and true to the times as possible. This is an imperfect process that relies necessarily on very limited information from a very limited number of ancient sources.

The three novels in this series cover the historical period of the wars between Dacia and Rome during the reign of King Decebal on the Dacian side and Emperor Domitian and Emperor Trajan on the Roman side. The focus is primarily but not exclusively on the largely untold story of the Dacians. It is not possible to tell the story fully without telling both sides of the story.

It is also not possible to make the historical period come to life without focusing on the rich cultures of both Dacia and Rome, and on the compelling cast of characters and personalities who shaped the events of their time. The military struggles that lasted for over two decades between Dacia and Rome were interesting and certainly consequential, but equally fascinating was the clash of cultures and the interplay between the major actors of that period. The cultures and humanity of the people of Dacia and Rome play a prominent role in these novels as they did in the real lives of people living in that era.

It was a stroke of historical good fortune that Julius Caesar not only wrote a detailed account of his wars against the Gauls, but that his books also survived the ravages of time. Emperor Trajan also wrote an extensive account of his wars with Dacia, but sadly all that survived over time is one fragment of one sentence. Posterity is much poorer for it. Emperor Trajan left us the majestic Trajan's Column, but as discussed below that is not the same as a book of history.

There are no detailed historical accounts of the wars between Rome and Dacia that survived to our time. Those readers who might wish for a description of such and such a legion, deployed in such formations, following such strategies against such barbarian forces, may find disappointment with the story that unfolds here. That kind of information from the Rome - Dacia wars simply does not exist.

Although Cassius Dio is often cited by historians as a go to source on Trajan's campaigns in Dacia, the information he provided about those events fills paragraphs, not books. The historians embellishing on Dio make their own assumptions and interpretations.

Trajan's Column is without question a masterpiece of art. It is also often treated as a history book, which unfortunately it is not. It is a work commissioned by Trajan and designed by his chief architect Apollodorus to celebrate his conquests in Dacia. It was constructed by artists who did not witness the scenes depicted on the column. The stories told on panel after panel are stylized images of heroic Roman soldiers getting the best of clearly inferior barbarians. The central character of course is Emperor Trajan himself.

It may be more objectively accurate to view Trajan's Column not as a history book but as a form of Roman hype. If it was a modern production it might very well be a video called *Trajan's Greatest Hits*. Its main purpose was to entertain the public and to glorify Trajan, which it has done very admirably for two millennia. It turns out that Apollodorus of Damascus was the Steven Spielberg of his time.

This is not to say that Trajan's Column has no educational value, because it certainly does provide a wealth of information. When treated as a historical record however we should take into account its designed purpose and intentional biases. Unfortunately the column provides no information regarding locations or dates, so the images require guesses and interpretations. Scenes from Trajan's Column were incorporated in many places in writing these novels, with the author's best assessment regarding locations and time frames.

Unfortunately we have no such works of art or history left to us by the people of ancient Dacia. Whereas there are many busts and full statues of Emperor Trajan, there are no statues of King Decebal that were produced in his time. It is thought that due to religious beliefs Dacians did not produce images of their gods and heroes. Decebal is depicted on Trajan's Column as having a strong physical build and a regal bearing.

Most of what we know about the culture and civilization of Dacia comes from modern day Romania, in the form of oral history about "the people of the mountains" and from folk songs and poetry. They are thought to have dressed in clothes similar in style to those worn by Romanian shepherds and farming villagers in more recent times. The men wore woolen trousers, long shirts that hung down over their hips, and deerskin or leather moccasins. The women wore skirts and dresses embroidered with string to make colorful patterns.

Dacian men wore their hair long and their beards trimmed short. Dacian women are depicted in images as proud and statuesque. Their principal god was Zamolxis, who preached that others should be treated with compassion. They believed their souls were immortal and did not fear death. After the era of King Decebal many Dacians became Christians, which was perhaps not a difficult transition.

Dacia was indeed described as "the land of wheat and honey" by Alexander the Great circa 330 BC. They also had abundant resources of gold, silver, iron, and other minerals in the Carpathian Mountains and were prolific miners. The vast haul of gold and silver captured by Trajan in Dacia financed his rebuilding of Rome.

The events depicted in this novel are based on historical fact when available and on best guesses when facts are missing or in dispute. We simply don't know, for example, exactly when Gnaeus Pompeius Longinus was captured (or tricked into attending peace talks) and committed suicide by taking poison. We don't know as historical facts when or where assassins tried and failed to kill Emperor Trajan while he was on campaign, or what the circumstances might have been of Decebal being involved in such a plot. The ancient sources mention these events in passing but provide no details.

Some common misconceptions are hopefully laid to rest, one of them being that Decebal was hunted down and took his own life shortly after the fall of Sarmizegetusa. In fact Decebal spent at least a month after the fall of the city leading resistance against the Romans in the eastern mountains of Dacia. Roman cavalry finally caught up with him in the first week of September 106 AD.

The fall of Sarmizegetusa happened mostly as described here based on the details that we know. The city was doomed when the water supply was cut off. Many people including Decebal and the royal family escaped via a tunnel system. The venerable Vezina was killed when the Romans took the city. There was a diaspora of Dacian civilians from the central regions to the northern and northeastern parts of Dacia. Those areas would never be conquered by the Romans.

After Trajan established the new province of Dacia Traiana the Romans called the Dacians living in the north "neighboring Dacians" (*Daci limitanei).* The Dacians called themselves "free Dacians" or just Dacians. They continued to cause problems for Rome for over one hundred and sixty years, until Emperor Aurelian in 274 AD finally evacuated all Roman troops and settlers from Dacia. Dacia Traiana was too difficult for the Romans to defend.

Decebal is remembered and still revered today as a national hero in modern day Romania, which is geographically the heart of what used to be ancient Dacia. Interestingly, so is Trajan. There are many folk songs and poems that sing the praises of the ruler called Traian. Both men left a lasting legacy on the culture and the psyche of the people in that region of Europe.

## ABOUT THE AUTHOR

Peter Jaksa, Ph.D. is an author living in Chicago, Illinois.
He is a lifetime student of European history during
the era of the Roman Empire. In particular he is a
student of the history and culture of ancient Dacia.

Books by Peter Jaksa

**Historical Fiction:**
*Decebal Triumphant*
*Decebal and Trajan*
*Decebal Defiant: Siege At Sarmizegetusa*

**Psychology and Self-Help:**
*Life With ADHD*
*Real People, Real ADHD*

Made in the USA
Monee, IL
15 June 2021

35959cfd-5da3-4158-ba20-97af0ae367dcR01